THE BLOODSTONE RING

Edward takes Emma, his betrothed to visit his Uncle and Aunt Lowther, at Musgrove Manor. Edward adored his uncle's first wife, Aunt Lilian, but she died in childbirth and her two children are unwanted at Musgrove. When Emma befriends the girls, Margaret, the eldest, is frightened. What is the secret of that odd household? Why does Lilian's ring have a strange effect on Emma when she wears it? Whilst Emma attracts the attention of two bachelors during her stay, she also has to cope with the antagonism of Aunt Prudence Lowther.

SARA JUDGE

THE BLOODSTONE RING

Complete and Unabridged

LINFORD
Leicester

First published in Great Britain in 1984 by
Robert Hale Limited
London

First Linford Edition

2. Large type books
I. Title
823.9'14 [F]

ISBN 1–84617–302–7

Published by
F. A. Thorpe (Publishing)
Anstey, Leicestershire

Set by Words & Graphics Ltd.
Anstey, Leicestershire
Printed and bound in Great Britain by
T. J. International Ltd., Padstow, Cornwall

This book is printed on acid-free paper

For Katie
Because she has the Ring

1

It took me longer than I would have imagined possible to adjust to the slums of St Giles once more.

Our house had become so much smaller in the four weeks that I had been away from it; it was dark and damp, the rooms were cold, and there was a strong smell of mouse. The people outside its walls, 'our' people, were pleased to see me again, at least, some of them were. Others, as Edward had so rightly declared, were beyond help and neither wanted, nor appreciated, my care.

On my first day back I prevented three urchins from killing a cat. I came across the boys as I passed down the alley which led to Masons' square, on my way to visit Peggy Fry. The children, they were no more than that, were filthy, bare-footed, under

1

nourished, and cruel.

The cat's paws had been bound together with a piece of twine, and they were throwing and kicking the furry bundle in a ferocious game of ball.

The boys jeered from a safe distance once I had shouted, and cuffed them into dispersing, and the cat, terrified, wounded, and equally fierce, had scratched me for my pains and then dragged itself to a hole in the nearby wall.

Pressing my lips together in angry frustration, I had marched past the sneering ruffians and gone on my way, wondering why I had bothered.

If they had intended eating the animal, because they were starving, I would have understood; but such senseless, wilful cruelty was unforgivable.

Yet I knew what Father would have said: They do not know any better, Emma. When have they ever been shown love or affection? When have they been fondled with tenderness?

They cannot be blamed for their actions, and we must never stop trying to reach out and claim their souls for Christ.

I called on Peggy Fry, who was a young girl of perhaps fifteen years, nobody knew her correct age, who was expecting a child within the next few weeks.

Peggy lived in a cellar where damp and slime ran down the walls, and which she shared with five other beings. Three of the men worked in a nearby sweat-shop, so were out all day, and Peggy was a prostitute. But now she was confined to her cellar and stayed there for most of the time, in the dark, with an old man who was blind, and a small girl of about three years.

None of the inhabitants of the room appeared to be related to each other, and nobody, least of all Peggy, knew the identity of her unborn baby's father.

Peggy looked upon me as a friend, and I had promised to attend her when her time came, and take with me a few of our own limited supply of candles.

After talking to Peggy for a while and feeling almost sick from the fetid smell of her dank cellar, I went on to see Granny Lane. She had been dying before I went to Musgrove, and was still in the process of dying one month later. She lived with her daughter and son-in-law and seven grandchildren, in two rooms on the second floor of a building off St Giles Street.

I sat and held her hand and told her all about my adventures in Sussex, those which could be repeated, that was, and promised her daughter that I would bring a packet of tea with me next time I called.

The rest of the day I spent with the family of Littleworths, helping the harassed mother to clean her rooms; soothing and playing with her three youngest children, all of whom were under the age of five; and taking home with me a bundle of washing which I would launder and return as soon as it was ready.

I knew that Martha would scold me, for she, like Edward, hated me to take in washing. But we, at least, had a range and a copper, and enough coal to heat the water. We also possessed a back yard in Flower Street, where laundry could be hung if the weather was clement. Mrs Littleworth had none of these things and, when she found time and water in which to wash, hung her wet garments all around the room in which the family lived, and the children played and slept.

The two sovereigns which Harry Varney had given me were still in their little leather bag, but it was very hard to decide how to spend them. Granny Lane must benefit, and I also hoped to do something for Peggy Fry and her baby; but everywhere one looked there was dire need and I dreaded having to make a decision about those precious coins.

I walked home that evening, spent and miserable, longing for hot water in a tub with which to wash away the sadness and grime of the city. Martha only allowed me to have warm water in the sink on a Saturday night. I thought of Musgrove and groaned inwardly, longing to walk in the sweet-smelling fields again, to breath the fresh air and hear the birds sing. I missed the clean, intelligent company of the three little girls, and all the comforts which that big house had provided.

Before I went away from London nothing had seemed so bad because I did not know anything better. But now comparisons were hard to bear.

The next few weeks passed in the same fashion, with Peggy becoming slower and heavier, and Granny Lane slipping tediously and painfully in and out of restless sleep. Then, one morning very early, I was summoned by one of the men who lived in Peggy's cellar, and I spent the whole day with her in that hell-hole, endeavouring to bring her comfort during her painful labour. A woman from the floor above had some knowledge of midwifery, and we stayed until nine o'clock that evening, working by the light of a flickering candle, watched idly by the three men when they came home from work, and the one curious child.

Peggy Fry lived but her baby boy was stillborn.

'I want it buried!' cried the girl, clutching feebly at my hands. 'I want it buried right and proper, Miss Emma.'

I stroked back her wet hair and promised that I would ask Father when I got home.

'An' take it with you — I don't want it left here the night.'

I placed the poor dead bundle in a cardboard box, which one of the men found for me, and stayed with the exhausted girl until she fell asleep. Then I limped home, dirty and fatigued, gripping the box beneath my arm.

Martha met me at the door, grim-faced and irritable.

'About time, Miss Emma,' she said sharply. There's a gentleman to see you and he's been here ages and won't go till he's spoken to you. Your father's not in yet, and the food's spoiling, and *I* don't know what to do with him. What you got there?' she ended abruptly, eyeing my burden.

'It's a dead baby and Father must bury it — I promised.' I pushed at a strand of hair which had fallen forward over my forehead. 'Oh, Martha, I'm so tired! Who is the man, and what does he want?'

'He didn't give a name, but he's one of them high and mighty folks you was spending your time with down in Sussex.'

Oh, no! I thought desperately, not that, not now.

I was at the end of my tether, could scarcely speak from weariness, and was as filthy and unkempt as any slum inhabitant. Was it Harry Varney? Or Mr Middleton? I could not face either of them, but I must.

If I could just have a few minutes to myself; to wash and change my gown;

to brush my hair and compose my troubled mind. Then I would be able to face my visitor and hear what it was he had come to tell me . . .

2

Edward and I arrived at Musgrove Manor on a cold and wet afternoon in April. He had been so looking forward to showing me the estate, and the house, but in the event he was too wretchedly tired and weak from our journey to be excited, and did no more than lift his head from time to time and whisper,

'Are we nearly there?' as we jolted along on that seemingly endless ride.

And I, gazing out of the rain-splattered windows of the carriage, could make out little of the countryside save for endless soggy fields, interspersed with dripping hedgerows and storm-lashed trees.

'Nearly there, dear,' I said, willing my words to come true.

We seemed to have been in the rattling vehicle for hours, and I was frightened by the increasing pallor of Edward's face. Fortunately, Edward's Uncle Lowther had sent his own conveyance to collect us, but the travelling took far longer than I had anticipated, and I feared for Edward's indifferent health.

However, eventually we arrived and Uncle and Aunt Lowther were there to greet us in their wide hall. I could not take in details at that time, but was nonetheless impressed by the spacious, wood-panelled interior which awaited us. Then we were ushered upstairs to our rooms in the west wing.

My room possessed a fireside rug, and a canopied fourposter bed with a pink coverlet, and pink curtains hung at the tiny, diamond-paned windows. A fire had been lit for me, and once I had washed my face and hands at the marble wash-stand I felt more refreshed and able to take an interest in my new surroundings.

Uncle Arnold's manservant had helped Edward to bed, and as soon as I had seen him comfortably settled, I followed the same man along the corridor and back down the wide oak staircase to the drawing-room.

There, Uncle Arnold and Aunt Prudence Lowther awaited me.

'You poor dear, come and take a seat by the fire and warm yourself. You must be famished, so we will dine early tonight,' said Aunt Prudence.

She was a very big woman, wearing a gown of dark green tarlatan, and with a black lace shawl around her generous shoulders. Her face was white, and a mass of yellow hair was bundled up on top of her head beneath a muslin cap. She also possessed soft white hands which clasped mine and drew me towards to hearth.

'Now, Emma dear, you are not to worry about Edward. Mr Lowther has insisted that you both remain here with us until Edward is fully returned to his former health.'

I smiled at her, removing my hands from her grasp, conscious of how rough and hard my skin was in comparison to hers.

Uncle Arnold stood to one side of the fireplace as we seated ourselves on the well-stuffed sofa before him.

The drawing-room was spacious, with whitewashed walls, and oak beams supporting the low ceiling; the fireplace was wide, with horse brasses shining brightly on either side of it, and a thick Turkish carpet covered the floorboards. Two sofas and several large armchairs were placed facing the roaring log fire.

It was not an elegant room, despite the chandeliers overhead and the long red velvet curtains at the windows, but it was a warm and friendly room.

There was a heavy oak dresser against one wall, which bore many pewter mugs and plates; there was also a large round table, polished to a rich shine, and numerous smaller tables stood about with china ornaments and pot plants upon them. There was a piano, and a writing desk, and various embroidered foot-stools. I had never seen so much furniture in my life before, and wondered how many maids there were at Musgrove, and how long it took them to polish and dust so many items, and if the other rooms in the big house were as cluttered as this one.

'So glad you were able to come,' said Uncle Arnold gruffly, a stocky, red-faced man, with greying hair and bright blue eyes. He looked the very picture of a country squire. 'When I received your letter telling me that my nephew had been ill, I knew at once that Musgrove was the place for him. Good country air and wholesome food will work wonders, Miss Emma, and it seemed imperative to me that you got him away from those London slums as quickly as possible.'

'It was most kind of you to invite us, sir.' I looked up at him gratefully. 'At first I did not think that Father would be able to spare me. But he insisted that my place was by Edward's side and, besides, he could never have managed the journey on his own.'

Uncle Arnold nodded. 'Doing splendid work there, I've no doubt, but can't be healthy, m'dear.' He leaned forward to peer at me. 'Could do with some colour in your face, too, I perceive. Right decision to make, right place to be.' He leaned back clearing his throat. 'We must, of course congratulate you on your betrothal — delighted to hear it — young Edward needs a wife to take care of him. Always was a delicate boy, even as a youngster. And you look a capable young lady. He's chosen right, quite right.'

'Thank you, sir.'

I was fortunate also, for a female of twenty-seven was definitely upon the shelf, and being blessed with neither beauty nor riches, I had given up all thought of marriage at an early age, and had thrown myself into charitable work, helping my father in the terrible slums of St Giles.

Father was a vicar, and a good and honest man, albeit somewhat fearsome in both manner and appearance. But he cared about people, and, heaven knew, there were more than enough unfortunates in our parish who needed care and attention.

When Edward Lowther arrived, some two years previously, anxious to serve the community, my father was delighted and I was pleased by the company of the earnest young curate.

'Suppose Edward told you that he was my heir?' said Uncle Arnold abruptly, startling me from my thoughts. 'That is of course, if Mrs Lowther and I do not have a son of our own?'

'But we will, Mr Lowther!' His wife gave a little bounce on the sofa beside me and gazed up at her husband with a laugh. 'We will have sons, dear sir, I am certain of it.' She turned to me and said coyly,

'Mr Lowther and I already have a young daughter, and you shall see her tomorrow.'

'I should like that.' I leaned towards

her eagerly. 'And there are other children I believe?'

Edward had told me that his uncle had two daughters by his first marriage.

'Oh, Lilian's two,' answered Aunt Prudence carelessly, 'yes, well, you shall see them all tomorrow. But I must warn you, dear,' she bent her large white face nearer in a confiding way, 'Lilian's eldest is not quite right here.' She touched some of the yellow curls which had escaped from her cap. 'Never got over her mother's death, did she, my love?' She turned her attention back to her husband, who rose up and down on his toes, looking slightly uncomfortable.

'No, well, er, she is not mentally retarded, if you understand, Miss Emma. But she, Lilian's eldest, that is, was most disagreeably affected by poor Lilian's death. And, er, is a very awkward child, very awkward indeed.'

'I think she should be placed in a special home. Oh, I don't mean a mental institution,' said Aunt Lowther quickly, 'but a special school, there are such places, you know, where she can be properly cared for.'

'But she is good with the other girls, m'dear,' remarked her husband.

'Yes, dear love, very useful for the time being. Mr Lowther will not hear of her going away,' she said to me, 'but they will soon outgrow her and she is a *most* depressing creature to have about the place, you must agree, dearest?'

'Yes, well, we shall have to see about that. Time to make decisions later on — no hurry for the present.'

'Perhaps I could help her,' I said, feeling pity for a child who had lost its mother so young. 'I have worked a lot with orphaned and bereaved children, and sometimes a stranger can help where family cannot.'

'Oh, you need not worry your head about Lilian's eldest!' laughed Aunt Prudence.

She had very small eyes in her otherwise large-featured face, and I could not make out their true colour in the candlelight. They were so small that one could not read their expression either, but her mouth was big and red-lipped, and she smiled often. Too often?

I was beginning to think that I did not care greatly for Edward's Aunt Prudence. But there, I told myself, be charitable. It was doubtless a hard task bringing up two little girls who had lost their mother, and perhaps resented the fact that their father had married again.

'I like children,' I said quietly, 'and would enjoy talking to them and taking them for walks.'

'You are here to *rest*, dear Emma, and I will not hear of you working as a nurse-maid. Lilian's eldest is remarkably self-possessed, most mature in many ways, but too silent and withdrawn. I wanted you to know beforehand so as not to be disconcerted when she appears. Now,' Aunt Prudence went on briskly, 'Let us eat at once, you must be weary and in need of an early night's rest. Tomorrow I shall hope to meet your Edward, and become better acquainted with Mr Lowther's nephew.'

That night I was in truth weary, and retired to my room where an attentive maid brought me hot water, and a copper warming pan for my bed. Edward had been asleep when I poked my head round the door of his chamber to bid him goodnight, and perhaps it was just as well, else I might have beleaguered him with questions.

There was so much I wanted to know. In London he had spoken a few times about Musgrove Manor, but we were always so busy and so tired by nightfall that I had learned little save for the fact that he loved the estate, had spent much time there in his youth, and had been extremely fond of his Aunt Lilian. I had hoped to learn more on our journey down to Sussex, but the constant jolting of the carriage had quickly tired him, so my knowledge of the Lowther family was far from complete.

What was really wrong with Lilian's

eldest? And what was her proper name? Why were the children not present when we arrived? It had not been late — barely six o'clock. Surely too early to banish children from the drawing-room?

And why had Aunt Lilian died? Edward had spoken about her with affection, remembering holidays spent with her on the estate, but all I knew was that she had died some years before, and that Aunt Prudence was his uncle's second wife, whom Edward had met briefly once before.

Tomorrow, I thought, climbing into my wide and comfortable bed with a sigh of pleasure, tomorrow I shall find out more about the children who appear unwanted because they are not boys.

★ ★ ★

The next day I saw the manor properly, and it was a well-preserved Tudor building with uneven floor-boards, and very thick walls, which tended to bulge out in odd places. It surprised me that Aunt Prudence did not have a house-keeper, but she was an extremely capable person, running the household of four maids, a manservant, and a cook, all by herself.

Uncle Arnold spent most of his days riding over his estate; he was an efficient and enthusiastic squire, Edward had informed me, and owned a great deal of land. Aunt Prudence, too, was always busy, supervising the servants, ordering meals, arranging flowers, and giving daily orders to the head gardener.

I saw her briefly that first morning, when I came downstairs after breakfast-ing in my room.

'We rise early, dear,' said Aunt Prudence, looking big and businesslike in her dark blue dress, covered by a white starched apron. 'I do hope that you slept well, and that Dolly brought you adequate sustenance this morning?'

'Yes, thank you,' I replied. 'If I eat as

well as that every morning I shall quickly be putting on weight!'

My companion laughed. 'Your Uncle Arnold rises at half-past six and likes a good meal in his stomach before going out for the morning. Edward only picked at his tray, I was sorry to see. But don't worry about him, dear, we'll have him up and about in a couple of days. Now, can you amuse yourself this morning?' She was obviously impatient to be off and about her day's business. 'There is a fire lit in the morning-room — I hope you have brought some embroidery with you? Yes? Well, that's splendid. Make yourself comfortable, Emma, and we'll meet in the drawing-room at half-past twelve. If there is anything you require, ring for one of the maids, won't you?'

'The children?' I said quickly, as she began to bustle away. 'Can I see the children?'

'Oh, not in the mornings, dear.' She looked quite shocked. 'They stay in the east wing and amuse themselves until the afternoon. But at five o'clock they always come downstairs and you'll see them then.' She nodded brightly before disappearing across the hall and down a further passage which led her to the rear of the house.

I was not fond of needlework. There was never time for dainty stitching at home in Flower Street, and I was used to being active, going out with Father and visiting the poor and needy. I never had time to sit down until after our evening meal, and then any sewing which had to be done was repairing my own, or my father's, clothes. Fancy embroidery was not for the likes of me and, although I had brought a tapestry firescreen with me, I had no intention of sitting bent over my needle when there was so much to be seen and learnt about this peculiar household.

I had seen Edward briefly before coming downstairs, but he was still weak from his journey and disinclined to talk. So the morning was mine, and I intended putting it to good use. Pulling my shawl about my shoulders, I crossed the hall and let myself out through the heavy oak door. The rain had cleared during the night and the air smelt fresh and cool. If I walked briskly the exercise would do me good, and I could explore the grounds and perhaps catch a glimpse of those mysterious children.

The drive led from the front steps round a clump of rhododendron bushes, down a tree-lined avenue, to the distant lodge gates. Before me, to the left, stretched a wide lawn, and at the far end of it stood a high yew hedge. A little paved path led over the wet grass to a gap in the hedge, so I decided to go and see what lay beyond.

After a few paces I paused to look back at the house. Musgrove stood weathered and softly beautiful in the morning sunshine. Its many chimneys lifted to a blue sky, and smoke curled lazily in the air. Birds sang, a cow lowed in the distance, and I breathed in the pure country air with a sigh of happiness. Then I turned and walked through the gap in the hedge to find myself in a rose garden. Little paths led off in four directions, intersecting the rose beds, and joined in the centre of the garden at a sun dial, mounted in a column of stone.

An old man in a faded blue smock was hoeing in a far bed, and lifted his head when he saw me and touched his forehead politely with his fingers.

I smiled and called out, 'Good morning,' then wandered across to the opposite opening in the hedge and discovered another lawn, which sloped gradually away to a duck pond. Beyond the water was a barn, and some sheds and outbuildings, which I presumed to be the boundary of the home farm.

One day soon, I decided, I would ask Uncle Arnold to show me round the farm. I had never seen a cow or a sheep, except in a picture book which I had possessed as a child. A neighbour of ours in Flower Street had once owned two ducks, but they had been stolen from him in the night.

No animal was safe in St Giles, I thought gloomily, beginning to retrace my steps. Even rats had been known to end their days in cooking pots, though not in our house. Martha, even if she were dying of starvation, would never have countenanced the eating of vermin.

★　★　★

I did not see the children until five o'clock that evening, precisely as Aunt Prudence had stated.

We were sitting in the drawing-room, Edward, too, for he had come down-stairs for tea and sat, his knees covered with a rug, as close to the fireplace as possible.

He still looked very pale and tired, but his eyes were more alert and I was thankful to see him beginning to take an interest in his surroundings. Uncle Arnold was telling him about the estate, and what new developments had occurred since last he visited Musgrove, and then the big grandfather clock in the hall struck five times and this was followed by a timid knock on the door.

'Ah, here they are,' announced Aunt Prudence brightly, and we all turned our heads to gaze at the three little girls who shyly entered.

'Good evening, children,' said Uncle Arnold, moving forward to greet them. 'Come along and meet some new members of our family. You haven't seen Lilian's two before, have you, Edward?'

'I saw the eldest once, if you remember. I came to her baptism. In fact, she is my god-daughter,' replied Edward, turning round in his chair and smiling at the little group.

'Come on then, he won't bite,' joked Uncle Arnold, pushing the youngest forward, who moved unwillingly, letting go of the taller girl's hand.

She could not have been more than three years old, and was a round-faced, fair-haired cherub, wearing a solemn expression.

'This is our Rachel,' declared her father. 'Now, make your curtsey to Mama and our visitors, and then you may sit by the fire.'

The little girl made a curious ducking motion, almost falling over in the effort, and her mother smiled, nodded her bushy head, and folded her hands together on her lap.

Not a kiss, nor a cuddle or an endearment, I thought in amazement, and watched as the little one toddled over to the hearth and sat down at Edward's feet, returning his gaze with serious, contemplative eyes.

'And this is Lilian's youngest,' went on Uncle Arnold, as the next child moved forward to make her curtsey. 'Tell Cousin Edward and Cousin Emma your name, dear.'

'My name is Elspeth and I am five years old,' whispered the child, before dropping her head and moving across to join her half-sister.'

She possessed very dark blue eyes, I noticed, in the fleeting moment when she raised her head, and her hair was black and cut short around her face. She looked rather like a medieval page boy, apart from her pinafore and long-sleeved dress, but perhaps it was the easiest way to keep such hair, for it was very thick with no trace of a curl.

Longing to turn my head and see 'Lilian's eldest,' the difficult one, I controlled my desire and waited for Uncle Arnold's next announcement.

'And that is Margaret, Lilian's eldest,' declared Uncle Arnold finally. 'But she is very shy and will not come forward, I think.'

I turned then, and stared over my shoulder at the slim, white-faced girl who stood straight and silent by the door.

'For goodness sake come forward and meet your Cousin Edward,' snapped Aunt Prudence from beside me. 'He says he is your god-father so you might show some respect, Margaret.'

'And meet your Cousin Emma,' said

Uncle Arnold, in a gentler tone than his wife. 'She is very fond of children and would like to get to know you.'

But the girl stood tense and motionless, as if she had not heard them. She was very plain and, I thought, looked rather ill.

Her dark brown hair was scraped back from her face with a ribbon, and hung lank and lustreless down her narrow back. She was pitifully thin, wearing a sad, limp gown of grey serge, and she looked older than her ten years.

'Well, we'll just ignore her — it is best so,' said Uncle Arnold, coming back to join us around the hearth. 'I do apologise for her odd behaviour, my dears, but we did warn you, did we not?'

'Impudent chit!' Aunt Prudence rearranged her skirts with an irritable little shake. 'I don't know why we bother to keep her — she should be sent away.'

'What ails her?' Edward sat forward, a look of concern on his face.

31

'Oh, you were not here yesterday when we spoke to Emma. Never got over her mother's death, so she would have us *believe*. But *I* put such behaviour down to jealousy and an un-christian spirit. She would not accept me as your uncle's second wife, and she resents our little Rachel.'

'But you told me she was good with the children,' I put in quickly, disliking this kind of talk in front of the girl, and wanting to find something pleasant to say. 'She cares for the younger ones, does she not? You do not have a nurse-maid for them?'

'Good gracious, no! Lilian's eldest must do some work whilst she lives with us, and yes, I must admit she is useful with — er — Elspeth, and our darling Rachel. But she is not *fond* of them, I can tell that. She shows no affection, you understand?'

'It must be hard to lose one's mother at an early age,' remarked Edward carefully. 'She was old enough to know her well, after all. What was she

— three, four, when Aunt Lilian died?'

'Almost four,' snapped Aunt Prudence, 'but that was years ago and this silly behaviour has gone on too long. The girl cannot be right in the head.' She tilted her chin at her husband.

'Yes, well, we will not discuss the matter for the moment,' said Uncle Arnold. 'Now tell me, girls, what have you learned today? Can you say your numbers yet, Rachel?'

His daughter put her thumb into her mouth and shook her head.

'Well, what about you Elspeth? Recite your numbers for our guests, if you please.'

So quietly that I could scarcely hear, the child breathed out the numbers from one to twenty.

'That is excellent, excellent,' said Uncle Arnold, beaming. 'You see, m'dear, Lilian's eldest is a fine little teacher.'

'How did Margaret learn?' I asked. 'Who gave her lessons?'

'She was often with her mother

during those early years,' replied Uncle Arnold. 'Lilian doted on the child and, of course, she learned a great deal from her mother, who spent many hours with her every day.'

'Spoiling her abominably,' said Aunt Prudence. 'That is the trouble.'

Uncle Arnold ignored her. 'Margaret could both read and write before poor Lilian died,' he said.

'When our Rachel is old enough she shall have a governess,' announced Aunt Prudence harshly. 'In a year, or so, Mr Lowther, you must engage a suitable person for our daughter. She will soon outgrow that girl's limited knowledge, and must have the best tuition in all the accomplishments of a young lady.'

3

Soon the children were forgotten as Aunt Prudence prattled on about the neighbouring gentry, and the people she wished us to meet during our stay at Musgrove.

'Tis a pity about Wadhurst Grange,' she said, 'for that is the nearest estate to ours, and a *very* beautiful house, so I have been told. But the owner is away in Australia, and I have never met him.'

'Nice chap, young Middleton,' nodded Uncle Arnold. 'Used to see quite a bit of him when — ' he paused, 'in the old days,' he went on quickly. 'But he was restless and impatient to see the world, so he's gone exploring. Left his land in capable hands, I must admit. Rowland's a good bailiff and manages the estate competently.'

'Mrs Varney is very pleasant,' broke in his wife, 'she is one of my best friends and lives on the other side of the village. We must also introduce you to the vicar and his wife. You will enjoy meeting them, dear Edward, once you are fit again. In fact, I shall give a little party for you in a few weeks time, and then you can meet all our friends. I don't suppose you have time for a social life in those miserable slums of yours, do you?'

No, I thought, staring into the golden flames of the fire, there was little time even to talk in the evenings. We were so weary when we arrived home that we only managed a bite of supper, prepared for us by Martha, and then all but fell into our beds. But life was tolerable because we were useful, and we cared.

I glanced at the two little girls on the rug in front of me, and thought of the still figure standing by the door.

No lonely child was passed without a caress or a cheerful word in our wretched community, and although we had few possessions and even less money, we had love in plenty and were not ashamed to show it.

Even Father, whom grown men and women respected and often looked at with an emotion close to fear, even Father softened his stern attitude when he saw a child. They were the innocents, he used to say. Men who were drunk and beat their wives, or women who sold their bodies for a piece of bread, were sinners and not to be forgiven, for they knew right from wrong and should behave morally no matter how poor they were.

I could not agree with such harsh judgement, but respected his rigid puritanical views.

Children, however, were innocent, no matter how savage life had made them, and Father would spend time, endless time, trying to save their souls.

'I said would you and Edward accept it, Miss Emma?' Uncle Arnold's voice broke in upon my reverie, and I raised my head, blushing at my rudeness, for I had not heard a word he said.

'Forgive me, please,' I answered, 'my thoughts were far away with Father, wondering how he was faring without me.'

Uncle Arnold nodded, and Edward, a slight frown upon his face, said clearly,

'My uncle has asked if we would accept a ring which belonged to Aunt Lilian. I remember her wearing it, a signet ring, was it not, Uncle?'

Uncle Arnold nodded again. 'Lilian would have liked you to have it and as you doubtless have little money for such trinkets, I thought perhaps Miss Emma would care to wear it as a sign of your betrothal?'

'It is of little value — a worthless bloodstone,' said Aunt Lowther.

'I should love to have it,' I answered eagerly. 'It is most kind of you to have thought of it.'

Edward and I had no money between us, and would be hard put to find enough money to buy a wedding ring for me when we eventually married.

'I shall fetch it now. No good just

lying there in a drawer, and my dear Mrs Lowther will not wear it — '

'I should think not!' said Aunt Prudence with a delicate shudder. 'The very idea!'

'Well, now, say goodnight, children, and then run along off to bed.' He had suddenly remembered the girls. 'We shall see you again tomorrow at five.'

Uncle Arnold followed his children from the room, and returned some minutes later with the ring. This he handed to Edward, who took it with a small smile.

'Yes,' he said softly, 'I remember her wearing it, on the little finger of her right hand. She was never without it.'

'Well, then, place it on your beloved's hand,' said his uncle jovially.

And I, embarrassed by the attention, and feeling that it was something which we should do privately, in some quiet place of our own choosing, slid to my knees beside Edward's chair and held out my right hand.

His fingers were cold and slightly damp, even though he sat close to the fire, and he fumbled for a moment before sliding the gold circle onto my little finger. It fitted perfectly; a wide gold band, with an oval of almost black background set in it, and tiny red marks streaking through the stone.

'Thank you,' I whispered.

'That's it, now give the girl a kiss,' boomed Uncle Arnold.

Blushing still further, I lifted my face and felt Edward's dry lips touch my brow.

'There, that's settled,' remarked Uncle Arnold comfortably. 'Pity it could not have been the correct finger, but no matter. You are now decently betrothed, my dear Miss Emma, and have a ring to prove it. All very satisfactory, don't you agree, m'dear?'

Aunt Prudence sniffed. 'I could have wished for a prettier ring,' she said. 'But perhaps, one day, Edward will be given the living of some prosperous parish and will be able to afford a diamond for his wife. Then she can discard Lilian's poor cheap thing and wear her ring with pride.'

'I am very satisfied with this ring,' I answered quietly, sitting back on my heels and gazing at my hand, 'and am proud to wear it.'

Aunt Prudence flashed me a look of contempt and then rose, shaking out her shirts. 'There's no accounting for some taste,' she said. 'Now if you'll excuse me I'll go and see Cook about the dinner.'

And she swept from the room in a huff.

We retired early to bed at Musgrove, for both Uncle and Aunt Lowther rose at half-past six and Uncle Arnold was out and about the estate by eight o'clock in the morning.

Normally I was glad to go to my bed, for I enjoyed the peace of the countryside, and the knowledge that there would be no interruptions, no hammering on the door after midnight with urgent pleas for help or shelter; no screams, or yells, or noise of nocturnal tumult with which we were forever disturbed in the heart of London.

But this night I felt strangely restless, and paced my bedchamber, wondering what troubled me. Was it those unfortunate children? So safe and secure in their big comfortable house, with enough food for their stomachs, and sufficient warm clothing in even the bitterest weather; yet lacking that one all-important quality of life, which no money could buy, the quality of charity. Was it their fate which so disturbed me?

I pondered, twisting the ring upon my finger, unused to the weight on my hand. Tomorrow morning I would go into the east wing, I decided. Aunt Prudence had not questioned me as to what I did with myself in the morning, and it would be easy to slip upstairs again once she was about her house-hold tasks, and explore that far wing of the house. If anyone should see me and want to know what I was doing there, it would be simple enough to say that I had taken the wrong turning and lost my way.

Having thus made up my mind, I prepared to go to bed. The maid, Dolly, had brought hot water to my room, and the bedcovers were neatly turned back, inviting repose. Yet still I paced, a strange heaviness in my heart, turmoil in my mind.

Was it Aunt Lowther who had upset me? I disliked her callous attitude towards the children, and did not care for her as a person, either. But she was giving Edward and me a place to rest, a home in which to find solace and comfort after our hard life at St Giles. I should be grateful for the pretty room, the luxurious surroundings, and the excellent food. I need not like the lady, but I should appreciate what she was doing for us.

Was it Edward? Slowly, I sat myself down in the chair before the fire and made myself sort out my thoughts, carefully, precisely.

Edward's illness, his continual weakness, his slow recovery to health, was this beginning to irritate me? He was young, some three years younger than me. Why had he succumbed to this fever, he, a man in his prime? I had been helping my father for as long as I could remember, in all weathers, with but meagre nourishment and scant clothing, yet neither Father nor I had ever spent a day in bed. Was I secretly disappointed in this weakness in the man who was to be my husband?

Yet I should be grateful for his love, for the knowledge that he desired to make me his wife. Edward was not much to look at, being tall and over-thin, with pale brown hair and a long, rather mournful face.

But who was I to criticise his looks?

Standing up suddenly, I went to stare at my own countenance in the mirror, before which the candle flickered uncertainly. I was no beauty.

Large, dark grey eyes stared back at me, with deep smudges beneath them, which showed the years of interrupted sleep and endless worrying. My brown hair, pulled back neatly and firmly into a bun at the back of my head, was a lank and lifeless as Margaret's had been. In fact, with my thin body and narrow, pale face, I could quite easily have been mistaken for her elder sister. Or her mother!

Smiling briefly at such fanciful thoughts, I put my hands to my head and removed the hair pins one by one, placing them in the porcelain dish on the dresser before me. There was some curl there, if it were encouraged. Gently I wound a strand around my finger, allowing it to fall back upon my shoulder, and it swung, curving into my cheek, softening the line of my face.

Leaning forward, I bit at my lips, making them red, and full, and softly moist, then I pinched my cheeks until the blood flowed. Suddenly my face became alive, almost pretty, and my eyes appeared even larger, smiling back at me with a mischievous gleam in the flattering light from the candle.

I could be attractive!

My waist was small, and my bosom high and firm, although it could do with more fullness. Critically I surveyed myself. If I possessed the right clothes; if I were properly laced and adequately gowned and petticoated; if my hair were tonged into ringlets; if I were to sport earrings, and a little paint on my cheeks —

I took a step back, drawing in my breath with a little gasp. What was I doing? My heart was racing in my breast and I put up my hands to try and still its rapid beating. Dear heavens, what had come over me?

Here I was, behaving like some — some loose woman, flaunting my body and my face in a most provocative manner. I, the vicar's daughter, brought up in a respectable, God-fearing home, learning at an early age that the wages of sin was death; that pride in one's looks, and the wearing of showy finery, was an abomination unto the Lord.

I had seen how the poor painted creatures in St Giles had lost their virtue, selling their bodies in the streets, in order to earn a few pence for their families; but dying young, often before the age of thirty, in childbirth, or of some dreadful disease. Yet here I was, daring to imitate them, attempting to make myself pretty, wanting to appear desirable.

Feverishly I removed the ring from my finger, tore off my clothes, and, fetching the cold water jug from its stand and putting the basin upon the floor, flung the contents of the jug over my quailing flesh.

There, I told myself, teeth chattering, reaching for the towel to rub myself dry, if you think such evil thoughts again this is the punishment you will receive. Wicked creature! Now get down on your knees and pray for God's forgiveness.

I spent a long time beside my bed, until my knees ached and my body trembled from fatigue and cold. The fire had died down and the room was very cold. But as I climbed into bed and pulled the covers over me, I was once again at peace, and fell asleep before many minutes had passed.

The following morning, once Aunt Prudence had left me alone in the morning-room, I peered out into the hall and then made my way swiftly upstairs again. I caught a glimpse of Dolly, through the open door of my bedroom, pummelling my pillows in readiness for bed-making, and I tiptoed past her along the corridor which ran the length of the middle part of the house. In this section was the bedroom belonging to the Lowthers, and Uncle Arnold's dressing-room, plus two other bedrooms. Then I faced the back stairs leading down to the kitchen area, and on my left another passage led to the east wing.

I walked along it slowly and carefully, listening for voices. One door, which I opened, led into the linen room, and the next was obviously the maids' bedroom. Finally, at the end of the passage, tucked away in the farthest corner of the east wing, were two doors. From behind the first one I heard somebody speaking.

'With what exhortation did John the Baptist preach the first Advent of Christ?'

'Repent ye, for the kingdom of heaven is at hand.'

'That's right, Elspeth, now, how was the second Advent of Christ preached by St Peter with the same exhortation?'

'Oh, I don't know!' It was a wail of despair and I decided to interrupt this painful lesson.

I knocked upon the door and there was an immediate silence, so, turning the handle, I went in.

It was a schoolroom, a big wide room, with bookshelves and a cupboard down one side of it, and a fireplace set in the other wall. There was a rocking-horse standing near the window, on which Rachel sat, holding a cloth doll before her, the thumb of her other hand in her mouth.

At the large wooden table in the middle of the bare floorboards sat Elspeth and Margaret, facing each other, books lying open before them.

All three children turned their heads towards me as I entered, and their expressions were both surprised and frightened.

'Please may I join you?' I said closing the door behind me. 'I am lonely downstairs and wanted so much to get to know you all better.'

Margaret immediately rose to her feet, smoothing down her pinafore and clasping her thin hands before her. She did not speak, but stood, head erect, facing me in a defiant pose. But there was flicker of fear in her eyes, and in the tight compression of her lips.

'I was most impressed with the way Elspeth knew her numbers last evening,' I said, moving forward to seat myself at the end of the table. 'Did you teach her all by yourself?' I looked at

Margaret. 'That was a very clever thing to do.'

Elspeth grinned shyly at me, pushing her hair behind her ears with ink-smudged fingers.

'I can read as well,' she announced.

'Well, I never!' I shook my head in amazement. 'Do you know that in St Giles where I come from, I see lots of children, boys and girls of all ages, and none of them can read or write.'

'Why not?' asked Elspeth.

At least here was one child with whom I had made contact. I ignored Margaret and went on talking, keeping my eyes fixed on Elspeth's round face.

'Because,' I said, 'they are very poor, some don't even have shoes to wear, and there is no money in that part of London for teachers, or school lessons.'

'Poor children.'

As we were speaking, Rachel clambered down from her rocking-horse with the aid of a stool set beside her, and came hesitantly round the table to stand before me, the rag doll dangling from her fist.

'What is the name of your doll?' I said, lifting the battered creature and setting it upon my lap.

'Dill,' answered the little girl, leaning against my knee with a small sigh.

'Dill?'

'She means Jill,' explained Elspeth, 'only she can't talk properly yet.'

'Poor Jill.' I examined the torn dress, and saw that one arm was almost separated from her soft body. 'She needs a little attention. Do you have a needle and thread?' I turned to look directly at Margaret. 'I am not much of a seamstress but can mend quite neatly.'

Margaret stared at me and I thought for a moment that she would not respond, but then she moved away from the table to one of the cupboards which stood against the wall. When she returned she held out a needle-case and a spool of black thread.

I did not comment on the colour,

but took the needle-case and thread from her with a smile. 'Thank you, Margaret.'

Carefully I sewed back the doll's arm and then began on the tattered dress. If I used very small stitches one would not notice the thread.

'Are you staying here long, Cousin Emma?' asked Elspeth.

'Don't ask personal questions, it is rude.'

Margaret's voice was high and sharp.

'I don't mind, Margaret. How can you get to know me if you do not ask questions? And it is all right here in this room,' I went on hastily, not wishing to under-mine her authority, 'but, of course, downstairs with the grown ups you must *never* ask questions, and *never* speak unless you are spoken to first.'

I put on a very stern frown, grossly exaggerated, and peered at Elspeth from under my brows. She let out a little spurt of laughter at my expression, and Rachel joined in at once. It was a pleasant sound, for I did not believe that these children often laughed. Indeed, what cause could they have for merriment?

'I shall be staying at Musgrove for a few weeks,' I went on, 'until Cousin Edward is quite recovered from his fever.'

Margaret pulled back her chair and sat down again.

'Now, tell me what you are learning today,' I said.

'We are learning the *Bible*,' Margaret answered, 'only Elspeth is lazy and does not try hard enough.'

'But the words are so long,' wailed her sister. 'I cannot understand them.'

'I shall explain, only you must try and remember, Elspeth. We went all through this yesterday and you have not remembered anything I told you.' There was a little frown between her eyebrows as she stared at her sister. 'What will Father say tonight if you cannot tell him anything new?'

Elspeth hung her head, and her thick,

shiny black hair swung forward, hiding her face.

'You learn the *Bible*,' I said quickly, 'and you learn numbers, what else do you learn?'

'That's all.' Margaret looked at me blankly. 'We read a lot, and we go for walks in the afternoon.'

'And Rachel?' I put my free arm around the sturdy little body at my side. She was leaning half across my lap, almost asleep. 'What does Rachel do?'

'Oh, she listens,' said Elspeth, from across the table, 'and she sleeps a lot, as well.'

'Where?' I looked round the room. With neither carpet nor curtains it was a spartan place, not designed for comfort.

'When she is tired she goes in there.' Elspeth indicated the door behind her with a nod of her head.

'Come,' I said to the drowsy child, 'shall we go and see?'

She took my hand and I stood up and began to lead her towards the closed door. Then I stopped. 'May I go in there?' I asked Margaret.

She nodded and sighed. 'Rachel is always tired. She wakes up so early, then she gets tired in the middle of the morning and has to sleep.'

Margaret could have done with some sleep, herself, I thought, looking at her pale tight face and shadowed eyes.

'Perhaps, Rachel could go to bed a little later in the evening,' I suggested. 'Then she might not wake up so early?'

'But *I* am tired at night,' cried Margaret, 'and I like some time to myself for reading, and unless I get Rachel and Elspeth to bed early, I have no time for myself.'

Anger flared in my heart. She sounded like a weary adult, as harassed and exhausted as Mrs Littleworth in St Giles. Why was there no nurse, no governess or able-bodied person to care properly for these three children?

'Do you clean the rooms and make the beds?' I asked. 'And what about meals?' Did this child have to do everything?

A smile lightened Margaret's gaunt face for a fleeting moment. 'Oh, no! I don't do any housework, although we do try to keep our rooms tidy. Bessie is the maid, and she cleans for us and brings us our meals on a tray'

I nodded. 'I see.' Then I led Rachel into the other room.

This was a smaller chamber than the schoolroom, but it was comfortably furnished, and there were three beds, all in a row, against the far wall, and rugs upon the floor and curtains at the window. There was a fire still smouldering in the grate, and a large cupboard against the other wall, and a jug and basin on a stand near the window

'Which is your bed?' I asked Rachel, and she pointed to the one in the corner. 'Well, now, let's take off your pinny and your dress, and we'll have your shoes, too, and you can have a nice lie-down. Then we'll play some games when you wake up. How about that?'

I helped her off with her outer garments, tucked her between the covers and smoothed back her soft fair hair. She put her thumb into her mouth and settled down with a sigh, closing her eyes before I had left the room.

'Can you draw?' I asked the other girls as I went back to join them. 'Have you paints and some paper?'

'That's not learning,' said Margaret, with a frown.

'Do you not think it would be fun, though?' I asked gently. 'Perhaps Elspeth cannot always remember things because her brain is too tired? Why don't you have a short rest in between lessons to enjoy yourselves? Won't you paint me a picture, Margaret? I should like that very much.'

She looked at me doubtfully, as Elspeth clapped her hands in delight.

'Oh, yes! Let's draw,' she said.

'I used to paint sometimes with my Mama,' said Margaret quietly. 'I used to like that.'

'You see? It can be fun, and you have

lots of time to learn, so share out the hours — some for study and some for pleasure.'

She nodded, and went across to the cupboard again, and bending down rummaged away in the bottom of it. After a few minutes, when she had almost disappeared into its depths, she came back, somewhat flushed, carrying a box of paints and some paper.

Whilst the girls were preparing their utensils, I roamed along the book-shelves looking for something suitable to read. The *Bible* was all very well but I felt that something lighter would be more beneficial whilst they painted. Eventually I found a beautifully illus-trated volume of *Gulliver's Travels*, and carried this back to the table.

'What shall we paint?' Elspeth was staring at her piece of blank paper.

'I know,' said Margaret, 'but it is a secret until I finish. You're not to look, Elspeth.'

'What about a pretty garden, Elspeth?' I said. 'With all the flowers, and perhaps a little cottage, and a twisty path, and a duck pond beside it?'

She nodded, chewing at her paint brush, casting a dubious eye at her sister, who was busily engaged on something which she was concealing behind an upended book.

'Whilst you paint I shall read to you,' I went on, and we sat companionably for nearly an hour as I read Mr Swift's enthralling tale to the two absorbed little girls.

By half-past eleven two pictures had been completed, and my voice was beginning to feel tired.

'Show me what you have done,' I said, putting the book to one side and holding out my hand.

Elspeth's offering was a crude, over-coloured affair, which was rather wet, and the red of the house had run into the green of the grass.

'That is not bad for a first attempt,' I remarked tactfully, 'Leave it to dry, Elspeth, and then I should like to keep it, if you will allow me?'

She nodded, her face breaking into a heart-warming smile.

Margaret's painting was surprisingly good. I stared for some moments at the little brown horse, which stood with proud head and swishing tail in a daisy-strewn meadow. She had caught the feeling of the animal, and it looked as if it would gallop off at any moment.

'Don't you like it?' Margaret's voice said anxiously.

'It is excellent.' I looked across as her and saw her cheeks redden at my praise. 'Do you like horses, Margaret?'

'Yes.' She ducked her head, and began scratching at a mark on the table with her finger nail.

'I should like to keep this painting as well, if you do not mind?' I peered at her, not wanting to offend, but when she did not reply I decided it was best to change the subject. She was still a tense and secretive child, and it would be foolish to pester her with further questions.

'Now,' I said, rising to my feet, 'I

shall waken Rachel and then we can have a few games before I go downstairs for lunch.'

'Games?' queried Margaret, frowning again. 'But we must do some more learning. Father will be cross if Elspeth hasn't learned anything new.'

'You can tell him that you have begun reading *Gulliver's Travels*,' I answered quickly, 'that will surely please him. And you can remember what I read you today, can't you, Elspeth?'

The child nodded. 'I like that story.'

'Then that will do nicely,' I said.

Once Rachel was dressed again we played Hunt the Thimble and Ring-a-Roses until noon. The girls were bright-eyed and rosy-cheeked with all the excitement, and I vowed to myself that I would return every morning to liven their dreary days. What would happen when I went back to London did not bear thinking about. That was for the future. For the present I was proving useful, and enjoyed being with them, and I hoped that the pleasure was mutual.

'At what time do you go out in the afternoons?' I asked Margaret, as I prepared to leave. 'Perhaps you would let me walk with you?'

'Yes, yes!' cried Elspeth, jumping up and down. 'You come too, Cousin Emma, and we'll show you all our favourite walks.'

'That will do, Elspeth.' Margaret's voice was cool and her sister immediately quietened. 'We leave the house at three o'clock, Cousin Emma, and go down the back stairs. There's a side door which leads into the yard.'

'Then I'll meet you by the stables, at three o'clock,' I said. 'But if I cannot manage it, don't wait for me.' Aunt Prudence sometimes paid calls in the afternoons, and would no doubt expect me to join her. 'I shall be there whenever I am free and look forward to it,' I said, and then went along to my room to freshen up and tidy my hair before joining the family for lunch.

4

On my way back I decided to stop and see if Edward was in his room. I wanted to talk to someone about the children. Surely he would understand and could, perhaps, say a word on their behalf to his uncle? After all, Edward was family and I was not.

But when I reached Edward's door, Aunt Prudence was coming out, and, on seeing me, she held a finger to her lips.

'He is sleeping, poor lad,' she said softly. 'He did not have a good night and I've told him to stay in bed. Maybe he will come down this evening, but sleep is all important, Emma, it will heal him. I am sure he worked far too hard in those slums of yours. Now his poor body needs repose.'

I hesitated, then nodded briefly before going on to my room. Was all this pampering necessary? Was he really making an effort to improve in health? It seemed to me as if Edward was enjoying being an invalid, and would never pull himself together if Aunt Prudence continued to treat him in this way. So much time and attention for him, I thought angrily, but none to spare for the three little girls beneath her roof. What a strange women she was..

Feeling guilty at having such uncharitable thoughts, I washed my face with cold water and felt better.

Poor Edward. I should not condemn him. He *had* been very ill in London, but the fever had abated over a week ago and the doctor had assured me that all he needed was rest and nourishing food. Well, he was certainly getting both at Musgrove. I hoped that this would soon set him on his feet again, and that we would both be able to explore the estate together and, hopefully, enjoy the children's company as well.

Smiling a little, I patted my hair and

then went out along the passage in the direction of the front stairs. My dream was to see the girls fully reunited with their parents, leading a normal and loving family life, before Edward and I had to return to London.

'I intend visiting friends this afternoon, Emma, dear,' announced Aunt Prudence as we finished our meal. 'We will have that party for Edward once he is fully recovered, so I want to make tentative arrangements and find out what dates are most convenient for people.'

'Quite right, the drive will do Miss Emma good,' said Uncle Arnold. 'Hope you are not too bored here in the country, m'dear?'

'Not at all,' I answered truthfully. 'I am enjoying my stay here very much.'

'Er — forgive me for being blunt,' put in Aunt Prudence, 'but do you possess another morning dress?'

I flushed, looking down at the brown velvet which encased my body. I had worn it on arrival, and every day at

Musgrove so far, but then it was my only one. I kept my body and my petticoats washed and clean, and Dolly sponged and brushed my velvet every evening. It would do — it had to. For evenings I had my grey silk, and my favourite and best gown was the dark green tarlatan, which was only worn on Sundays.

'You look very neat,' said Uncle Arnold, noticing my embarassment, 'very neat and tidy, I must say.'

'This is the only day dress I have with me.' I lifted my eyes to face Aunt Lowther's enquiring stare. 'The little money we possess has to be spent on more important items than clothing.'

'Naturally, I understand, dear. You must forgive me for being impertinent. Only I wondered if you would care to look through some of poor Lilian's garments? There is a trunk in the attic, full of very good stuff, too good to throw out. And you are slim — I do believe some of the things might fit you. What do you say, Mr Lowther? You would not mind? They are just lying about up there waiting for the moth and the mice.'

Uncle Arnold nodded slowly. 'Why not?' he said. 'Miss Emma is welcome to anything she can find there — glad to be of help. Take whatever you fancy, dear girl.'

'Thank you,' I said.

No one had bothered to ask me if I should care to wear the dead woman's clothes. But I supposed that my feelings did not matter. What did matter was the fact that Aunt Prudence should not feel ashamed of me when introducing me to her friends.

That first afternoon I sallied forth in my tired brown velvet, with my black shawl pinned across my bosom with Mother's cameo brooch. I also wore my shabby brown bonnet, and Aunt Lilian's signet ring. Amazingly, I did not feel dowdy or insignificant beside Aunt Lowther's large and colourful figure.

I felt alive and excited and rather pleased with myself, emotions quite unlike my normal dull reticence. But Musgrove, I decided, was having a rejuvenating effect on me, and hopefully it would soon work its magic for poor Edward.

Aunt Prudence wore cerise-coloured satin; her face very white above the frills at her throat, and her bushy yellow hair was concealed beneath a bonnet of red velvet, lined with matching watered silk. Her soft white hands were encased in black lace mittens, through which numerous rings glittered.

'We shall visit Mabel Varney first,' announced Aunt Prudence. 'Such a dear friend of mine, but I hope her wretched son is not at home. Mabel dotes on him, but he is a complete rascal and horribly spoilt. Father died some years back, and dear Mabel finds it hard to cope with that boy. But *she* is a kind, sweet soul and one of my very best friends.'

Mrs Varney was small and plump, in a mustard silk gown, and a heavily fringed cashmere shawl covered her shoulders. She possessed a kind of faded prettiness with her pale blue eyes and soft fair hair beneath her muslin cap.

The Varneys lived in a charming house set back in one corner of the village, with weeping willows and a small pond at the bottom of their front lawn. Mrs Varney led us into her sitting-room, where the sofa and chairs were covered in a striped silk, and the furniture was of the light Georgian style, very different to Musgrove's heavy dark wood.

Mrs Varney motioned us to sit down and then cocked her head at me enquiringly.

'You remind me a little of someone, Miss Garnet. Are you related to the Lowthers?'

'Soon to be, by marriage,' simpered Aunt Prudence. 'Have you met Edward? So sorry he is not with us today but he needs time to recover from his wretched illness.'

'I saw him only as a young lad, many

years ago,' answered her friend. 'He came over and played with Harry one holiday, I remember. Seemed such a sensible boy, I did hope that he would have a good influence on my son. But there — ' she sighed and shrugged. Then she turned her attention back to me. 'Will you be staying long at Musgrove, Miss Garnet? The countryside must be such a relief after those dreadful London slums! Prudence told me how hard Edward had to work there, and such unrewarding labour, to be sure. Do you feel very low at times?'

She was looking at my unfashionable clothes and worn shoes, and I felt irritation rise in my bosom. What could these people know of poverty and dirt and destitution? They had their comforts, and their three meals a day, and their horses and carriages, and spoke of 'my' slums with a suppressed amusement behind their horror.

'Yes, naturally I feel depressed at times,' I answered quickly, 'but as long

71

as people need us we shall be there to aid them.'

'What do you actually *do*?' asked Mrs Varney, her pale eyes staring at me with interest.

'I visit the sick and talk to them. Although St Giles is grossly over-crowded nobody seems to have the time to sit down and talk. I fetch water for the elderly, and for the women who are expecting babies and should not carry heavy loads.'

'You carry water!' Mrs Varney's mouth fell open, and Aunt Prudence moved restlessly on her chair.

'Yes.' I nodded, enjoying their unease. 'I fetch it from the stand pipe in the nearest yard. We usually have to queue for it because water is only laid on for a few hours each day.'

'Why does your father not do such things? It is not right for a young lady to carry buckets like — like a servant.'

'Father probably does, in some other court, or yard. He and Edward never stopped working, and were constantly visiting people and assisting them in every possible way.'

'Do you mean to tell us, Emma, that you go about *alone*?' said Aunt Prudence, in a voice of shocked awe. 'That you wander those streets unchaperoned?'

'Heavens, yes!' I smiled at her obvious dismay. 'We would never get half the work done if we went around together. And I am quite safe, I assure you. The people know me and I have never been molested. Although I should not like to go out on my own late at night,' I admitted.

'It is shocking!' exclaimed Aunt Prudence, adjusting her bonnet.

'It would be more shocking if we did nothing to help,' I said clearly, 'and whilst I am down here experiencing all the luxuries and comforts of life in Sussex, I intend asking all your friends to make a contribution towards our work in St Giles. We need money so urgently, I am sure people here will give generously once they know about the terrible conditions of those less fortunate folk in London.'

I had had no previous intention of doing any such thing, but now the idea seemed a good one, and my words wiped the looks of disdain off my companion's faces, replacing them with expressions of stunned disbelief. I folded my hands on my lap and gazed serenely at Mrs Varney.

'We need a great deal of money,' I went on, 'and kind Aunt Prudence has suggested that we make calls and see if we cannot collect a really grand sum for my poor.'

Aunt Prudence stared at me, not daring to gainsay me in front of her friend.

'I say,' broke in a new voice from the hallway, 'what a splendid idea!'

A tall young man, with curly fair hair, strode into the room. He bowed over my hand as we were introduced, and I liked the humour in his blue eyes.

'I heard what you were saying, Miss Garnet, and I find it a capital notion.

But we must not be niggardly in our contribution, Mother, for others will see what we have given, and if it is a lot they will be unable to give less than the Varneys, for fear of appearing mean. You shall return to London with a small fortune, Miss Garnet, depend on it.'

I smiled up at him gratefully, whilst Aunt Prudence heaved with wrath at my side, and his mother twittered on the sofa like an agitated robin.

'It is no use begging from Parson Roberts,' went on Harry Varney, with enthusiasm, 'for he is too busy looking after his own flock, though their needs are few, I suspect. But you must take Miss Garnet to see the Coulsdons, Mrs Lowther, and to the Packhams, and also to Wadhurst Grange — '

'Mr Middleton is abroad,' said Aunt Prudence shortly.

'But returning soon, so I have heard,' answered the young man, 'having done very well for himself in Australia, or so the gossip goes.'

I stared at Mr Varney in admiration;

he was wearing very tight grey trousers, an elaborate waistcoat of green and yellow and orange flowers, and a frock-coat of a deeper grey, which was extremely waisted and showed his elegant frame to advantage. I had never seen such a well-dressed man, and his enthusiasm for my cause delighted me.

'Well, really!' Aunt Lowther sounded most put out. 'I cannot expect my friends and acquaintances to hand out money willy-nilly. It is so impolite to ask. Whatever gave you such an idea, Emma? All I wanted was to introduce you socially — I have no intention of using these visits for ulterior motives. No, indeed!'

'But you must.' Young Mr Varney leaned forward from his great height and smiled engagingly at my aunt. 'Don't you see what a perfect opportunity this is? Miss Garnet speaks so well and authoritatively, everyone will want to help her and Edward in their magnificent work. Such a chance is not to be missed. Come, Miss Garnet,' he held out his hand to me — 'we will seat ourselves at the writing desk over there, and I shall make out a list for you of all the people whom you must contact in the district.'

Demurely I rose to join him, and whilst the two ladies muttered behind us, he settled himself at the desk and drew pen and paper towards him.

I looked down on his shiny fair curls, and at the back of his white neck, and thought what an attractive young man he was. And so dynamic and determined. Why was Edward not like this? Why was he so weak and sickly?

'There!' Harry Varney looked up at me and smiled, and I smiled back. 'Now, I have the very thing for you. A leather bag into which you will put your store of gold. Come with me.'

He led the way from the room, and I was conscious of the ladies' frowning faces as we passed them and went out into the hall.

'It is very good of you to spare time and thought on such a venture,' I said breathlessly, for he went at a great pace, across the hall and down a passage to a room on the other side of the house.

'Nonsense — it's a pleasure. I have been spoilt all my life, Miss Garnet, and have never known hunger or want. Your talk of poverty touched my heart and it was particularly moving to see how sincere you were.' He stopped with his hand on the door, and looked down at me. 'You are very pretty, if you will excuse the impertinence, and it is unusual amongst my acquaintances to find a young lady who cares for others more than she does for herself.'

'Gracious, Mr Varney!' I felt my cheeks redden at this compliment, and wondered that he could find me attractive in my shabby brown velvet. 'I only do what any other female would do under the circumstances. I have been brought up to it, you see, and have never known any other life until now.'

He shrugged, then moved to a desk by the window and, pulling out a drawer, removed a soft leather pouch from its depths.

'Behold the receptacle for your treasure.' Smiling he held it out for me. 'Before you leave Musgrove that bag must be filled, Miss Garnet. But I hope you will not accomplish your task too soon — I should like to see more of you.'

I lowered my lashes, hiding my eyes from his intent gaze. This was ridiculous! The boy was far younger than I was and, besides, there was Edward to consider. Poor ailing, serious Edward.

'You should not be speaking to me in such a manner, Mr Varney. And I must remind you that I am betrothed to Aunt Prudence's nephew.'

'Is he as gloomy as ever?' asked my irrepressible companion. 'You would be wasted on him, Miss Garnet. Edward Lowther and I were at school together although he is some three years older than me. And would you care to know his nickname?' His glance was wicked and I should not have been prepared to listen, but I could not help myself. The

Lowthers were dull, and Edward was dull, and this young man was charming. There had been no golden-haired young men in my life before, so throwing caution to the winds I looked up at him and smiled.

'Tell me,' I said.

'Your betrothed, Miss Garnet, the man with whom you will spend all the days of your life, and it may be a very long life — was called by some Earnest Edward, and by others, Lowther the Pious. Now, can you imagine spending the rest of your days with one such as him? For I cannot believe that he has changed much since last I saw him. Has he?'

Biting my lips to suppress a giggle, I shook my head.

'Go on — laugh,' said my companion. 'I do not think you have laughed for a long time.'

'Perhaps because there has not been much to laugh at,' I answered more soberly.

'You can be certain that there will be

nothing amusing about marriage to Edward Lowther,' replied Varney.

'I shall not listen,' I cried, turning away from him. 'Dearie me, I do not know what has come over me this afternoon. I have been behaving quite unlike my normal self. For *I* am rather earnest, too, Mr Varney. At least, I was. And am therefore a good match for Edward. But today everything seems to have got rather out of hand.'

'For heaven's sake call me Harry — we are friends, Miss Emma, are we not?'

'For today, if you wish. But this evening I must return to Musgrove and be serious and respectable again. Father would not approve of all this frivolity,' I said.

'But think of the bag, Miss Emma.' Harry Varney patted the pouch and then placed it in my hand. 'Frivolity or not, we'll have that bag filled in a month and your father will not find fault with *that*, I am sure.'

'No,' I said, 'only if he learns that a handsome young man gave it to me, who flirted abominably and was impertinent about my poor Edward.'

'Poor Edward! What an excellent description of him. You will be wasted on him, Miss Emma, I can assure you of that.'

'That is for me to decide,' I said firmly, 'and now we must return to the drawing-room. I dare not imagine what they are saying about my behaviour this afternoon.'

'Let them talk. It will do the two old dears good to have a good gossip. My poor mother despairs of me and she will be able to pour out her woes to your Aunt Lowther.'

'Then we make a fine pair,' I said, 'for I am sure my aunt feels the same way about me.'

We walked slowly back down the passage and crossed the hall.

'Perhaps you would be kind enough to ride over and see Edward one day?' I suggested. 'It might help his recovery to see an old friend.'

Harry frowned at me. 'Not a friend,

Miss Emma, a mere acquaintance.'

'But your mother said you used to see each other in the holidays?'

'Mother believes what she fondly imagines to be true. She liked Edward — most adults did — he was so *sensible*. In actual fact we loathed each other both in and out of school, and he spent his time preaching at me, and would not join in any pranks'

'Then I expect you were a naughty boy and Edward was quite right not to get involved in your mischief.'

'Edward is — ' he stopped. 'No, I shall not be rude about your beloved. In fact, I shall take you up on that offer, Miss Emma, and come and visit. But it won't be to see Edward, you realise? It will be solely to see you.'

'Such nonsense!' I tossed my head and walked quickly before him into the drawing-room, but my heart was pounding with excitement and I felt exhilarated.

The atmosphere in the room was distinctly cool and we ate our cake in a chill and disapproving silence, interspersed only by Harry Varney's attempts at conversation. Soon afterwards we took our leave, and as we climbed into our carriage for the drive home, I realised that Aunt Prudence was furious.

'Never have I experienced such outrageous behaviour! I do not know what Mr Lowther is going to say. And as for poor Edward — to think that you are betrothed to him, and then spend half-an-hour alone in another room with a young man. A young man, moreover, who has a quite dreadful reputation. Poor Mabel simply does not know what to do with him — and you led him on — I could see by your expression — it was quite dreadful! How could you behave in such an unladylike fashion?'

'You must realise, Aunt Prudence, that I am not a young lady any more,' I said coolly, 'I am nearly twenty-eight years of age, and Harry could not have been — '

'Harry!'

'Could not have been more helpful,' I went on firmly. 'He is genuinely interested in our work in St Giles and this is his way of helping.' I touched the leather bag on my lap which now held two gold sovereigns.

'I have *never* been so embarrassed,' said Aunt Prudence, beginning again. 'When you two disappeared and stayed away all that time — why *no* female, no matter what her age, should have been without a chaperone in the company of *that* young man.

'I liked him. And he is coming over to Musgrove to see Edward. They were friends at school.'

'To see Edward!' she scoffed. 'He will be coming to see you, miss, and I shall tell Edward so. I saw the way he was looking at you — the allure of the older woman, I suppose.' She sniffed, 'And you were smiling and giggling there with him like some chit from the school-room. Oh, I saw, I tell you, and I was ashamed.'

The tirade went on for the entire journey home, and when we eventually arrived, I fled up the stairs to my room, thankful to get away from her grating voice.

I do not care, I told my reflection defiantly, as I unpinned the brooch from my shawl and stared at my thin form in its shabby brown cloth. What had he seen in me? He had called me pretty — could it be true? I leaned forward, examining my face in the mirror. My cheeks were flushed and my eyes sparkled, I was animated, alive with the thrill of being admired by a member of the opposite sex. Yes, perhaps I really was almost pretty.

But why did not Edward make me feel this way? He had never once complimented me on my appearance. But then I never glowed for him.

Had our relationship become stale, I pondered, did familiarity breed contempt? Yet, looking back, I could not remember feelings, or words, or looks of love between us. I had felt relief, enormous gratitude, because he had offered me marriage and given me hope for the future. He was the first man who had looked upon me with admiration, and I had grasped at his proposal of marriage knowing that it was my last chance. I had never loved him, but had felt affection for him and knew that I could and would care for him.

Now realisation had dawned on me that other men might find me attractive; that Edward might not be my last chance of wedded bliss. If a twenty-one year old lad could flirt with me, what about other men in the district? Here in Sussex I might have the opportunity to meet gentlemen of breeding and intelligence, which was an impossibility in St Giles . . .

Blinking, I put my hands to my face. What was happening to me? It must be the house — it must be Musgrove, for I had never had such odd thoughts and doubts about Edward in London. But this strange new world was rather pleasant — I had come alive — discovered a new person within my body whom I had never dreamt existed before.

Carefully, I removed my worn brown velvet and hung it in the cupboard. Then I lifted out my grey silk and rang for Dolly to assist me.

By the wall stood a massive trunk, its lid half-open, and I decided that I would have a splendid time in the coming days, rummaging through its contents and finding new gowns and shawls and slippers for the new me. I did not know for how long we would be staying at Musgrove, but intended making the most of my visit for nothing like this would ever happen to me again, of that I was certain.

Dolly helped me to arrange my hair in a different style that evening; she piled it high on top of my head, then pulled a few strands loose onto my cheeks, coaxing them around her finger so that they curled in a captivating manner.

My neck was long, and the lace collar

which adorned my silk cried out for a brooch of emeralds, or sapphires, and with my hair so high, I needed drop earrings of matching gems.

Casting a sidelong look at the trunk, which had belonged to Aunt Lilian, I wondered if any jewellery had been left amongst the clothes. But this did not seem likely, and as there was no time to go through the things before dinner, I sighed and pinned Mother's cameo at my throat. It would have to do. I still wore Lilian's signet ring, and with such adornment I would have to be content.

'My, you do look pretty tonight, Miss,' said Dolly, in admiration, standing back and clasping her hands together. 'And when we gets them old dresses out I reckon we'll find some beauties for you to wear later on.'

'Do I look all right?' I was moved by her interest and enthusiasm, and went back to the mirror and pinched my cheeks. There! The colour made my eyes look brighter and yes, with the new hair style I did look quite nice. Wishing that Harry Varney could see me now, I turned from the mirror and went out of the room.

That was a dreary meal. Edward had come downstairs and Aunt Prudence had obviously said her piece, for the atmosphere was cool and nobody remarked on my appearance, although I noticed Uncle Arnold looking at me with appreciation.

Edward was stiff in his manner towards me, Aunt Prudence was frigidly polite, and Uncle Arnold cleared his throat and began talking in a jolly way, but then subsided into silence after a swift look from his wife.

We ate our way through five courses in an uncomfortable quiet and when my companions retired to the drawing-room, I excused myself on account of a headache and went back to my room.

I am not surprised, said Aunt Prudence's eyes, glimmering at me in a venomous way. A headache is just reward for such appalling behaviour.

Have I made a terrible mistake? said

Edward's sombre face. Marriage to a flighty female would be quite intolerable.

'Sleep well, m'dear,' said Uncle Arnold out loud, no doubt hoping that all would be forgiven and forgotten by morning.

But I could not forget and it was far too early to go to bed. I felt strangely feverish, although my brow was cool, and paced the room, unable to sit quietly, or compose myself for the night.

I had to get out — away from the house and all the stuffy people in it. Fresh air and brisk exercise was needed, then, maybe, sleep would come.

On top of Lilian's trunk, spilling half onto the floor, were folds of what looked like a black velvet cloak. I lifted the lid and drew the soft, rich material towards me. It was a cloak, long and hooded, and I swathed it around my body, luxuriating in its warmth and comfort. Then I stole along the passage towards the east wing and went down the back stairs.

There was the sound of clattering of dishes and a murmur of voices from the kitchen quarters, but I saw no one and let myself out of the side door which led into the yard. Walking quickly, I went round the side of the house and across the lawn to the rose garden. With the high yew hedge all around I felt secure, and was sheltered from the cold breeze.

Holding the cloak firmly around my body, I marched up and down the paths between the rose beds until I was quite breathless, and gradually my ill-temper eased and my irritation gave way to a gentle calm. Eventually I stood, regaining my breath, looking down at the sun dial which showed up clearly in the moonlight.

Suddenly a man's voice broke the silence.

'Lilian!'

I stood, dumbfounded, as strong hands gripped my shoulders from behind and spun me round. Then two arms enveloped me, and my face was pressed against a rough textured coat.

'I have come back, my love!'

We both stepped away from each other at the same moment, I, in stunned horror, he, in shocked amazement.

'By God!' the stranger exclaimed at last. 'Who are you?'

'It might be more appropriate if you told me who you were,' I said, losing my fear and wondering if I were dreaming. 'And what are you doing in the Lowther's garden at this hour of the night?'

He was a very tall man, with curly hair and a straight nose, and a wide and generous mouth. I could see that much with the moon shining full upon him, but I could not make out the colour of his hair or eyes. 'Who are you, sir?'

He was a very handsome gentleman, and my heart leaped within my breast at the sound of his deep voice.

Forgive me for startling you.' He was looking down at me with some amusement now that he had recovered from his shock. 'I do not make a habit of embracing unknown females, I do assure you.'

'Your name, sir?'

'Charles Middleton, ma'am,' and he bowed.

I caught my lip between my teeth. So this was the neighbour who had gone off to Australia, and who had made a fortune for himself overseas? But why had he called me 'Lilian', and 'my love'? I shivered suddenly, drawing the cloak closer around me. Did he not know that she was dead?

'And your name?' he queried.

'Emma Garnet. I am staying with the Lowthers because I am betrothed to Edward Lowther.'

'Ah.' The man let out a long sigh. 'Young Edward, if I remember rightly, Lilian's beloved nephew? How are they all at Musgrove? I must ride over shortly and greet the family in daylight.' He smiled down at me, and his expression was rueful. 'I cannot expect you to forget this meeting, Miss Garnet, but I do beg for your discretion.' He lifted his hands in a small, helpless gesture. 'No doubt you will feel angry with me, and with Lilian, for deceiving her husband. But I ask you to guard your tongue and say nothing which will jeopardise Lilian's happiness at Musgrove. I have been away several years — perhaps you can understand my, er, enthusiasm at seeing her again. She is very beautiful, is she not?'

My thoughts were in a turmoil — how could he not know? Did no one write letters? Had he heard nothing on his arrival back home? Why had his servants not spoken? Surely Lilian Lowther's death, so young, would have been a momentous event in this quiet countryside?

'When did you return, sir?' I asked, unable to say more.

'I arrived but late this afternoon and came straight — straight here,' he replied softly. 'And seeing you, in that cloak, and with your hair so — ' he paused, lifting his hand as if to touch me. 'You look so very like her, I can still scarce believe it.' He bent over me, gazing into my face. 'Why do you look like that? Is she well? Is Lilian all right?'

I swallowed and lowered my head, there was no way in which I could break the news gently. 'Lilian is dead,' I said.

'Ah, no!' It was a harsh gasp of sound. 'But how? Why?' His hands came up and grasped my shoulders, giving them a little shake. 'Tell me, quickly, how can that be? She was young, so young and lovely — how can she be dead? Was she ill? A hunting accident? Tell me!' His hands and his voice were rough, and his fingers bit into my flesh, through the thick folds of velvet. 'When did it happen? Oh, God, why was I not informed?'

'You are hurting me.' I pulled away from him, angered by the ferocity of his action. It had happened so long ago, and I had not known her, it was nothing to do with me.

'I don't know what caused her death, but she must have died about five years ago. I have but recently come to Musgrove and Edward told me only that his Aunt Lilian was dead and that his uncle had married again.'

Mr Middleton turned abruptly from me, head bowed, and went to lean his tall frame against the sun dial. His chin was sunk into his chest and he stood very still.

'It was a long time ago,' I repeated.

She was another man's wife, and mother of two children. How *could* she have behaved in such a wanton manner? Meeting another man, holding secret trysts in the rose garden? It was a despicable way to behave.

And yet as I looked at Charles Middleton, at his tall manly form and strong profile, and remembered the warmth of his hands on my shoulders, and the tenderness of that first embrace, something rose within my breast and filled my heart with longing. He was a very handsome man. I thought of Uncle Arnold, small and inclined to plumpness, with greying hair and a jovial manner. He was kind, I knew, and a decent honest squire, but he was not the sort of man to lift one's heart, not the kind to make a female burn with passion.

But he was her husband, I told myself firmly, and thus worthy of loyalty and affection.

Feeling disagreeably affected by all this emotion, caught up in events which had long passed and had nothing to do with me anyway, I decided to leave the stranger to his grief and return to the house. I was both disturbed and shocked by what I had experienced, and wanted no more drama for that night.

'Wait!' I heard Mr Middleton's voice call behind me, so I halted and looked back. 'You will not speak of this meeting, Miss Garnet?' He came quickly down the path towards me, his face stern. 'I can be sure of your discretion?'

I nodded curtly. 'It is not my affair,' I said.

'Thank you. Then when we meet again, as I am certain we shall, my emotions will be under control and I shall greet you as a stranger. I trust you will understand.'

Charles Middleton bowed and then swung away towards the far entrance to the garden. I watched him go, wondering why my heart was heavy, and I felt so terribly alone.

5

The next morning I lay for a while after waking, trying to shape my thoughts into some sort of order.

What was happening to me? I lay flat upon my back, with my fingers clenched at my side; I was behaving in the most outrageous fashion and, indeed, did not feel at all like myself at times.

What had possessed me to encourage young Mr Varney? And to stand by and listen to his derogatory remarks about Edward? I had offended Aunt Prudence, I shuddered at the memory of her rage, and I had forgotten all about the children at five o'clock yesterday evening. Aunt Prudence and I had been back from our drive by then, but I had not gone down to the drawing-room to see them.

I had spent far too long making

myself attractive the night before. Why had I allowed Dolly to arrange my hair in such a frivolous style? And I had met, yes, and found desirable, a man who was a complete stranger and, moreover, an adulterer.

I had thought it before, and it was becoming more certain with every passing day, that Musgrove was having a very bad effect on me.

Flinging the bedcovers from me, I stomped across the room to the wash stand. There I ignored the jug of warm water which Dolly had brought up for me, and emptied the cold water jug into the basin. Removing my nightgown, and clenching my teeth, I sponged myself down with the icy water, punishing my shrinking limbs with vigour. There! It was the only way I could think of to chastise myself. But if I had been a nun, I thought savagely, rubbing at my goose-pimpled body, I would have taken a knotted rope and flayed my shoulders until they bled.

What *would* Father think of me?

Thank heavens he was not present to see the way in which his daughter abused his strict and pious upbringing.

And Edward? Poor dear Edward. I had scarcely seen him since we had been at Musgrove. He was my betrothed, and I had betrayed his trust by flaunting myself about the county, making sheep's eyes at strange men.

But today sanity had returned. I was aware of my numerous faults, truly repentant, and resolved to lead a more orderly, restrained and sober life from now on.

Let it never be thought that I, Emma Garnet, was like that wretched Lilian Lowther. I knew what my father would have thought of *her*. She was a trollop. She might have been Edward's adored aunt, and a very beautiful woman, also. But she was a trollop nonetheless, and Uncle Arnold was well rid of her and her cheating ways. No wonder Aunt Prudence was a little harsh with the children. Whether she had known Lilian and guessed at her behaviour, I did not know, but the two older girls possessed tainted blood in their veins and must be brought up in the firmest manner.

Poor Uncle Arnold. No wonder he had chosen Aunt Prudence as his second wife, no one could be less like Lilian, and her sensible and careful morals must have been a great relief to him after his first wife's appalling trumpery.

I put on my brown velvet. Aunt Prudence would have to get used to seeing it for daily wear; I would only don Lilian's clothing and her ring if visits, or visitors, were expected. It would not be pleasant to wear that creature's soiled raiment.

I screwed my hair back into its tight bun at the back of my head and went down the passage to see Edward.

He was sitting in a chair beside a roaring fire, wearing a maroon-coloured dressing-gown, and with a rug draped over his knees.

'Good morning, dear.' I went across and placed a kiss upon his forehead. 'I have come to apologise for my behaviour yesterday. I do not know what came over me and am truly sorry for hurting, or offending you.' I looked down into his pale face and saw relief in his eyes. 'Forgive me.' Kneeling beside his chair, I took one of his hands in mine.

'I forgive you, Emma, and pray that you will not act in such a foolish manner again. I felt so ashamed and Aunt Prudence was most put out.'

'I shall apologise to her, also,' I said contritely.

'That would be desirable.' Edward's voice was low and strained. 'My uncle and aunt are giving us a home here and your behaviour was a most selfish and unpleasant way of repaying their hospitality. Aunt Prudence says she does not like the thought of taking you visiting again, she is so fearful of what you might do or say.'

'I have said I am sorry, Edward, and can assure you it will not happen again. Do you feel any better, dear?' I held his hand to my cheek. 'Will you come downstairs later this morning?'

He shifted in his chair and cleared his throat. 'I don't know, Emma. You must not be impatient with me. Aunt Prudence says it will be quite wrong if I force myself to a normal way of life just yet, it might do my body irreparable harm.' He removed his hand from mine and put it to his brow.

'Poor Edward. I am sorry if you do not feel quite well yet, but I should so like your company downstairs. You were going to show me round the estate, and all your boyhood haunts, remember?'

'There is plenty of time for that,' he answered irritably. 'We can stay here for weeks, months, if we like. Aunt Prudence has told me so. Do not rush me, I beg.'

'I am not rushing you, Edward, but *I* cannot remain here indefinitely.' I rose to my feet and gazed down at his hunched form. 'Father cannot manage for too long on his own, and I did not intend staying more than three weeks at the most.'

'Your place is at my side. I am your husband-to-be and I do hope you will not be putting your father's wishes before mine once we are married, Emma?'

'Of course not, but I worry about Father and you know how busy we were, and Peggy Fry is expecting her baby, and Granny Lane will want — '

'Your father has Martha to cook and clean for him, and as for the others, they will have to manage without you for a time,' interrupted Edward. 'Now it is *I* who matter, and my health is of the utmost importance.' He sounded quite peevish, and I realised that my visit was probably tiring him.

'I will leave you in peace now,' I said, making for the door. 'Take care, and I'll see you downstairs this evening when the children come down. They are dear little things, do you not think so?'

'Lilian's eldest is unpleasantly spoilt, a hopeless case, I fear. But the younger ones are not too bad.'

I paused, my hand on the door. 'Why did Aunt Lilian die?' I asked, looking back at him.

'In childbirth. Elspeth lived but her mother passed away soon after her second daughter was born.'

'Oh,' I said. So Lilian must have died five years ago as I had told Mr Middleton. 'And Aunt Prudence?' I queried. 'How did Uncle Arnold meet her? Was she from the neighbourhood? When did they marry?'

'So many questions, Emma.' Edward pulled at the rug on his knees and his face twitched with impatience. 'I do not know all the details and for goodness sake do not go pestering the family about it all. It shows bad manners and a curiosity which is not appealing. Aunt Prudence is Mrs Lowther now, and an excellent wife and mother. Accept that fact and be a little more courteous towards her, if you please. I think she is rather distressed by your attitude towards her on occasion.'

'Yes, Edward,' I said meekly, and left his room.

How strange that he lacked interest now, when he had spoken often of his beloved Aunt Lilian in London. I had looked forward to learning more about her, the woman who had given him a home when she married, for Edward had been orphaned at a young age. However, that was all in the past and none of my business anyway. What little I had discovered about Lilian Lowther had not been pleasant, and it would be just as well if we forgot all about her.

Treading lightly down the stairs I descended to the dining-room. But the children could not be so easily cast aside, I decided, helping myself to the bacon and eggs which Bessie brought in for me. Neither my uncle nor aunt were present, so I ate slowly and with enjoyment, planning my day ahead.

Since my first morning at Musgrove, I had been coming downstairs for breakfast; to eat in my room was pure luxury and not in any way necessary, and I felt it would save Dolly's legs, for she had enough to do without running up and down stairs for me.

Edward was being well cared for and did not need me for the present, but the children did. Until Edward was up and about again, I intended seeking companionship with the three little girls as often as was possible.

'You did not come for a walk yesterday,' Elspeth said accusingly, when I entered the schoolroom later that morning. 'We waited and waited but you did not come.'

'That will do, Elspeth,' said Margaret quickly. 'Cousin Emma has plenty to do without wasting time with us.'

'But I did *think* about you,' I said untruthfully, bending to lift Rachel in my arms. She had run forward as soon as I came into the room, and now snuggled against me, her head tucked between my neck and shoulder. 'Sometimes I shall not be able to see you, but I shall always try and come up here whenever I can in the mornings.'

I walked forward and sat down at the table, cuddling Rachel on my lap.

'I like you,' she whispered.

'And I like you, dearest.' I bent to kiss her soft curls. 'Now, tell me what you have done since yesterday morning.'

'We walked and came home and went to bed.'

'*And* we saw Father,' added Margaret.

'Yes,' Elspeth nodded. 'And Cousin Edward. Is he ill? Will he die soon, like Mama?'

'Elspeth!' Margaret glared at her sister. 'Do not say such hateful things!' Her little white face was drawn with anger and her eyes flashed dangerously.

'It is all right, Margaret,' I said soothingly, 'your Cousin Edward is not very ill, Elspeth, dear. But he has had a fever and must stay quietly here and recuperate in the country.'

'What's recuperate?' She looked at me with her deep blue eyes.

'Get better. Now that's a good word

to learn — write it down and I'll spell it for you. Then you will have learnt a whole new word today.'

'But don't say that to Father,' cut in Margaret brusquely.

I stared at her. 'Why not?'

'I don't like talk of illness, or things like that — not with Father,' she answered.

I wondered why it mattered. Her mother had died so long ago. Margaret should almost have forgotten her by now. But that was the strange thing, the unnatural thing about her; she should not be continually living in the past, harbouring grudges still, carrying her resentment like a flag. Five years had passed since Lilian's death, no normal child should still be so implacably alienated to a new way of life. But perhaps, shut away in the east wing, as they were, with little contact with either family or friends, such behaviour was not so very odd?

'Do you remember your mother?' I asked gently. If she could bring herself to speak about Lilian perhaps she would feel better?

'I don't want to talk about her.' Margaret's mouth clamped shut and she turned her head away from my gaze.

'Very well. Let us talk about happier things. Shall I read to you again from *Gulliver's Travels*?'

'When we have done our work,' said Margaret. 'Elspeth has three more verses to learn before she may rest.'

Whilst the older girls carried on working, I took Rachel into the other room and sang some songs to her before putting her down in her bed. She slept for over an hour, and I read to Margaret and Elspeth while they painted. Before leaving, I promised to meet them for their walk, as I did not think that Aunt Prudence would pay calls for two days running. In this I was right, and managed to meet the girls in the stable yard and have a splendid walk, across the park and into the woods.

As we were returning to the house, with Margaret and Rachel a little way behind us, Elspeth caught hold of my hand and lifted her face to me.

'Would you like to see my Mama?' she whispered.

I was stunned, holding onto her hand rather too tightly. 'Why, Elspeth, your mama is — is with the angels in heaven.'

She nodded. 'I know *that*, but we keep her picture up in the attic and we go up and visit her every morning. You mustn't tell Margaret I've told you, or she'll be cross.'

'When do you go up there?'

'In the mornings, after breakfast. One of us always stays with Rachel, because it's not *her* mama, you see, and she's too young to keep a secret. So we take it in turns and I'd like to show you, Cousin Emma. Please come.'

I hesitated, wondering if it would be sensible to encourage her, knowing that so long as Lilian's picture was there for them to see daily, Margaret

113

would never forget.

'Do come, Cousin Emma. It's my turn tomorrow and I'll meet you by the back stairs — I want to show you.' She wriggled her hand free from mine. 'Ooh, you do squeeze tight!'

'Sorry.' I bent and touched her shoulder. 'Very well, Elspeth, I shall try and come tomorrow. What time will you be ready?'

'After breakfast,' she said again, and I realised that she could not tell the time yet. But the girls doubtless ate earlier than I did, so if I went along to the east wing before breakfasting myself, I should probably time it right.

'All right, dear,' I said. 'I will see you tomorrow morning by the back stairs.'

She nodded and gave a little skip. 'But don't tell.'

'I won't,' I promised.

When we arrived back in the stable yard I told them to run upstairs and make themselves tidy.

'Then you will be ready to come down at five o'clock,' I said. 'And don't say that you have already seen me today — that will be our secret.'

The children smiled and nodded and went on their way to the east wing, whilst I went to my room to divest myself of my shawl and bonnet.

My conscience pricked me at the thought of what I was doing. Was it deceitful to see the girls and say nothing to their parents? Yet I knew that if I spoke of them to Aunt Prudence, she would not want me to spend time with them; she had made that clear on my arrival. But why should I not see them? I would obey any sensible orders with alacrity, but to sit alone with my sewing each day, whilst they buried their heads in work above me, seemed a foolish waste of time. I believed that I made their lives happier, and more interesting, and all the time that Edward was ill, and Aunt Lowther so occupied with her household, why should I not be with the children?

Sighing, I decided that the secret must be kept for a while longer, at least until Edward was well and I could take him into my confidence.

The following morning, before going down to breakfast, I went along to the east wing and found Elspeth waiting at the top of the back stairs.

'*You* took a long time,' she said accusingly.

'I'm sorry, dear, have you been waiting long?'

'Ages,' she nodded, 'but it's all right now you're here. Come with me,' and she smiled and took hold of my hand.

Round the back of the stair well, in a corner so dark that I had not noticed it previously, was a small door. Elspeth pushed it open and a narrow, dusty flight of stairs met my gaze. She motioned me to go ahead of her, and closed the door behind us. Gradually my eyes became accustomed to the gloom and, lifting my skirts, I began to climb.

At the top of the flight I found myself in an enormous attic, or loft, which must have stretched the entire length of

116

the house. I had to keep my head lowered to avoid bumping it against the rafters, and numerous festooning cobwebs.

'Ugh!' I exclaimed, as one touched my cheek and clung in my hair. 'Where do we go now?'

There was light from several small windows which were set low in the walls, close to the floor, and I followed Elspeth past old pieces of furniture, and packing cases, and wicker baskets, and dust-filled trunks.

'Over here,' she said.

Hidden away behind a lopsided chest was a small, swept area, with an oil painting of Lilian Lowther propped up against a packing case. The portrait faced the window and the early morning sun shone into the attic, lighting up the face of a very beautiful woman.

Elspeth possessed her mother's colouring, I decided, looking at the raven black hair which was piled high upon a small, proud head, and the dark blue eyes which gazed serenely out from her little pointed face. The mouth was full-lipped and red, with a hint of petulance, and I imagined that the arched brows could draw together with fiery temper when the lady was angry.

I could not see any resemblance to Margaret.

Lilian wore a gown of a light material which looked like silk, and it was as blue as her eyes, with white lace at her throat and more lace edging the elbow-length sleeves. A white cashmere shawl lay over the back of her chair, and one raised hand bore a sapphire ring. The other, I saw with a shock of recognition, bore my signet ring.

In front of the picture was a glass jar, filled with a posy of wild flowers, and there was also a moth-eaten cushion, and two candles beside a tinder box. It looked for all the world like a shrine, I thought uncomfortably.

'I must just say a little prayer,' said Elspeth composedly, and to my consternation she dropped down upon the cushion, folding her hands together and shutting her eyes.

I stood quite still, staring at the woman's lovely face, wondering what life would have been like if she were still mistress of Musgrove; wishing suddenly that she had not died. I knew that she had been wicked and flighty, and unfaithful to her husband, but she had also been a good mother, if Margaret could be believed, and certainly her daughters' lives would have been happier if she were still here.

'There,' said Elspeth, rising to her feet, 'we'd better go back now or Margaret will wonder where I've got to. Don't tell her you've seen Mama, will you?'

'No, Elspeth,' I said, shaking my head, 'and thank you for bringing me. Your mother was a very beautiful lady.'

'She was, wasn't she?' remarked Elspeth cheerfully.

Then she blew a kiss at the portrait and we made our way carefully out of the attic and down the stairs again.

Later, as the girls and I were engaged in a somewhat noisy game of Blind Man's Bluff, and I wore the kerchief over my eyes and had just caught a small and squirming body which I knew was Rachel's, the door to the schoolroom was flung open and Bessie stood there, out of breath and red in the face.

'You must come at once, miss. Madam has been looking for you everywhere, and Dolly said you wasn't gone out because your shawl and outdoor shoes were still in your room. And there's been such a commotion — you must come at once!'

I pulled the kerchief from my eyes and stared back at her.

What now? How to explain my disappearance? The children had become as still as mice and we all stood motionless, but my thoughts were racing.

Of course, I *could* tell Aunt Prudence where I had been, but if she forbade me to see the children again, I could not obey her. Suppose she enlisted Edward's aid? He seemed to admire her greatly, then I would have to defy him, too. Oh, no, I could not do that — could not disobey the man I was to marry.

I glanced down at Margaret, thin, pale, overburdened Margaret, whom I was growing to love. And who was beginning to act like a child now, instead of a harassed and weary adult.

And Elspeth? She of the shiny black hair and inquisitive mind? I loved her, too.

A small hot hand slid into mine, looking down, I saw Rachel burying her face in my skirts. She, also, was most precious. I could not desert them, not yet.

Bessie, who cared for the children's needs, had no doubt guessed before now where I spent my mornings, and she was fond of the girls and would not, I believed, give away our secret. Fortunately she had known where to find me. How terrible if it had been Aunt Prudence, herself, standing swelling with rage at the schoolroom door!

'Well, now,' I said quickly, easing my hand from Rachel's grasp, 'I suppose I'd better go down and see what all the fuss is about.'

'But what will you *say*, Cousin Emma?' Margaret, at least, was aware of the difficulty.

'I shall think of something,' I said firmly. 'Carry on with your work until lunch time and *perhaps* I'll see you on your walk. I can't promise, mind.'

'She'll forbid you.' Margaret's mouth was tight. 'We'll not see you again.'

Rachel let out a wail of anguish at these words and I hushed her quickly, taking her small fist and placing it in her elder sister's hand.

'Don't be foolish, Margaret, I shall see you again either this afternoon, or else in the drawing-room at five o'clock. I want to hear Elspeth tell her father what she has learnt today.'

'Oh, come, miss!' Bessie was screwing up her apron with nervous red-fingered nails. 'You must hurry!'

I nodded, putting a hand to my

ruffled hair, trying to smooth it into a more orderly shape.

'I have been in the attics, Bessie,' I said, following her trim form down the passage. It was a half-truth, after all. 'You heard my footsteps overhead and came to call me. I'll manage the rest.'

'Very well, miss.'

'I don't like telling lies, Bessie,' I went on, 'but it's for the children, you understand that?'

'Oh, yes, miss, and I'm ever so glad. But I won't let on to the others, miss, 'case it comes to Mrs Lowther's ears.'

'Thank you. What is this all about anyway, do you know? Why am I needed so urgently?'

There's a visitor, miss. A gentleman called and he's now with Master Edward, and Mrs Lowther she said call Miss Garnet at once, see?'

I nodded and moved swiftly down the passage to the west wing. There was no time to do my hair or tidy myself up, but I could not descend by the back stairs, and must present myself to Aunt

Prudence and make my excuses before losing another minute.

At least I was in a better state of mind than on Wednesday night, and could face Mr Middleton with serenity. Presumably, he had recovered from his grief and felt able to face me and the Lowther family, with suitable composure.

'Where in heaven's name have you been, Emma?' Aunt Prudence came out of the drawing-room and faced me in the hall. 'We have been looking everywhere for you, and it has really been *most* annoying.'

'I am sorry to have caused you trouble, but I was up in the attics,' I said.

'The attics!' Her voice rose in a little shriek. 'What were you doing there? I had the trunk brought down to your room on Wednesday.'

'I found one glove and was seeking its pair,' I said, hoping that the excuse was not too weak. It was all that I could think of in a hurry. 'Why do you wish to see me?'

'Not me — Edward. Go up to his room at once. He was worried to death about you. It is really most selfish and thoughtless of you to leave him on his own so much, and now, with a visitor, it looks bad if you are not together.'

Sighing, I turned and made my way upstairs again. When I did try to see Edward he was either asleep, or too tired to talk to me. However, now my presence was desired, and I went quickly along to his room.

Perhaps Edward would be glad to see Charles Middleton, and maybe, the strong, vigorous man would imbue some of his own force into my betrothed? Maybe Edward was reminiscing about the old days when Lilian was alive? He could not talk about her in front of Aunt Prudence, so perhaps he and Mr Middleton were now exchanging memories? Painful for the latter, no doubt, but it would serve him right for behaving so badly towards Uncle Arnold. Although now that I had seen for myself the measure of Lilian's beauty, it was difficult to condemn any man for loving her.

'Come in,' called Edward, in answer to my knock, and I marched in to see him in his usual place beside the fire, and opposite him sat Harry Varney.

'My dear Miss Garnet!' Young Varney rose at once and crossed the room to greet me, his eyes snapping with amused delight. 'What a pleasure to see you again, and what a relief that you have been found.'

He was wearing fawn-coloured breeches, and a different embroidered waistcoat, of pinks and blues this time, I noticed, and a blue silk cravat was around his neck. He looked young, very smart, and very healthy beside Edward's huddled form.

'Emma, where have you been?' Edward's voice was peevish. 'I wanted to see you and was told you couldn't be found.'

'I am sorry, dear.' I removed my hands from Mr Varney's warm embrace, and walked over towards my betrothed. Then I drew forward a stool which was standing by the window, and sat down beside him. 'I was exploring the attics when Bessie came to call me.'

'The attics!' Edward's voice rose, as Aunt Lowther's had done. 'What on earth were you doing up there?'

'Looking for treasure?' Harry Varney came back from the door and seated himself opposite us.

I looked at him coldly. 'I was searching for a glove.'

'A glove!' He threw back his head and let out a bellow of laughter. 'My dear Miss Garnet, you are the most fascinating and unpredictable of women! Edward, I must compliment you on your choice of bride — she is entrancing.'

Edward looked sour and I stared with icy eyes at the young man. He needed putting in his place, and was far too forward for my liking. Aunt Prudence had been right; my stupid behaviour on Wednesday afternoon had given him the wrong impression of me.

'Emma, I have been hearing of the most extraordinary scheme — I could not believe it when Aunt Prudence described it to me, but apparently it is true. Harry says that you intend begging money from all the neighbouring families. You *cannot* be serious?'

'It was a joke, I do assure you,' I said soothingly, laying my hand on his arm. 'I happened to be telling Mrs Varney about our work in London and Mr Varney heard and thought up this wild notion. Of course we were not serious, it was merely a prank on Mr Varney's part.'

'Now, now,' said Harry Varney, shaking his head at me. 'I dare not call you a liar, Miss Garnet, but it was *you* who suggested this idea, and you took my leather pouch and the two sovereigns we gave you, with every sign of enthusiasm. You must agree to that, ma'am?'

'I accepted your money because you were so insistent, sir,' I replied quietly, 'and of course it was a most generous gesture. But I was in a strange mood quite unlike myself, sir and, on thinking it over since, have realised that Edward is right and I could not possibly ask other people for money.'

'I should think not!' said Edward.

'But if we, here in the country, care to make donations to a just and worthy cause, why should we not?' asked the young man, sticking out his chin in a stubborn way.

'Because I shall not ask,' I answered, 'and beg that you forget all that was said on Wednesday. My behaviour was most out of character, and I was not myself.'

'I see.' Varney rose to his feet, looking down at me in a curious fashion. 'Then I shall bid you farewell, Edward, and wish you a speedy recovery. Perhaps you would be so kind as to see me out, Miss Garnet?'

I nodded and walked before him to the door. 'Will you be coming down-stairs for lunch, Edward?'

'I don't think so. I shall have a rest now, all this talk has wearied me greatly,' he answered, leaning his head back in the chair and closing his eyes. 'My regards to your mother, Varney.'

'What a marvellous performance!' said Mr Varney, as he followed me down the passage. 'But you must see what I mean, Miss Emma, Edward is *not* the right man for you.'

'I do not know what you are talking about, Mr Varney.' I paused at the top of the stairs. 'I meant every word that I said in there.'

'Dear Miss Garnet.' He put a hand on my arm and his blue eyes were puzzled. 'You cannot have changed so much since your visit to us? You must see for yourself that marriage to Edward would be intolerable — he has no sense of fun, and is so horribly boring. You *must* agree? Why, we laughed about him on Wednesday!'

I shook myself free from his touch, quivering with anger. 'Do not keep calling me *dear* Miss Garnet, and it is you who are boring, and also incredibly rude, sir!' I snapped. 'I am sorry if I gave you the wrong impression last time we met, but that was not the real me, so please forget all about that meeting. Please go now, and do not call again unless it is to see Edward, and that, you must agree, seems hardly likely.'

Varney frowned and stepped back from me, studying my face with reflective eyes. 'It is odd,' he remarked, 'but you even look different today. And that hair style — all scraped back — it is not becoming. I must admit that I preferred the attractive young lady whom I met on Wednesday. However,' he went on hastily, 'before you bite my head off I shall depart. If you *should* change your mind, I shall always be delighted to see you. But as you are now, Miss Garnet, you and Edward are well suited.'

He looked at me for a long moment, and then bowed and went whistling down the stairs before I could think of a fitting reply.

6

That afternoon Uncle Arnold gave me a short tour of the home farm. I was still feeling ruffled by Harry Varney's unexpected visit, and when Uncle Arnold enquired if I should care to join him, I leapt at the chance. Aunt Prudence looked sour, but insisted that *she* had no time to waste, so we left her behind and, after putting on my stout walking boots, I followed Uncle Arnold out into the stable yard.

The stable block was bordered by a high wall and in this was a door to which my uncle led me. Beyond was the farm.

'Edward will see a great difference when he is well,' said my companion, 'for I have invested heavily in a new under-drainage system. The soil here is mainly clay and in winter Musgrove becomes a morass and the land is virtually unworkable. But now, over two hundred acres have been drained and Hilton assures me that we will produce some fine crops next spring.'

'How many acres do you possess?' I asked.

'Six hundred, m'dear. But if that seems large to you, Charles Middleton owns a thousand acres at Wadhurst.'

'A lot of land,' I said.

'And at five pounds per acre to drain, a lot of money,' nodded Uncle Arnold.

'And here?' I stopped and gazed at a group of labourers who were engaged in constructing a building of some kind.

'Here we will have a new barn, a better-designed dairy, and a bullock yard,' announced Uncle Arnold. 'You will see the old ones in a minute and will realise there is room for improvement. I am also pulling down several of the old cottages, terrible wattle and daub affairs, and building proper brick and slate houses for my workers. I shall rent each one for a shilling a week, because the worth of such dwellings must be appreciated.'

'I am sure they will be, and only wish that there were such caring landlords as yourself in St Giles. Tell me, what is the average wage of one of your labourers?'

'Eight shillings and five pence a week, and they get their ale allowance each day, of course, and a flitch of bacon once a month.'

We paused at one of the pig sties and Uncle Arnold placed his hand on the low wall before him, his eyes studying the pink, nostril-twitching animals with affection; they were so much bigger than I had anticipated, looking back at me with mutual interest from their small, intelligent eyes.

'My dream, Miss Emma,' said my uncle, 'is to possess a model farm with everything new and clean and well-made and efficient.'

'I should imagine that dream will come true very quickly,' I answered smiling. 'For already many things have changed, and your labourers will work diligently because they will benefit from the changes.'

Uncle Arnold nodded and breathed out a long sigh of satisfaction. 'Contented, well-housed labourers, contented, well-housed animals — and the land showing a healthy profit year after year, that is what I wish above all else.'

'Yes,' I said softly, feeling that I could grow to love this place as much as he so obviously did.

People worked hard on the land, but it was natural work; with fresh air and sunshine, and the honest dirt of animals, and the good Lord's soil beneath their feet. Those who laboured in the cities were surrounded by man-made filth and squalor; working in airless sweat-shops, or factories, and returning home at night to unhealthy, evil-smelling hovels.

'You like the country, Miss Emma?' He had turned, and was watching my face. 'You like Musgrove?'

'I love it, and could not desire a more perfect existence.'

Uncle Arnold smiled and took hold of my arm, beginning to lead me back to the house. 'I am glad that you are to be Edward's wife, my dear. And you know, Miss Emma, at times you remind me very much of my — of Margaret's mother. She loved this land, also. It pleases me to realise that Musgrove will be in such good hands when I am gone.'

*　*　*

When Bessie brought me my breakfast next day, I decided to ask her about the children. One should not question servants, or take them into one's confidence, but I had to find out more about this strange household. I also knew that Bessie was fond of the girls and, since our fright the morning before, felt that she would be on my side and could be trusted.

'For how long have you been at Musgrove?' I asked, as she poured out my coffe. 'Did you know the first Mrs Lowther?'

'No, miss. Me and Dolly was engaged by the present Mrs Lowther after she married the master.'

'And the other servants?' I queried. 'Have they been here long?'

'Mr Martin, he's bin with Mr Lowther goodness knows how long, and Cook's bin here ages, too. The other maids — ' she paused, raising her eyes to the ceiling — 'Min's newer than us, and Elsie were here before we come.'

I pondered. It would be impossible to have a heart-to-heart with Martin, Uncle Arnold's manservant, and I seldom saw the other maids, who worked mainly in the kitchen and scullery. Cook would probably know all the gossip, but I never saw her, either.

'Do you know why the children are not allowed downstairs, Bessie? It seems a little strange to me that they always have to stay in their rooms.'

'Cept at five o'clock, miss, they always come down then and see their parents.'

'Yes, I know, but that's a very short time each day.'

Perhaps she did not find this puzzling? Perhaps this was normal in big houses? I, being motherless from the age of six, had spent much time with Father, and he had taken me with him everywhere he went. But maybe such behaviour would be considered odd by other people? I had no experience of how the upper class lived, and knew only the close-knit family life of the crowded St Giles slums.

'Course, Mrs Lowther is terribly houseproud,' remarked Bessie, 'and it wouldn't do to have the girls running all over the place. They go out for walks every afternoon, miss, but they have to use the side entrance. We couldn't have them tramping all over the carpets in muddy boots, now could we?' She gave a quick grin and began to leave the room. 'Children should be seen and not heard, I believe 'tis said, and they're best off up there with all them books and toys.'

So she accepted Aunt Prudence's rules without question; well, perhaps she was right. But these children were not even *seen* very much, I thought grimly. And with that shrine to Lilian, one could call it nothing else, their isolation was positively unhealthy. Mentally, that was. I did not fear for their bodies, but was worried about their minds.

'Thank you, Bessie, I have everything I need,' I said, as she hovered by the open door.

She smiled gratefully and scurried away, no doubt anxious not to be caught prattling in the breakfast room by her mistress.

I still had not discovered why *I* should not see the girls; Bessie had answered the question as to why they were shut away upstairs. Well and good, Aunt Prudence was an excellent housekeeper and kept Musgrove in beautiful order, she would not want the children running through the rooms causing a rumpus. But why should I be stopped from seeing them? Why should we all live in fear lest my visits be found out? Perhaps I had not tried hard enough? Maybe I had misunderstood her intentions?

When Aunt Prudence came briefly into the room, as was her wont, to wish me good morning and to enquire if I had slept well, I tried once more.

'I wondered if I might go upstairs and see the girls this morning?' I said brightly. 'I can take my sewing with me, and should enjoy their company for a few hours whilst Edward is still unwell.'

'I would rather you did not, Emma. They have plenty of studying to do and their social time is at five o'clock every evening, as you know.' She smiled at me with her mouth, but her eyes were cold. 'You could always talk then, but I haven't noticed that you take much interest when they come downstairs. Is it vulgar curiosity, Emma? I can assure you that they have pleasant rooms, and good food, and Bessie cares for all their wants.'

'I thought they seemed a little shy,' I said defensively, 'and do not like to question them too much for fear of embarrassing them.'

'Question them too much? You do not even say one word to them!'

It was true that I kept silent when the girls came down, but this was because I was frightened lest Rachel gave our secret away. Knowing that the other two could be relied upon to remain aloof, I still kept my distance, fearful lest little Rachel run across and climb into my lap if I so much as smiled at her.

'It might be necessary to go poking and prying into the affairs of those poverty stricken creatures in your slums, Emma, but I can assure you that such attention is not needed here at Musgrove. The children are fit and happy, as you have seen, and must learn to be self-reliant. Mr Lowther and I are very occupied with our own affairs, so we set aside that half-hour for the girls every evening. I think that is quite sufficient. I am sorry if you are bored with life here in the country, perhaps it would be as well if you returned to your father in London? Edward is, alas, not well enough to return to that arduous work, but we would care for him in your absence, and you could come down again in the summer, perhaps?

I gazed at her for a moment, unable to speak. She wanted me gone. For some strange reason she was trying to separate us, and would like nothing better than to have me gone. But why? She was an enigma; I neither knew nor liked her, and was determined not to please her on this matter. I would not be parted so easily from Edward, neither would I leave the children — not yet.

'You are very kind to Edward,' I answered sweetly, 'and I do appreciate how difficult it must be having an invalid in the house. But I shall stay a little longer, if you don't mind. He would miss me if I went, and has already stated most emphatically that my place is by his side. I also want to get to know the estate better, and to meet more of Edward's friends from the past. If Musgrove *is* to be our future home, I should like to know it well.'

There, that would not please her! She had made clear her intention of providing Uncle Arnold with a son and heir on our first evening at Musgrove, but whether she would achieve this aim I rather doubted. Aunt Prudence was not a young woman, although it was impossible to guess her age, and Rachel was nearly four years old. If there was no boy-child to follow her, the estate would be Edward's in time.

I watched Aunt Prudence through narrowed eyes, wondering if she would mind giving up her home to us, and with sudden clarity I realised that she would mind, very much indeed.

'Stay, if you will.' She shrugged her big shoulders, but her neck had become red and blotchy, and looked rather too fat for her white lace collar. 'Do not become too fond of Musgrove, Emma, I intend giving Mr Lowther more children before my child-bearing days are over, and if we do not have a son — ' she paused, and her little eyes stared at me, unblinking and malevolent. 'It is possible for Wills to be changed and, moreover, for a daughter to inherit. This land is not entailed, you know.'

'Then it must go to Margaret,' I said softly, 'for she is the eldest.'

'It will never go to Lilian's eldest,' she replied flatly. 'And I do not wish you to entertain false hopes, either.'

'Edward hopes that it will come to him in time,' I said, 'he has always loved it.'

'Edward.' She smiled, without humour. 'Edward is weak and timid and your uncle is realising that now. He is not of the right calibre to manage a large estate.'

No, but I could, I thought suddenly. And Uncle Arnold likes me. If I were Edward's wife, and he inherited Musgrove, I could learn how to keep it prosperous. Was that why she wanted me gone? Was she aware of her husband's fondness for me?

'You are not seeing Edward at his best,' I said. 'He is a most responsible and caring person when he is well. Father had nothing but praise for him in London. And Edward was often speaking about Musgrove, and the happy holidays he spent here when his Aunt Lilian was alive.'

Aunt Lowther's face closed, and her neck became redder.

'Lilian was a silly, feckless creature and best forgotten,' she snapped. 'Oh, the men adored her, so pretty and gay and light-hearted, they all said. Light-headed, was nearer the truth! Spending money like water — all those clothes — you've seen them. What must they have cost, I ask you? And forever at her mirror, prinking and patting and doing her hair in a hundred different ways; wasting time with that child all day long, painting pictures, and whatnot. And no order in the house — ' she stopped, aware that her tongue had run away with her.

'So you knew Lilian?' It had not occurred to me that the two women had met. Aunt Prudence must have lived in the neighbourhood. Here at last was the knowledge I had been seeking; here was someone who had known Lilian. But she had not liked her. The understandable emotion of a plain female for a beautiful one.

'I was housekeeper here for a year before she died,' answered Aunt Prudence. 'Now, I have wasted enough time talking and must leave you to your own devices. There are books in the library, if you wish to read, and I hope you have managed to find some new gowns in the trunk.' She glanced at my brown velvet with distaste. 'Alter any you wish, but do find yourself something new. That gown does not become you, and with all those other dresses at your disposal you must surely find something appropriate. I cannot abide waste,' she said.

Two days later Aunt Prudence and I took the carriage and went to have tea with Parson Rogers and his wife. This had been Uncle Arnold's suggestion.

'I trust we are entertaining you enough, Miss Emma?' he had said. 'You must not go back to the city believing that life in the country is dull. And with Edward still indisposed, your days must be long and dreary.'

'Oh, no, indeed!' I had answered, for in truth I was happily occupied with the children.

'Take her visiting,' he said to his wife. 'She must meet more people, m'dear, and have a gayer time. There can be little chance of chatter and light-hearted entertainment in the St Giles slums.'

So Aunt Prudence spoke to the parson after service on Sunday, and we were duly invited to tea the following day.

I spent a little time with Edward

before we went, feeling somewhat guilty at leaving him on his own so much, then Dolly assisted me with a new gown which we had found in Lilian's trunk.

It was of pale green silk, with a matching silk mantelet, trimmed with ruches of lace. Dolly had also discovered a straw hat, which had a green satin ribbon around the crown, and which tied in a large bow at the side of my head, held in place by my bun.

'Oh, what a fuss!' I declared, wishing that I could have remained in my simple brown velvet. 'Hurry up, Dolly, my aunt will be calling in a minute.'

Dolly fiddled and tweaked at the silly bow, wanting to get just the right effect, and I was in such an impatience to be off and away from her irritating fingers, that when Aunt Prudence called for me I left without my brooch or my ring.

'I am in a great rush,' said my aunt, ushering me out of the hall towards the waiting carriage, 'because I intend leaving my card at Wadhurst Grange on our way to the village. I hear that Mr Middleton has returned, and had hoped to have seen him in church yesterday only he was not present. Now we will just pop round and see if he is at home, I wish to invite him to our party once we have been introduced.'

As we drove up the long, tree-lined drive which led to Wadhurst, I wondered how the man would react when he saw me again. I certainly had no desire to see him, but a meeting could not be avoided, it seemed.

He would be relieved to know that I had held my tongue, I thought grimly, but then whom was there for me to gossip to? I never seemed to have a proper conversation with Edward these days, Uncle Arnold was only interested in his estate, and Aunt Prudence was not the sort of person with whom one gossiped.

I wondered if anyone had guessed at Charles Middleton's relationship with Lilian Lowther? Aunt Prudence had said she was admired by all the gentlemen, which probably meant that Lilian had flirted with every one of them, therefore any attention which Mr Middleton had shown her would not have been remarked upon.

'Did you know Mr Middleton before he went to Australia?' I asked.

'If you remember, Emma, I was merely the housekeeper in those days,' she answered snappishly, 'and thus remained well out of sight. Now I can meet Mr Middleton as an equal, and look forward to seeing his home. I don't suppose he will be in at this hour — ' she leaned forward and peered out of the window — 'but I shall be invited inside one day, and leaving my card will be the first step in that direction. Look! There is the house, is it not magnificent?'

Over her shoulder I glimpsed a large white house, with many long windows reflecting the afternoon sun in their panes, and two fine pillars were set before the front door. It was an immensely elegant building, but did not, I felt, possess the quiet charm of Musgrove.

As we drove up to the front steps a man came out through the door and stared at us. He was wearing cream-coloured breeches, a dark green jacket, and shiny black riding boots.

'Why, I do believe it is Mr Middleton himself!'

Aunt Prudence called out to the coachman to stop and was opening the door almost before the wheels had ceased rolling. I stared straight ahead. It *was* Mr Middleton, and I did not wish to speak to him.

My heart was beginning to pound in a queer fashion, and the palms of my hands were moist within my gloves. I remembered the warmth of his embrace, and felt sick. How dreadful to have been taken into the enveloping arms of a complete stranger! And now, to have to face him with that memory clear in my mind — it was intolerable. I prayed that Aunt Lowther would hand him her card and leave at once. We had arrived unexpectedly, unannounced, and she had no right to linger.

'Emma! Come down at once, Mr Middleton has kindly invited us in!' Her voice was shrill with excitement.

'We are due at the Vicarage for tea,' I called back, 'we do not have time.'

'There is plenty of time.' She came bustling back to the carriage, her face unusually red. 'Get down this minute, girl, how can you be so impertinent!'

Angrily, I gathered up my skirts and made to leave the carriage.

'Allow me.' Mr Middleton appeared beside my aunt, hand outstretched, and as our fingers touched I felt a tremor shoot along my arm and pierce my resisting body.

'This is Miss Emma Garnet, my niece-to-be,' I heard Aunt Prudence explain in a foolish, high voice, as I alighted in the drive at his feet and bowed my head.

He was very tall, I had forgotten how tall he was, even bigger than Harry Varney, and this made it easier for me to avoid his gaze. I lifted my eyes to the height of one of his waistcoat buttons and murmured, 'How do you do?'

'Enchanted,' said his deep voice above me, with a trace of amusement in it, and then turned to follow my aunt who went prattling up the front steps and into the house.

Mr Middleton took us on a very quick tour of the downstairs rooms, and I remained stubbornly silent as Aunt Prudence exclaimed and made trite remarks about the lavish furnishings, and the paintings, and the exquisite porcelain ornaments which were out on display.

'The rooms are almost ready now,' remarked Charles Middleton, 'for everything of value was stored away whilst I was abroad. It has taken time to put everything back in its rightful place. But Mrs Bridges, my housekeeper, has taken splendid care of my home and I am delighted with Wadhurst all over again, seeing it with new eyes, as it were.'

We were on the first floor now, walking down a long gallery which ran the length of the house, and where family portraits and other fine oil paintings hung along the wall facing the windows.

'My ancestors, and others,' said Mr Middleton drily.

'Have you no bride in mind?' asked Aunt Prudence coquettishly, eyeing the paintings with awe. 'It would be too sad if there were to be no more Middletons to grace these walls. Did you not meet any attractive young ladies on the other side of the world?'

I did not hear his reply. I was staring at the last painting in the row, at a boy in a black velvet suit, whose arm lovingly encircled a small dog, which stood on a chair beside him. There was something about the glossy dark hair and the large enquiring eyes which seemed familiar. My spine tingled with fearful recognition — where had I seen that face before? That pensive, intelligent little face? It was Elspeth!

'A flattering portrait, Miss Garnet,' said Mr Middleton's voice, breaking in on my reverie, 'painted after my father's death, hence the mourning suit. Can you see a resemblance to the man as he is today? Do you like it?'

I forced my eyes away from the picture and looked up into his interested gaze. His hair was not so dark now, doubtless lightened by the strong Australian sun, and his eyes were hazel, unlike Elspeth's vivid blue. She had inherited her mother's colouring, but her expression, and her features, were too like that small boy's for me to be mistaken.

'I like the child but not the man,' I answered shortly, and walked away from him to join Aunt Prudence, who was admiring a chinese vase.

'Is your niece always so quiet, Mrs Lowther?' asked Mr Middleton. 'I had thought that the fair sex always had plenty to say for themselves.'

Aunt Prudence flashed me a look of displeasure. 'Emma is a moody creature,' she replied. 'Sometimes she is far too voluble and at other times she sulks. I fear we are wasting your time, my dear sir,' she went on quickly, 'and must be on our way to the Vicarage. I cannot thank you enough for showing us your beautiful home, and I do so hope that you will come over and renew acquaintances with Mr Lowther and my nephew in the near future. We shall be giving a small party shortly, to which you will of course receive an invitation, and you must on *no* account refuse, dear sir!' She tapped his arm playfully with her finger, and he smiled in response and led us along a further corridor to the head of the staircase.

'I shall be delighted to come to your party, ma'am, and will also try to visit Musgrove shortly.'

'You knew Edward as a boy, of course?' she queried, adjusting her bonnet as we entered the hall and made ready to depart.

'Indeed, yes. Edward used to come over in the holidays and we often rode together. I look forward to seeing him again.'

And what of your daughter? I thought fiercely. Do you know that a child of yours also lives at Musgrove?

'Yes, well, poor Edward has not been well of late,' said Aunt Lowther sighing. 'But with a good long rest here in the country I'm sure he'll mend in time.'

'What ails him?' asked Charles Middleton.

'He has been doing far too much in the slums, you know. Emma and her father work in St Giles and the conditions are quite dreadful there. Poor Edward went down with a fever some weeks ago and that was why Mr Lowther invited him to Musgrove.'

'You live in St Giles?' Mr Middleton turned to me, surprise in his voice. 'You live and work in those slums?'

I opened my mouth and then shut it again.

'Oh, yes, she and her father are fighting poverty, but it really doesn't *do*, Mr Middleton!' Aunt Prudence gave a light laugh. 'The poor are always with us, alas, but they are not receptive to new ideas and it is a thankless task trying to teach them about cleanliness, and good food, and the like. Rather a waste of time, if you ask *me*, but then Mr Garnet is a clergyman and bent on doing Good Works, don't you know?'

I turned and walked down the steps, needing to get some fresh air, to escape from Aunt Lowther's cruel tongue. I strode quickly across the gravel and climbed into the carriage, seething with rage. How dared she mock our work and scorn the poor people who had not enough to eat, and neither clean clothes to wear, nor water in which to wash their wretched bodies? And he was as bad as she was, listening to her with that inane smile upon his lips! Adulterer. He, who loved another man's wife, and produced a bastard into the bargain — how I despised them both.

The carriage lurched as Aunt Prudence heaved her bulk into the seat beside me.

'Goodbye,' called Mr Middleton, but Aunt Prudence was leaning forward blotting out my vision, so I did not have to look at him again. 'I shall be calling at Musgrove soon. Goodday to you, Mrs Lowther, and to you, Miss Garnet, I will see you again shortly.'

'Well, really Emma, I found your conduct most impolite.' Aunt Prudence shifted her position, resettling her shawl about her plump shoulders. 'You were impossibly rude to that charming man and I shall have to tell Mr Lowther. I really do not think I can take you visiting again.'

'Aunt Prudence,' I said, turning in my corner to look across at her, 'last time you said I talked too much, and was over-friendly and forward. Now you accuse me of sulking. I really do not know what you really want of me.'

'I expect politeness without frivolity,' said my aunt, 'and talk, not prattle. Dear me, girl, haven't you been taught how to behave in company? No, I suppose not. You do not entertain in

159

those slums of yours and are unused to gentlefolk. Well, for heaven's sake speak a few words to the vicar and his wife, or it will be all round the county that Edward is marrying a mute!'

'I shall do my best, but we are going to be very late and they have probably had tea already.'

'Nonsense! They know we are coming and will have waited for us.'

She was right, of course. Parson Rogers and his wife had indeed waited, and when they heard the reason for our delay they were full of envious enquiries. How did Mr Middleton look? Had he brought a bride back with him? Was he as handsome as ever? Did he intend settling down in England for good now?

They gossiped and tittered and talked a lot of foolish nonsense, admiring the man for his wealth and looks, not knowing the unsavoury truth about him, which I longed to divulge. I sat in stony silence, far too insignificant for them with my plain countenance and borrowed clothing. Mrs Rogers glanced at me from time to time and I felt sure that she knew she had seen my gown before, and that it did not suit me as well as it had Lilian's fair form. Fortunately they were all so busy discussing Mr Middleton, that I could remain silent without exciting Aunt Prudence's wrath. She was in her element, describing all that she had seen at Wadhurst, and they listened with envy and admiration.

What made me even more irritable was the fact that their home was spacious and very comfortable; not for them a dark, narrow house in a rat-infested alley. Of course, Father could have lived in a better house nearer his church, which was in a square off the High Street. But he had stubbornly refused comfort, insisting that his place was amongst the poor and needy, so Martha and I made the best of our damp home in Flower Street, and I had never realised its inadequacies until I came to Sussex.

Seeing Parson Rogers with his fat

stomach, and his well-clad wife, who presided over a tea table groaning with rich fruit cake, buns and biscuits, made me envious and cross. This clergyman was not interested in his parishioners' souls, all he wanted to know about was the state of their purses, and he judged them accordingly. Mr Middleton was deemed a fine and worthy gentleman because he owned a large house and one thousand acres of land.

Aunt Prudence was very quiet on the way home, she did not criticise me again, and that evening I realised where her thoughts lay.

'Mr Lowther, would you mind if I invited my sister, Alice, to stay?' she said brightly, having regaled her husband and Edward with our afternoon's adventures. 'I have not seen her for over a year, and she would be company for Emma.'

'Good idea, good idea,' nodded Uncle Arnold. 'Nice little thing, if I remember right. Still at school, is she?'

Aunt Prudence nodded, glancing

quickly at me and Edward. 'Of course, Alice is no longer a schoolgirl,' she said, 'but works for Miss Hetty in her establishment, and earns a small living. There is so little employment for genteel young girls with impoverished means. If Miss Hetty can spare her I should love her to come, and with that charming Mr Middleton coming to the party, I must provide some unattached females for his amusement.'

'Good idea,' said Uncle Arnold again. 'Be pleasant for Miss Emma, too. You girls will be bound to get on famously together. Splendid notion, Mrs Lowther, send word to your sister at once.'

My heart sank at these words. I did not need company, and if this wretched Alice were present how was I ever going to slip away and spend time with the children?

7

The following afternoon I managed to get away and meet the girls in the stable yard. It was round the corner, out of sight of the house, so even if Aunt Prudence should have been in the kitchen, I could not have been observed from the window.

'Can we go and see the sheep?' said Elspeth, giving her accustomed little skip. 'I want to see the lambs — they are so pretty, Cousin Emma.'

'You must show me the way,' I said, holding Rachel's hand and following the two older girls along the path which led through the kitchen garden. It was a way I had not been before, and out onto a rough furrowed track, which was bordered by fields.

It was a sunny, fresh day and the air was wonderfully clear; although I had been at Musgrove for over a week, I was still surprised by the wide open spaces and clear air, and I breathed in deeply, awed by the beauty all around me, yet saddened by the fact that so few people could share my joy. How many thousands were there, I wondered, thronging the mean streets and alleys of London, living in cramped, stench-filled dwellings, dying of starvation and disease, whilst I sauntered at my leisure through acres of uninhabited and lovely countryside?

If there were only enough money, I thought grimly, I would bring out all the orphaned children and give them a home, and let them run and shout and leap in the fields; craftsmen would be engaged to teach the boys how to work with wood, and leather, and metal, and the girls would be taught how to spin and weave.

Dearie me, what a dream! But how rewarding such a life would be. They would have to return to the towns and cities eventually, I realised, for who here on the land would require a dozen carpenters, or weavers? This was the reason so many families had drifted to the cities; they needed work, which was no longer to be found in the country. But, at least, my children would begin with healthy bodies, and with a trade; I would give them a decent start in life. As mistress of Musgrove, I could do so much . . .

'There's the field!' called out Elspeth, rushing ahead, and Rachel let go of my hand and ran to join her at the fence.

'There's someone coming,' remarked Margaret, moving sedately at my side, and I looked ahead and saw a horse and rider on the track.

'I wonder who it can be?' I strained my eyes, hoping that it was no one from Musgrove. But there — if it came to Aunt Prudence's ears that I had been out walking with the children, I should not deny it. I had gone for a walk, met the girls en route, and joined them on their ramble. She could not find fault with *that*.

As the horseman advanced, I saw

that it was Charles Middleton. Dear heavens — why did it have to be him? Margaret had slipped away to join her sisters at the fence, so I had to face the gentleman alone.

He was bare-headed, looking very sun-bronzed and healthy, wearing the same green jacket and with a pale green silk cravat tied around his neck. As he drew rein he looked down at me, a half-smile upon his lips.

'Goodday to you, Miss Garnet. Dare I enquire as to whether you are in a talkative, or a sulky mood this afternoon?'

'I find that remark offensive. Pray do not spoil our walk, sir.'

'Ah, sulky, I perceive.'

'I am *not* sulky,' I retorted, 'And never have been. That was purely Aunt Lowther's way of showing she was cross with me. The first time she took me visiting she declared that I talked too much, but when I am quiet she accuses me of sulking!'

'You cannot win, it seems.' He swung

down from his horse and began walking by my side. 'Then perhaps I may join you and we can indulge in a little pleasant conversation? Brutus will doubtless be glad of the rest for he has led an idle life these past years.'

I looked at the beast doubtfully. 'He is very large.'

'Do you not ride, Miss Garnet?'

'You forget, sir, that horses are only seen in St Giles on rare occasions, and then they are pulling drays. There is nobody to give riding lessons in the slums.'

'I am put firmly in my place. Tell me, Miss Garnet, why do you dislike me? I did not notice it on our first meeting, but it is clear to me now that you feel aversion. Is it because of my past indiscretion with — '

'Hush!' I warned, as Margaret left the others and crept nearer, her eyes on the horse. 'She would dearly love to ride. Margaret, come and meet Mr Middleton who owns this beast.'

It would do her good to meet

someone new, I thought, and perhaps, with her love of horses, she would lose her shyness and be able to speak to the man.

Charles Middleton looked down at the girl and then held out the reins to her. 'Can you lead him for a while?' he asked. 'My arms are tired and he is a placid brute, grown fat and lazy, I'm afraid.'

Margaret's little face lit up with excitement and she took the reins from him, then stretched out her free hand and stroked the horse's velvety nose.

'He is beautiful,' she whispered, and began to lead him ahead of us down the track.

There was something infinitely moving about the sight of that huge animal, and the small, slender girl in her grey bonnet and gown.

'Is that Lilian's daughter?' asked my companion quietly.

I nodded, wondering about Elspeth. Should I say something about her? She was still at the fence, chattering away to

Rachel about the lambs, her bonnet concealing her face.

'And the other two?' Mr Middleton jerked his head in their direction. 'More Lowther's? Or have you children here to play?'

'I think not, Mr Middleton.' I looked up at him and he must have been warned by the expression on my face.

'What do you mean by that?' He stared back at me, a startled look appearing in his hazel eyes.

'Rachel is the youngest and belongs to Aunt Prudence and Uncle Arnold, but Elspeth — ' I shrugged, pulling my shawl closer around my body, ' — see for yourself.'

Charles Middleton turned and walked swiftly away towards the fence, where he stopped and lowered his head to speak to the two younger children.

I hurried to catch up with Margaret and smiled at her. 'You are doing that as to the manner born,' I said, 'are you not afraid of such a big animal?'

'No, Cousin Emma, he is wonderful!'

170

There was colour in her face, and her eyes were alive, sparkling with happiness. I had never seen her so animated, and realised that she might grow up to be a very pretty woman — if she were happy. Oh, the pity of it all!

Uncle Arnold would have to be confronted, I decided suddenly. Before going back to London, I would try and see that Margaret had the chance of riding, of possessing a pony of her own. Surely he would agree to that?

'I think we had better go back in a minute,' I said, 'or you won't be in by five.'

'Yes,' she replied with a little sigh, and pulled the horse to a halt. Then she stretched up and planted a kiss on its nose. The horse threw back its head and snorted, drawing up its top lip and looking most comical.

'Look, Cousin Emma — he is laughing!'

'He likes you.' Mr Middleton had come up on the far side of the horse, and now took the reins from her outstretched hands. 'How about having a ride on him?'

And with a small shriek of surprise, she was lifted into the air and placed on the saddle, her skirts bunching beneath her.

'That was rather unexpected,' I said, moving quickly to pull down her dress. But sitting astride, as she was, it was impossible to make her appear more ladylike. 'Really, Mr Middleton, it is not right to perch her up there — what if she should fall?' I hovered anxiously, holding on to Margaret's right leg, terrified lest harm befall her.

'Nonsense,' replied Mr Middleton, 'Lilian's daughter will not fall. She will be like her mother, a fearless and expert horsewoman, given the chance.'

I saw Margaret's face go white, and my heart sunk. He was going to undo all the good which had been done that afternoon.

'Did you know my mother?' she asked, in a small clear voice.

I held my breath, keeping my face

down, praying that he would say the right thing.

'I knew your mother, Margaret,' said Mr Middleton cheerfully, plodding along beside her. 'And she was a brilliant rider, taking every jump, afraid of nothing. You should have seen her out hunting, she practically led the field and put most men to shame.' He looked up at the girl as I glanced swiftly across at him, and he was smiling into her tense face. 'Do you know? I believe you could be just as good as she was. You have light hands and a nice straight back. You're a natural, my love, must have inherited it from Lilian.'

Margaret nodded slowly, and I gave a sigh of relief.

'I would like to get down now, if you please,' she said, and I saw that the house and outbuildings were in sight.

Mr Middleton swung her down on his side, saying, 'Any time you feel like a ride just ask your father to bring you over to Wadhurst and I'll give you some lessons. I've a nice little pony there just about ready for schooling, and we'll tackle him together. How would you like that?'

She came round into my sight, straightening her bonnet and smoothing down her skirts. 'It will not be possible, but thank you all the same,' she said. 'Come, Elspeth, Rachel, we must go in.' She took her sisters by their hands and led them away from us, a stiff, erect little finger in her crumpled gown.

'Well, now, what was that all about?' Charles Middleton was frowning in bewilderment. 'I thought she would jump at the chance.'

'There is a lot you do not understand, sir,' I said bitterly. 'We live in a strange household, where the children are shut away in the east wing, unwanted and unloved. If you call at Musgrove, I beg you to be cautious. Do not make their lives more difficult than they already are.'

'Wait, Miss Garnet,' he called, as I

began to walk rapidly after the girls, 'you must explain.'

'There is no time — and no explanation. Ask Aunt Lowther if you really want to know. Maybe she knows the answer, for I assuredly do not.'

Later that afternoon when I went down to join the family for tea, I found Mr Middleton sitting in the big armchair opposite Edward, chatting in an easy manner to Aunt Prudence. My aunt looked a trifle strained, I thought, and was unusually pleased to see me. Probably because the men had been recalling the old days, and the happy times spent with Lilian.

'Oh, it is you, Emma,' she said, as I entered the room, 'I had hoped it was Mr Lowther. We have a visitor, dear, Mr Middleton has ridden over from Wadhurst. Isn't that nice?'

I smiled in suitable surprise, as Mr Middleton rose and bowed to me.

'Miss Garnet,' he said gravely, 'how pleasant to see you again.'

'Where have you been, Emma?' said

Edward. 'You always disappear at the most inconvenient times.'

'I have been out for a walk and hope that you will join me soon. It was really quite warm this afternoon and the air was most refreshing. A short walk would do you the world of good.'

'Edward must take care not to catch a chill,' said Aunt Prudence, pouring out tea for her visitor. 'There, Mr Middleton, and please do have a slice of cake. Cook's cherry cake is famous in the district.'

I took my usual seat beside my aunt on the sofa, praying that Mr Middleton would heed my earlier remarks and not cause trouble for the children when they appeared.

'We were just discussing the party, Emma, and the seventeenth is a convenient date for Mr Middleton, so we must start writing out the invitations tomorrow. Edward feels much stronger now, so in — let me see — in eight days time he should be quite fit enough for our little celebration. I am having my young sister to stay,' Aunt Prudence smiled across at our visitor, 'and that will give her plenty of time to come down here and make herself at home before the seventeenth.'

Mr Middleton looked politely interested at this information, and I chewed stoically at my cake, waiting for the clock to chime. At five o'clock Uncle Arnold had still not arrived, but the three little girls appeared and came into the room, Margaret remaining by the door.

Aunt Prudence made the introductions, and I saw Mr Middleton's eyes settle on Elspeth's bright face. Without her bonnet, her hair shone thick and glossy, and the resemblance to that portrait in the gallery at Wadhurst was unmistakable.

What now? I thought. Will he be able to accept the way in which his daughter is forced to live? Or will he shock the country and lay claim to her?

Elspeth recited further doings of Gulliver on his travels, so Aunt

Prudence was satisfied, and Rachel sat with her thumb in her mouth on the hearth-rug, but her eyes smiled up at me and I had to look hastily down at my tea cup.

'Who is that child over by the door?' asked Mr Middleton quietly. 'Why does she not come forward?'

'Oh, that is Lilian's eldest,' answered Aunt Prudence with a light laugh. 'She is a difficult, unfriendly girl who looks after the younger ones and will soon be off to a boarding establishment. I really cannot cope with her impossible behaviour any longer.'

'How tiresome for you,' murmured Mr Middleton.

'Lilian spoilt her,' put in Edward. 'Mind you, she spoilt *me*, too, when I was a lad but I did not turn out badly.' He gave a self-satisfied smile and glanced across at me. 'You are not wearing your ring, Emma,' he said, his smile fading, 'I wish you would not take it off. Uncle Arnold kindly gave me Lilian's signet ring,' he explained to the visitor, and my fingers clenched into my palms.

Why did he have to bring up this subject now? So much talk of Lilian was not right, not in front of Margaret. How could he be so tactless.

'Perhaps you remember it, sir? She always wore it on her little finger — a bloodstone, it was. Yes? Well, I have given it to Emma and she should wear it always.' His voice became fractious. 'I cannot understand you, Emma, I thought females liked jewellery and such-like?'

'I am very proud to wear it,' I answered softly, 'but it seems to me better worn on special occasions. I find it strange to wear such adornment during the day, perhaps because I am unused to jewellery.'

'Of course, rings do draw attention to one's hands,' said Aunt Prudence, 'and your skin was dreadfully rough and red when you came here, Emma. I cannot imagine what you did to get it in such a state. You have a maid, have you not?'

'I helped some women,' I said

defensively, 'with their babies. And I cleaned rooms and — '

'She took in washing,' remarked Edward, 'although I told her not to.'

'Washing!' cried Aunt Prudence in horror. 'You cannot mean — '

'Somebody had to do it,' I said, lifting my chin and returning her stare. 'And we had a good water supply at our house, and a range to heat it on. Some of the homes I visited had no water at all.' My face grew red as I spoke, but I was not ashamed and would not defend my actions.

'And now that you are away, who is continuing your good deeds?' asked Aunt Prudence sarcastically. 'What is the point of it all, Emma? You are not being kind. On the contrary, you have shown those creatures a better way of life, which they cannot continue with on their own but, having once known it, they will be all the more miserable because of deprivation. It is all quite futile, if you ask me, and a waste of your time.'

'I do not believe that showing kindness is *ever* a waste of time,' I replied hotly.

'Do not contradict your aunt,' said Edward. 'What she says makes very good sense. I have been thinking a great deal about our life in London, whilst I have been here convalescing, and I intend taking Aunt Prudence's advice and seeking a living in the countryside, or in some small and prosperous town. I really cannot face that miserable existence in St Giles any more, and must take care of my health.'

'Edward!' I exclaimed. 'How can you say such things? And what about Father?'

'Your father is a most Christian man — I'll allow that — but misguided, Emma, an idealist and not a practical man. For how long have we all been working in St Giles? And what have we achieved? Nothing, I tell you. Look at the drunkards, for example; sobbing tears of remorse and shame one minute, begging for forgiveness, vowing to give up liquor and spend their gin money on milk for their babies. And what happens? Next time you see them they are intoxicated all over again, but promising to repent in the very near future — very ashamed and all that.' He jerked back his head and let out a bark of a laughter. 'Pah! Aunt Prudence is quite right and it's all a complete waste of time.'

'Do they ever go to church?' asked Aunt Prudence, leaning forward.

'Only if bribed.' Edward glanced at me. 'Emma wants to open a soup kitchen in the vestibule. Get them to come to church, then offer them soup afterwards as a reward!'

'Just as I thought.' Aunt Prudence sat back, folding her hands complacently upon her lap.

'We must try!' I cried out. 'No matter how often we are disappointed, we must never stop *trying*!'

At that moment Uncle Arnold entered the room, and it was as well he did, for I was close to tears and found that I was beginning to dislike Edward with astonishing intensity.

'Middleton, my dear fellow, how good to see you again!' Uncle Arnold strode forward, as Charles Middleton rose and shook him by the hand. 'Well, well, what a pleasant surprise. Sorry I was late, dear,' he turned to his wife, 'but Hilton kept me longer that I intended, discussing the new shed.'

Aunt Prudence nodded, then turned swiftly towards the children. 'Now, girls, run along upstairs and let your father have a chat in peace.'

Elspeth and Rachel stood up obediently and left the room with Margaret. I watched them go with sombre eyes, wishing that I, too, could gain my freedom.

*　*　*

The following week was extremely hectic and I had little time for the girls. Aunt Prudence was in a tither about the party, and we were all involved in the work. The drawing-room had to be cleared of carpet and furniture, in preparation for the dancing; the chandeliers had to be taken down and cleaned, and the curtains and window drapes had likewise to be removed and washed.

Chairs had to be brought in from other rooms and placed around the walls, and the morning-room and dining-room had to be swept and dusted, for we were to use both those rooms for the food. The menu was discussed at length and Cook became frantic, for Aunt Prudence changed her mind at least twice a day. All the best china had to be sorted out and washed, and glasses and linen brought out from storage. Invitation cards had to be written and addressed, and musicians engaged for the evening.

In the midst of all this confusion, Alice arrived.

I need not have worried about her; she was a plump, timid girl with the white skin and fair hair of her sister, but showing none of the older woman's aggression.

Alice was given a room in the main body of the house, down the passage from the Lowther's bedroom, and she seemed genuinely grateful for any kind word, or helpful gesture. She called her sister Prue, which I found somewhat disconcerting, it being a cheerful little name and ill-suited to the big dominant woman.

'You must see to Alice,' announced Aunt Prudence, bustling about with her sleeves rolled back and her cap at an absurd angle on her bushy hair. 'I have not the time for her at present, so show her around, Emma, and then come and help me. There is so much to do, we'll never get through in time!'

She refused to engage extra help from the village. 'What a waste of money!' So we were all made irritable by her constant nagging.

'Poor Prue,' sighed Alice, as we sat sewing in my bedroom the day after she arrived. 'She means well but she tries

185

too hard and must always have everything done to perfection.'

I did not feel that Aunt Prudence needed sympathy, but perhaps I did not know her well enough. 'Are there just the two of you in your family?' I asked, wondering at the difference between meek Alice and aggressive Prudence.

Alice nodded, bending her fair head over the taffeta on her lap. 'There were three others between us,' she said, 'but they all died. Prue brought me up when our parents died of the typhoid, and she was always talking about bettering our position in life.' She smiled, lifting her head and showing pretty, very small white teeth. 'She sent me away to Miss Hetty's establishment when I was nine, and it was understood that if I worked in the house and helped with the cleaning, and looked after the littlest girls, I would get some tuition free of charge.'

Alice shrugged and turned again to her sewing. 'I learned to read and write, and I copied some of the older girls, so

I know how to speak well, but I fear that Prue was not pleased with my accomplishments. Now, I assist Miss Hetty by teaching reading and writing to the youngest girls, and she pays me a small wage, for which I am grateful.'

'Do you like it there?' I wondered if this was the place to which she intended sending Margaret in due course.

'I do not like it or dislike it, though Miss Hetty can be harsh at times. I know Prue desires me to make a Good Marriage, but as I never meet any gentlemen, I do not see how that will be possible.'

If Aunt Prudence had hopes of an alliance with Charles Middleton, I feared that she would be disappointed; to a man who had admired Lilian Lowther's beauty and vivacity, little Alice would appear as insipid and colourless as buttermilk.

The children did not come downstairs at all that week, for we were having to take our meals in the kitchen, and the entire household routine was disrupted. Uncle Arnold stayed out as much as possible, and spent a good deal of his time over at Wadhurst Grange, and Edward took to his room in a huff.

I managed to visit the girls twice, for very short periods, and explained to them the reason for all the unusual commotion, and they were surprisingly delighted by my news.

'Will we be able to hear the music?' asked Elspeth. 'I shall tiptoe down the corridor and listen at the top of the stairs.'

'Me, too,' said Rachel.

'There used to be music when Mama was alive,' said Margaret wistfully, 'and she wore lovely shiny ball gowns.'

'What will you wear, Cousin Emma?' squeaked Elspeth. 'And will you promise to come and show us before you go down?'

'If I can, if there is time,' I said.

I had left Alice reading to Edward and was thus able to slip away for a few precious minutes, but I could not stop long.

'Are you sewing a dress, Cousin Emma? What colour is it?'

'I am not sure what I shall be wearing, Elspeth.' I knew that it would have to come from Lilian's trunk, and feared lest Margaret remember it.

Alice, too, had few clothes, and Aunt Prudence had told her to take something suitable from the trunk. But Alice was small and plump and it was not going to be easy to dress her. Any spare minute was spent in feverish cutting, and snipping, and sewing, and Aunt Prudence demanded much attention for she had ordered material for herself and was making her own gown, with my reluctant assistance.

Fortunately, I discovered a rose-pink satin gown which fitted me perfectly, but Alice's blue taffeta had to be let out and shortened, and altered quite considerably.

Aunt Prudence had chosen a purple silk, with numerous frills and bows, which did not compliment her large form. It was far too fussy and decorative a style, and Bessie and Dolly were ordered to help as well, or it would never be finished in time.

On the afternoon of the party, Alice came to my room and we helped each other to get ready. The maids were all too busy in the kitchen and Dolly, I believe, was assisting Aunt Prudence with her toilette.

I discovered that Alice was clever with her hands and enjoyed playing with hair, so I allowed her freedom with mine and she created a masterpiece. I had washed my hair the day before so it was very shiny and slippery, but Alice smoothed it flat on my head, from a centre parting, and then took the tongs and managed to create a mass of ringlets which were wide apart on my temples and descended low on my cheeks. Numerous combs and pins held the weight of the ringlets in place over my ears, and I found to my delight that the style made me appear considerably younger than my twenty-seven years.

'What a pity you do not have any jewellery,' said Alice, stepping back and surveying her handiwork in the mirror. 'With that low-cut bodice you look a trifle naked. I know!' She clapped her hands together. 'I have the very thing.'

Away she flew, back to her own room, returning with a piece of rose-coloured velvet ribbon in her hands.

'I use it for my hair but it will go beautifully with your dress.'

'What shall I do with it?' I asked in bewilderment.

'Why, wear it round your neck, so.' She placed it at my throat. 'And I'll fasten it in front and you can have your cameo brooch over the fastening so it doesn't show.'

The effect was good. My skirts billowed about me, held out by the hooped petticoat which had also belonged to Lilian. My hair, thick and full at the sides, made my narrow face appear rounder, and the pink velvet at my throat was a magical touch. I slipped on my ring and then stood up and gave a twirl of satisfaction.

'Don't forget your gloves,' said Alice.

'I'll put them on when I've helped you.' The gloves were of white kid, elbow-length, and felt luxurious and very feminine against my skin. There was also an ivory fan painted with tiny rosebuds, which we had discovered amongst Lilian's things.

'Oh, dear, Emma, I do hope my lacing is tight enough. I haven't eaten all day and I *should* be able to get into it — but it was rather a battle last time I tried it on.'

I tugged and squeezed and pulled, and managed to do up all the buttons at the back of her straining bodice, but she bulged alarmingly, and I wondered if the fastenings would hold. We had had to let out every seam to the limit so there was nothing more which could be done.

'Don't eat this evening, either, and do be careful when you dance.'

She looked fresh and pretty, with her white skin, and pink cheeks; and her unruly fair hair was bundled into a blue-sequinned net. I felt sure that the gentlemen would find her appealing. And me? Plain Emma Garnet from St Giles — what would they think of me? I turned again to the mirror and sucked at my lips to make them red and moist.

'You look beautiful, Emma, and so young!' Alice spoke from behind me, and I knew that she was right. A great surge of joy swept through me, making me feel elated, confident, and very excited.

'We are going to have a lovely party,' I said, and heard myself giggling for the first time in my life. 'Now, go and fetch Edward.' I spun round and gave Alice a little push. 'Make sure he looks smart, and tell him he is handsome, that will please him. Then go downstairs and if Aunt Prudence asks for me, tell her I'll be down in a minute.'

Obediently, Alice went off to see

Edward, and I took my candle in the opposite direction, hearing my skirts swish about me with a delicate whisper of sound, as I made for the east wing.

'I've come,' I said, closing the door of the schoolroom behind me and walking across to place my candle on the table.

'Do you like my dress?'

The children gasped with wonder, Rachel and Elspeth running to me, stroking the shiny satin, exclaiming with awe at the beautiful fabric, and admiring my hair. Then I looked up and saw Margaret staring at me.

'What is it?' I ignored the younger girls and went quickly to her, holding out my arms. 'What is it, little one? Do you not like me like this?'

'You look like my mama,' she said, then her face crumpled and she burst into tears.

I took her thin, trembling body into my arms, not caring that her tears streaked my bodice, or that the satin creased and crumpled as she lay against me. "There, there, darling, don't cry. I love you, Margaret, you know that, don't you?'

I could feel her nod and I hugged her closer. She was mine, my own darling, and no none was going to hurt her ever again.

'You're my midget, my little one,' I crooned, rocking her against me, feeling a tenderness I had never felt before.

'Don't cry, darling, we are going to have such fun together, and you shall have your pony, Margaret, I am quite determined and will speak to Papa about it tonight.'

She lifted her great tear-sodden eyes and smiled a watery smile. 'You are my mama now, aren't you?'

I nodded. Then turned and held out my free hand to the others, who were standing forsaken, looking at us from a distance. 'And you, too. Rachel and Elspeth, you are my own dear ones also. Come, my cherubs!'

They came running, clutching at my

skirts, hiding their faces in the slippery satin of my gown. 'And we are going to have such fun together, wait and see! No more hiding away up here — but you'll come down and join in the meals, and we'll go for walks, and have children in to play, and be a proper family.' I gave them all a quick hug and a kiss, then disentangled myself from their clinging arms. 'I must go now, I can hear the music starting. But tomorrow I'll come again and tell you all about the party.'

As I took up my candle and began moving towards the door, Margaret came up behind me and touched my skirts.

'Be careful,' she said.

I looked down at her in surprise. 'Why, Margaret, what do you mean?'

Her little face looked pinched again, thin and strained, and her red-rimmed eyes looked up at me filled with fear. 'Don't let the bear get you like it did my mama.'

An ice-cold finger touched my spine

and I stiffened in a strange, half-remembered terror. 'Bear?' I whispered. 'What bear?'

'The one that comes in the night — the one that killed my mama — oh, I don't want you to die too!' It was a cry of anguish and she threw herself at me again, burrowing her face into my bosom.

'Margaret, compose yourself — you are frightening the others. And I must go.' The strains of music were clear now, and the faint sound of voices. 'Our guests are arriving and I must hurry.' I thrust her away from me, swallowing down my panic. 'Look after the others and I'll see you tomorrow, I promise.'

She nodded, and I left her staring after me as I closed the door.

What on earth was she talking about? I shook my head and walked down the corridor and along the further passage to the head of the stairs. Then I extinguished my candle and left it on the table on the landing.

The hall was brightly lit below and

197

there was a plesant comforting noise of voices, and laughter, and music. Tonight was the party and I was going to enjoy myself. I put all thoughts of Margaret and the other children to the back of my mind, shook out my skirts, and smoothed my long gloves. Then I gave my ringlets a little pat and began to descend the staircase.

8

There were already several guests in the hall, and I saw young Harry Varney chatting to Edward and Alice, and Aunt and Uncle Lowther were standing before the open door of the drawing-room, speaking to two more newcomers. Bessie and Dolly, very smart in their best black dresses, with starched pinafores and glistening caps, were taking cloaks and wraps and darting with them into the study; whilst Martin came gravely out from the kitchen passage and made his way towards the drawing-room, carrying a tray of glasses.

As I paused at the top of the last flight of stairs, Mr Varney raised his eyes and saw me.

'By Jove,' I heard him say, 'doesn't she look exquisite!'

Edward turned and I saw him look up and frown, my appearance did not please *him*, it seemed. But I did not care about dull old Edward, and skimmed down the last few steps holding out my hands to Harry Varney.

'How splendid to see you again, dear sir. And how handsome you look tonight!' I placed my hands in his, enjoying the admiration in his blue eyes.

'I am in favour again, I see. Well, that pleases me no end, Miss Garnet. May I say that you look quite extraordinarily beautiful, and may I have the first dance, please?'

'Of course,' I slipped my arm through his and led him towards the drawing-room.

Aunt Prudence waited there, large and plain in her purple furbelows. She looked cross, and for an instant I imagined a glimpse of some other emotion in her tiny eyes, but then she was rustling forward, smiling her expansive smile at Mr Varney. I turned from her show of geniality, and saw honest admiration and affection in

Uncle Arnold's red face.

'Do not forget to claim a dance from me,' I told him with a tap of my fan, and then Mr Varney was leading me out onto the polished wooden floorboards of the drawing-room, and we joined the other couples who were rotating to the lilting melody of a waltz.

I had never danced before and had worried earlier lest my feet disgrace me. But Harry Varney was an accomplished dancer, and led me firmly and smoothly through the steps, so that my feet quickly found the rhythm. I felt the warmth of his hand on my back, and allowed myself to relax in his firm embrace.

How elegant he was, and how handsome, in his black tails and white frilled shirt. He smiled down at me, his eyes glowing with delight, and I lowered my lashes, hoping that he would notice how long they were.

'You look so delicious tonight, Miss Emma, I could eat you up,' he breathed in my ear.

'There is food in plenty, sir,' I responded, 'so I do not think you need start on me.'

'Not even one peck from those sweet lips?' He was staring down at my mouth, and I felt my blood quicken at the thought of his mouth on mine.

He was so clean, and young, and ardent — why should I not indulge in a mild flirtation? And I was beautiful, and this was my night. Why did Edward never make me feel like this? So gay, and light-hearted, and abandoned? On thinking of my betrothed, I turned my head and surveyed the other dancers.

'Have you seen Edward?' I asked.

'Do not worry about him. Tonight you are mine, Miss Emma.' Varney's hand tightened about my waist, and I thrilled at the sensual tone of his voice. 'I do not know what has changed you, but something miraculous has happened since we last met, and I do not intend allowing you to languish in Edward Lowther's arms.'

'Poor Edward!' we both said together,

and then burst out laughing.

At that moment he passed us, waltzing stiffly with Alice in his rigid arms, and she did not look happy. It was not surprising, for I saw that Edward's face was white with anger, and his eyes, as they alighted on me, were icily reproving.

'Poor Edward does not look as if he is enjoying the party,' whispered Harry Varney. 'Shall we remove ourselves from his vision and from the room? Methinks the sight of us offends him.'

He took my hand and led me to the doors at the end of the room, which were open onto the terrace. Lights from the windows were shining out into the garden, and it was a still night, pleasantly warm for May.

'This is better,' said Varney, pulling me round to face him. 'Now then, Emma Garnet, are you going to kiss me? Or will you scream with fright and slap my face?'

'I am going to kiss you,' I said, and

stood on tiptoe, putting my mouth to his.

His arms went round me and he held me hard against him, and for a moment the earth spun and I had to clutch at him for support.

'That was almost perfect, Emma,' murmured Harry Varney against my cheek. 'Shall we try again?'

We were standing locked together, when I felt a hand on my shoulder and heard a deep voice say,

'I do believe the next dance is mine.'

We both turned, and I gazed up into the expressionless countenance of Mr Middleton.

'How *dare* you!' I said, stamping my foot. He had no right to come interfering in what was, after all, a very private business.

'I say, old man, that is not correct,' put in Varney quickly, 'Miss Garnet has promised *me* the next.'

'I'm afraid you're mistaken.' Mr Middleton placed his hand firmly on my arm and almost pulled me away from my companion. 'Come, Miss Garnet, the music is starting again.'

He was rough and very strong, and had me back in the ballroom before I could think properly. But it was rather nice to be carried off in such a fashion, I decided, as his arm went round me. Fancy being fought over by two handsome men! I melted into his arms and felt that life was wonderful. Charles Middleton did not dance as smoothly as Mr Varney, but he made up for this deficit by being bigger, and broader, and more of a man.

I looked up into his face and fluttered my eyelashes, feeling my ringlets bob against my cheeks. 'You are very masterful, sir, and really quite rude. But I forgive you.' I gazed at his set mouth and steady eyes. 'Why don't you smile? Do you not find me pretty?'

'What has come over you?' he asked shortly. 'And where did you get that dress?'

'Aha! You remember it?' I threw back my head and half-closed my eyes. 'I am

Lilian tonight, my dearest Charles. May I call you that? Do you not see the resemblance? And I am going to dance and laugh and flirt until the dawn.'

'Stop it!' he said harshly. 'Stop play-acting and pull yourself together. You are making a spectacle of yourself.'

'Oh, no, I am not. I am beautiful and happy and flirting with you. And all the others are staring because the women are jealous, and the men wish they were in your shoes. Do you not find me attractive, Charles? Of course, you do! You loved Lilian and so you must love me.' I gave a little giggle. 'You may take me outside, if you wish, and kiss me.'

'Have you been drinking?' His face was a mask of distaste.

'I have not — what a question! Do you not believe that I could find you desirable unless I were intoxicated? You underestimate your charms, sir!'

I leaned against his arm and smiled. 'Do not look so fierce. If I do not please you then let me go back to Harry. He, at least, appreciates me and I want to be admired. I intend enjoying myself to the full tonight, and rather think I am going to make love to someone. But not to Edward.' I straightened and looked about me. 'If you see Edward do not let him come near me — he is such a *bore* — I really cannot abide his mournful face and accusing eyes. Do you not think I should be wasted on him?'

'You are not yourself,' said my partner grimly, 'and you had better go to your room and sleep off this extraordinary mood.'

'Will you come too?' I laid my head against his chest, allowing my body to rest against his. 'Take me to my room, if you will, but do not leave me there alone.'

As I was speaking, a hand touched my arm, and Uncle Arnold was at my side, smiling down at me.

'Will you forgive me, Middleton, and allow me to make off with my niece? She promised me a dance, and is proving so popular that I must lay claim to her whilst I can.'

'I was just going to take Miss Garnet for some refreshment,' said Mr Middleton quickly. 'She was feeling a little faint and I believe some sustenance is indicated.'

'Of course,' Uncle Arnold stepped back, dropping his hand from my arm. 'Go with him, Miss Emma, and eat. I shall have a dance with you when you return.'

'But I don't want — ' I began, but my partner pushed me ahead of him, propelling me through the dancers to the door into the hall.

'You are hurting me,' I said crossly, trying to shake off his grip.

'I shall hurt you more in a minute,' replied Mr Middleton in a harsh whisper, 'get on out of here, and hurry!'

I walked beside him, holding my head high, although my eyes were smarting from the pain of his hold. He was going to spoil my evening, he was not in the mood for frivolity, and was turning out to be an irksome and disapproving companion. Where was

Mr Varney? I searched the faces in the hall, seeking the tall young man who was friendly, and who appreciated me. Mr Middleton was proving as big a bore as Edward.

To my surprise we passed the dining-room and I found myself being steered down the passage towards the kitchen.

'Where are we going?'

'Upstairs,' he said grimly, and once out of sight of the guests in the hall, I was lifted in his arms and carried up the back stairs.

'Oh, you are strong!' I leaned against his chest, nestling my head beneath his chin. He was better than Edward — Edward could never do this. 'And you are an ardent and passionate man. You are going to take me to bed, are you not?'

He was breathing heavily, carrying me at a great pace along the passage to the west wing.

'Can you see? Do not drop me, I beg!'

There was some light coming in from the windows, but the passage was dark nonetheless, and I clung to him, scared in case he should stumble and have us both on the floor.

'Which room is it?' He dumped me ungraciously upon the landing, and reached for the candle.

In there.' I pointed, and then opened the door for him and followed him into my chamber.

As he placed the candle upon the dresser, I went up behind him and put my arms around his neck. 'Now you can kiss me, dear love.'

Mr Middleton unwound my arms and gave me a push backwards so that I lost my balance and collapsed upon the bed.

'Tell me,' he said, in a very quiet, controlled voice, 'what is this all about?'

'I don't know what you mean.' I rubbed my arm above the wrist where it was beginning to ache.

'You have made mock of Lilian,' he said slowly, 'and you have dressed in her clothes and done your hair in similar fashion. But you are not Lilian, Miss Garnet, and never will be. Get that into your wooden head and get out of that dress. I cannot bear to see it on you.'

'My dress?' I gasped. 'But it's beautiful and — '

'The gown may be, but you ruin it. Take it off, I say.'

'I will not!' I rose, and ran round the side of the bed, my heart beginning to thud with fear, but he came after me and his hands reached out, ripping the satin at my breast.

'Take it off, damn you! And that stupid hair!' His hand grabbed my hair and he began pulling at the curls, so that the pins fell and my hair fell over my face. I screamed, for his hands were rough and I felt as if he would drag the very roots from my scalp.

'Stop!' I cried, wriggling and panting in a frenzy, but he held me around the waist with one arm, and tore at my head with the other.

'And that ribbon.' Middleton's fingers caught at the velvet at my throat and the ribbon came apart. My cameo brooch flying onto the floor with a clatter. 'Now the dress.' He fumbled with the hooks, then cursed and threw me upon the bed, face down, and began undoing the fastenings with clumsy fingers.

I lay motionless, my anger fading and fear beginning to take its place. What had gone wrong? Why was he behaving like a madman?

Charles Middleton pulled me round to face him and drew the dress off my shoulders. 'Now stand up and get out of it.'

Swallowing my tears, trembling in every limb, I divested myself of the gown which he bundled up in his arms and threw into a shimmering heap to one dark corner of the room.

'Now that ridiculous hoop thing, and those gloves. Everything that once belonged to her.'

Wretched and miserable, aware of my

near nakedness before his fiery gaze. I untied the lacing at my waist and stepped out of the hoop. Then I rolled down my gloves. Was he going to ravish me? Suddenly the idea did not seem appealing and I wished that I had not flirted so blatantly with this dangerous man. He was still very attractive, but he was also strong, and very angry. I had the feeling that he might enjoy hurting me, and my body flinched at the thought of his hands bruising my flesh.

'Now get into bed and stay there. I shall leave you the underwear, although that is no doubt borrowed, as well. And don't you ever imitate Lilian again in my presence, or I shall thrash you so hard you will be unable to sit down for a week. I shall tell them downstairs that you have a headache and have retired to your room for the night.' Middleton strode to the door, as I crept beneath the covers, then he paused and looked back at me. 'I shall be staying here until the last guest has left, so do not imagine that it is safe to come down. You will remain here until morning, and, please God, you will be in a saner frame of mind when you awake.'

After Charles Middleton had departed I got out of bed, removed my chemise and pantaloons, took off my ring, brushed out my tangled hair, and washed my face and hands. Then, clad in my nightgown, and feeling cleaner and more composed, I went back to bed and blew out the candle.

But I did not sleep. I wanted to think, to ponder and remember, to consider all that had happened since coming to Musgrove.

In a way, Mr Middleton's brutal handling had brought me to my senses; the Emma Garnet who had dressed in the rose-pink gown, who had gone in to the children to show off her finery, who had cuddled and kissed them with such lavish affection, was *not* the Emma Garnet of Flower Street.

Nor was the girl who had flirted with Harry Varney and kissed him — *kissed* him! My body cringed with self-loathing and my face went hot with shame.

And the extraordinary and stupid way in which I had behaved with Mr Middleton was incomprehensible. I would never act in such a way. But I had. The Emma Garnet of Musgrove had acted like flighty Lilian Lowther — had almost *been* Lilian. What was it all about?

And Margaret. Little, timid, worried Margaret, telling me to be careful, fearful lest the bear get me. What did she mean? What bear? It sounded like some childish game — 'Beware the bear!' — But Margaret's look had not been childish; she had worn the pinched, anxious expression of an old woman. There had been no play-acting in her gesture of terrified anxiety.

But what bear, for heaven's sake? And how could she believe that a bear had killed her mother?

I rolled over onto my side, pressing my fist against my mouth. Was I going mad? But these strange events were not of my imagination; Margaret's worry had been real; Harry Varney had found me beautiful and desirable; Mr Middleton *had* thought I looked like Lilian, and not only this night. He had mistaken me for her that first evening in the rose garden.

I sat up suddenly, frowning into the darkness. It was not Musgrove which was affecting me. It was Lilian Lowther.

A shiver ran through my body and I felt the same icy tingle of fear down my spine, as I had felt when Margaret mentioned the bear. At certain times, but not always, Lilian was taking over my body.

It was when I wore her ring! With sudden certainty the fact struck me; that time I went visiting the Varneys with Aunt Prudence, I had acted quite out of character, and I had been wearing the bloodstone. The night in the rose garden, when I was first attracted to Charles Middleton, the ring was on my finger. And this night, this awful, never-to-be-forgotten night of the party, I had been wearing the ring.

Yet when I left it off I became once again the serious, responsible, rather dull creature which I really was.

So, what now? Should I fling it from me, throw it from the window, lose it forever? But that would not solve the mystery, would not explain why Lilian was haunting me. There were many odd happenings, many secrets in this house, and maybe Lilian knew the answers and wanted to communicate them to me.

Dear Heavens. I shut my eyes and fell back upon the pillows. If only there were someone in whom to confide. I needed advice and moral support. My life had become a nightmare and I did not wish to face the consequences alone.

Edward was too reproving, and would never understand. Mr Middleton disliked me, and would not want to discuss his beloved Lilian with me. If only events had turned out differently, he was the kind of man whom I could love; he was so sure of himself, yet gentle with children, and pleasant enough to me, before I repulsed him. He was a very attractive man . . . no, not Charles Middleton, think of someone else, quickly!

Harry Varney? He liked me and, I believed, would listen to me. Although he was young, he seemed to have experience of life, and I had to talk to somebody.

Aunt Prudence? Never! Uncle Arnold? I was fond of him, but did not really know him, and it would not be kind to discuss Lilian with him, anyway. Alice was sweet, but too young and unworldly to be of use.

So, Mr Varney it must be, and the sooner the better.

There was a timid knock on the door and Alice put her head into the room.

'Are you asleep, Emma?' she whispered.

'No, but I have a dreadful headache

and have to lie down.'

'Mr Middleton said you were not feeling well. Oh, I am so sorry.' She came softly into the room and gazed down at me in the semi-darkness. 'You have not drawn the curtains and — what's that? Oh, Emma, it's your lovely dress on the floor.'

Alice lit the candle, tutting to herself, then she drew the curtains across the diamond shaped panes, and went over to pick up my gown.

'Is it over? Have they all gone?' I asked.

'The guests are beginning to disperse, and as Edward was weary and wished to retire I decided to come up with him.'

Aunt Prudence's large figure suddenly emerged through the doorway. '*What* is the matter with you, Emma? Poor Edward was so put out by your sudden departure — you really *should* have thought of him. And it was most odd that Mr Middleton had to make excuses for you.' She came over and stared down at me, a belligerent expression on her pale face. 'Well, what is wrong? You were certainly acting very strangely earlier in the evening, but you did not *look* ill!'

'I have a bad head,' I said weakly, 'I get them sometimes and have to lie down in the dark and rest.'

'Hm,' grunted Aunt Prudence, 'I'll tell Dolly to bring you up some warm milk, but I really think you should go back to London, dear. You have been acting in a most odd manner for some time now, even Edward has remarked on it, and we think you are probably missing your father and all that splendid work you do. You've had a nice little holiday, but now it is time you were fully occupied again.'

I was not leaving Musgrove. Not until this mystery had been cleared up. And I couldn't leave the children — not yet.

'That is most thoughtful of you, and I shall consider what you have said, but I think a few more days would be appropriate. Father believes that I shall be away for three weeks,' I answered carefully.

'You had better discuss it with Edward in the morning,' she said huffily. 'But he is not happy, not happy at all.' Then she turned to Alice, who had been quietly sorting and folding away my garments as we were speaking.

'Did you dance with Mr Middleton, Alice? You must push yourself forward a bit more, dear, or you will never be noticed. It was kind of Edward to dance with you — ' she gave me a spiteful, sidelong look — 'he is so good-hearted, and partnered you as Emma was not available. But I wished you and Mr Middleton to become better acquainted.'

'I did have one dance with him, Prue, but — ' she faltered — 'he frightens me rather.'

'Frightens you! That charming man?'

'He seemed so, so aloof, as if his thoughts were elsewhere, and he did not talk at all,' she said softly.

'Then *you* should have made conversation. Oh, dear, I wash my hands of you, I really do. Have you learnt nothing at Miss Hetty's? What an unfortunate party, it was not as I planned at all.' She stomped to the door remarking crossly, 'Emma behaves in a most outrageous manner and then disappears because of a headache, and you spend most of your time with Edward and do not even *try* to be attractive and interest the other young men in the room.'

'But I know Edward, and I did not know the other gentlemen, Prue.'

'It was a waste of time and money.' Her sister ignored her. 'And the whole evening was ruined by the pair of you. I shall not try to entertain again whilst you are here — such a waste of money,' she snapped. 'Now come out and leave Emma alone, and we'll all get some sleep. I am worn to a ravel and have not enjoyed the evening at all.'

Nor have I, I thought bitterly, as the door closed behind them. And Alice is not the right girl for Mr Middleton. How foolish of Aunt Prudence to imagine that her simple little sister would catch that gentleman's eye. He admired vivacious, beautiful and seductive females, those like Lilian Lowther. He would never be attracted to a little mouse like Alice, nor to a sober and conscientious spinster like Emma Garnet.

Before Dolly brought me the hot milk, my mind had begun fretting again, and this time I worried about the children. I had promised Margaret a pony, had said they would all be able to come downstairs, have friends in to play, lead a normal, sociable life from now on. What a fool I was! Nothing had changed, nothing had been resolved, but one thing was certain.

As I sipped the milk I made up my mind on one point. I would not leave Musgrove until something had been sorted out about the children's future. Perhaps Mr Varney could help me there, too.

9

Two days later I was still at Musgrove. I had made my peace with both Edward and Aunt Prudence, realising that the only way in which I would be allowed to remain there was to bow to their will, agree with everything they said, and be as meek and amenable as possible. With Lilian's ring off my finger, I could behave in a suitably contrite manner.

On Thurdays Bessie had her afternoon off, so I asked her if she would kindly drop a letter in at the Varneys when she went to the village. It was the only way I could think of contacting Harry Varney.

The village was over two miles from Musgrove, and Bessie walked there after lunch to visit her mother, so she informed me, and left at five o'clock the next morning, in order to be back for work at Musgrove on the Friday.

I could have walked the one way, and Mr Varney would no doubt have brought me back in his carriage. But I could not risk the chance that he might be away from home, if I called unexpectedly; nor could I think of an adequate excuse for my absence, should I be seen returning to Musgrove in the young man's company.

It was safer to send a note by Bessie.

'Dear Mr Varney,' I wrote. 'I need to see you on a matter of some urgency, and beg you to ask your mother to invite Edward and Alice and me over for tea one afternoon, as soon as possible. My reason for seeing you must remain private, and please think of some way in which we can talk together without arousing suspicion. I have been behaving in a most odd manner of late and, when I see you, will endeavour to explain the reason. I am in *desperate* need of advice. Yours, Emma Garnet.'

Harry Varney acted with commendable speed, so much so that I feared he might have misconstrued my meaning, and was hoping for a lovers' tryst. But the note from Mrs Varney was short and to the point, inviting us to tea with her on Saturday.

Fortunately, Edward decided not to come.

'You girls go,' he said, 'I cannot imagine that Mrs Varney wants me to go and chatter over the teacups, and invited me solely out of politeness. And I do not care for her son at all, so it would be pointless going to see him. She does not mention Harry, however, so hopefully he will not be there.' Edward glanced swiftly in my direction. 'I beg that you do not encourage him, Emma, should he appear. Varney is not an honourable young man, and might well seek to pester you for attention, particularly after the way in which you behaved at the party.'

I lowered my eyes. 'I told you that I regretted my behaviour on that evening, Edward, and can only explain my actions by claiming that I was unwell. I am ashamed of myself and assure you it will not happen again.'

He grunted. 'Alice will be with you, anyway, and she is a most sensible and well-behaved young lady. Go and enjoy yourselves, and pray make my excuses to Mrs Varney.'

Aunt Prudence was a bit put out at not receiving an invitation for herself, but she supposed it to be a tea party for young people, and she still had a great deal to do in the house, clearing up from the party.

Mrs Varney greeted us in a most flattering and warm-hearted way, and her son behaved in a restrained manner towards both Alice and me. We were given a delicious tea in the garden, but I could not enjoy it fully because I kept wondering how Harry could speak to me on my own. Then, when we had finished eating, Mrs Varney suggested showing Alice her pretty home.

'You have been here before, Emma, have you not? So I shall not bore you with my little excursion. Take Emma over to the lawn, Harry, and we shall join you for a game of croquet in a few minutes.'

We all rose, everyone pleased with this arrangement, and as soon as Mrs Varney and Alice had entered the house, Harry escorted me over to the side lawn.

'Now, tell me quickly what you have to say,' he said.

I told him and he listened gravely, nodding his head and being most sensible, when I had feared that he might make mock of my ideas.

'You do believe me?' I said finally. 'You do not presume it to be all my imagination?'

'I believe you, Miss Emma, because I have noted the quite extraordinary changes in you. At first I decided that you were simply a fickle and unpredictable female, but when I see you as you are *now*, it is clear that you are a sane and practical young woman.' He gazed down at me, his eyes kind and very comforting.

'Thank goodness I can confide in you

— I am becoming quite desperate. Tell me, Mr Varney, what shall I do?'

He bent his tall frame over one of the croquet hoops and began hammering it more firmly into the lawn. 'You could always ask the church to help. Is your father not a vicar? I would not advise Parson Rogers, you have met him, haven't you? A rather stupid man, I fear. But the Church is supposed to exorcise spirits — why not that, Miss Emma?'

'My father would never believe me! He thinks I have too vivid an imagination already! He would call my ideas fanciful and have no patience with me. Besides, I don't think I *want* Lilian's spirit, or whatever it is, exorcised. I want to know why this is happening to me? Is she trying to communicate with me? What is this all about?'

'Tell you what.' He lifted his head. 'You must visit Aunt Maggie. She'll know what to do.'

Who is Aunt Maggie?'

'No relation, I hasten to add. She is a witch, Miss Emma, but a good one,' he went on quickly, as I exclaimed in dismay. 'In fact, she may not be a witch at all. I don't know for sure. But she is called Mad Aunt Maggie by some, and everyone is a little afraid of her. The children tease her but take care never to pass her cottage after dark, and even I, as a boy, used to go and steal her apples, and throw pebbles at her windows in daylight.'

He shrugged and pulled a comical grimace. 'I really only got to know her when I was a lad of some thirteen years and Mother despaired of the warts on my hands. She took me to London specialists, she badgered our poor local doctor until he was sick to death of my revolting hands. But no cure could be found. Then Mother thought of Aunt Maggie, and she took me to her cottage one dark night, terrified lest any of her friends should see us, and scared of what she might discover in that cottage, I've no doubt. But the old girl cured me, Miss Emma. See?' He held out his hands to me. 'And I've not had a wart since.'

'What did she do?' I asked doubtfully. 'Did she have a cauldron simmering on the fire, and make you drink some dreadful concoction?'

'No.' He grinned, looking like a small, mischievous boy. 'She gave me some ointment and we came hastily away. But do you know what was in that cream?'

I shook my head.

'Snails!' he said, with relish.

'Oh, Harry, how awful!' I put my fingers to my mouth.

'Awful or not, they did the trick and she is the person for you. Quick, hit the ball and look businesslike, they're coming to join us.'

I bent to attack the ball with my mallet. 'How can we arrange a meeting?' I asked, with my head down.

'Ah, there you are. What a lovely afternoon for a game. There, Alice, dear, you take that mallet and I'll have this one. Well played, Emma!' said Mrs Varney.

'That's it, Miss Alice, now I'll go — so — now it's your turn, Mother.'

As Mrs Varney walked off after her ball, Harry said quietly,

'I'll arrange something. It will have to be at night. Can you slip out without anyone seeing you?'

'Good shot, Alice!' I called. 'Yes, I think so, headaches are most useful.'

'Bad luck, Mother, and don't cheat. She has a deplorable habit of concealing the ball beneath her skirts and then manoeuvring it into a different position when she thinks nobody is looking.'

'I do *not*, Harry, how naughty of you!' said Mrs Varney, her cheeks pink. 'There, that was perfect and achieved by *skill*, my son. See if you can better that stroke.'

Harry bit his lip, then aimed a good long shot which made Alice and Mrs Varney concentrate and then move further away from us.

'I think you have missed your turn, Miss Emma.'

'No matter. Tell me where I should meet you, and when.'

'Next Tuesday, that will give me time to see Aunt Maggie beforehand. Come out and wait in the rose garden, it is nicely secluded, and I'll meet you there. Can you ride, Miss Emma?'

'No.' I shot him a look. Why did he decide on the rose garden? Dear heavens, had Lilian met him there in the past? But no, I decided, she died six years ago and Harry Varney would have been but fifteen years of age. I could not imagine Lilian Lowther would have wasted her charms on a mere schoolboy.

'Pity, but I've a good steady horse and he will take both our weights if we go slowly. You can sit up behind me, Miss Emma, and I'll get you to Aunt Maggie and back without mishap.'

'Come on, Harry, you're keeping us waiting,' called his mother.

'Very well,' I said quickly. 'I'll be

waiting in the rose garden at nine o'clock on Tuesday evening, and thank you.'

On Tuesday I kept very quiet all day but only Alice appeared to notice.

'Are you not feeling well?' she asked, as we went upstairs to change for dinner.

'I fear I have another migraine coming,' I said, 'It is such a nuisance, but if I go to bed straight after dinner it will go.'

'Poor Emma,' she said consolingly. 'Why do you not go to bed now and I'll ask Prue if something can be brought to your room?'

It was too early for that, and I did not fancy lying in bed for several hours, fretting about going out, and having to ride a horse, and having to meet Mad Aunt Maggie. It was better by far to be occupied and in the company of other people for as long as possible.

'I'll come down,' I said, 'it might improve.'

During the meal I played with my food, eating very little although I was hungry. When I announced that I would retire early, nobody appeared to mind and I went upstairs with relief. There I rang for Dolly, and said there was nothing more I wanted that evening and only desired to sleep. Then I put on my old brown velvet, which had not been worn for some time, placed a bolster in my bed and pulled up the covers.

At ten minutes to nine I made sure that my curtains were drawn, wrapped my cloak about me, and went out closing the door softly behind me. I had to wait a while at the top of the back stairs because the servants were still clearing away in the dining-room, and kept tramping up and down the passage to the kitchen. As I stood, willing them to hurry up and finish, strains of music floated up to me from the drawing-room. Alice could play the piano quite competently, and since she had come to Musgrove, it had become a habit for her to play every evening after dinner, when the family assembled in the drawing-room.

Eventually the lights in the dining-room were extinguished and the last footsteps echoed down the passage in the direction of the kitchen. I slipped down the stairs, across the hall, and out of the side door. Not knowing at what time Martin locked up, I prayed that the door would still be open on my return. If not, I should just have to throw pebbles at Alice's window and get her to come down and let me in. I could always say that I had gone out for some fresh air on account of my head.

Once in the yard I began to run, and fled across the lawn, gathering up my skirts with one hand, the other holding my cloak firmly about my body. It must have been well past nine o'clock, but surely Harry Varney would have waited for me?

As I entered the rose garden between

the high yew hedges, I saw a tall figure standing beside the sun dial, and for an instant my heart leapt and I remembered that other night, and the man who had taken me into his arms in that warm embrace. Then the figure turned to face me and I saw that it was Varney, and my heart returned to its normal beating.

'You are late, we must hurry,' he said briskly. 'I've left my horse behind the trees over there. Take my arm, Miss Emma, and I'll show you the way.'

The horse appeared enormous, looming out of the darkness, standing high above my head. But Mr Varney lifted me up onto its back without hesitation, then swung himself up before me and I clung to him for dear life. He rode without a saddle so it was not too uncomfortable for me, but my cloak and petticoats were dreadfully crushed, and my legs dangled in a distressing way. I clutched at Mr Varney's firm back, praying that I would not fall and that we would soon be there.

★ ★ ★

'Good evening, Miss Garnet, come and sit yourself by the fire.'

Aunt Maggie was small and thin, with white hair wound in plaits on top of her head, like a coronet. She had a calm, sun-browned countenance, and the lightest blue eyes I had ever seen. She looked clean and neat, wearing a blue dress with a white collar, and the room was surprisingly cheerful; there were red curtains across the windows, red cushions upon the chairs, a gaily coloured woven rug was upon the floor, and the table in the middle of the small room was covered by a crocheted lace cloth.

There was nothing frightening about either the woman, or her house, and I smiled as I walked across to sit opposite her at the hearth.

'Mr Varney informed me that you would be coming, and I shall try to help you.' Aunt Maggie's clear eyes gazed serenely at me. 'Won't you taste a little of my dandelion wine?' she went on, offering me a glass from the table beside her.

It was a golden liquid with a pleasant taste, and I sipped it gratefully as I gathered my thoughts.

'I do not understand what is wrong,' I began, 'but some peculiar things have been happening to me, and I believe you are the right person to advise me.'

Then I told her about everything which had occurred since my arrival at Musgrove. Aunt Maggie sat quite still, nodding her head from time to time, her eyes fixed upon my face.

'Well, now,' she said, when I had finished my tale, 'I have been able to heal people's bodies on occasion, but the mind — oh, dearie me — that is a different matter.'

'Do you think it is possible that Lilian Lowther is haunting me?'

'It would seem as if her spirit is not at rest,' answered my companion slowly. 'What exactly do you feel when you wear her ring?'

I thought for a moment. 'Confident, happy, and very light-hearted. There is certainly no misery, or worry, or fear. I say and do things quite out of character and enjoy the attentions of gentlemen.' My face burned.

Aunt Maggie nodded. 'Just like the first Mrs Lowther.'

'Did you know her?'

'Anyone who visits me can rely on my discretion. But Lilian Lowther has been dead for many years now, and you do seem to be greatly involved with her, and her affairs, so I do not think it would matter if I confided in you.' She paused. 'Mrs Lowther came to me when she first knew that she was to have a baby. And she wanted a boy. Of course there was nothing I could do about the sex of her child, but she begged and pleaded so I gave her a few old country potions, which, as it turned out, did no good at all.' She smiled slightly. 'Poor lady, she did not enjoy child-bearing and hoped that if the baby were a son she would not need to have more.'

'But she loved Margaret!' I cried.

'Yes, she loved that little girl. But her figure was slight, too slender for the bearing of children, as we sadly learned when her last was born. She also adored riding, Miss Garnet, and did not welcome the tedious months spent out of the saddle. Are the girls well?' she asked suddenly. 'I see them sometimes on a Sunday, when they go to church, and I do not feel that they are happy children.'

'They are not, and lead an isolated life shut away at the top of the house. Aunt Lowther is not cruel, I must admit, but she ignores them for most of the time, and they lack loving.'

'Have you spoken to the eldest about her mother? She must still remember her?'

I told her then about Margaret's silence, and about the shrine, and the strange remark about the bear.

'Was there a travelling fair visiting the village at the time of Lilian's death? Did

Margaret perhaps see a bear and have nightmares about it? I cannot understand the connection between that animal and her mother's death.'

'You must speak to the child, Miss Garnet. I have the feeling that the girl holds the key to this mystery.'

I sighed. 'Margaret will not discuss her mother with me, she gets too upset if I try to talk about Lilian.'

'Maybe you should upset her. Perhaps a good weeping is what the little one needs. All her emotions are locked up within her breast and she needs to let go, allow them to burst from her. Such reticence can be doing her no good at all. Have you brought the ring with you?' she asked, abruptly changing the subject. 'I should like to see it.'

I felt in the pocket of my cloak and drew out the bloodstone, wrapped in a handkerchief.

The old woman held it in her hands, leaning back in her chair and closing her eyes. 'No,' she said, after a while, 'I cannot feel anything from that.' She returned the ring to me, and I wrapped it carefully and returned it to my pocket. 'Give me your hands, Miss Garnet, let me see if I can feel anything about you. Sometimes I can.'

I placed my hands in hers, and her skin was warm and surprisingly soft. She did not look at my palms but held my hands between her own, cradling them lightly.

'Yes,' she said quietly, 'yes, you are strong — strong and good. But you will need your strength, my dear. There is danger very near.' Her grip tightened, and her pale eyes shone fiercely into mine. 'Do be careful. I think perhaps your aunt is right and you should go away from here. Leave Musgrove, you can change nothing. Go back to London, Miss Garnet, and the sooner the better.'

Aunt Maggie seemed suddenly agitated, and she let go of my hands and sprung to her feet, walking about the room, touching the tablecloth, giving the curtains a little tweak.

'You came to see me for advice, Miss Garnet, and I say to you go! Go now, before it is too late.'

'Too late?' I stared at her, panic rising in my breast.

'Too late for what?'

'For living,' she answered bleakly. 'I have a terrible feeling of foreboding; there is evil surrounding you and death is very close. Now it may be that you are so closely linked with the first Mrs Lowther, that it is her death I feel. But do please heed my advice and leave Musgrove at once.'

'But the children!' I rose to my feet, a chill creeping through my limbs. 'I cannot leave them now. They need me.'

'They managed well enough before you came, and will cope once you have gone. Children are remarkably resilient, Miss Garnet, and *their* safety is not in question.'

I nodded and pulled my cloak about me, making for the door.

'I'm sorry,' whispered Aunt Maggie, touching my arm and looking up at me with worried eyes. 'I am sorry I could not help you more. But give that ring back, do not wear it again, and go!'

I did not feel like talking on the way home, but Harry Varncy, who had waited patiently for me out in the lane, naturally wanted to know what had passed between us. I told him a little of what Aunt Maggie had said.

'Danger? For heaven's sake be careful, Miss Emma, and do not fall down the stairs.'

'I am more likely to fall off this horse,' I answered, trying to make light of the matter. Aunt Maggie had frightened me more than I cared to admit.

'I'll ride over,' went on Varney, his back warm and strong beneath my hands, giving me confidence, 'I'll ride over to Musgrove twice a week from now on to make sure you are all right.'

'That is kind of you, Harry, but I am sure it won't be necessary. I believe Aunt Maggie was muddling me with Lilian Lowther. She is very much a part of me now, although I do not act like her unless I wear her ring.'

'Do you think like her, though?'

I hesitated. Perhaps, more than I realised. Certainly I was more critical; finding Aunt Prudence irksome and too domineering; looking down upon Alice because she was so sweet and immature. I was also thinking about Mr Middleton too often, and enjoying the company of Harry Varney, yes, and liking the feel of his body beneath my hands. None of these emotions would have been possible before I came to Musgrove, a brief three weeks earlier.

'Maybe I am beginning to think like Lilian,' I said slowly. 'I have certainly changed a great deal since coming to Musgrove, and do not know what Father will say about me when I go back.'

'You had better return to him soon, Miss Emma.' Harry Varney jumped to the ground and then helped me to alight beside him. 'Do not tempt Fate, I want you safe and sound.' He leaned forward and planted a kiss upon my brow. 'There, that will keep you from all evil until next we meet. Go in quickly now, and I'll see you in a few days.'

I thanked him, then walked swiftly across the lawn to the side door. It was still open. I slipped inside, made for the back stairs, and walked along the passage to my room.

When I opened the door I saw Edward sitting in the chair by the fire. The candle was lit and the bedcovers had been ripped back to disclose the bolster.

10

'Where have you been?' Edward's face was as white as my bed linen, and there was a sheen of perspiration on his skin, which glistened in the candlelight. His hands were clenched so tightly upon his knees that his knuckles protruded, yellow and shiny. He did not look weak, or sickly, but was burning with impotent rage.

'Where have you been, Emma? I demand an explanation.'

'She has been out, and not alone.' Aunt Prudence came softly into the room behind me, and moved across to join Edward by the fireplace. Her large white face was expressionless. 'Emma was in the company of a man. I saw him riding away as she came up the stairs.'

'This is unforgiveable!' Edward's voice rang out harshly, and he thumped his fists down on his knees. 'Who was he, Emma? And what were you doing with him? Where did you go?'

I sighed and turned away from the pair of them, unwrapping my cloak and flinging it down upon my untidy bed. Then I faced them again, feeling remarkably calm and composed. Matters had come to a head and it would be futile to lie. They should hear the truth. It would be interesting to see what they made of it.

'I was with Harry Varney. He took me to see Aunt Maggie. I was in need of advice,' I said.

'I knew it!' Aunt Prudence looked triumphant.

'You have been setting your cap at that young man ever since you came here. Shame on you, girl, for such reprehensible behaviour! How could you treat dear Edward in such a wicked fashion?'

'Who is Aunt Maggie?' Edward asked, ignoring his aunt's words.

'She is — ' I paused, then said

hurriedly, 'she is a wise woman who lives in the village. I have been behaving strangely of late, as you must have noticed, and I sought her advice.'

'Behaving strangely?' Aunt Prudence snorted. 'That is to put it mildly, my dear. Your behaviour has been atrocious and Edward has every right to terminate your engagement.'

Edward nodded. 'I cannot tolerate this running about with Varney. I was your betrothed, Emma, and you should have come to me. Why did you not seek my aid?'

'Because you would not have believed me.'

'And what is this secret matter which troubled you?' asked Aunt Prudence scornfully. 'What was so important that you had to go rushing off to Harry Varney, and could not bring yourself to speak about it to any of us here at hand?'

I lifted my chin and returned her gaze with disdain.

'Lilian Lowther is haunting me.

Every time I wear her ring she seems to take over my body, and I wanted to know the reason for this.'

'You are out of your mind!' Edward cried, jerking forward on his chair. 'How dare you speak so about the dead!'

'What an extraordinary statement to make,' remarked Aunt Prudence, her small eyes watching me intently.

'I really must insist on being released from my promise to marry you, Emma,' said Edward, wiping his brow with a limp hand. 'The situation has become intolerable. I shall write to your father tonight and explain my decision. Kindly return the ring, then we shall be free to go our separate ways, and the sooner you go back to London the better it will be for all of us. I must apologise for all the distress she has caused you,' he said to his aunt, 'she is obviously distraught and does not know what she is saying.'

'I know very well what I am saying, and am determined to find out the truth before leaving Musgrove. I *become* Lilian when I wear her ring, you must have noticed it, and I intend finding out why.'

'You are not well, Emma,' said Aunt Prudence, moving towards me, 'and must go to bed at once. I shall call Dolly to assist you. But first, the ring. Kindly return it to Edward.' She held out her hand.

'No. I release Edward from his proposal of marriage, and can quite understand that a union between us would be impossible. But the ring is mine and I feel very strongly that Lilian wishes me to keep it.'

Aunt Lowther's eyes flashed, and for a moment I thought that she would strike me, but then a shadow passed over her face, her eyelids drooped, and she regained her composure.

'As you will,' she said quietly. 'Let us all go to bed now and get some sleep. In the morning we can discuss this matter further. Emma, you look exhausted — I hope you are not sickening for something? I shall send

Dolly up with some hot milk for you, and then we can all retire for the night. This has been a *most* upsetting evening.'

She walked from the room and Edward rose to follow her.

'You have lied and cheated and behaved in a most outrageous manner,' he said stonily, his hand on the door. 'And to think that you blame it all upon poor Aunt Lilian! I am sorry if your father is shocked by what he is about to hear. No doubt you are after Varney's money? Well, I wish you joy of it. Marrying a man so much younger than yourself will bring nothing but misery, but no doubt that is what you deserve. I shall never forgive you for the hurt and anxiety you have caused my aunt and uncle Lowther.

'I have no intention of marrying Harry Varney,' I replied curtly, 'but if I *did*, I can assure you that he would prove a more loving and loyal husband than you would ever be. You have shown neither consideration for my feelings, nor patience with my problems, and have been totally absorbed in your own imaginary aches and pains. You are no loss to me, Edward Lowther, nor to our people in St Giles, and Father shall hear *my* side of things, also. I can assure you of that.'

He flinched at my words and then stalked from the room, slamming the door behind him.

I was well rid of him. But what had I done, apart from becoming a free woman? There was no way in which I could remain at Musgrove without the goodwill of Aunt Prudence, and I knew that she would ask me to leave in the morning.

As I began to disrobe, Dolly appeared, and with a little tut of surprise she ran to my bed and began rearranging the covers. When she had smoothed them to her satisfaction, she turned her attention to me and hung away my cloak in the cupboard, and helped me to prepare for bed. Then she fetched a tray bearing a mug of hot chocolate, and a few biscuits, and saw me comfortably reclining against the pillows before leaving me for the night.

As I sipped the drink I began to relax. I was more weary than I had realised with all the tensions of the evening, and the unaccustomed ride, and the shock of Aunt Maggie's words. As I slid effortlessly into slumber, I decided that all future plans could be safely left until morning.

When I woke the sun was shining in at the open window, and Alice was sitting beside my bed, an odd expression on her face.

'Gracious me,' she said, leaning forward and patting my hand, 'I thought you would never wake up!'

I blinked at her features which appeared distorted and muzzy, and tried to focus my eyes on the room behind her.

'What time is it?' I asked, but my tongue felt thick in my mouth, and my eyes would not open properly.

'Are you all right, Emma?' Her face

swam before my gaze, so I closed my eyes, allowing myself to drift back into comforting sleep. 'Wake up, Emma!' Alice was shaking my shoulder, rousing me against my will. 'You cannot keep sleeping, it is two o'clock in the afternoon!'

'Leave me be,' I muttered, hunching away from her onto my side.

There were muffled footsteps, the sound of a door opening and closing, voices whispering, and then strong hands lifted me, propping me up against the pillows, and a voice said,

'Here, drink this, it will do you good.'

I felt a cup pressed to my lips and sipped obligingly, although my head felt like lead and would have fallen to one side if a shoulder had not been there to support it.

'I wonder if we should call the doctor?' Aunt Prudence spoke in my ear.

'Shall I tell Mr Lowther to send for him?' asked Alice, in a tearful whisper.

'We'll wait one more day — this

should do the trick,' answered Aunt Prudence.

It was so strange hearing their voices, knowing that they were concerned about me, and yet feeling quite removed from them all. All I wanted was to be left in peace, to sleep.

There followed a succession of faces and voices and odd muted sounds; hands held me and administered to me, and drinks were pressed upon me. Alice seldom left my side, and Aunt Prudence billowed in and out of my dreams like a ship in full sail. Uncle Arnold swam into my vision on one occasion, huffing and blowing like a grampus, and looking very ill-at-ease. I longed to comfort him and say there was no pain, I was most comfortable and just wished to be left alone. But my head was too befuddled to think out the words, and my mouth was too dry to speak them.

Only one thought niggled, returning over and over again, gnawing at a corner of my mind. It would not allow me to rest and eventually I had to accept that there was something which had to be done. What was it? What was of such urgency that I could not find repose? Ah, I had it. The ring. Lilian's ring was of vital importance — it must not be left in my room. It must go. Go where? In a dim, uncertain haze I thought of Margaret. She must be given her mother's ring.

Tell someone. Careful, not Edward, he wanted the ring. Not Aunt Prudence, she was not to be trusted. Turning my hand I opened my eyes and saw Alice. Sweet, uncomplicated, gentle Alice.

'What is it, Emma?' She leaned forward and took hold of my hand. 'Would you like some water?'

'The ring,' I muttered.

'Do not distress yourself, dearest, you will recover soon. Just rest, dear, lie back and rest.'

'The ring,' I lifted my head with a gigantic effort and gazed about the room. 'Take my ring.'

'What, dear? Oh, I wish you would not agitate yourself. Prue says you must be kept quiet.' Her cheeks were flushed and she tried to push me back against the pillows.

'Give my ring to Margaret.' The words suddenly came out clearly and I felt an enormous rush of pleasure. 'Where is it Emma? . . . ' Alice was on her feet, looking down at me perplexedly. 'It is not on your finger.'

'Cloak — in pocket.'

Alice went to my cupboard and brought out the black velvet cloak. Then she fumbled in the pocket and drew out the handkerchief wrapped around the bloodstone ring. 'Here it is.'

My head fell back and I closed my eyes. 'Take it to Margaret,' I said thickly, 'secret — don't tell. Only Margaret.'

Alice came over and stood beside the bed looking down at me. 'I should give it to Margaret — the funny quiet one?' She frowned. 'Are you sure that is what you want, Emma?'

I nodded with a supreme effort. 'Now. Go now.'

'All right, dear, if it will please you. I shan't be long.'

When I next opened my eyes it was night, for the room was dark but a candle flickered, throwing shadows onto the white-washed walls of my chamber. I heard quiet, stealthy movements, and although nobody sat beside my bed, I knew that someone was in the room moving about just out of sight. I could not lift my head, but found that I could roll it sideways, and there in the corner was a large white shape. It was Aunt Prudence in her nightgown. She had a night cap upon her head, and was carefully opening and shutting all the drawers in my chest.

I watched her furtive movements and realised that she was searching for something. My body still felt limp, totally without strength, but my mind had cleared somewhat. The ring, I thought with satisfaction, she is looking for the ring.

As I watched, her shadow moved on the wall beside her, thrown up huge and bulging by the candlelight. Through half closed eyes I saw the shadow bow and straighten as she rummaged through my belongings. Then, as she bent again, the end of her night cap must have fallen forwards over one shoulder, for the shadow thrown up on the wall became a large body, a small head, and a long snout. It looked for all the world like a big fat bear.

A bear! Even in my semi-conscious state I felt my heart skip a beat, and then that ice-cold ripple of fear snaked through my body. Margaret's bear! The bear which had killed her mother!

I must have made some sound, a whimper of fear, or exclamation of terror, for the shadow straightened with a jerk, changed shape, and then Aunt Prudence padded into my view.

She looked very big, very white, and

very menacing as she advanced on the bed. Then she looked down at me and a small, secret smile twisted her lips.

'So,' she said softly, 'you have hidden the ring. Well, that will not do, Emma.'

I stared up at her, my tongue clinging to the roof of my mouth, my palms clammy with sweat, yet I could not utter, was unable to scream or shout, could not move.

She raised her hands and gently removed one of the pillows beneath my head.

'This won't hurt, dear, it will be quick and very peaceful. But you must join Lilian now — I cannot have you around any longer causing so much trouble.'

As she lifted the pillow I tried to turn my head away, but it was a useless act and the soft featherdown descended upon my waiting face.

As I slipped into suffocating blackness, I thought I heard somebody screaming.

11

The following Monday I was still at Musgrove, but recovered in both mind and body and making ready to depart. Aunt Lowther had been taken away, and the house seemed strangely empty at first without her commanding presence. But normality was returning, and there was nothing more for me to do save return to Father and Flower Street.

Mr Middleton had been the first visitor, even before Harry Varney, and had taken Uncle Arnold away with him; poor, broken Uncle Arnold. We did not know if he would ever recover from his shock, but Mr Middleton, with firm cheerfulness, had announced that he would take Uncle Arnold to stay with him for a while.

It had been Margaret who had screamed that fateful night, thus waking the household and saving my life.

'How did you *know*, Margaret?' I asked her, as I lay propped up in bed on the second day. Margaret sat on the chair beside my bed, and Elspeth and Rachel perched on either side of my feet. 'How did you know to come to my room? After all, it was the middle of the night. Were you not asleep?'

'I don't know why I came.' She frowned in concentration. 'All I remember is waking up with a sort of a jolt and feeling that something dreadful was about to happen. I had to come and see you, although I didn't want to.' She lowered her head, clenching her hands on her lap. 'I was frightened — especially after last time — when Mama died.'

'Tell me about that.' I said gently, 'it will do you good to talk about it. You have never told anyone, have you?'

She shook her head, eyes still cast down. 'It was so long ago — I can't remember all of it — but some things are quite clear. I have never forgotten the bear.'

She shuddered, and the other two children seemed to freeze in silent terror on the end of the bed.

'Tell me,' I repeated, watching their faces, knowing that this must be brought out into the open. We had all experienced fear and shock and must talk about them, air them for once and all, and never allow secrets and dread to rule our lives again.

'Mama had that other room, next to Father's, down the main corridor,' said Margaret softly, 'and I did not understand about the baby, and her being sick, and everything. I was very unhappy because they would not let me see her.'

'They?' I queried.

'The woman who came up from the village and took care of Elspeth after she was born, and — and *her*.'

I presumed the woman to be the wet nurse, and the other, whom Margaret could not bear to name, would have been Aunt Prudence, no doubt about that.

'That night I wanted to see Mama — I hadn't seen her all day, and everyone kept rushing about and telling me to get out of the way. It was horrible.' She gave a little shiver. 'So I went along to Mama's room at night, when I thought everybody would be sleeping. I opened her door very carefully so as not to disturb her and I saw — I saw — ' she broke off, raising her head, and looked at me with great tears welling in her eyes. 'I saw a big white bear bending over Mama's bed!'

Margaret let out a sob of anguish and flung herself forwards, pressing her face against my hand. Her thin shoulders heaved with sobs, and Elspeth and Rachel joined their voices with hers.

'There,' I said, stroking her back, thankful that she could cry at last, 'you are a fine, brave girl and I shall never forget how you saved my life. Perhaps it was the ring, Margaret? Do you think it might be? Perhaps that was what made you come to my room? Alice gave it to you, didn't she?'

Margaret sniffed and nodded. 'It is too big for me,' she said in a muffled voice, 'but I have put it on a ribbon and wear it around my neck. I *wish* I could have saved Mama's life, too. I *wish* I could have!' She began to weep again and I leaned forward and put my arms around her trembling body.

'You were too small then, Margaret, and too young to know what to do. Did *she* see you looking? Did she know you were there?'

Make her talk, Aunt Maggie had said, and I intended doing just that. Every grim detail must be remembered, every wretched memory resurrected and assessed; then, maybe, Margaret would be able to live in the present and put the haunted past behind her.

'I still thought it was a bear, I could not have been properly awake for I was certain it was an animal, and it was pressing down on Mama's face. Then it turned and looked at me and — and it had *her* face!'

'What did you do then?' I asked, holding her tightly in my arms.

'I turned and ran and ran back to my own room, and got into bed and waited for the bear to come and get me. I couldn't sleep — I didn't sleep well for ages after that, I still don't sleep well some nights. But now with Elspeth and Rachel it is better.' She looked across at her sisters and gave a watery smile.

'And nothing was said to you? In the morning did Aunt Prudence say nothing?'

'No.' Margaret's mouth clamped shut and she put a hand up to her face and rubbed fiercely at her wet cheeks. 'Father was gentle and kind and told me that Mama was dead — but *she* was horrid. I did not see much of her — she hated to have me around and I spent most of my time in my room. But I *knew*, you see, and that's why she wanted to send me away, although Father would not permit it.'

'Could you not have told your father what you saw?'

'No. I was very frightened at first, in case she did something to *me*, so I kept quiet and hoped that she would forget all about me. Then Bessie came and looked after me, and then they married and I couldn't say anything after that.'

Yes, I thought, once Prudence married Arnold Lowther she was totally secure in every way, and would have remained so if I had not come to Musgrove.

Was the ring bewitched? I wondered, as the children kissed me and then departed. They had been told not to tire me and only stayed for a short time each day. But at least they had the freedom of the house now and were not imprisoned like caged birds in their two upper rooms.

Was the ring bewitched? Or was it purely my imagination? That vivd imagination which I had possessed since childhood, and which Father had often told me would prove my undoing.

Had I, perhaps, by listening to Edward when he told me about his gay and beautiful aunt, subconsciously mimicked her characteristics, allowing my thoughts to become frivolous and vain whenever I wore her ring? Maybe I did look a little like her, particularly when I wore her clothes and did my hair in a similar style. And perhaps, because Margaret had heard that I was ill and confined to my bed, her imagination had taken hold of her and she had come to my room, re-enacting the nightmare of her mother's sickness and death?

I would never know the answers, but liked the idea of a magic ring, and hoped that Lilian Lowther's spirit might have had something to do with the latter events. Now she could rest in peace, poor ill-fated lady, I thought, leaning back and shutting my eyes. Justice would be done, and Musgrove and the three little girls could begin a new and more tranquil life without the awesome presence of Prudence Lowther.

Edward and Alice would marry in time, I was convinced of that. Once the horror of the last few days receded and they had time to think and plan, their marriage was inevitable. Alice would be kind to the children, and that thought soothed me, although the loss of Musgrove was hard to accept. I had grown to love the house, as I had the girls, and would dearly have liked to be mistress there. But I had to go, there was no place for me now in the household and Father needed me in St Giles.

For the time being Edward was in charge of the estate; Uncle Arnold was in no condition to be interested in the land, indeed, he was scarcely interested in life itself, so Edward, as his heir, took on the task of squire. And Alice was to remain as housekeeper, and to care for the children.

'You do not hate me, Emma?' she asked brokenly, when she first saw me after Aunt Lowther was taken away. 'I cannot help being Prue's sister, but I pray that you do not hold that against me?'

'Of course not, silly.' I smiled into her miserable face. 'We have been friends, Alice, and I hope will always remain so.'

'If only I had *known* — perhaps I should have guessed? But I was only a schoolgirl when the first Mrs Lowther died, and although I knew Prue to be ambitious I never dreamt that she was wicked. I still cannot believe it, Emma. The doctor said she was giving you her sleeping powders. She never slept well — all her life she suffered from insomnia, so it was the easiest thing in the world to keep putting the powders in your drinks.' Her cheeks became suddenly pink and she went on with a rush — 'Edward is very upset, he wants to see you and apologise. He — I do hope that you will make it up and decide to marry after all. He is a good man, you know, but Prue deceived him totally.'

'I do not blame Edward for any-thing,' I said, 'but we will never marry. I have learned many things here at Musgrove, and I am not the right person for him. But maybe you are, Alice.'

Her face became even redder beneath my gaze. 'Oh, I am not worthy of him,' she said softly. 'But I do admire him and feel most — most comfortable with him, Emma.'

'Time will tell. Stay here and look after the house and the children, and in a few months I shall expect to receive an invitation to your wedding.'

She smiled and ducked her head, and I knew that she would be right for Edward.

'Take care of the girls,' I said more soberly. 'They have been grossly neglected, and Margaret, especially, has been hurt and frightened. Give them freedom to laugh and run and have other children here to play. And see that Margaret has her pony, Alice, she would so love that. They need the security of a happy home, particularly now that their father has gone. I do so hope he will recover soon and come back to them, but you must do your best until then.'

'Mr Middleton will make him better. He will do it if *anyone* can.'

Yes, Uncle Arnold was in good hands, I thought gratefully, but wished that the same could be said about Musgrove. Edward was not a born countryman and I feared for the future of the estate. I would have a word with Charles Middleton before I left, I decided. Edward was difficult and stubborn, but he respected Middleton, and if that gentleman could be persuaded to keep an eye on Musgrove, it might yet be safe.

Musgrove — my lovely home — the house I had so dearly wanted to possess. But it was not to be; I was almost ready to depart, and my dreams would be but memories, to be taken out and looked at and cherished for a few short minutes of the day or night, when I became depressed or discouraged in my efforts in St Giles.

Harry Varney rode over to wish me

God-speed, the day before my departure for London.

'I hope you will forgive me, Miss Emma,' he said, his blue eyes for once serious, and his manner unusually grave. 'I blame myself for not taking greater care of you, especially after Aunt Maggie's warning. But how could we have guessed it was going to be that fiend of a woman!'

'Everyone seems to be begging my forgiveness,' I answered, smiling slightly, 'yet no one was to blame — apart from her.' Like Margaret, I found it difficult to speak her name. 'Apparently she was giving me her sleeping powders. But I cannot understand how she dared to do it. Surely someone would have been suspicious if I had died?' I shivered at the thought.

'I doubt it.' Varney shook his head. 'You had visited Aunt Maggie the evening before you became ill, and you told me yourself that she had given you some of her home-made brew. Prudence Lowther had only to tell the doctor where you had been and the assumption would have been clear. The old witch had poisoned you! Aunt Maggie is disliked by many in the village, so it would have been her word against the respectable Mrs Lowther's, and it is obvious which of the two would have been believed. If you had died, my dear, why should any suspicion have fallen on your aunt? She had nothing to gain from your death, had she?'

'But why did she not kill me at once, at night in my sleep? Why bother with drugging me?'

'Because the sudden death of a healthy young woman would have been *too* suspect. All right, she could have blamed it all on to Aunt Maggie, but how much better it would be for you to sicken from some unknown ailment, gradually become weaker, and *then* expire. Dear heavens, what an evil mind! Let us talk of happier things. How is little Margaret? I shall always bless her for saving your life.'

'She is well, and quite calm now. It amazes me how resilient children are. Another instance of Aunt Maggie's wisdom — she told me the very same thing.'

'I suppose the child is fortunate in still being alive. Edward informed me that she actually saw Prudence Lowther smothering her mother.'

I shuddered. 'Yes, Margaret has been through a great deal, poor love. Small wonder she was so strange and withdrawn all these years.'

'And *you* had to go because you were becoming too like Lilian, and that creature was terrified that you might learn the truth?' Varney sighed. 'Here we go again, Miss Emma, talking about evil things which are best forgotten. I *insist* that we change the subject at once!' He moved suddenly and came towards me, where I sat in a chair by the open window of the drawing-room. 'Dearest Emma, I shall call you that and you cannot stop me. Will you marry me?'

I was so startled by his words that my mouth fell open and I could only stare in astonishment.

Varney knelt beside my chair, taking one of my hands in his warm ones. 'I realise that you do not know me well, but we have been through a great deal together in a short space of time, and I can think of no other female whose company I enjoy as much as yours. We are good companions, are we not?' He peered up at my face with loving intensity.

'Dear Harry, of course we are good friends, and I like you very much indeed.' I put my free hand over his, not wanting to hurt him, yet knowing that the truth must be told. 'But I cannot marry you.'

'Why not? You are no longer betrothed to Edward, and I realise that I am a bit younger than you but it does not worry me, so why should you care? We would have such fun together, Emma, can't you see that?'

'Yes,' I said soberly, 'but there is more

to marriage than having fun, and I know that the serious side of my nature would not appeal to you. I *am* too old for you, Harry, and too dull.'

'You are not a bit dull, and that is no answer at all,' he said stubbornly. 'You cannot refuse me on those grounds, Emma.'

'Well, then, I do not love you,' I remarked flatly, 'and although it might be a silly, romantic notion, I could never marry a man whom I did not love.'

'But you did not love Edward Lowther and you were betrothed to him!'

'That was before I came to Musgrove, and since being here I have changed. Lilian has affected me more than I realised. But the truth is that I am returning to London tomorrow, a different woman, but a free one, and will continue with my work there trying to make less fortunate people a little happier.'

'May I come and see you in London?'

'By all means,' I replied quickly, 'I shall always be glad to see you, Harry.'

'Then I shall not give up hope, my dear Emma,' he said defiantly.

★ ★ ★

That afternoon I drove over to Wadhurst Grange, to say goodbye to Uncle Arnold, and to have a quiet word with Charles Middleton. Unfortunately, it very soon became apparent that my visit was a waste of time.

Mrs Bridges, the housekeeper, opened the door to me and smiled in a pleasant, friendly manner, although she must have been bursting with curiosity. Gossip about my near death and Prudence Lowther's arrest must have swept the country by now. She showed me into the library and said she would inform Mr Middleton of my arrival.

Sitting in a high-backed chair, his hands lying listlessly on his knees, sat Uncle Arnold. He did not turn his head at my approach, but continued to gaze before him at the carpet.

'I have come to say goodbye,' I said gently, bending forward to kiss his cheek. 'I am going back to London tomorrow and wanted to see you before my departure.'

He made no reply, did not move so much as his eyes, and continued to gaze before him like a blind man.

I sat down on a chair opposite him, wishing that Mr Middleton would come and join us. It was impossible to hold a conversation with someone who neither looked at one, nor appeared to listen. It was like talking to a piece of furniture, and I was all the more grateful to Mr Middleton for having Uncle Arnold to stay — he must have been a most depressing guest.

Still, I did my best, telling him about the three little girls, and of Margaret's desire for a pony; I explained that Alice was to remain and look after the house, and said I hoped that she and Edward would marry in due course. I chattered on, in desperation, hearing my own voice sounding false and strained in the silence of the high-ceilinged library.

Then the door opened and Charles Middleton strode briskly into the room.

'Uncle Arnold is no better,' I said, looking up at his tall figure. 'What are we going to do? I have been trying to talk to him but he cannot, or will not, respond.'

Middleton drew up a chair which had been set against the table, and leaned back on it, sighing. 'It will be a lengthy business, I fear, Miss Garnet. But, as you once so courageously remarked, we must never stop trying.'

I remembered that day, when Aunt Prudence and Edward had been so disparaging about my work in the slums, and it seemed like years before, instead of a matter of days. 'Yes, I suppose one must never give up. But this — ' I gestured at the man opposite me, seeing how he had aged in the last week, how his face had become drawn and lined with despair and shock, how his body appeared to have shrunk within his clothing — 'this is terrible. Is there any hope for him?'

'To learn that your first wife was murdered, and that your second wife was the murderess cannot be a pleasant experience,' said Mr Middleton matter-of-factly. 'But yes, the doctor believes there is hope.' He stretched out his long legs, glancing at the older man beside him. 'I talk to him every evening, telling him about my affairs, and all the problems and little incidents which occur on the estate each day. And if I have visitors, I always make sure that we sit in the same room as Lowther. Something, some day, may awaken his interest in life.'

'You are very kind to him, sir.'

'I am atoning for my sins, Miss Garnet.'

Charles Middleton flashed me a look which made the blood rush to my face. I did not wish to be reminded of his behaviour with Lilian; thoughts of her brought back too many memories; of his arms about me in the rose garden, of my outrageous conduct at the party, and his brutal manner towards me afterwards. The ring was no longer in my possession, Lilian's ghost was laid, and I wanted only to return to being the cool and virtuous spinster I really was.

'So, what now?' asked my companion, tactfully changing the subject. 'When are you and Edward to wed?'

I stared at him in surprise. 'I thought you knew? Everybody else seems to. Edward and I are no longer betrothed and I leave for London tomorrow.'

Middleton shook his head, his face expressionless. 'I had no idea. But why this rush to leave, Miss Garnet? I imagine they could all make use of your advice and numerous abilties. The children, particularly, have grown fond of you and will not find it easy to do without both their father and their friend.'

'I must leave Musgrove,' I answered swiftly, 'and return to the life which I know best, and where I am needed more. Alice will be staying on to look after the house and the girls, and they will manage well enough without me. But that brings me to my second reason for calling here,' I hesitated, 'I have a favour to ask.'

Suddenly the words would not come easily, and I wondered at my boldness in expecting this man to do more for the Lowther family. He had taken on the task of caring for Uncle Arnold, was that not enough? Now I intended asking him to keep an eye on Edward, to see that Margaret got her pony, to visit his daughter from time to time and make sure that all the little girls were all right. What presumption! He was a busy landowner with, no doubt, a varied social life. And here I was, about to beg further favours.

'Yes?' queried Middleton, his eyes intent on my face. 'You have surprised me with your first news, now shock me with your plea — I can always say no, Miss Garnet.'

Why was I not at ease with him, as I

was with Harry Varney? Why did I blush and hesitate, whereas with Harry I would have come straight out with my request without a qualm?

There were too many memories of Lilian, I thought dismally. Charles Middleton was too involved with the Lowther family, and my knowledge of this would always lie between us, like a dark shadow.

'For one who is normally so self-assured and businesslike, you are remarkably hesitant, Miss Garnet. Pray speak your mind before I expire from curiosity.'

If there had been amusement in his voice, or a hint of laughter in his eyes, how much easier it would have been. But I could not tell what he was thinking; did not know him, nor understand him. His face was blank, his voice cool.

'Would you keep an eye on Edward?' I blurted out, finding words at last. 'I realise that it is a great deal to ask, but he is taking over the running of the estate, and has no experience of such matters.'

'Hilton is a very good bailiff and his judgement is sound. If Edward listens to him no harm will come to the land. But why this interest, Miss Garnet? I should have thought that recent events would have made you feel nothing but horror for the place.'

'I am glad to be leaving, of course, but — ' I paused, 'but I did love it. That first morning when I went out and explored the grounds, and saw the house properly in daylight, I fell in love with it. And the children — ' I stopped abruptly.

The children were nothing to me now. I had my own life to lead, and they would have to adjust to theirs without me.

'The children will be well cared for by Alice,' I continued. 'But perhaps you would ask Margaret to come over and see that pony, as you once suggested? I have told Alice about her love of horses, but she will have her hands full with the house and everything, and she might forget about Margaret,' I ended lamely.

'And Elspeth?' he asked. 'Pray tell me what I should do about her.'

I rose to my feet, brushing down my skirts. He was mocking me, and I had no time for banter. 'You must do what you think best. I apologise for my interference but certain things had to be said.'

I went over to Uncle Arnold and touched one of his lifeless hands. 'Goodbye,' I said gently, 'I hope you will soon feel better. Musgrove needs you.'

I turned away, and Charles Middleton rose and escorted me to the door.

'I wish you a safe journey home, Miss Garnet, and envy all those people in your slums. They have a most capable and efficient lady to look after them and put their world to rights.'

He thought I was an inquisitive busybody, and perhaps he was right. But if I cared for people I had to make sure that they received all the loving attention it was possible to give them 'Forgive me for taking up so much of your precious time,' I said, holding out my hand.

'It was a pleasure, Miss Garnet, and I hope to see you again when you next visit Musgrove.' He bowed over my hand. 'Such a conscientious person will surely return to make sure that all her instructions are being properly carried out.'

I returned to London in a very unhappy state of mind; angry with myself for not handling my visit to Wadhurst Grange with more tact, annoyed with Mr Middleton for not accepting my advice with better grace, and miserable at having to leave the children.

The journey back to St Giles was long and irksome on my own, and when I arrived in the cobbled streets, the stench and degradation of humanity there filled me with a greater depression. I had forgotten about the smells! For one month I had been away from filth and poverty, my lungs had been filled with pure country air; I had walked in green pastures and had experienced space in living, and walking, and breathing. Now I was back in the slums, and aware of everything with new eyes, my senses sharpened and acute. And I did not like what I saw and heard and smelt.

Father was as fierce as ever, engaged in a losing battle, but fighting for every soul with a lion's courage. And grumpy, faithful Martha was there to welcome and nag me on my first evening home.

'So you recovered from your sickness, Emma? Father said, as we sat down to our meal of broth and dry bread. 'Edward wrote and told me that you had not been well.'

But he had said no more than that. Once I had recovered, and Aunt Lowther had gone, I had begged Edward to say nothing to Father about the circumstances of her attack on me, and her arrest. Father was unlikely ever to visit Musgrove, he had not known the Lowther family, and it was not necessary to burden him with the sad and involved tale. I intended forgetting all about the past, and it would be best if no one at home knew the truth.

'You look different, Miss Emma.' Martha's eyes, although old, were sharp and perceptive. She would be less easy to deceive than Father.

'I *am* different,' I replied, more cheerfully than I felt. 'I have been away from London for the first time in my life, and have experienced a different world. How I wish that I could take you and Father, and all those wretched souls out there — ' I nodded towards the window — 'away with me to the countryside. We would not have the sickness and the deaths with which we are plagued in this forsaken place.'

'But *you* were sick there,' said Martha.

'Oh, only a slight chill,' I answered carelessly. 'Now tell me what has been happening since I've been away.'

'When is Mister Edward returning?'

Martha would not be side-tracked. She had looked after me and Father since Mother died, and believed this gave her the right to know everything about us. She firmly believed that she was 'family'.

'Edward and I are no longer engaged to be married. Did he not write that in his letter?'

Father looked surprised. 'He did not. Why this sudden and surprising decision, Emma? He was a most humble and caring young man, and I liked him.'

'We got to know one another rather better during these last weeks,' I said truthfully, 'and it became plain to us both that we were not suited. We parted amicably, and as Edward's uncle is not well at present, Edward is to stay on at Musgrove and manage the estate.'

'Seems like a lot of illness down there in Sussex,' muttered Martha.

Father ignored her. 'Edward was to inherit the place, I believe? Well and good, his place is there, I have no doubt. But I am glad to see you back,

Emma. We have all missed you and there have been many enquiries for you whilst you've been away.'

Wishing that I felt the same gladness, I smiled and then made ready to go to bed. 'It has been a tiring day,' I explained, kissing him goodnight, 'and I must be fresh and ready for work tomorrow.'

'If you are fit for it,' remarked Martha, going ahead of me up the narrow stairs. 'You don't look right, Miss Emma, and there's more to all this than you're telling. Have you fallen in love with another man?' She turned sharply on the landing, and the candle in her hand flickered and almost went out.

'Don't be silly, Martha,' I said brusquely, pushing past her so that she could not see my face. 'Light me to my room and then get some sleep yourself. Who knows what the morrow holds in store for us?'

'It is a man.' Martha nodded in a smug way and placed the candlestick beside my bed. 'Never mind, dearie, you're best off with your father and me. Never was made for marriage, I reckon, and your life is meant to be here with us in Flower Street.'

12

Now I stood in the draughty passage, facing Martha with her lamp, and feeling cold and tired and dirty. A visitor awaited me, whom I did not wish to see, but whom I could not avoid meeting.

'Bring some water to my room quickly! I shall have to wash, and change this gown, and do something to my hair. Tell him I'll be down in a few minutes,' I said to her.

But even as I spoke, the door to the front parlour opened and Charles Middleton's tall figure filled the doorway.

'Miss Garnet?' His voice was puzzled as he peered out into the passage, seeing me unclearly in the subdued light from Martha's lamp.

Hastily I pushed the cardboard box into her hand, then stepped forward to confront him, just as I was. What did it matter now? Let him see for himself how the other half lived.

'Good evening,' I said quietly, moving past him into the parlour, where I was thankful to see that a fire had been lit. 'I have only just returned and must apologise for keeping you waiting.' I moved to the chair by the hearth and sank down, my limbs so heavy that they would not have borne me up a minute longer. 'Why did you want to see me?'

Mr Middleton's eyes took in every detail of my dishevelled appearance; my dirt-encrusted, stained gown, my lank uncovered hair, my torn shawl and bloody hands.

'My God!' he breathed, moving slowly forward as Martha set the lamp down upon the table. 'What have you been doing? Is this your usual time for returning home?'

I smiled slightly, despite my fatigue, amused by his lack of self-control, the slipping of his normally expressionless mask. Perhaps it was just as well that he saw me like this; it would make him realise that my work was vital; that people here did live under the appalling conditions which I had once tried to describe; that I was desperately needed to help fight poverty and destitution.

'Martha,' I said, 'please bring us food as soon as possible. I am famished and no doubt Mr Middleton could do with something, also.'

She opened her mouth as if to argue, thought better of it, and went away to the kitchen bearing the cardboard box with her.

Our visitor seated himself opposite me, his eyes never leaving my face. 'Dear heavens, it is pitiful to see you in such a condition. Tell me, what have you been doing?'

'I have been helping to deliver a baby, but it was born dead.'

'I am sorry.' He looked genuinely concerned.

'You need not be. It will mean one less mouth to feed for the mother, and she will be free to work again as soon as she is stronger.'

'Oh, well, then I suppose it is all to the good.' He watched me closely. 'Was she a friend of yours? You seem bitter in some way.'

'Only about the fact that this will happen again in a year, or so. Peggy will have another baby, which may or may not live, and then another. And nobody will look after her because she is not married, and hers is the age-old profession, Mr Middleton. She is also but fifteen years old,' I said.

He stood up abruptly and went to lean one elbow on the mantelshelf. 'We shall finish with this morbid and unpleasant subject at once,' he said harshly. 'You told us a little about life in St Giles, but I must confess that I had no idea how truly dreadful it was! Now, Miss Garnet, I wish to say my piece and bring some sanity into your life.'

He paused. 'How your father can allow you to live and work in this Hades is beyond my understanding. However,' he lifted a hand as I made to speak. 'Allow me to finish, if you please. I have come here today to beg a favour from you, Miss Garnet. The children are missing you very much and we all decided that I should come and beg you to return to us.'

'The children?' I stared up at him in fright. 'Are they all right? What has happened at Musgrove?'

'The children are fine but lonely without you. I have them staying with me now, you see, because Uncle Arnold began to recover and wished to go home. He went back to Musgrove three weeks ago, but is still in a confused state of mind.

'Alice is doing her best, poor child, but she really could not cope with the sick man, and the household tasks, and the three little girls. So I have taken them to Wadhurst where they have settled down well, and Mrs Bridges does her best for them. But she is no longer young, Miss Garnet, and — '

'And you want a nursemaid for

them,' I ended for him.

How strong he looked, standing there before me, how vigorous and healthy and handsome! I had not seen a whole man since leaving Sussex, for even Father was becoming bowed and aged with the rigours of our slum existence.

How splendid Mr Middleton looked! And how totally alien to my way of life.

'I could not return, sir. I am needed here, and much as I still love the girls, they are blessed with so much, whereas the people here have nothing.'

'You misunderstand me, Miss Garnet. I came to ask you to return to Wadhurst Grange, not as a nursemaid but as my wife.'

For a moment I thought that I would faint, it was too much, coming on top of a long and painful day. I leaned forward, putting my face in my hands.

Martha marched in at that moment, bearing a tray which she banged down upon the table.

'Now what have you done to her?' She came stomping round to my side,

300

and I felt the weight of her arm across my shoulders. 'So tired and wore out and needing her sleep. What did you say to upset her? Miss Emma don't want you here, pestering and annoying her. It's best if you leave us alone and get back where you belong.'

'It's all right, Martha.' I lifted my head. 'Mr Middleton must stay and eat with us. Please lay the table and just keep some back for Father.'

She huffed and snorted, making a fine display of her temper, then she left us alone with our bowls of soup and chunks of home-made bread.

'Well,' said Mr Middleton, eyeing me from over the top of his raised bowl, 'you have not answered my question?'

I sipped a few mouthfuls of the nourishing liquid, allowing it to warm my stomach, giving me strength to respond.

Once I had believed that I would be mistress of Musgrove; had desired nothing more in life. Now Wadhurst Grange was being offered to me. That fine house, far larger than Musgrove, and the chance of being with the children forever, and of possessing the wealth, and the time, to enjoy them and spoil them. Mrs Charles Middleton of Wadhurst Grange. It was unbelievable. Wife to this man, whom I had loved ever since he took me into his arms that night in the rose garden, the man who infuriated me, puzzled me, and whom I found infinitely attractive. But who did not love me.

'I realise that you do not love me, Miss Garnet,' he was saying, 'but marriages can be built on mutual respect and affection. I have admired you ever since I first met you, and know that you would make me very happy and very proud if you would consent to being my wife.'

And Lilian? I thought. How can I ever forget her, and the hold she has upon your heart?

'I have never been in love before,' he went on softly, looking away from me, 'and perhaps I should not be baring my soul to you. But it seems that you need some persuading, my dearest Miss Garnet, and I do assure you that my love for you is genuine and deep.'

'You loved Lilian Lowther!' I declared stiffly.

'Indeed I did not. And do not look so angry! I was amused by Lilian, I admired her beauty, and I enjoyed flirting with her, that is all. Why else should I have gone off to Australia for so many years? She was becoming too possessive, too careless and demanding, you see. Oh, all right, I used her, I suppose, it was partly my fault. But I did not love her and would never have married her, if she had been free.'

'But that night — ' I stared at him — 'that night when we first met — you called me Lilian, and my love, and you embraced me, thinking it to be *her*!'

'I shall never forget it.' He smiled at me, and my face went hot at his look. 'Remember that I had been away for a long time and yes, I was looking forward to seeing her again. I *liked* her immensely, you see, and enjoyed her company. Perhaps I was over-fervent, but it was a superficial, light-hearted fervour, not the feeling of true love.'

'You used her for your own pleasure, then? How despicable!'

Charles Middleton sighed and put down his empty bowl.

'My past behaviour has often been despicable, Miss Garnet, and there are many incidents in my life which I deeply regret. But they cannot be made undone, and all I ask is that you will take me in hand and teach me to become a good and loving husband. I think you are quite capable of that.'

'Why were you so angry with me at the party? When I dressed in Lilian's gown, and had my hair arranged in that foolish style?'

How well I remembered his look of wrath, and his rough handling, and the furious tone of his voice! I gave an involuntary shiver at the memory of that painful night.

'Don't you see, my dearest Emma?'

Mr Middleton leaned forward across the table, his eyes filled with compassion. 'It was because I loved you, and could not bear to see you wearing her clothes and apeing her flirtatious manner. You were too good for such nonsense, and I wanted you as I had grown to love you — brisk, old-fashioned, and very warm hearted. I do not desire a beautiful and seductive charmer as my wife. I want a sensible, kind and at times rather daunting, Emma Garnet.'

'Why did you not tell me all this before? When I came to see you and Uncle Arnold at Wadhurst? Why did you let me come back to London?'

Mr Middleton sighed. 'Because I needed time to think, because I had Arnold Lowther to consider, because — '

Martha threw open the door and marched in to disturb us once more.

'Have you finished?' she said. 'Here's a piece of treacle pudding and when are you going to bed, Miss Emma? You look exhausted. It's too bad keeping you up so late — some folk have no consideration for others. Just because they have money and fine clothes and talk grand, they think the sun rises and sets for them.' She removed our empty bowls, muttering under her breath, but loud enough for us to hear her quite plainly.

I looked at her lined, bad-tempered face, and saw the dark scullery behind her through the open door; I looked down at my hands, realising that I had eaten without washing; I wondered what my face and hair must look like.

'I'm leaving your father something on the stove and I'm off to bed. Can't stay up a minute longer. I'll be waking you at five tomorrow, Miss Emma, so if this gentleman has any kindness in him he'll go and let you have some rest.'

She went out banging the door behind her.

There lay my future, I thought bleakly. A life ahead of Martha, and Granny Lanes, and Peggy Frys, and dirt and poverty and disaster. How could I refuse Wadhurst Grange in the face of all that?

'I accept your proposal, sir,' I said, looking at the man opposite me; wishing, in a small corner of my mind, that he had said he found me beautiful. 'On one condition.'

Mr Middleton stood up and came round the table to stand beside me.

'What now?' he asked, gazing down at me.

'May I have a place at Wadhurst, a place for a few children, or families? Where they can come for a holiday once a year? I would ask Father to look for people in real need of peace, and fresh air, and space in which to breathe for a short time in their miserable lives.'

'I have an old dilapidated barn,' said Mr Middleton slowly, 'which was about to be pulled down. But we can repair it and make it into a decent shelter for your unfortunate people. You may do whatever you wish, my dearest Emma, just as long as you have time for me, also.' Then he leaned forward and pulled me to my feet. 'I want to kiss your poor white face, and make you forget all the terrible things which you have seen and experienced in your short life.'

His arms went round me and I sank against him, feeling comforted and strengthened and loved, all in one tumultuous rush of emotion. Then his hands cupped my face and he brought his lips down on mine with infinite tenderness.

I knew then that Lilian's ghost need never be feared again, and that beauty was of no importance at all.

THE END

We do hope that you have enjoyed reading this large print book.

Did you know that all of our titles are available for purchase?

We publish a wide range of high quality large print books including:
**Romances, Mysteries, Classics
General Fiction
Non Fiction and Westerns**

Special interest titles available in large print are:
**The Little Oxford Dictionary
Music Book, Song Book
Hymn Book, Service Book**

Also available from us courtesy of Oxford University Press:
**Young Readers' Dictionary
(large print edition)
Young Readers' Thesaurus
(large print edition)**

For further information or a free brochure, please contact us at:
**Ulverscroft Large Print Books Ltd.,
The Green, Bradgate Road, Anstey,
Leicester, LE7 7FU, England.
Tel:** (00 44) **0116 236 4325
Fax:** (00 44) **0116 234 0205**

Other titles in the
Linford Romance Library:

TUDOR STAR

Sara Judge

Meg Dawlish becomes companion to Lady Penelope Rich whom she loves and admires. Her mistress, unhappily married, meets the two loves of her life — Sir Philip Sidney, and Sir Charles Blount . . . Meg partakes in the excitement of the Accession Day Tilts and visits the house of the Earl of Essex . . . When Meg falls in love she has to decide whether to leave her mistress and life at court, and follow her lover to the wilds of Shropshire.

SAY IT WITH FLOWERS

Chrissie Loveday

Daisy Jones has abandoned her hectic London life for a more peaceful existence in her old home town. Taking on a florist business is another huge gamble, but she loves it and the people she meets. Her new life brings a new love and her life looks set for happiness . . . until the complications set in. Nothing is quite what it seems and she sets off on an emotional roller coaster. Who said life in a small town is peaceful?

ENCHANTED DESERT

Isobel Scott

A strange man takes Cindy Charles from a jeweller's in London's Bond Street to the deserts of Saudi Arabia. The man, an Arab with green eyes, is Sheikh Al Adham. He is handsome with an air of mystery that the flowing robes of Arabia emphasise . . . At the first opportunity, Cindy escapes the influence of the man whom she finds so disturbing. But on reaching England she finds him impossible to forget. And then Cindy is sent on a straightforward journey, which has an unexpected meeting in store for her.

Dick Francis

WILD HORSES

PAN BOOKS

First published 1994 by Michael Joseph

This edition published 1995 by Pan Books
an imprint of Macmillan General Books
25 Eccleston Place, London SW1W 9NF
and Basingstoke

Associated companies throughout the world

ISBN 0 330 34142 1

7 9 8

A CIP catalogue record for this book is available from
the British Library

Typeset by CentraCet Limited, Cambridge
Printed and bound in Great Britain

Wild Horses

Dick Francis has written thirty-three international bestsellers and is widely acclaimed as one of our finest thriller writers. His awards include the Crime Writers' Association's Cartier Diamond Dagger, for his outstanding contribution to the crime genre, and an honorary Doctorate of Humane Letters from Tufts University of Boston. He and his wife, Mary, divide their time between England, Florida and the British West Indies.

We are spirits clad in veils;
Man by man was never seen;
All our deep communing fails
To remove the shadowy screen.

Christopher Pearse Cranch
(1813–1893)

CHAPTER ONE

Dying slowly of bone cancer, the old man, shrivelled now, sat as ever in his great armchair, tears of lonely pain sliding down crepuscular cheeks.

That Tuesday, his last, his stringy grip on my wrist tightened convulsively in a long silence while I watched his mouth tremble and move in abortive struggles to speak.

'Father.' The words finally wavered out; a whisper, desperate, driven by ultimate need. 'Father, I must make my confession. I must ask . . . absolution.'

In great surprise and with compassion I said, 'But . . . I'm not a priest.'

He paid no attention. The feeble voice, a truer measure of affairs than the fiercely clutching hand, simply repeated, 'Father . . , forgive me.'

'Valentine,' I said reasonably, 'I'm Thomas. Thomas Lyon. Don't you remember? I've come to read to you.'

He could no longer see newsprint or anything straight ahead, though peripheral vision partly remained. I called in more or less every week, both to keep him up to date with the racing columns in the newspapers and also to let his beleaguered and chronically tired old sister go out for shopping and gossip.

I hadn't actually read to him on that day. When I arrived he'd been suffering badly from one of his intermittent bouts of agony, with Dorothea, his sister, feeding him a teaspoon of liquid morphine and giving him whisky and water to help the numbness work faster.

He hadn't felt well enough for the racing papers.

'Just sit with him,' Dorothea begged. 'How long can you stay?'

'Two hours.'

She'd kissed me gratefully on the cheek, stretching on tiptoes, and had hurried away, plump in her late seventies, forthright in mind.

I sat as usual on a tapestry stool right beside the old man, as he liked the physical contact, as if to make up for sight.

The fluttery voice persisted, creeping effortfully into the quiet room, determined and intimate. 'I confess to God Almighty and to Thee, my Father, that I have sinned exceedingly ... and I must confess ... before ... before ...'

'Valentine,' I repeated more sharply, 'I'm not a priest.'

It was as if he hadn't heard. He seemed to be focusing all the energy left in him into one extraordinary spiritual gamble, a last throw of hell-defeating dice on the brink of the abyss.

'I ask pardon for my mortal sin ... I ask peace with God ...'

I protested no more. The old man knew he was dying; knew death was near. In earlier weeks he had

2

discussed with equanimity, and even with humour, his lack of a future. He had reminisced about his long life. He'd told me he had left me all his books in his will. Never had he made any mention of even the most rudimentary religious belief, except to remark once that the idea of life after death was a load of superstitious twaddle.

I hadn't known he was a Roman Catholic.

'I confess,' he said, '... that I killed him ... God, forgive me. I humbly ask pardon ... I pray to God Almighty to have mercy on me ...'

'Valentine ...'

'I left the knife with Derry and I killed the Cornish boy and I've never said a word about that week and I accuse myself ... and I lied about everything ... *mea culpa* ... I've done such harm ... I destroyed their lives ... and they didn't know, they went on liking me ... I despise myself ... all this time. Father, give me a penance ... and say the words ... say them ... *ego te absolvo* ... I forgive your sins in the name of the Father ... I beg you ... I beg you ...'

I had never heard of the sins he was talking about. His words tumbled out as if on the edge of delirium, making no cohesive sense. I thought it most likely that his sins were dreams; that he was confused, imagining great guilt where none lay.

There was no mistaking, however, the frantic nature of his repeated plea.

'Father, absolve me. Father, say the words ... say them, I beg you.'

I couldn't see what harm it would do. He was desperate to die in peace. Any priest would have given

3

him absolution: who was I cruelly to withhold it? I was not of his faith. I would square it later, I thought, with my own immortal soul.

So I said what he wanted. Said the words, dredging them from memory. Said them in Latin, as he would clearly understand them, because they seemed less of a lie that way than in bald English.

'*Ego te absolvo*,' I said.

I felt a shiver through my body. Superstition, I thought.

I remembered more words. They floated on my tongue. '*Ego te absolvo a peccatis tuis, In nomine Patris et Filii et Spiritus Sancti. Amen.*'

I absolve you from your sins in the name of the Father and of the Son and of the Holy Ghost. Amen.

The greatest blasphemy of my life to date. God forgive me my sin, I thought.

The dreadful tension subsided in the old man. The rheumy near-blind eyes closed. The grip on my wrist loosened: the old hand fell away. His face relaxed. He faintly smiled, and then grew still.

Alarmed, I felt for a pulse under his jaw and was relieved to feel the threadlike beat. He didn't move under my touch. I shook him a little, but he didn't wake. After five minutes I shook him again, more strongly, without results. Indecisively then I got up from my seat beside him and, crossing to the telephone, dialled the number prominently written on a notepad nearby, to get through to his doctor.

The medicine man was less than pleased.

'I've told the old fool he should be in hospital,' he

4

said. 'I can't keep running out to hold his hand. Who are you, anyway? And where's Mrs Pannier?'

'I'm a visitor,' I said. 'Mrs Pannier is out shopping.'

'Is he groaning?' demanded the doctor.

'He was, earlier. Mrs Pannier gave him some pain-killer before she went out. Then he was talking. Now he's in a sort of sleep from which I can't seem to wake him.'

The doctor growled a smothered curse and crashed his receiver into its cradle, leaving me to guess his intentions.

I hoped that he wouldn't send a wailing ambulance with busy figures and stretchers and all the rough paraphernalia of making the terminally ill feel worse. Old Valentine had wanted to die quietly in his own bed. Waiting there, I regretted my call to the doctor, thinking that I'd probably set in motion, in my anxiety, precisely what Valentine had most wanted to avoid.

Feeling stupid and remorseful, I sat opposite the steadily sleeping man, no longer on a stool beside him but in a more comfortable armchair.

The room was warm. He wore blue cotton pyjamas, with a rug over his knees. He sat near the window, bare branched trees outside giving promise of a spring he wouldn't know.

The study-like room, intensely his own, charted an unusual journey through time that had begun in heavy manual labour and ended in journalism. Born the son of a farrier, he'd been apprenticed to the forge in childhood, working the bellows for his father, skinny arms straining, young eyes excited by the noise and the fire. There had never been any question that he would follow in the trade, nor had he in fact veered towards anything else until his working pattern had long been settled.

Framed fading photographs on his walls showed a young Valentine with the biceps and pectorals of a giant, a prizewinning wielder of brute power with the wide happy grin of an innocent. But the idyll of the village smithy under the chestnut tree had already long gone. Valentine in his maturity had driven from job to job with his tools and portable brazier in a mobile working van.

He had for years shod a stableful of racehorses trained by my grandfather. He'd looked after the feet of the ponies I'd been given to ride. He had seemed to me to be already a wise man of incredible age, though I knew now he'd been barely sixty-five when I was ten.

His education had consisted of reading (the racing newspapers), writing (bills for his customers) and arithmetic (costing the work and materials so that he made a profit). Not until his forties had his mental capacity expanded to match his muscles. Not until, he'd told me during the past debilitated weeks, not decisively until in his job he was no longer expected to make individual shoes to fit the hooves of horses, but to trim the hooves to fit mass-produced uniform shoes. No longer was he expected to hammer white-hot iron bars into shape, but to tap softer metals cold.

He had begun to read history and biography, at first all to do with racing but later with wider horizons. He had begun in shy anonymity to submit observations and anecdotes to the newspapers he daily studied. He wrote about horses, people, events, opinions. One of the papers had given him a regular column with a regular salary and room to grow a reputation. While still plying his original trade, Valentine had become an honoured institution in print, truly admired and enjoyed for his insights and his wit.

As physical strength waned, his journalistic prowess had grown. He'd written on into his eighties, written into semi-blindness, written indeed until four weeks earlier, when the cancer battle had entered the stage of defeat.

And this was the old man, amusing, wise and revered, who had poured out in panic an apparently unbearable secret.

'I killed the Cornish boy . . .'

He must have meant, I thought, that he was blaming himself for an error in his shoeing, that by some mischance a lost nail in a race had caused a fatal accident to a jockey.

Not for nothing had Valentine adopted often enough the doctrine of doing things thoroughly, quoting now and then the fable of the horseshoe nail. For want of a nail the kingdom was lost . . . little oversights led to great disasters.

A dying mind, I thought again, was scrambling old small guilts into mountainous terrors. Poor old Valentine. I watched him sleep, the white hair scanty on his scalp, big blotchy freckles brown in his skin.

For a long time, no one came. Valentine's breathing grew heavier, but not to the point of snoring. I looked round the familiar room, at the horses' photographs I'd come to know well in the past few months, at the

7

framed awards on the dark green wall, the flower-printed curtains, the worn brown carpet, the studded leather chairs, the basic portable typewriter on an unfussy desk, the struggling potted plant.

Nothing had changed from week to week: only the old man's tenure there was slipping away.

One wall, shelved from floor to ceiling, held the books that I supposed would soon be mine. There were years and years of form books listing thousands upon thousands of bygone races, with a small red dot inked in beside the name of every horse Valentine had fitted with racing shoes for the test.

Winners, hundreds of them, had been accorded an exclamation mark.

Below the form books there were many volumes of an ancient encyclopaedia and rows of glossily jacketed life stories of recently dead racing titans, their bustling, swearing vigour reduced to pale paper memories. I'd met many of those people. My grandfather was among them. Their world, their passions, their achievements were passing into oblivion and already the young jockeys I'd star-gazed at ten were grandfathers.

I wondered who would write Valentine's life story, a worthy subject if ever there was one. He had steadfastly refused to write it himself, despite heavy prompting from all around. Too boring, he'd said. Tomorrow's world, that was where interest lay.

Dorothea came back apologetically half an hour late and tried without success to rouse her brother. I told her I'd phoned the doctor fruitlessly, which didn't surprise her.

'He says Valentine should be in hospital,' she said.

'Valentine refuses to go. He and the doctor swear at each other.' She shrugged resignedly. 'I expect the doctor will come in time. He usually does.'

'I'll have to leave you,' I said regretfully. 'I'm already overdue at a meeting.' I hesitated. 'Are you by any chance Roman Catholic?' I asked. 'I mean ... Valentine said something about wanting a priest.'

'A priest?' She looked astounded. 'He was rambling on all morning ... his mind is going ... but the old bugger would never ask for a *priest*.'

'I just thought ... perhaps ... last rites?'

Dorothea gave me a look of sweet sisterly exasperation.

'Our mother was Roman Catholic, but not Dad. Lot of nonsense, he used to say. Valentine and I grew up outside the Church and were never the worse for it. Our mother died when he was sixteen and I was eleven. A mass was said for her. Dad took us to that but it made him sweat, he said. Anyway, Valentine's not much of a sinner except for swearing and such, and I know that being so weak as he is he wouldn't want to be bothered by a *priest*.'

'I just thought I'd tell you,' I said.

'You're a dear to come here, Thomas, but I know you're mistaken.' She paused. 'My poor dear boy is very ill now, isn't he?' She looked down at him in concern. 'Much worse?'

'I'm afraid so.'

'Going.' She nodded, and tears came into her eyes. 'We've known it would come, but when it happens ... oh, dear.'

'He's had a good life.'

9

She disregarded the inadequate words and said for-lornly, 'I'll be so *alone*.'

'Couldn't you live with your son?'

'No!' She straightened herself scornfully. 'Paul is forty-five and pompous and domineering, though I hate to say it, and I don't get on with his wife. They have three obnoxious teenagers who switch on deafening radios all the time until the walls vibrate.' She broke off and smoothed her brother's unresponsive head fondly. 'No. Me and Valentine, we set up home here together when his Cathy died and my Bill passed on. Well, you know all that ... and we always liked each other, Valentine and me, and I'll miss him. I'll miss him something awful, but I'll stay here.' She swallowed. 'I'll get used to being alone, same as I did after Bill went.'

Dorothea, like many elderly women, it seemed to me, had a resolute independence that survived where youth quaked. With help once daily from the district nurse, she'd cared for her failing brother, taking on ever more personal tasks for him, exhausting herself to give him comfort and painkillers when he lay awake in the night. She might mourn him when he'd gone, but her dark-rimmed eyes showed she was much overdue on rest.

She sat down tiredly on the tapestry stool and held her brother's hand. He breathed slowly, shallowly, the sound rasping. Fading daylight from the window beside Valentine fell softly on the aged couple, light and shadow emphasising the rounded commitment of the one and the skeletal dependence of the other, the hovering imminence of death as plain as if the scythe had hung above their heads.

I wished I had a camera. Wished indeed for a whole camera crew. My normal day-to-day life involved the catching of emotion on the wing, the recording of ephemeral images to illumine a bedrock of truth. I dealt with unreality to give illusion the insight of revelation.

I directed films.

Knowing that one day I would use and re-create the quiet drama before me, I looked at my watch and asked Dorothea if I might use her telephone.

'Of course, dear. On the desk.'

I reached Ed, my earnest assistant, who as usual sounded flustered in my absence.

'It can't be helped,' I said. 'I'm running late. Is everyone there? Well, get some drinks sent over. Keep them happy, but don't let Jimmy have more than two G and Ts, and make sure we have enough copies of the script alterations. Right? Good. See you.'

I regretted having to leave Dorothea at such a time, but in fact I'd squeezed my visit into a day's schedule that had made no provision for it, keeping the promise I'd given week after week.

Three months back, in the preliminary pre-production stage of the film I was currently engaged on, I'd called to see Valentine as a brief matter of courtesy, a gesture to tell him I remembered him in the old days in my grandfather's time, and had always admired, even if from a distance, his emergence as a sage.

'Sage my foot!' He'd disclaimed the flattery but enjoyed it all the same. 'I can't see very well these days, boy. How about reading to me for a bit?'

He lived on the outer edge of Newmarket, the town long held to be the home and heart of the horseracing industry worldwide. 'Headquarters', the racing press called it. Fifteen hundred of the thoroughbred élite rocketed there over the windswept training gallops and over the wide difficult tracks, throwing up occasional prodigies that passed their glorious genes to flying generations of the future. An ancient wealth-producing business, the breeding of fast horses.

I was on the point of leaving when the front doorbell rang, and to save Dorothea's tired feet I went to answer it.

A short thirtyish man stood there looking at his watch, impatient.

'Can I help you?' I asked.

He gave me a brief glance and called past me, 'Dorothea?'

Regardless of fatigue, she appeared from Valentine's room and said miserably, 'He's ... in a coma, I think. Come in. This is Thomas Lyon who's been reading to Valentine, like I told you.'

As if on an afterthought, she finished the introduction, flapping a hand and saying, 'Robbie Gill, our doctor.'

Robbie Gill had red hair, a Scots accent, no small-talk and a poor bedside manner. He carried a medical bag into Valentine's room and snapped it open. He rolled up the ill man's eyelids with his thumb and pensively held one of the fragile wrists. Then he silently busied himself with stethoscope, syringes and swabs.

'We'd better get him to bed,' he said finally. No mention, I was glad to notice, of transportation to hospital.

'Is he – ?' Dorothea asked anxiously, leaving the question hovering, not wanting an affirmative answer.

'Dying?' Robbie Gill said it kindly enough in his brusque way. 'In a day or two, I'd say. Can't tell. His old heart's still fairly strong. I don't really think he'll wake again, but he might. It partly depends on what he wants.'

'How do you mean, what he wants?' I asked, surprised.

He spent time answering me, chiefly, I thought, for Dorothea's sake, but also from a teacher's pleasure in imparting technical information.

'Old people,' he said, 'very often stay alive if there's something they particularly want to do, and then after they've done it they die quite quickly. This week I've lost a patient who wanted to see her grandson married. She went to the wedding and enjoyed it, and was dead two days later. Common occurrence. If Valentine has no unfinished business, he may slip away very soon. If he were looking forward to receiving another award, something like that, it might be different. He's a strong-willed man, and amazing things can happen even with cancer as advanced as this.'

Dorothea shook her head sadly. 'No awards.'

'Then let's get him settled. I've arranged for Nurse Davies to pop in late this evening. She'll give him another injection, which will keep him free from any pain he might feel in the night, and I'll come back first thing in the morning. The old codger's beaten me, dammit. He's got his way. I'll not move him now. He can die here at home.'

13

Dorothea's tears thanked him.

'It's lucky he has you,' the doctor told her, 'and don't make yourself ill.' He looked from her to my height assessingly, and said, 'You look bigger than both of us. Can you carry him? Nurse Davies would help Dorothea move him, as she always does, but usually he's conscious and doing his best to walk. Can you manage him on your own?'

I nodded. He weighed pathetically little for a man once as strong as horses. I lifted the tall sleeping figure in my arms and carried him from his armchair, through the small hallway and into his bedroom, putting him down gently on the white sheet, revealed by Dorothea peeling back the bed covers. Her brother's breathing rasped. I straightened his pyjamas and helped Dorothea cover him. He didn't wake. He had died inside, I thought, from the moment he'd believed in his absolution.

I didn't bring up the subject of a priest again with Dorothea, nor mention it to the doctor. I was convinced they would both disapprove of what I'd done, even though Valentine was now dying in peace because of it. Leave things as they are, I decided. Don't add to Dorothea's distress.

I kissed the old lady, shook hands with the doctor and, offering vague but willing future help, drove back to my job.

Life, both real and imaginary, was loud and vigorous along in Newmarket, where the company I was working for had rented an empty racing stable for three months, paying the bankrupt owner-trainer enough to keep him in multiple child-support for ever.

Although a good hour late for the script conference I'd called for five-thirty, I did not apologise, having found that the bunch I was working with took regrets for weakness, chiefly because of their own personal insecurities. It was essential, I understood, for them to regard me as rock, even if to myself sometimes the rock was no more durable than compressed sand.

They were gathered in what had earlier been the dining-room of the trainer's cavernous house (all the furniture having passed under the bankruptcy hammer, satiny green and gold striped paper still adhering richly to the walls) and were variously draped round a basic trestle table, sitting on collapsible white plastic garden chairs on the bare boards of the floor. The drinks provided by the catering unit had barely lasted the hour: no one on the production was wasting money on excess comfort.

'Right,' I said, ousting Ed from the seat I wanted, halfway along one side of the table, 'have you all read the alterations and additions?'

They had. Three were character actors, one a cinematographer, one a production manager, one a note-taker, one an assistant director – Ed – and one a scriptwriter that I would like to have done without. He had made the current changes at my reasonable insistence, but felt aggrieved. He believed I was intent on giving a slant to the story that departed at ninety degrees from his original vision.

He was right.

It was disastrously easy to make bad horseracing

pictures and only possible to do it at bankable level, in my view, if racing became the framing background to human drama. I'd been given the present job for three reasons that I knew of, the third being that I'd previously stood two animal stories on their heads with profitable results, the second being that I'd been trained in my work in Hollywood, the source of finance for the present epic, and – first – that I'd spent my childhood and teens in racing stables and might be considered to know the industrial terrain.

We were ten days into production: that is to say we had shot about one-sixth of the picture, or, putting it another way, roughly twenty minutes a day of usable footage, whole cloth from which the final film would be cut. We'd been scheduled to finish in sixty working days; a span of under ten weeks, as rest days were precious and rare. I, as director, decided which scenes would actually be shot on which days, though I'd made and distributed in advance a programme to which we mostly adhered.

'As you've seen,' I said generally, 'these changes mean that tomorrow we'll be shooting on the railed forecourt in front of the Jockey Club's headquarters in the High Street. Cars arrive and leave through the gates. The local police will help with the town's regular traffic from eleven to twelve only, so all of our arrivals and departures will be condensed into that time. The Jockey Club has agreed to our using their front door for entering and leaving shots. The internal sets have, of course, been built here in this house. You three . . .' I said to the actors, '. . . can put some useful poison into your various encounters. George, be sly. Iago stuff. You are now secretly engineering Cibber's downfall.'

The script-writer moaned, 'That's not the right interpretation. I don't like what you've made me do. Those two are very good friends.'

'Only up to the point of opportunist betrayal,' I said.

Howard Tyler, the writer, had already complained about small earlier changes to the producer, to the accountant and to the film company's top brass, all without getting me fired. I could put up with his animosity in the same way as I stifled irritation at his round granny glasses, his relentlessly prim little mouth and his determination to insert long pointless silences where only movement and action would fill cinema seats. He adored convoluted unspoken subtleties that were beyond most actors' powers. He should have stuck to the voluminous moody novels whence he came.

His book that he'd adapted for the present film was loosely based on a real-life story, a twenty-six-year-old Newmarket racing scandal very successfully hushed up. Howard's fictional version purported to be the truth, but almost certainly wasn't, as none of the still living real participants had shown the slightest sign of indignant rebuttal.

'You'll find you each have a plan of the Jockey Club forecourt,' I said to the meeting. They nodded, flicking over pages. 'Also,' I went on, 'you've a list of the order of shooting, with approximate times. The three cars involved will be driven to the forecourt first thing in the morning. Get all the crews alerted so that lights and cameras can be set up where shown on the plan. If

17

everyone's willing and ready, we should finish well before the daylight yellows. Any questions?'

There were always questions. To ask a question meant attention had been paid and, as often happened, it was actors with the smallest parts who asked most. George, in this case, wanted to know how his character would develop from the extra scene. Only, I enlightened him, as just one more factor in Cibber's troubles. Cibber, eventually, would crack. Bang. Fireworks. Cibber said 'Hallelujah' gratefully. George compressed his mouth.

'But they were friends,' Howard repeated stubbornly.

'As we discussed,' I said mildly, 'if Cibber cracks, your motivation makes better sense.'

He opened his little mouth, saw everyone else nodding, folded his lips and began to act as if Cibber's cracking was all his own idea.

'If it rains tomorrow,' I said, 'we'll shoot the internal Jockey Club scenes instead and trust it will be fine on Thursday. We are due to complete the first Newmarket segment on Saturday. On Sunday, as I think you know, we're shifting the horses forty miles west to Huntingdon racecourse, to the stable block there. Actors and technicians will travel early on Monday morning. Rehearsals, Monday, from noon onwards. Shooting Tuesday to Friday, return here the following weekend. Ed will distribute times and running order to everyone concerned. OK? Oh, and by the way, the rushes from yesterday are fine. Thought you'd like to know. It was a lot of hard work, but worth it.'

The resulting sighs round the table came from relief. We'd spent the whole day in the stable yard, the human action in the foreground taking place against a background of routine equine life. Never could rows of horses have been mucked out, fed, watered and groomed more times in any twelve hours before: but we had enough shots in the can to give the fictional stable unending life.

The script meeting over, everyone dispersed except a tall thin, disjointed-looking man in an untidy beard and unkempt clothes whose unimpressive appearance hid an artistic confidence as unassailable as granite. He raised his eyebrows. I nodded. He slouched in his seat and waited until all backs but our own had passed through the door.

'You wanted me to stay?' he asked. 'Ed said.'

'Yes.'

Every film with any hope of acclaimed success needed an eye that saw all life as through a camera lens. Someone to whom focus and light intensities were extrasensory dimensions taken for granted. His title on the credits might variously be 'cinematographer' or 'director of photography'. I'd had a mathematical friend once who said he thought in algebra: Moncrieff, director of photography, thought in moving light and shadows.

We were used to each other. This was our third film together. I'd been disconcerted the first time by his surrealist sense of humour, then seen that it was the aquifer of his geysers of visual genius, then felt that to work without him would leave me nakedly exposed in the realm of translating my own perceptions into revelations on the screen. When I told Moncrieff what I wanted an audience to understand, he could instinctively slant a lens to achieve it.

We had once staged a 'last rites' scene for a man about to be murdered by terrorists: the ultimate cruelty of that wicked blasphemy had been underscored by Moncrieff's lighting of the faces; the petrified victim, the sweating priest and the hard men's absence of mercy. *Ego te absolvo* ... it had brought me death threats by post.

On that Tuesday in Newmarket I asked Moncrieff, 'Have you seen the railings outside the Jockey Club? The ones enclosing the private parking forecourt?'

'Tall and black? Yes.'

'I want a shot that emphasises the barrier qualities. I want to establish the way the railings shut out everyone but the élite. Inside can be mandarins of racing. Outside, *hoi polloi.*'

Moncrieff nodded.

I said, 'I also want to give an impression that the people inside, Cibber and George, the Jockey Club members, are themselves prisoners in their own conventions. Behind bars, one might say.'

Moncrieff nodded.

'And,' I said, 'take a five-second shot of the hinges of the gates as they open, also as they close.'

'Right.'

'The scene between Cibber and George is shot to begin with from outside the bars. I'd like the zoo aspect made clear. Then track the lens forward between the railings to establish where they're standing. The rest of that conversation is in close-ups.'

Moncrieff nodded. He seldom made notes while we talked, but he would write a meticulous worksheet before bedtime.

'We're not being judgmental,' I said. 'Not heavy handed. No great social stance. Just a fleeting impression.'

'A feather touch,' Moncrieff said. 'Got you.'

'Contributing to Cibber's crack-up,' I said.

He nodded.

'I'll get Howard to write that crack-up tomorrow,' I said. 'It's mainly a matter of a shift in intensity from the calm scene already in the script. Howard just needs to put some juice into it.'

'Howard's juice is watered cranberry.' Moncrieff picked up a vodka bottle from among the drinks clutter, and squinted at it against the light. 'Empty,' he commented morosely. 'Have you tried vodka and cranberry juice? It's disgusting.'

Howard drank it all the time.

'Howard,' Moncrieff said, 'is radioactive waste. You can't get rid of it safely.'

He knew as well as I did that Howard Tyler's name on the billboards would bring to the film both the lending library audience and attention from upmarket critics. Howard Tyler won prestigious prizes and had received honorary doctorates on both sides of the Atlantic. Moncrieff and I were considered lucky to be working with such a luminous figure.

Few authors could, or even wanted to, write screenplays of their own novels: Howard Tyler had been nominated for an Oscar at his first attempt and subsequently refused to sell his film rights unless the

21

package included himself. Moncrieff and I were stuck with Howard, to put it briefly, as fast as it seemed he was stuck with me.

Our producer, bald, sixty, a heavily-framed American, had put a canny deal together for the company. Big-name author (Howard), proven camera wizard (Moncrieff), vastly successful producer (himself) and young but experienced director (T. Lyon), all allied to one mega-star (male) and one deliciously pretty new actress; money spent on the big names and saved on the actress and me. He, producer O'Hara, had told me once that in the matter of acting talent it was a waste of resources employing five big stars in any one picture. One great star would bring in the customers and maybe two could be afforded. Get more and the costs would run away with the gross.

O'Hara had taught me a lot about finance and Moncrieff a lot about illusion. I'd begun to feel recently that I finally understood my trade – but was realistic enough to know that at any minute I could judge everything wrong and come an artistic cropper. If public reaction could be reliably foretold, there would be no flops. No one could ever be sure about public taste: it was as fickle as horseracing luck.

O'Hara, that Tuesday, was already in the Bedford Lodge Hotel dining-room when I joined him for dinner. The studio bosses liked him to keep an eye on what I was doing, and report back. He marched into operations accordingly week by week, sometimes from London, sometimes from California, spending a couple of days watching the shooting and an evening with me going over the state of the budget and the time schedule.

Owing to his sensible planning in the first place, I hoped we would come in under budget and with a couple of days to spare, which would encourage any future employers to believe I had organisational talents.

'Yesterday's rushes were good, and this morning went well,' O'Hara said objectively. 'Where did you get to this afternoon? Ed couldn't find you.'

I paused with a glass of studio-impressing Perrier halfway to my mouth, remembering vividly the rasping of Valentine's breath.

'I was here in Newmarket,' I said, putting down the water. 'I've a friend who's dying. I called to see him.'

'Oh.' O'Hara showed no censure, registering the explanation as a reason, not an excuse. He knew anyway – and took it for granted – that I'd started work at six that morning and would put in eighteen hours most days until we'd completed the shooting.

'Is he a film man?' O'Hara asked.

'No. Racing . . . a racing writer.'

'Oh. Nothing to do with us, then.'

'No,' I said.

Ah, well. One can get things wrong.

CHAPTER TWO

Fortunately, Wednesday morning dawned bright and clear, and Moncrieff, his camera crew and I attended sunrise beside the Jockey Club's railings, filming atmospheric barred shadows without interruption.

Rehearsals with Cibber and George went fine later on the forecourt, with Moncrieff opening his floods easily to supplement the sun, and with me peering through the camera eyepiece to be sure the angles brought out the spite developing in the erstwhile 'best friends'. By eleven we were ready for the cars-inward, cars-outward sequences, the police cooperating efficiently in the spirit of things.

Our male mega-star, laconic as always, patiently made three arrivals behind the wheel of a car, and four times uncomplainingly repeated a marching-to-execution type entrance through the hallowed front door, switching his fictional persona on and off with the confidence and expertise of a consummate pro. As if absentmindedly, he finally gave me an encouraging pat on the shoulder and left in his personal Rolls-Royce for the rest of the day.

At midday we broke for a well-earned hour for lunch.

O'Hara came in the afternoon to watch George's Iago touch (which basically needed only an inoffensive 'cool it just a bit' comment from myself) and sat smiling in a director's chair for most of the afternoon. O'Hara's hovering smile, though I was never sure he knew it, acted like oil on the actors and technical crews, getting things smoothly done: under his occasional slit-eyed disapproval, problems geometrically increased.

After wrapping things up on the forecourt O'Hara and I went together to Bedford Lodge for an early beverage (light on alcohol, following the film company's overall puritanical ethos), discussing progress and plans before he left fantasy land en route for marketing and advertisement in offices in London. Making the film was never enough; one had to sell the product as well.

'I see you've booked our chief stuntman for Monday,' he said casually, standing to leave. 'What do you have in mind?'

'Untamed horses on a beach.'

I answered him lightly, giving him the option of believing me or not.

'Do you mean it?' he asked. 'It's not in the script.'

I said, 'I can fit in the beach reconnaissance with the stuntman very early on Monday morning Dawn, in fact. I'll be back in good time for rehearsals. But ...' I paused indecisively.

'But what?'

'In the past you've given me an extra day here or there,' I said. 'What if I could use one this time? What if I get an idea?'

Twice in the past, granted latitude, I'd slanted his productions into a dimension the public had liked. Without demanding to know details in advance of a process I found came only from spur-of-the-moment inspiration in myself, he gave me merely a five-second considering stare, then a brief nod, and then a virtual carte blanche.

'Three days,' he said. 'OK.'

Time was very expensive. Three days equalled trust. I said, '*Great.*'

'If you hadn't asked,' he said reflectively, 'we'd be in trouble.'

'Don't you think it's going well?' I had anxieties always.

'It's going professionally,' he said. 'But I hired you for something more.'

I didn't feel flattered so much as increasingly pressured. The days when not much had been expected had been relatively restful: success had brought an upward spiral of awaited miracles, and one of these days, I thought, I would fly off the top of the unsteady tower and crash down in Pisa, and no sane finance department would consider my name again.

On the doorstep of the hotel, with his chauffeured car waiting, O'Hara said, 'You very well know that in the matter of film making there's power and there's money. On big budget productions the money men dictate what the directors may do. On medium budget productions, like this one, the power lies in the director. So use your power. *Use* it.'

I gazed at him dumbly. I saw him as the mover behind this film, saw *him* as the power. He, after all, had made the whole project possible. I saw that chiefly I had been trying to please *him*, more than myself; and he was telling me that that wasn't what he wanted.

'Stand or fall,' he said, 'it's your picture.'

I thought that if I were shooting this scene, it would be clear, whatever he said, that the real power lay in the older, craggily self-assured, lived-in face atop a wide-shouldered gone-to-overweight but comfortable body, and not in the unremarkable thirty-year-old easily mistaken for an extra.

'The power is yours,' he said again. 'Believe it.'

He gave me an uncompromising nod, allowing me no excuses, and went onwards to his car, being driven away without a farewell glance.

I walked thoughtfully across the drive to my own car and set off along the road to Valentine's house, aware of being at the same time powerful and obscure, an odd mixture. I couldn't deny to myself that I did quite often feel a spurting ability to produce the goods, a soaring satisfaction that could nosedive the next minute into doubt. I needed confidence if I were to give life to anything worthwhile, yet I dreaded arrogance, which could at once mislead into sterile *folie de grandeur*. Why, I often wondered, hadn't I settled for a useful occupation that didn't regularly lay itself open to public evaluation, like, say, delivering the mail?

Valentine and Dorothea had bought a four-roomed single-storey house, taking two rooms each as bedroom and sitting room, constructing an extra bathroom so that they had their privacy, and sharing one large kitchen furnished with a dining table. Living that way had, they had both told me, been an ideal solution to their widowed state, a separate togetherness that gave them both company and retreat.

Everything looked quiet there when I parked outside on the road and walked up the concrete path to the front door. Dorothea opened it before I could ring the bell, and she'd been crying.

I said awkwardly, 'Valentine . . .?'

She shook her head miserably. 'He's still alive, the poor poor old love. Come in, dear. He won't know you, but come and see him.'

I followed her into Valentine's bedroom, where she said she had been sitting in a wing-chair near the window so that she could see the road and visitors arriving.

Valentine, yellowly pale, lay unmoving on the bed, his heavy slow breath noisy, regular and implacably terminal.

'He hasn't woken or said anything since you went yesterday,' Dorothea said. 'We don't need to whisper in here, you know, we're not disturbing him. Robbie Gill came at lunchtime, not that I had any lunch, can't eat, somehow. Anyway, Robbie says Valentine is breathing with difficulty because fluid is collecting in his lungs, and he's slipping away now and will go either tonight or tomorrow, and to be ready. How can I be ready?'

'What does he mean by ready?'

'Oh, just in my feelings, I think. He said to let him know tomorrow morning how things are. He more or less asked me not to phone him in the middle of the night. He said if Valentine dies, just to phone him at home at seven. He isn't really heartless, you know. He still thinks it would be easier on me if Valentine were in hospital, but I know the old boy's happier here. He's peaceful, you can see it. I just know he is.'

'Yes,' I said.

She insisted on making me a cup of tea and I didn't dissuade her because I thought she needed one herself. I followed her into the brightly painted blue and yellow kitchen and sat at the table while she set out pretty china cups and a sugar bowl. We could hear Valentine breathing, the slow rasping almost a groan, though Nurse Davies, Dorothea said, had been an absolute brick, injecting painkiller so that her brother couldn't possibly suffer, not even in some deep brain recess below the coma.

'Kind,' I said.

'She's fond of Valentine.'

I drank the hot weak liquid, not liking it much.

'It's an extraordinary thing,' Dorothea said, sitting opposite me and sipping, 'you know what you said about Valentine wanting a priest?'

I nodded.

'Well, I told you he couldn't have meant it, but then, I would never have believed it, this morning a neighbour of ours – Betty from across the road, you've met her, dear – she came to see how he was and she said, did he get his priest all right? Well! I just stared at her, and she said, didn't I know that Valentine had been rambling on about some priest our mother had had to give her absolution before she died, and she said he'd asked her to fetch that priest. She said, what priest? I mean, she told me she never knew either of us ever saw a priest and I told her of course we hadn't, hardly even

29

with our mother, but she said Valentine was talking as if he were very young indeed and he was saying he liked to listen to bells in church. Delirious, she said he was. She couldn't make sense of it. What do you think?'

I said slowly, 'People often go back to their childhood, don't they, when they're very old.'

'I mean, do you think I should get Valentine a priest? I don't know any. What should I do?'

I looked at her tired lined face, at the worry and the grief. I felt the exhaustion that had brought her to this indecision as if it had been my own.

I said, 'The doctor will know of a priest, if you want one.'

'But it wouldn't be any good! Valentine wouldn't know. He can't hear anything.'

'I don't think it matters that Valentine can't hear. I think that if you don't get a priest you'll wonder for the rest of your life whether you should have done. So yes, either the doctor or I will find one for you at once, if you like.'

Tears ran weakly down her cheeks as she nodded agreement. She was clearly grateful not to have had to make the decision herself. I went into Valentine's sitting-room and used the phone there, and went back to report to Dorothea that a man from a local church would arrive quite soon.

'Stay with me?' she begged. 'I mean . . . he may not be pleased to be called out by a lapsed non-practising Catholic.'

He hadn't been, as it happened. I'd exhorted him as persuasively as I knew how; so without hesitation I agreed to stay with Dorothea, if only to see properly done what I'd done improperly.

We waited barely half an hour, long enough only for evening to draw in, with Dorothea switching on the lights. Then the real priest, a tubby, slightly grubby-looking middle-aged man hopelessly lacking in charisma, parked his car behind my own and walked up the concrete path unenthusiastically.

Dorothea let him in and brought him into Valentine's bedroom where he wasted little time or emotion. From a bag reminiscent of the doctor's he produced a purple stole which he hung round his neck, a rich colour against the faded black of his coat and the white band round his throat. He produced a small container, opened it, dipped in his thumb and then made a small cross on Valentine's forehead, saying, 'By this holy anointing oil . . .'

'Oh!' Dorothea protested impulsively, as he began. 'Can you say it in Latin? I mean, with our mother it was always in Latin. Valentine would want it in Latin.'

He looked as if he might refuse, but instead shrugged his shoulders, found a small book in his bag and read from that instead.

'*Misereatur tui omnipotens Deus, et dimissis peccatis tuis, perducat te ad vitam aeternam. Amen.*'

May almighty God have mercy upon you, forgive you your sins, and bring you to everlasting life.

'*Dominus noster Jesus Christus te absolvat . . .*'

Our Lord Jesus Christ absolves you . . .

He said the words without passion, a task undertaken for strangers, giving blanket absolution for he knew not what sins. He droned on and on, finally repeating, more or less, the words I'd used, the real thing now but without the commitment I'd felt.

'*Ego te absolvo ab omnibus censuris, et peccatis tuis, in nomine Patris et Filii et Spiritus Sancti. Amen.*'

He made the sign of the cross over Valentine, who went on breathing without tremor, then he paused briefly before removing the purple stole and replacing it, with the book and the oil, in his bag.

'Is that all?' asked Dorothea blankly.

The priest said, 'My daughter, in the authority vested in me I have absolved him from all blame, from all his sins. He has received absolution. I can do no more.'

I went with him to the front door and gave him a generous donation for his church funds. He thanked me tiredly, and he'd gone before I thought of asking him about a funeral service – a requiem mass – within a week.

Dorothea had found no comfort in his visit.

'He didn't *care* about Valentine,' she said.

'He doesn't know him.'

'I wish he hadn't come.'

'Don't feel like that,' I said. 'Valentine has truly received what he wanted.'

'But he doesn't *know*.'

'I'm absolutely certain,' I told her with conviction, 'that Valentine is at peace.'

She nodded relievedly. She thought so herself, with or without benefit of religion. I gave her the phone number of the Bedford Lodge Hotel, and my room number, and told her I would return at any time if she couldn't cope.

She smiled ruefully. 'Valentine says you were a real little devil when you were a boy. He said you ran wild.'

'Only sometimes.'

She stretched up to kiss my cheek in farewell, and I gave her a sympathetic hug. She hadn't lived in Newmarket when I'd been young and I hadn't known her before coming back for the film, but she seemed already like a cosy old aunt I'd had for ever.

'I'm always awake by six,' I said.

She sighed. 'I'll let you know.'

I nodded and drove away, waving to her as she stood in Valentine's window, watching forlornly in her sorrowful vigil.

I drove to the stable yard we were using in the film and stood in the dark there, deeply breathing cool March evening air and looking up at the night sky. The bright clear day had carried into darkness, the stars now in such brilliant 3D that one could actually perceive the infinite depths and distances of space.

Making a film about muddy passions on earth seemed frivolous in eternity's context, yet, as we were bodies, not spirits, we could do no more than reveal our souls to ourselves.

Spiritus sanctus. Spiritus meant 'breath' in Latin. Holy breath. *In nomine Spiritus Sancti.* In the name of the Holy Spirit, the Holy Breath, the Holy Ghost. As a schoolboy I'd liked the logic and discipline of Latin. As a man, I found in it mystery and majesty. As a film director I'd used it to instil terror. For Valentine, I'd usurped its power. God forgive me, I thought ... if there is a God.

The mega-star's Roller whispered gently into the

yard and out he popped, door opened for him as always by his attentive chauffeur. Male mega-stars came equipped normally with a driver, a valet, a secretary/assistant and occasionally a bodyguard, a masseur or a butler. For female mega-stars, add a hairdresser. Either could require a personal make-up artist. These retinues all had to be housed, fed and provided with rented transport, which was one reason why wasted days painfully escalated the costs.

'Thomas?' he asked, catching sight of me in the shadows. 'I suppose I'm late.'

'No,' I assured him. Mega-stars were *never* late, however overdue. Mega-stars were walking green lights, the term that in the film world denoted the capacity to bring finance and credence to a project, allied with the inability to do wrong. What green lights desired, they got.

This particular green light had so far belied his pernickety reputation and had delivered such goods that he'd been asked for in good humour and with sufficient panache to please his fans.

He was fifty, looked forty, and stood eye to eye with me at a shade over six feet. Though his features off-screen were good but unremarkable, he had the priceless ability of being able to switch on inside and act with his eyes. With tiny shifts of muscle he achieved huge messages in close-up, and the smile he constructed with his lower eyelids had earned him the tag of 'the sexiest man in films', though to my mind that smile was simply where his talents began.

I'd never before been appointed to direct such an actor, which he knew and made allowances for: yet he'd told me, much as O'Hara had, to get on with things and use my authority.

The mega-star, Nash Rourke, had himself asked for this night's meeting.

'A bit of quiet, Thomas, that's what I want. And I need to get the feel of the Jockey Club room you've had built in the trainer's house.'

Accordingly we walked together to the house's rear entrance, where the night-watchman let us in and logged our arrival.

'All quiet, Mr Lyon,' he reported.

'Good.'

Within the barn of a house the production manager, with my and O'Hara's approval and input, had reconstructed a fictional drawing-room within the original drawing-room space, and also re-created the former trainer's office as it had been, looking out to the stable yard.

Upstairs, removing a wall or two and using old photographs as well as a sight of the real thing, we had built a reproduction of the imposing room still to be found within the Jockey Club headquarters in the High Street, the room where, in the historic past, enquiries had been held, with reputations and livelihoods at stake.

Real official enquiries had for forty years or more been conducted in the racing industry's main offices in London, but in Howard Tyler's book, and in our film, a kangaroo court, an unofficial and totally dramatic and damning enquiry, was taking place within the old forbidding ambiance.

I switched on the few available lights, which gave only a deadened view of a richly-polished wood floor,

Stubbs and Herring on the walls and luxurious studded leather armchairs ranged round the outer side of a large horseshoe-shaped table.

The constructed replica room, to allow space for cameras, was a good deal larger than the real thing. Also, complete with cornices and paintings, the solid-seeming walls could obligingly roll aside. Bulbs on ceiling tracks, dark now, waited with a tangle of floods, spots and cables for the life to come in the morning.

Nash Rourke crossed to one side of the table, pulled out a green leather armchair and sat on it, and I joined him. He had brought with him several pages of newly rewritten script which he slapped down on the polished wood, saying, 'This scene we're doing tomorrow is the big one, right?'

'One of them,' I nodded.

'The man is accused, baffled, angry and innocent.'

'Yes.'

'Yeah. Well, our friend, Howard Tyler, is driving me crazy.'

Nash Rourke's accent, educated American, Boston overtones, didn't sit exactly with the British upper-class racehorse trainer he was purporting to be, a minor detail in almost everyone's eyes, including my own but excluding (unsurprisingly) Howard's.

'Howard wants to change the way I say things, and for me to play the whole scene in a throttled whisper.'

'Is that what he said?' I asked.

Nash shrugged a partial negative. 'He wants what he called "a stiff upper lip".'

'And you?'

'This guy would *yell*, for Christ's sake. He's a big powerful man accused of murdering his wife, right?'

'Right.'

'Which he didn't do. And he's faced with a lot of stick-in-the-muds bent on ruining him one way or the other, right?'

'Right.'

'And the chairman is married to his dead wife's sister, right?'

I nodded. 'The chairman, Cibber, eventually goes to pieces. We established that today.'

'Which Howard is spitting blue murder about.'

'Tomorrow, here,' I waved a hand around the make-believe courtroom, 'you yell.'

Nash smiled.

'Also you put a great deal of menace into the way you talk back to Chairman Cibber. You convince the Jockey Club members, *and* the audience, that you do have enough force of personality to kill. Sow a seed or two. Don't be long-suffering and passive.'

Nash leaned back in his chair, relaxing. 'Howard will bust a gut. He's mad as hell with what you're doing.'

'I'll soothe him.'

Nash wore, as I did, unpressed trousers, an open-necked shirt and a thick loose sweater. He picked up the sheets of script, shuffled them a bit, and asked a question.

'How different is the whole script than the one I saw originally?'

'There's more action, more bitterness and a lot more suspense.'

'But my character – this guy – he still doesn't kill his wife, does he?'

'No. But there's doubt about it right to the end, now.'

Nash looked philosophical. 'O'Hara sweet-talked me into this,' he said. 'I had three months free between projects. Fill them, he said. Nice little movie about horseracing. O'Hara knows I'm a sucker for the horses. An old real-life scandal, he tells me, written by our world-famous Howard, who of course I've heard of. Prestige movie, not a sink-without-trace, O'Hara says. Director? I ask. He's young, O'Hara says. You won't have worked with him before. Too damn right, I haven't. Trust me, O'Hara says.'

'Trust me,' I said.

Nash gave me one of the smiles an alligator would be proud of, the sort that in his Westerns had the baddies flinging themselves sideways in shoot-outs.

'Tomorrow,' I said, 'is the opening day of the main Flat racing season in England.'

'I know it.'

'They run the Lincoln Handicap on Saturday.'

Nash nodded. 'At Doncaster. Where's Doncaster?'

'Seventy miles north of here. Less than an hour by helicopter. Do you want to go?'

Nash stared. 'You're bribing me!'

'Sure.'

'What about insurance?'

'I cleared it with O'Hara.'

'Be damned!' he said.

He stood up abruptly in amused good humour and began measuring his distances in paces round the set.

38

'It says in the script,' he said, 'that I stand on the mat. Is this the mat, this thing across the open end of the table?'

'Yes. It's actually a bit of carpet. Historically the person accused at a Newmarket horseracing enquiry had to stand there, on the carpet, and that's the origin of the phrase, to be carpeted.'

'Poor bastards.'

He stood on the carpet and quietly said his lines, repeating and memorising them, putting in pauses and gestures, shifting his weight as if in frustration and finally marching the inside distance of the horseshoe to lean menacingly over the top chair, which would contain Cibber, the inquisitor.

'And I yell,' he said.

'Yes,' I agreed.

With the fury at that point silent, he murmured the shout of protest, and in time returned to his former seat beside me.

'What happened to those people in real life?' he asked. 'Howard swears what he's written are the true events. O'Hara tells me you're sure they're not, because no one's screaming foul. So what really did happen?'

I sighed. 'Howard's guessing. Also he's playing safe. For a start, none of the people who were really involved are called by their real names in his book. And I don't honestly know more than anyone else, because it all happened in this town twenty-six years ago, when I was only four. I can't remember even hearing about it then, and in any case the whole thing fizzled out. The trainer you're playing was a man called Jackson Wells. His wife was found hanged in one of the boxes in his stable yard, and a lot of people thought he'd done it. His wife had had a lover. His wife's sister was married to a member of the Jockey Club. That's about as far as the known facts go. No one could ever prove Jackson Wells had hanged his wife and he swore he hadn't.'

'Howard says he's still alive.'

I nodded. 'The scandal finished him in racing. He could never prove he *hadn't* hanged his wife and although the Jockey Club didn't actually take away his licence, people stopped sending him horses. He sold his place and bought a farm in Oxfordshire, I think, and got married again. He must be nearly sixty now, I suppose. There apparently hasn't been any reaction at all from him, and Howard's book's been out over a year.'

'So he won't come bursting onto the set here swinging a noose to lynch me.'

'Believe in his innocence,' I said.

'Oh, I do.'

'Our film is fiction,' I said. 'The real Jackson Wells was a middle-ability man with a middle-sized training stable and no outstanding personality. He wasn't the upper-class powerful figure in Howard's book, still less was he the tough, wronged, resourceful conqueror we'll make of you before we're done.'

'O'Hara promised an up-beat ending.'

'He'll get it.'.

'But the script doesn't say who *did* hang the wife, only who didn't.'

I said, 'That's because Howard doesn't know and can't make up his mind what to invent. Haven't you read Howard's book?'

'I never read the books scripts are written from. I find it's too often confusing and contradictory.'

'Just as well,' I said, smiling. 'In Howard's book your character is not having an affair with his wife's sister.'

'Not?' He was astonished. He'd spent a whole busy day tumbling about in bedclothes half naked with the actress playing his wife's sister. 'However did Howard agree to *that*?'

I said, 'Howard also agreed that Cibber, the sister-in-law's husband, should find out about the affair so that Cibber could have an overpowering reason for his persecution of your character; in fact, for the scene you're playing here tomorrow.'

Nash said disbelievingly, 'And *none* of that was in Howard's book?'

I shook my head. O'Hara had leaned on Howard from the beginning to spice up the story, in essence warning him 'No changes, no movie.' The shifts of mood and plotline that I'd recently introduced were as nothing compared with O'Hara's earlier manipulations. With me, Howard was fighting a rearguard action, and with luck he would lose that too.

Nash said bemusedly, 'Is the real Cibber still alive as well? And how about the wife's sister?'

'About her, I don't know. The real Cibber died three or so years ago. Apparently someone dug up this old story about him, which is what gave Howard the idea for his book. But the real Cibber didn't persecute Jackson Wells as relentlessly as he does in the film. The real Cibber had little power. It was all a pretty low-key story, in reality. Nothing like O'Hara's version.'

'Or yours.'

41

'Or mine.'

Nash gave me a straight look verging on the suspicious and said, 'What are you not telling me about more script changes?'

I liked him. I might even trust him. But I'd learned the hard way once that nothing was ever off the record. The urge to confide *had* to be resisted. Even with O'Hara, I'd been reticent.

'Devious,' O'Hara had called me. 'An illusionist.'

'It's what's needed.'

'I'll not deny it. But get the conjuring right.'

Conjurors never explained their tricks. The gasp of surprise was their best reward.

'I'll always tell you,' I said to Nash, 'what your character would be feeling in any given scene.'

He perceived the evasion. He thought things over in silence for a long full minute while he decided whether or not to demand details I might not give. In the end, what he said was, 'Trust is a lot to ask.'

I didn't deny it. After a pause he sighed deeply as if in acceptance, and I supposed he'd embraced blind faith as a way out if the whole enterprise should fail. 'One *should* never trust a director . . .'

In any case he bent his head to his script, reading it again swiftly, then he stood up, left the pages on the table and repeated the whole scene, speaking the lines carefully, forgetting them only once, putting in the pauses, the gestures, the changes of physical balance, the pouncing advance down the horseshoe and the over-towering anger at the end.

Then, without comment, he went through the whole thing again. Even without much sound, the emotion

42

stunned: and he'd put into the last walk-through even the suggestion that he could be a killer, a murderer of wives, however passionately he denied it.

This quiet, concentrated mental vigour, I saw, was what had turned a good actor into a mega-star.

I hadn't been going to shoot the scene in one long take, but his performance changed my mind. He'd given it a rhythm and intensity one couldn't get from cutting. The close shot of Cibber's malevolence could come after.

'Thanks for this,' Nash said, breaking off.

'Anything.'

His smile was ironic. 'I hear I'm the green light around here.'

'I ride on your coat tails.'

'You,' he said, 'do not need to grovel.'

We left the set and the house and signed ourselves out with the night-watchman. Nash was driven away in the Roller by his chauffeur, and I returned to Bedford Lodge for a final long session with Moncrieff, discussing the visual impacts and camera angles of tomorrow's scene.

I was in bed by midnight. At five, the telephone rang beside my head.

'Thomas?'

Dorothea's wavery voice, apologetic.

'I'm on my way,' I said.

CHAPTER THREE

Valentine was dead.

When I arrived at his house I found not the muted private grief I expected, but a showy car, not the doctor's or the priest's, parked at the kerbside, and bright lights behind the curtains in every window.

I walked up the concrete path to the closed front door and rang the bell.

After a long pause the door was opened, but not by Dorothea. The man filling the entry was large, soft and unwelcoming. He looked me up and down with a practised superciliousness and said, almost insultingly, 'Are you the doctor?'

'Er . . . no.'

'Then what do you want so early?'

A minor civil servant, I diagnosed: one of those who enjoyed saying no. His accent was distantly Norfolk, prominently London-suburban and careful.

'Mrs Pannier asked me to come,' I said without provocation. 'She telephoned.'

'At this hour? She can't have done.'

'I'd like to speak to her,' I said.

'I'll tell her someone called.'

Down in the hall behind him, Dorothea appeared from her bathroom and, seeing me, hurried towards the front door.

'Thomas! Come in, dear.' She beckoned me to sidle past the blockage. 'This is my son, Paul,' she explained to me. 'And Paul, this is Valentine's friend Thomas, that I told you about.'

'How is he?' I asked. 'Valentine?'

Her face told me.

'He's slipped away, dear. Come in, do. I need your help.' She was flustered by this son whom she'd described as pompous and domineering; and nowhere had she exaggerated. Apart from his hard bossy stare he sported a thin dark moustache and a fleshy upturned nose with the nostrils showing from in front. The thrust-forward chin was intended to intimidate, and he wore a three-piece important dark blue suit with a striped tie even at that hour in the morning. Standing about five feet ten, he must have weighed well over fourteen stone.

'Mother,' he said repressively, 'I'm all the help you need. I can cope perfectly well by myself.' He gestured to me to leave, a motion I pleasantly ignored, edging past him, kissing Dorothea's sad cheek and suggesting a cup of tea.

'Of course, dear. What am I thinking of? Come into the kitchen.'

She herself was dressed in yesterday's green skirt and jumper and I guessed she hadn't been to bed. The dark rings of tiredness had deepened round her eyes and her plump body looked shakily weak.

'I phoned Paul later, long after you'd gone, dear,'

she said almost apologetically, running water into an electric kettle. 'I felt so lonely, you see. I thought I would just warn him that his uncle's end was near . . .'

'So, of course, although it was already late, I set off at once,' Paul said expansively. 'It was only right. My duty. You should never have been here alone with a dying man, mother. He should have been in hospital.'

I lifted the kettle from Dorothea's hands and begged her to sit down, telling her I would assemble the cups and saucers and everything else. Gratefully she let me take over while the universal coper continued to rock on his heels and expound his own virtues.

'Valentine had already died when I got here.' He sounded aggrieved. 'Of course I insisted on telephoning the doctor at once, though Mother ridiculously wanted to let him sleep! I ask you! What are doctors for?'

Dorothea raised her eyes in a sort of despair.

'The damned man was *rude* to me,' Paul complained. 'He should be struck off. He said Valentine should have been in hospital and he would be here at seven, not before.'

'He couldn't *do* anything by coming,' Dorothea said miserably. 'Dying here was what Valentine wanted. It was *all right.*'

Paul mulishly repeated his contrary opinions. Deeply bored with him, I asked Dorothea if I could pay my respects to Valentine.

'Just go in, dear,' she said, nodding. 'He's very peaceful.'

I left her listening dutifully to her offspring and went into Valentine's bedroom which was brightly and brutally lit by a centre bulb hanging from the ceiling in an inadequate lampshade. A kinder lamp stood unlit on a bedside table, and I crossed to it and switched it on.

Valentine's old face was pale and smoothed by death, his forehead already cooler to the touch than in life. The laboured breathing had given way to eternal silence. His eyes were fully closed. His mouth, half open, had been covered, by Dorothea, I supposed, with a flap of sheet. He did indeed look remarkably at peace.

I crossed to the doorway and switched off the cold overhead light. Dorothea was coming towards me from the kitchen, entering Valentine's room past me to look down fondly at her dead brother.

'He died in the dark,' she said, distressed.

'He wouldn't mind that.'

'No . . . but . . . I switched off his bedside light so that people wouldn't see in, and I was sitting in that chair looking out of the window waiting for Paul to come, listening to Valentine breathing, and I went to sleep. I just drifted off.' Tears filled her eyes. 'I didn't know . . . I mean, I couldn't help it.'

'You've been very tired.'

'Yes, but when I woke up it was so dark . . . and absolutely quiet, and I realised . . . it was *awful*, dear. I realised Valentine had stopped breathing . . . and he'd died while I was *asleep*, and I hadn't been there beside him to hold his hand or anything . . .' Her voice wavered into a sob and she wiped her eyes with her fist.

I put an arm round her shoulders as we stood beside Valentine's bed. I thought it lucky on the whole that she hadn't seen the jolt of her brother's heart stopping, nor heard the last rattle of his breath. I'd watched my own mother die, and would never forget it.

47

'What time did your son get here?'

'Oh, it must have been getting on for three. He lives in Surrey, you see, dear. It's quite a long drive, and he'd been ready for bed, he said. I told him not to come ... I only wanted someone to talk to, really, when I rang him, but he insisted on coming ... very good of him, dear, really.'

'Yes,' I said.

'He closed the curtains, of course, and switched on all the lights. He was quite cross with me for sitting in the dark, and for not getting Robbie Gill out. I mean, Robbie could only say officially that Valentine was dead. Paul didn't understand that I *wanted* just to be in the dark with Valentine. It was a sort of *comfort*, you see, dear. A sort of goodbye. Just the two of us, like when we were children.'

'Yes,' I said.

'Paul means well,' she insisted, 'but I do find him tiring. I'm sorry to wake you up so early. But Paul was so cross with me ... so I phoned you when he went to the bathroom because he might have stopped me, otherwise. I'm not myself somehow, I feel so weak.'

'I'm happy to be here,' I assured her. 'What you need is to go to bed.'

'Oh, I couldn't. I'll have to be awake for Robbie. I'm so afraid Paul will be rude to him.'

A certainty, I thought.

The great Paul himself came into the room, switching on the overhead light again.

'What are you two doing in here?' he demanded. 'Mother, do come away and stop distressing yourself.

The old man's had a merciful release, as we all know. What we've got to talk about now is your future, and I've got plans made for that.'

Dorothea's frame stiffened under my embracing arm. I let it fall away from her shoulders and went with her out of Valentine's room and back to the kitchen, flicking the harsh light off again as I went and looking back to the quiet old face in its semi-shadow. Permanent timeless shadow.

'Of *course*, you must leave here,' Paul was saying to his mother in the kitchen. 'You're almost eighty. I can't look after you properly when you live so far away from me. I've already arranged with a retirement home that when Valentine died you would rent a room there. I'll tell them you'll be coming within a week. It's less than a mile from my house so Janet will be able to drop in every day.'

Dorothea looked almost frightened. 'I'm not going, Paul,' she contradicted. 'I'm staying here.'

Ignoring her, Paul said, 'You may as well start packing your things at once. Why waste time? I'll put this house on the market tomorrow and I'll move you immediately after the funeral.'

'No,' Dorothea said.

'I'll help you while I'm here,' her son said grandly. 'All Valentine's things will need sorting and disposing of, of course. In fact, I may as well clear some of the books away at once. I brought two or three empty boxes.'

'Not the books,' I said positively. 'He left his books to me.'

49

'*What?*' Paul's mouth unattractively dropped open. 'He can't have done,' he said fiercely. 'He left everything to Mother. We all know that.'

'Everything to your mother except his books.'

Dorothea nodded. 'Valentine added a codicil to his will about two months ago, leaving his books to Thomas.'

'The old man was ga-ga. I'll contest it.'

'You can't contest it,' I pointed out reasonably. 'Valentine left everything but the books to your mother, not to you.'

'Then Mother will contest it!'

'No, I won't, dear,' Dorothea said gently. 'When Valentine asked me what I thought about him leaving his books and papers to Thomas, I told him it was a very nice idea. I would never read them or ever look at them much, and Valentine knew Thomas would treasure them, so he got a solicitor to draw up the codicil, and Betty, a friend of mine, and Robbie Gill, our doctor, witnessed his signature with the solicitor watching. He signed it here in his own sitting-room, and there was no question of Valentine being ga-ga, which both the solicitor and the doctor will agree on. And I can't see what you're so bothered about, there's just a lot of old form books and scrap books and books about racing.'

Paul was, it seemed to me, a great deal more disconcerted than seemed natural. He seemed also to become aware of my surprise, because he groped and produced a specious explanation, hating me while he delivered it.

'Valentine once told me there might be some value

50

in his collection,' he said. 'I intend to get them valued and sold . . . for Mother's benefit, naturally.'

'The books are for Thomas,' Dorothea repeated doughtily, 'and I never heard Valentine suggest they were valuable. He wanted Thomas to have them for old times' sake, and for being so kind, coming to read to him.'

'*Ah-hah!*' Paul almost shouted in triumph. 'Valentine's codicil will be invalid because he *couldn't see* what he was signing!'

Dorothea protested, 'But he *knew* what he was signing.'

'*How* did he know? Tell me that.'

'Excuse me,' I said, halting the brewing bad temper. 'If Valentine's codicil is judged invalid, which I think unlikely if his solicitor drew it up and witnessed its signing, then the books belong to Dorothea, who alone can decide what to do with them.'

'Oh, *thank you*, dear,' she said, her expression relaxing, 'then if they are mine, I will give them to you, Thomas, because I know that's what Valentine intended.'

Paul looked aghast. 'But you *can't*.'

'Why not, dear?'

'They . . . they may be *valuable*.'

'I'll get them valued,' I said, 'and if they really are worth an appreciable amount, I'll give that much to Dorothea.'

'No, dear,' she vehemently shook her head.

'Hush,' I said to her. 'Let it lie for now.'

Paul paced up and down the kitchen in a fury and came to a halt on the far side of the table from where I sat with Dorothea beside me, demanding forcefully, 'Just who are you, anyway, apart from ingratiating yourself with a helpless, dying old man? I mean, it's *criminal*.'

I saw no need to explain myself to him, but Dorothea wearily informed him, 'Thomas's grandfather trained horses that Valentine shod. Valentine's known Thomas for more than twenty years, and he's always liked him, he told me so.'

As if unable to stop himself, Paul marched his bulk away from this unwelcome news, abruptly leaving the kitchen and disappearing down the hall. One might have written him off as a pompous ass were it not for the fugitive impression of an underlying, heavy, half-glimpsed predator in the undergrowth. I wouldn't want to be at a disadvantage with him, I thought.

Dorothea said despairingly, 'I don't *want* to live near Paul. I couldn't bear to have Janet coming to see me every day. I don't get on with her, dear. She bosses me about.'

'You don't have to go,' I said. 'Paul can't put this house up for sale, because it isn't his. But, dearest Dorothea . . .' I paused, hesitating.

'But what, dear?'

'Well, don't *sign* anything.'

'How do you mean?'

'I mean, don't sign *anything*. Ask your solicitor friend first.'

She gazed at me earnestly. 'I may *have* to sign things, now Valentine's gone.'

'Yes, but . . . don't sign any paper just because Paul wants you to.'

'All right,' she said doubtfully.

I asked her, 'Do you know what a power of attorney is?'

'Doesn't it give people permission to do things on your behalf?'

I nodded.

She thought briefly and said, 'You're telling me not to sign a paper giving Paul permission to sell this house. Is that it?'

'It sure is.'

She patted my hand. 'Thank you, Thomas. I promise not to sign anything like that. I'll read everything carefully. I hate to say it, but Paul does try too hard sometimes to get his own way.'

Paul, to my mind, had been quiet for a suspiciously long time. I stood up and left the kitchen, going in search of him, and I found him in Valentine's sitting-room taking books off the shelves and setting them in stacks on the floor.

'What are you doing?' I asked. 'Please leave those alone.'

Paul said, 'I'm looking for a book I loaned Valentine. I want it back.'

'What's it called?'

Paul's spur-of-the-occasion lie hadn't got as far as a title. 'I'll know it when I see it,' he said.

'If any book has your name in it,' I said politely, 'I'll make sure that you get it back.'

'That's not good enough.'

Dorothea appeared in the doorway, saw the books piled on the floor and looked aghast and annoyed at the same time.

53

'Paul! Stop that! Those books are Thomas's. If you take them you'll be *stealing*.'

Paul showed no sign of caring about such a minor accusation.

'He won't take them,' I told her reassuringly.

Paul curled his lip at me, shouldered his way past and opened the front door.

'What is he doing, dear?' Dorothea asked, perplexed, watching her son's back go purposefully down the path.

'It seems,' I said, 'that he's fetching one of his boxes to pack the books in.' I closed the front door and shot its bolts, top and bottom. Then I hurried through into the kitchen and secured its outside door in the same way, and made a quick trip through all the rooms, and both bathrooms, to make sure the windows were shut and locked.

'But Paul's my son,' Dorothea protested.

'And he's trying to steal Valentine's books.'

'Oh, *dear*.'

Paul began hammering on the front door. 'Mother, let me in *at once*.'

'Perhaps I *should*,' Dorothea worried.

'He'll come to no harm out there. It's nowhere near freezing and he can sit in his car. Or go home, of course.'

'Sometimes Paul isn't *likeable*,' Dorothea said sadly.

I put the stacks of books back on Valentine's shelves. The ones that Paul had chosen to steal first were those with the glossiest covers, the recently published racing biographies, which were, in commercial resale terms, almost worthless. I guessed that chiefly it was Paul's vanity that was reacting against being thwarted by his mother and by me.

I had never underestimated the virulence of outraged vanity since directing a disturbing film about a real-life fanatical body-builder who'd killed his girl-friend because she'd left him for a wimp. I'd had to understand him, to crawl into his mind, and I'd hated it.

Paul's heavy hand banged repeatedly on the door and he pressed unremittingly on the doorbell. This last resulted not in a shrill nerve-shredding single note, but in a less insupportable non-stop quiet ding-dong; quiet because Dorothea had turned down the volume to avoid disturbing Valentine as he'd grown weaker.

I looked at my watch: five minutes to six. Perhaps an hour before we could expect the doctor but only thirty minutes before I should start my own workday.

'Oh, dear,' Dorothea said for about the tenth time, 'I do wish he'd stop.'

'Tell him you'll let him in if he promises to leave the books alone.'

'Do you think he'll agree?' she asked dubiously.

'A good chance,' I said.

He wouldn't want to lose too much face with the awakening neighbours, I reckoned: only a fool would allow himself to be seen to be shut out like a naughty boy by his aged mother.

With evident relief she relayed the terms, to which her son with bad grace agreed. She unbolted the door and let him in, an entrance I carefully didn't watch, as the slightest smile on my face would be interpreted by him as a jeer which would set him off again. Motorists had been shot for cutting in.

I stayed for a while in Valentine's sitting-room with the door shut while mother and son sorted themselves out in the kitchen. I sat in the armchair opposite the one no longer occupied by the old man, and thought how easy it was to get embroiled in a senseless fracas. Without expecting it, I'd made an enemy of Paul Pannier: and I surmised that what he really wanted was not so much the books themselves, but to get me and my influence out of his mother's life, so that he could control and order her future as best suited his beneficent view of himself.

At least, I *hoped* that was the case. Anything worse was more than I felt like dealing with in the middle of making a film.

I stared vacantly at the wall of books, wondering if after all there were anything there of value. If so, I was sure Valentine had been unaware of it. When I'd mentioned the possibility of an autobiography and he'd vetoed the idea, he hadn't referred to any diaries or other raw material that could be used as sources by anyone else but, sitting there, I wondered if by any chance Paul had made some sort of deal with a writer or publisher, to trade Valentine's papers for a share of the profits. No biography of Valentine's would make a fortune, but Paul, I guessed, would be content with modest pickings. Anything was better than nothing, one might hear him say.

Howard Tyler's book was not on the shelves.

Valentine had asked me, the first time I'd called on him, what had brought me back to Newmarket, and when I'd explained about Howard's book – *Unstable Times* – and the film we were to make of it, he'd said he'd heard of the book but he hadn't bought it, since at the time of its publication his eyesight had been fast deteriorating.

'I hear it's a load of rubbish,' he said.

'Is it?'

'I knew Jacksy Wells. I often shod his horses. He never murdered that mousey wife of his, he hadn't got the guts.'

'The book doesn't say he did,' I assured him.

'And I hear it doesn't say he didn't, neither.'

'Well, no.'

'It wasn't worth writing a book about it. Waste of time making a film.'

I'd smiled. Film-makers notoriously and wilfully distorted historical facts. Films knowingly based on lies could get nominated for Oscars.

'What was she like?' I asked.

'Who?'

'Jackson Wells's wife.'

'Mousey, like I said. Funny, I can't remember her clearly. She wasn't one of those trainer's wives who run the whole stable. Mouths like cesspits, some of them had in the old days. Jackson Wells's wife, you wouldn't have known she existed. I hear she's halfway to a whore in the book, poor little bitch.'

'Did she hang herself?'

'Search me,' Valentine said. 'I only shod the horses. The fuss died down pretty fast for lack of clues and evidence, but of course it did Jackson Wells in as a trainer. I mean, would *you* send your horses to a man who'd maybe killed his wife?'

'No.'

'Nor did anyone else.'

'The book says she had a lover,' I said.

'Did she?' Valentine pondered. 'First I've heard of it,' he said. 'But then, Dorothea could have a lover here under my nose and I wouldn't care. Good luck to her, if she did.'

'You're a wicked old man, Valentine.'

'Nobody's an angel,' he said.

I looked at his empty chair and remembered his desperate half-whisper . . . 'I killed the Cornish boy . . .'

Maybe the Cornish Boy was a horse.

Steps sounded on the path outside and the doorbell rang, ding-dong. I waited so as not to appear to be usurping Paul's desired status as head of the household, but it was in fact Dorothea who went to answer the summons.

'Come in, Robbie,' she said, the loud relief in her voice reaching me clearly. 'How dear of you to come.'

'That son of yours!' The doctor's voice held dislike.

'Sorry, sorry,' Dorothea said placatingly.

'Not your fault.'

Dorothea let him in and closed the front door, and I opened the door of Valentine's sitting-room to say hello.

Robbie Gill shook my hand perfunctorily. 'Glad you've got company,' he told Dorothea. 'Now, about Valentine?'

All three of us went quietly into the old man's dimly-lit room, followed importantly by Paul who immediately flooded the scene again with the overhead bulb. Perhaps it was only the director in me, I thought, that found this harsh insistence unpalatable. Certainly

58

Robbie Gill made no protest but set about establishing clinically what was evident to any eye, that Valentine – the he who had lived in that chemical shell – had left it.

'What time did he die?' he asked Dorothea, his pen poised over a clipboard.

'I don't know to the minute,' she said unhappily.

'Around one o'clock,' I said.

'Mother was asleep,' Paul accused unforgivingly. 'She confessed it. She doesn't know when he died.'

Robbie Gill gave him an expressionless stare and without comment wrote 0100 on his clipboard, showing it to me and Dorothea.

'I'll see to the paperwork for you,' he said to Dorothea. 'But you'll need to get an undertaker.'

'Leave it to me,' Paul interrupted. 'I'll take charge of all that.'

No one demurred. Taking important charge of relatively minor matters suited Paul's character perfectly: and perhaps, I thought, he would be so fulfillingly involved that he would forget about the books. There was no harm, however, in seeking to give Dorothea a close line of defence.

'How about,' I suggested to her, 'letting me go across to your friend Betty's house, and asking her to come over to keep you company?'

'Good idea,' Robbie Gill agreed emphatically.

'No need for that!' Paul objected.

'It's a bit *early*, dear,' Dorothea protested, looking at the clock, but seeming hopeful nevertheless.

I crossed the road to the friend's house and woke the friend's husband, whose initial irritation turned to a resigned shrug.

'Poor old sod,' he said, apparently referring to Valentine. 'We'll look after Dorothea.'

'Her son Paul is with her,' I told him.

'Betty,' he said intensely, 'will be over *straight away*.'

I smiled at the owner of the bristly chin and the crumpled pyjamas and dressing gown. Paul had a galvanic effect on everyone else's good nature, it seemed.

I waited until Betty had bustled across, plump and loving like Dorothea, and until Robbie Gill had left, during which period Paul half a dozen times told me I had no need to remain. While he was at one point busy patronising the doctor, Dorothea confided to me guiltily that she had *locked* Valentine's sitting-room door, dear, just in case, and had hidden the key in the pink vase in her bedroom.

I kissed her cheek, smiling, and drove off to work, half an hour late again but offering no apology.

Rehearsal and lighting took all morning. Each of the non-speaking characters, Jockey Club members, had to be positioned in his armchair and taken through the responses to Nash Rourke's long vehement defence.

'Act scandalised here,' I prompted, 'then disbelieving, then throw up hands, throw down pencil, look angry, you think the man's guilty and lying. Right everyone, we go through it again.'

And again and again, with Nash's stand-in repeating the speech and pausing step by forward step for Moncrieff's lighting plans to be finalised. Cibber, at the head of the table, kept making fruity jokes as usual and running down the government in the normal bored manner of an old character actor who'd long abandoned hopes of Hamlet. Cibber – I called most of the cast by their script names as I found it less confusing all round – Cibber was going to give a crack-up later of such truth and misery that he would garner good critical mentions while detesting me for a long time after, but as yet he coasted along on 'heard the one about the sperm and the lawyer, old boy?'

Cibber had been chosen by the casting director because of his upper-class appearance and voice; and I had no complaints about these, but only with his facile assumption that they were *enough*, when to me they were merely a start.

We broke briefly for lunch. Nash Rourke arrived in good time for make-up, and did one silent walk-through under the lights, for Moncrieff to check he had the same colour temperatures as with the stand-in.

Owing to Nash having rehearsed in private the evening before, the 'Jockey Club members' were not prepared for what they were going to see, and as I particularly wanted to record their spontaneous reactions in advance of their rehearsed version, I announced that the first take was in this case not to be considered to be a rehearsal, but would be the real thing: that action, failing only the set falling to pieces, would continue from start to finish, whatever was seeming to go wrong.

'Continuous,' I said. '*No stops. Right?*'

Everyone nodded, even if doubt could be spotted here and there. Except for unrepeatable effects involving five hundred extras, first takes were rarely those seen on the screen.

With the world-weariness of unlimited experience, Nash understood what I wanted, but that didn't guarantee that he would deliver. That day, however, from some motive of his own, he decided generously to go along with the all-out take one, and performed with such vibrating power that the mouths round the table fell open with real incredulity. Moncrieff said the hairs on his own neck stood up, let alone those of the cast. Cibber instinctively slid down in his chair as Nash came to a thunderous halt leaning over him, and after a second or two of dead silence, when I said a shade breathlessly, 'Cut, and print,' the crews and actors as if of one mind *applauded*.

Nash shrugged it off. 'Well, it's strongly written . . .'

He retraced his steps to leave the horseshoe and came over to where I stood.

'Well?' he said.

I was practically speechless.

'Go on,' Nash said. 'Say it. Say "Do it again".'

His eyes smiled.

'Do it again,' I said.

We repositioned and reloaded the cameras and repeated the scene twice more. All three takes went miraculously without glitches, and all three were printable, but it wasn't only I who thought the first electric beyond insulation.

'That man could murder,' Moncrieff said of Nash thoughtfully.

'He was acting.'

'No.' He shivered slightly. 'I mean, in fact.'

CHAPTER FOUR

Howard had heard that the enquiry scene had given a galvanising, positively animating jolt to the whole production. He'd been told, by about ten different people, that Nash had said 'It's strongly written': and Howard knew that he hadn't written what Nash had yelled.

'*You*,' he said furiously, facing me after dinner across a small table in the Bedford Lodge Hotel bar, far too public a venue for his emotions, '*you* changed the script.'

'Well,' I said peaceably, 'not very much. Most of it was your words exactly.'

'But not the feeling,' he complained. 'You wilfully misinterpreted my intention. You told Nash to lose control and threaten Cibber. *You* told him to look like a killer, you must have done, otherwise he wouldn't have thought of it, not from what I wrote.'

'Look, Howard,' I said with resignation, 'we'd better come once and for all to an understanding. I don't want to quarrel with you. I want us to work together to produce a good film, but you did sign a contract –'

'What *you* think is a good film,' he interrupted, 'and what *I* think is a film truthful to my book, are totally opposite. All *you* care about is how much money it makes.'

I took a large bracing mouthful of post-prandial cognac (to hell with the non-alcohol ethos) and decided to explain a few basic facts of movie life to the unrealistic idealist opposite me, his prim round glasses gleaming over earnest brown eyes and his small mouth contracting further in pique.

'I'm a name,' he insisted. 'My readers expect subtlety, understatement and psychological depth. What you're giving them is sex and violence.'

'Have another vodka and cranberry juice?'

'No.'

'Howard,' I said, 'don't you understand what you agreed to? O'Hara put together a package that brought finance from one of the top seven studios. However much one may regret it, they don't fund moody films to play in art houses. They are strictly in the business for profit. The bottom line, Howard.'

'Obscene,' he said, disapprovingly.

I said, 'O'Hara's chief bargaining promise with the big-seven movie company was that we would, between us, produce a film that at least wouldn't *lose* them money. Your own soft-focus view of an ancient scandal obviously worked fine as a novel, and there's much of that that I've insisted on retaining. I've fought for you, whatever you may think.'

'What, precisely, have you retained?' he demanded, hurting.

'You wrote the whole first quarter as a semi-ghost story about the dream lovers of the wife who ended up hanged.'

'Yes.'

'Her dreams and illusions are in the screenplay,' I reminded him. 'Her lovers are jockeys, the way you wrote them. But who were the real jockeys? Did they ride the horses her husband trained?'

'They were in her mind.'

'But why did she hang, Howard? Was she topped by one of the dream lovers? Did she do it herself? Did her husband kill her?'

After a pause he said, 'No one knows.'

'I know they don't,' I said. 'At least, no one ever told. But an ending of no explanation at all isn't going to get people paying to see the film.'

He said sarcastically, 'That bottom line again.'

'I'll give you the dream lovers,' I said. 'And you'll allow me an earthly explanation.'

'That's not fair.'

I gazed at him. He was old enough to know that few things were fair. Most five-year-olds had already discovered it.

'What we are dealing with here,' I said, changing tack, 'is three versions of the same story.'

'What do you mean?'

'We have the story you wrote in your book. We have the story we're shooting in the film. And somewhere out of sight, way back in history, is what actually happened. Three views of the same facts.'

Howard didn't argue.

I said, 'By Sunday, Howard, I'd like you to come up with a rational explanation of the wife's death.'

'But it's already Thursday evening!' he exclaimed, horrified.

'You've had literally years to work it out.'

'But no one knows!'

'Then guess.'

'I can't,' he protested belligerently, 'I've tried.'

'Then I'll do it,' I said. 'I'll work with you on the necessary scenes. We'll use most of your script as written, but your inconclusive ending is impossible.'

'But it's what *happened*. There wasn't any ending to the story.'

'For the film, there has to be.'

'Don't you *care* about the facts?'

'Perhaps, if we look closely enough,' I said, only half meaning it, 'we might ourselves uncover those facts. What if we actually could find out what really happened?'

'You can't,' Howard said flatly. 'No one knows.'

'No one's saying. That's different.' I paused. 'What did Jackson Wells tell you, when you went to see him?'

O'Hara had asked Howard the same thing, he'd told me, and Howard, to O'Hara's utter disbelief, had said he hadn't consulted Jackson Wells at all. Howard hadn't thought it necessary. Howard didn't want to risk unwelcome anti-climactic disclosures from Jackson Wells that might upset his lyrical tale of the dream lovers and the semi-mystical death.

Moncrieff, strolling into the bar, seeing us, and crossing without hesitation to join us, saved Howard from having to answer.

Howard and Moncrieff disliked each other without making much overt display of it. Moncrieff, no reader of novels, thought Howard a prissy, impractical, pseudo-intellectual nuisance on the set. Howard's

66

expression made no attempt to disguise his disparagement of Moncrieff's unkempt appearance with the small straggly beard that was halfway between an artistic statement and a lazy approach to shaving.

Neither of them had the least understanding of the other's function. Moncrieff, endlessly creative within the effects of lighting, needed to be given the actors, the scene and the intention of the storyline, but his enormous input was a moonshot outside the range of Howard's comprehension. Each of them, being acclaimed as individualists, wholly believed that it was he who was indispensable to any chance of esteem for the finished film.

As Nash Rourke tended to think the same, also O'Hara, also myself and also the film editor who would cut some of his own opinions into our work, it was unlikely that anyone would end up wholly satisfied, even if the public approved. Howard, though he didn't seem to appreciate it, at least had more control of his own work than most authors.

'What about those dream lovers, then?' Moncrieff asked abrasively.

Howard became predictably defensive. 'The wife imagines them. You don't need to worry about it.'

'Oh, yes, he does,' I corrected mildly. '*She* may be imagining the jockeys, but we, the onlookers, are going to see them standing in her bedroom.'

Howard looked aghast, to Moncrieff's amusement.

'One at a time,' I explained. 'She sees one in her bedroom. Another time, she sees another. And another. We have three tall ultra-handsome unknowns coming to dress up as the dream lovers. They won't look like real jockeys. They don't speak, and don't worry, Howard, they won't get into bed. The wife watches her husband from her bedroom window as he rides out with his string of horses to their morning exercise, then she turns into the room and conjures up her dream jockey lover. Moncrieff will light the jockey to make it clear that he's imaginary. Another day the wife will wave to her husband, and then turn and imagine a *different* lover.'

Moncrieff nodded. 'Easy.'

'She dances with the third lover. Slowly, orgasmically. She's transported,' I said.

Moncrieff happily nodded again.

'So there you are, Howard,' I said. 'The lovers are how you wrote them. No sex.'

'All highly unlikely,' Moncrieff laughed. 'Any jockey worth his salt would have her nightie off before her husband was out of the stable yard.'

'She hanged,' I said. 'No dream.'

Both of them stared, silenced.

Why did she hang, I wondered. The further we went with the filming, the more I wanted to know, yet until then it had been the results of that death, the accusations against her husband, and his handling of them, that had been the focus both of Howard's book and, more especially, of our film version.

I gave a mental shrug. I hadn't time for any inept detective work, trying to unearth a secret twenty-six years buried. I had only to bully Howard into inventing a good reason and giving Nash a huge satisfactory last scene in which he discovered the truth – Howard's version of the truth – to end the film in perhaps cynical heroism.

'What made you write the book?' I asked Howard.

'You know what did. A newspaper article.'

'Do you still have it?'

He looked surprised and, as usual, displeased. 'Yes, I suppose so,' he said grudgingly, 'but not here.'

'What paper was it in?'

'I don't see that it matters.'

Howard himself, in the ensuing pause, seemed to agree that he'd been unnecessarily ungracious.

'The *Daily Cable*,' he said. 'It was an obituary of the member of the Jockey Club that I called Cibber in the book.'

I nodded. That much I knew. 'What was Cibber's real name?'

'Visborough.' He spelled it.

'And who wrote the obituary?' I asked.

'I've no idea,' Howard replied, still obstructively but this time with a surprise that gave his statement credence.

'Didn't you follow it up?' I asked.

'Of course not.' Howard became condescending. 'You've no idea how a creative author writes. The *inconclusiveness* of the obituary was its own inspiration. I received the *idea* from the obituary and the book grew in my mind.'

'So,' Moncrieff said, 'you never even tried to find out what really happened?'

'Of course not. But I didn't *alter* the account given in the obituary, not like O'Hara and Thomas have made

69

me alter things for the film.' He was acridly bitter. 'My readers will *hate* the film.'

'No, they won't,' I said, 'and hundreds of thousands of new readers will buy your paperbacks.'

He liked that idea, however he might carp. He preened, smirking. Moncrieff's dislike of him visibly grew.

Howard had had enough of Moncrieff, and of me too, no doubt. He got to his feet and left us, making no pretence of social civility.

'He's an oaf,' Moncrieff said, 'and he's belly-aching all over the place, to anyone who will listen, about the bastardising of his masterpiece. A few dream lovers won't shut him up.'

'Who has he been belly-aching *to*?' I asked.

'Does it matter?'

'Yes, it does. His contract forbids him to make adverse criticism of the film in public until six months after it has had a general release. If he's talking to the actors and the crews, that's one thing. If he's complaining to strangers, say in the bar here, I'll have to shut him up.'

'But can you?' Moncrieff asked with doubt.

'There are prickly punitive clauses in his contract. I had a sight of it, so I'd know what I could ask of him, and what I couldn't.'

Moncrieff whistled softly through his teeth. 'Did O'Hara write the contract?'

'Among others. It's pretty standard in most respects. Howard's agent agreed to it, and Howard signed it.' I sighed. 'I'll remind him tactfully tomorrow.'

Moncrieff tired of the subject. 'About tomorrow,' he

said. 'Still the six-thirty dawn call out in the stable yard?'

'Definitely. The horses have to be exercised. I told all the stable lads this evening we'd be shooting them mounting and riding out through the gate to the exercise ground. They'll be wearing their normal clothes: jeans, anoraks, crash helmets. I reminded them not to look at the cameras. We'll take the overall scene of the lads mounting. Nash will come out of the house and be given a leg-up onto his mount. We'll rehearse it a couple of times, not more. I don't want to keep the horses circling too long. When Nash is mounted and comfortable the assistant trainer can lead the string out through the gate. Nash waits for them to go, and follows, last. As he leaves, he'll look backwards and up to the window from where his wife is supposedly watching. You've arranged for a camera crew up there to do the wife's point of view? Ed will be up there, supervising.'

Moncrieff nodded.

I said, 'We'll cut the main shot once Nash is through the gate. I hope we won't have to do many retakes, but when we're satisfied, the string can go on and get their regular exercise, and Nash can come back and dismount. We're going to be repeating the whole thing on Saturday. We'll need a new view from the wife's room and different jackets et cetera on Nash and the lads. We'll need close shots of hooves on the gravel, that sort of thing.'

Moncrieff nodded. 'And Sunday?'

'The Jockey Club people are letting us film out on the gallops, as there won't be many real horses-in-training working that day. You and I will go out by car on the roads on Saturday with a map for you to position the cameras. I know already where best to put them.'

'So you should, if you were brought up here.'

'Mm. Sunday afternoon, the horses go to Huntingdon racecourse. I hope to hell we have three fine mornings.'

'What if it rains?'

'If it's just drizzle, we go ahead with filming. Horses do go out in all weathers, you know.'

'You don't say.'

'Tomorrow afternoon,' I said, 'we'll be indoors up in the enquiry-room set again, like today. The schedule you've got is unchanged. There are more exchanges between Cibber, Nash and others. Apart from the wide establishing shots, it's mostly short close-ups of them speaking. The usual thing. We'll complete Nash's shots first. If the others don't fluff their lines too much, we might get through most of it tomorrow. Otherwise we'll have to carry on on Saturday afternoon as well.'

'OK.'

Moncrieff and I finished our drinks and went our separate ways, I upstairs to my room to make an arranged phone call to O'Hara in London.

'How did the Jockey Club scene go?' he asked immediately.

'Nash wowed them.'

'Good, then.'

'I think ... well, we'll have to see the rushes tomorrow ... but I think it was a sit-up-and-take-notice performance.'

'Good boy.'

'Yes, he was.'

'No, I meant . . . well, never mind. How's everything else?'

'All right, but,' I paused, 'we need a better ending.'

'I agree that the proposed ending's too weak. Hasn't Howard any ideas?'

'He *likes* the weak ending.'

'Lean on him,' O'Hara said.

'Yes. Um, you know he based his book on the obituary of the man he called Cibber? His real name was Visborough.' I spelled it, as Howard had done. 'Well, could you get me a copy of that obituary? It was published in the *Daily Cable*, Howard says. It must have been at least three years ago. Howard doesn't know who wrote it. He never followed anything up in any way. He says simply that the obituary, and especially its inconclusiveness, was what jolted his imagination into writing the book.'

'You don't ask much!'

'The *Daily Cable* must have a cuttings library. You'll certainly be able to get that obituary. Could you fax it to me here at Bedford Lodge? If I knew exactly what started Howard's imagination working in the first place, perhaps I could help him find an explosive denouement.'

'You'll have the obituary tomorrow,' O'Hara promised.

'Thanks.'

'How's your friend?' he asked.

'What friend?'

'The one who's dying.'

'Oh.' I paused. 'He died during last night.'

'Bad luck.'

'He was old. Eighty something. A blacksmith turned top racing journalist, grand old character, great unusual life. Pity we can't make a film of *him*.'

'Films of good people don't have much appeal.'

'Ain't that the truth.'

'What was his name?'

'Valentine Clark,' I said. 'The *Daily Cable* might do an obituary of him too, you never know. He wrote for the *Racing Gazette*. Everyone in racing knew him. And ... um ... he knew the real trainer, Jackson Wells, the basis of the character that Nash is playing.'

'Did he?' O'Hara's attention sharpened down the line. 'So you surely asked him what he knew of the hanging?'

'Yes, I did. He knew no more than anyone else. The police dropped the case for lack of leads. Valentine said Jackson Wells's wife was an unmemorable mouse. He couldn't tell me anything helpful. It was all so very long ago.'

O'Hara almost laughed. 'It was very long ago for *you*, Thomas, because you're young. I'll bet twenty-six years is yesterday to Jackson Wells himself.'

'I ... er ...' I said diffidently, 'I did think of going to see him.'

'Jackson Wells?'

'Yes. Well, Valentine, my dead friend, he was originally a blacksmith, as I told you. He used to shoe my grandfather's horses regularly, and he did say he'd also sometimes shod the horses Jackson Wells trained. So perhaps I could make some excuse ... following Valentine's death ... to make a nostalgic visit to Jackson Wells. What do you think?'

'Go at once,' O'Hara said.

'He won't want to talk about the wife who hanged. He has a new life now and a second wife.'

'Try, anyway,' O'Hara said.

'Yes, I thought so. But he lives near Oxford ... it'll take me half a day.'

'Worth it,' O'Hara said. 'I'll OK the extra time.'

'Good.'

'Goodnight,' he said. 'I've a lady waiting.'

'Good luck.'

He cursed me – 'You son of a bitch' – and disconnected.

I'd always loved early mornings in racing stables. I'd been down in my grandfather's yard dawn by dawn for years, half my day lived before the first school bell. I tended, for the film, to make the horses more of a priority in my attention than perhaps I should have, moving about the yard, in close contact with the creatures I'd grown up among, and felt at home with.

I'd ridden as an amateur jockey in jump races from the age of sixteen, with most of my family expecting horses in some way to be my life for ever, but fate and finance – or lack of it – had found me at twenty engaged in organising horses in Arizona for the cavalry in a Western drama. By twenty-one I'd become the director of a bad minor film about rodeo riders, but that had led to the same post in a noble native-American saga that had modestly hit the jackpot. After that I'd spent a year working for film editors, learning their craft, followed by another year on soundtracks and music, and by twenty-six I'd been let loose as director on an unconsidered romance between a boy and a puma that had made astonishing profits. O'Hara had been the producer: I had never since been long out of work. 'The boy's lucky,' O'Hara would say, selling my name. 'You can't buy luck. Trust me.'

For this present film I'd suggested to O'Hara early in the pre-production stage that this time we should *buy*, not rent or borrow for fees, our stableful of horses.

'Too expensive,' he'd objected automatically.

'Not necessarily,' I'd contradicted. 'We can buy cheap horses. There are hundreds that have never done well in races, but they *look* like good thoroughbreds, and that's what's important. Also we won't have any problems with insurance or recompense for injuries, we can travel them where and when we like, and we can work them without anxious owners fluttering round to fuss about their feed or exercise. We can sell them again, at the end.'

One of O'Hara's chief virtues, in my eyes, was his ability to evaluate facts very fast and come up with quick decisions. So, 'Buy them,' he said, and he'd liberated sufficient funds for a bloodstock agency to acquire the fourteen good-looking no-hopers currently eating oats and hay in our yard.

The actors' unions having agreed we should use real-life stable personnel for the horses, I'd recruited a young assistant trainer from a prestigious Newmarket yard and installed him in charge of our whole horse operation, giving him the title of horsemaster and also the riding but non-speaking role of assistant trainer in the film.

He was already busy getting lads and horses ready for the morning action when I arrived in the yard at dawn. Moncrieff's crew had laid felt carpeting over the gravel to silence the progress of the rolling camera dolly. He himself had strategically planted his lighting. Ed, he reported, was already in position upstairs.

The weather was cold and windy with dark scudding clouds. Moncrieff liked the moodiness, humming happily as he arranged for ominous shadows to fall across Nash's stand-in, who looked hopelessly un-trainerlike in riding gear. When Nash himself – in character – strode out of the house and yelled bad-tempered instructions to the lads it was as real as any such bona fide moment I'd ever seen.

There were annoyances with the camera truck – one of its wheels squeaked despite the felt path. Oil and oaths fixed it. Moncrieff and I fretted at the delay because of light values. Nash seemed less irritated than resigned.

Only two takes were necessary of the assistant trainer giving Nash a leg-up onto his hack; the horse amazingly stood still. Nash wheeled away and sat on his mount in and out of shot while the assistant trainer heaved himself into his own saddle and led the circling string of by now mounted lads out through wide open stable gates onto the Newmarket training grounds beyond. Nash followed last, remembering to look back and up to the bedroom window. When his horse had walked him well out of sight I yelled 'Cut', and the whole string ambled back into the yard, the hooves scrunching on the gravel, the lads joshing each other like kids out of school.

'How did it go?' I asked Moncrieff. 'Cameras OK?'

'OK.'

'Print, then.' I walked among the horses to speak to their riders. 'That was good,' I said. 'We'll do it again, now, though. Two snaps are better than one.'

They nodded. By then they all considered themselves expert film-makers. The second take didn't go as smoothly, but that didn't necessarily matter: we would use the version that looked more natural on film.

I followed them on foot out of the gate to where Nash and all the lads were circling, awaiting my verdict.

'Same again tomorrow morning,' I said, patting horses' necks. 'Different clothes. Off you all go, then. Remember not to get in the way of any real racehorses. Walk and trot only on the grounds we've been allotted.'

The string filed off to exercise and Nash returned to the yard, dismounting and handing his reins to the lad left behind for the purpose.

'Is it still on for tomorrow?' he asked, turning in my direction.

'Doncaster, do you mean?'

He nodded.

'Of course it is,' I said. 'The stewards have asked you to their lunch, so you can use their box all afternoon and have as much or as little privacy as you want. They've sent tickets for two, for you to take a companion.'

'Who?'

'Whoever you like.'

'You, then.'

'*What?* I meant a friend, or perhaps Silva?' Silva was the bewitching actress he'd tumbled around with in bed.

'Not her,' he said vehemently. 'You. Why not? And don't say you'll still be doing close shots in the enquiry room. Let's make damned sure they all get completed this afternoon. I want you because you know the drill on a British racecourse, and the racing people know *you*.'

Green lights got what they wanted. Moreover, I discovered it was what I wanted also.

'Fine, then,' I said. 'Helicopter at eleven-thirty.'

Watching his familiar back walk off to his ever-waiting Rolls, I called Bedford Lodge from my mobile phone and by persuasive perseverance got the staff to find Howard Tyler, who was in the bar.

'Just a word, Howard,' I said.

'Not *more* script changes?' He was acidly sarcastic.

'No. Um . . . simply a word of warning.'

'I don't need your words of warning.'

'Good, then. But . . . er . . . I just thought I might remind you, knowing how you feel, that you agreed not to bellyache about the film until after its release.'

'I'll say what I damned well please.'

'It's your privilege. I don't suppose you care about the penalties in your contract.'

'What penalties?'

'Most film contracts include them,' I said. 'I'm sure yours does. Film companies routinely seek ways to stop a disgruntled writer from sabotaging the whole film just

79

because he or she dislikes the changes made to the original work. They put in clauses allowing themselves to recover substantial damages.'

After a lengthy pause Howard said, 'I never signed such a contract.'

'Fine, then, but you might check with your agent.'

'You're trying to frighten me!' he complained.

'I'm just suggesting you might want to be careful.'

Silence. Howard simply put down his receiver. So much for tactful advice!

True to his intention, Nash did make damned sure that we completed the enquiry-room shots that day, even if not until past eight in the evening. In want of a shower and a reviving drink, I drove back to Bedford Lodge and found waiting for me a long fax from O'Hara, starting with the *Daily Cable* obituary.

Rupert Visborough's life was dedicated to serving his country, the neighbourhood and the Sport of Kings.

Commissioned into the Scots Guards, he retired with the rank of major to enter local politics in his home county of Cambridgeshire. Many committees benefited from his expert chairmanship, including . . .

The list was long, virtuous and unexciting.

A landowner, he was elected a member of the Jockey Club following the death of his father, Sir Ralph Visborough, knighted for his patronage of many animal charities.

Highly respected by all who knew him, Rupert Visborough felt obliged to remove his name from a shortlist of those being considered for selection as parliamentary candidate, a consequence of his having inadvertently been involved in an unexplained death closely touching his family.

His wife's sister, married to Newmarket trainer Jackson Wells, was found hanged in one of the loose boxes in her husband's stable yard. Exhaustive police enquiries failed to find either a reason for suicide, or any motive or suspect for murder. Jackson Wells maintained his innocence throughout. The Jockey Club, conducting its own private enquiry, concluded there was no justification for withdrawing Wells's licence to train. Rupert Visborough, present at the enquiry, was justifiably bitter at the negative impact of the death on his own expectations.

Reports that Jackson Wells's wife was entertaining lovers unknown to her husband could not be substantiated. Her sister – Visborough's wife – described the dead woman as 'fey' and 'a day-dreamer'. She said that as she and her sister had not been close she could offer no useful suggestions.

Who knows what Rupert Visborough might not have achieved in life had these events not happened? Conjecture that he himself knew more of the facts behind the tragedy than he felt willing to disclose clung to his name despite his strongest denials. The death of his sister-in-law is unresolved to this day.

Visborough died last Wednesday of a cerebral haemorrhage, aged 76, with his great potential sadly unfulfilled.

He is survived by his wife, and by their son and daughter.

O'Hara had handwritten across the bottom, 'Pious load of shit! No one on the paper knows who wrote it. Their obits often come in from outside.'

The pages of fax continued, however.

O'Hara's handwriting stated, 'This paragraph appeared in the *Cable*'s irreverent gossip column on the same day as the obituary.'

Secrets going to grave in the Visborough family? It seems Rupert (76), Jockey Club member, dead on Wednesday of a stroke, never discovered how his sister-in-law hanged twenty-three years ago in who-dunnit circs. Bereaved husband, Jackson Wells, now remarried and raising rape near Oxford, had 'no comment' re the Visborough demise. Answers to the 23-year-old mystery *must* exist. Send us info.

O'Hara's handwriting: 'The Cable got about 6 replies, all no good. End of story as far as they are concerned. But at great expense they searched their microfilmed records and found these accounts, filed and printed at the time of the hanging.'

The first mention had earned a single minor paragraph: 'Newmarket trainer's wife hanged'.

For almost two weeks after that there had been daily revelations, many along the lines of 'did she jump or was she pushed?' and equally many about the unfairness – and personal bitterness – of the nipping in the bud effect of Visborough's ambitions for a political career.

A hanging in the family, it seemed, had discouraged not only racehorse owners; the blight had spread beyond Jackson Wells to canvassers and prospective voters.

The story had extinguished itself from lack of fuel. The last mention of Jackson Wells's wife announced untruthfully, 'The police expect to make an arrest within a few days.' And after that, silence.

The basic question remained unanswered – *why* did she hang?

I had dinner and went to bed and dreamed about them, Visborough as Cibber, his cuckolding wife as the pretty actress Silva, Nash as Jackson Wells and the fey, hanged woman as a wisp of muslin, a blowing curtain by the window.

No insight. No inspiration. No solution.

CHAPTER FIVE

Delays plagued the going-out-to-exercise scene the next morning. One of the horses, feeling fractious, dumped his lad and kicked one of the camera-operating crew. Light bulbs failed in mid-shot. One of the stable lads loudly asked a silly question while the cameras were rolling, and a sound engineer, who should have known better, strolled, smoking, into the next take.

Nash, emerging from the house, forgot to bring with him the crash helmet he was supposed to put on before he mounted. He flicked his fingers in frustration and retraced his steps.

By the time we finally achieved a printable result it was no longer dawn or anywhere near it. Moncrieff, cursing, juggled relays of coloured filters to damp down the exuberant sun. I looked at my watch and thought about the helicopter.

'Once more,' I shouted generally. 'And for Christ's sake, get it right. Don't come back, go on out to exercise. Everyone ready?'

'Cameras rolling,' Moncrieff said.

I yelled, 'Action', and yet again the lads led their long-suffering charges out of the loose boxes, hauled themselves into the saddle, formed a straggly line and skittered out of the gate. Nash, following them, forgot to look up at the window.

I yelled, 'Cut' and said to Moncrieff, 'Print.'

Nash came back swearing.

'Never mind,' I said. 'We'll cut it in. Would you ride out again and turn and look up *after* you're through the gate, as if the other horses had gone out of shot ahead of you? We'll also do a close shot of that look.'

'Right now?'

'Yes,' I said. 'Now, because of having the same light. And how about a touch of exasperation with the wife?'

The close shot of the exasperation proved well worth the extra time taken in raising a camera high. Even Moncrieff smiled.

All Nash said was, 'I hope the Doncaster stewards wait lunch.'

He whisked off in the Rolls but when I followed a minute or two later I found him still standing in the hotel lobby reading a newspaper, rigidly concentrated.

'Nash?' I enquired tentatively.

He lowered the paper, thrust it into my hands and in explosive fury said, '*Shit!*' Then he turned on his heel and stalked off, leaving me to discover what had upset him.

I saw. I read, and felt equally murderous.

BUMMER OF A FILM ON THE TURF

First reports of 'Unstable Times', now in front of cameras in Newmarket, speak of rows, discord and screeching nerves.

Author Howard Tyler's vibrant tale, ten weeks on

bestseller lists, is mangled beyond recognition, my sources tell me. Nash Rourke, superstar, rues his involvement: says 'Director Thomas Lyon (30), ineffectual, arrogant, insists on disastrous last-minute script changes.'

Lyon vows to solve a 26-year-old real-life mystery, basis of Tyler's masterpiece. The police failed at the time. Who is Lyon kidding?

Naturally those closely touched by the tragic unexplained hanging death of a leading Newmarket trainer's wife are distressed to have cold embers fanned to hurtful inaccurate reheat.

Lyon's version so far has the hanged wife's trainer-husband – Rourke – tumbling her sister, prompting apoplectic revenge from consequently cuckolded top Jockey Club steward, later ga-ga. None of this happened.

Why do the giants of Hollywood entrust a prestigious film-of-the-book to the incompetent mercies of an over-hyped bully-boy? Why is this ludicrous buffoon still strutting his stuff on the Heath? Who's allowing him to waste millions of dollars on this pathetic travesty of a great work?

Isn't Master Thomas Lyon ripe for the overdue boot?

There was a large photograph of Nash, looking grim.

Blindly angry, I went up to my rooms and found the telephone ringing when I walked in.

Before I could speak into the receiver, Nash's voice said, 'I didn't say that, Thomas.'

'You wouldn't.'

'I'll kill that son of a bitch, Tyler.'

'Leave him to O'Hara.'

'Are we still going to Doncaster?'

'We certainly are,' I said. Anywhere but Newmarket, I thought. 'Ready in half an hour?'

'I'll be down in the lobby.'

I phoned O'Hara's mobile phone and reached only his message service.

I said, 'Read the *Daily Drumbeat*, page sixteen, feature column headed, "Hot from the Stars". Nash and I are going to the sports. I'll have my mobile. Take Prozak.'

Howard Tyler's phone rang and rang in his room, unanswered.

I showered in record time, put on steward-lunching clothes and went down to ask questions of the helpful soul behind the reception desk.

'Mr Tyler isn't here,' she confirmed. 'He left.'

'*When* did he leave?'

'Actually,' she said, 'he picked up a newspaper from the desk here and went into the dining-room to have breakfast, as he always does. It's so nice to have him here, and Mr Rourke too, we can hardly believe it . . . So Mr Tyler hurried out of the dining-room five minutes later – he didn't eat his breakfast – he went upstairs and came down with his suitcase and said he didn't know when he'd come back.' She looked worried. 'I didn't ask him for payment. I hope I haven't done wrong, but I understood everything should be charged to the film company.'

'Don't worry about that,' I reassured her. 'Did Mr Tyler say where he was going?'

He hadn't, of course. He'd been in a great hurry. The receptionist had asked him if he'd felt ill, but he hadn't answered. He'd taken the newspaper with him, but the staff had had another copy. They had all read the column. She'd thought it best to show it to Mr Rourke. Her virtuousness nearly choked her.

'What will happen, do you think?' Nash asked, ready for the races, listening to a repeat from the receptionist.

'Short-term, we've got Howard off our backs.'

We went out to the Rolls and along to where the helicopter waited.

'I'll sue the bastard,' Nash said furiously, strapping himself in, 'saying I rue my involvement!'

'Did you?'

'Did I what?'

'Say it.'

'Shit, Thomas. I said I was sorry not to be staying home with my wife. And that was on day one. I don't in the least regret it now.'

'She could have come with you.'

He shrugged. We both knew why his wife had stayed at home: her insecurity in a four-months pregnancy with complications. She'd been annoyed with him for agreeing to Newmarket. He'd made too public an apology.

'As for all that trash I was supposed to say about you personally . . .'

'Howard put his own words into your mouth,' I said. 'Forget it.'

The helicopter lifted off from the Newmarket grass and swung round north-west.

However glibly I might say 'forget it', I had uncomfortable suspicions that the parent movie company, our source of finance, would come thundering down like a posse to lynch me from the nearest crossbeam. Any bad odour clinging to their investment called for dismissals to exorcise it. O'Hara might have to dump me: might even want to.

Bye-bye career, I thought. It had been great while it lasted. I couldn't believe what was happening.

Smart move on Howard's part to decamp out of reach of my fists. I could have killed him. I sat quietly in the helicopter looking out at Lincolnshire passing beneath and felt queasy from the turmoil in my gut.

I accepted that in general the most disliked person in the making of any film was the director. The director required people to do things they considered unnecessary/ridiculous/wrong. Directors (a) demanded too much from actors and (b) ignored their well-thought-out interpretations. Directors were never satisfied, wasted time on detail, worked everyone to death, ignored injured feelings, made no allowance for technical difficulties, expected the impossible, screamed at people.

I accepted also on the other hand that a director needed an overall vision of the work in progress, even if details got changed en route. A director had to fight to bring that vision to revelatory life. Excessive sympathy and tolerance on the set were unproductive, vacillating decisions wasted money and inconsistency left an enterprise rudderless. A successful movie was a tight ship.

It was more in my nature to be a persuader than an ogre, but sometimes, as with Howard, when persuasion failed to work, the ogre surfaced. I knew, too, that it was what O'Hara expected and in fact required of me. Use your power, he'd said.

Now everyone working on the film would read the piece in the *Drumbeat*. Half of Newmarket also. Even if O'Hara left me in charge, my job would be difficult to impossible, all my authority gone. If I had to, I would fight to get that back.

The helicopter landed near the Doncaster winning post, where a senior official was waiting to give Nash a suitable greeting and to lead him to the mandarins. The minute I followed him onto the grass my mobile phone buzzed, and I told him to go ahead, I would join him after I'd talked to O'Hara; if it were in fact O'Hara.

He looked at me straightly and asked the official to pause for my call.

I answered the phone's summons. 'Thomas,' I said.

'Thomas!' O'Hara's voice was loud with annoyance. 'Where are you?' Nash could hear him shouting: he winced.

'Doncaster racecourse.'

'I've had Hollywood on the line. It's not yet five in the morning there but the company is already furious. Someone made a phone call and then sent a fax of the *Drumbeat*.'

I said stupidly, 'A *fax*?'

'A fax,' he confirmed.

'Who sent it?'

'The mogul I talked to didn't say.'

I swallowed. My heart raced. The hand holding the instrument visibly trembled beside my eye. Calm down, I thought.

'Who did Tyler talk to?' O'Hara demanded furiously.

'I don't know.'

'You don't *know*?'

'No. He was grumbling to everyone who would listen. He may not have known he was spouting to a journalist – or to someone who *knew* a journalist.'

'What does he say about it?'

'The hotel says he blasted off the minute he saw the paper. No one knows where he's gone.'

'I tried his home number,' O'Hara shouted. 'They say he's in Newmarket.'

'More likely the moon.'

'The mogul I talked to is one of the very top guys, and he wants your head.'

This was it, I thought numbly: and I couldn't think of anything to say. I needed an impassioned plea in mitigation. Drew a blank.

'Are you there, Thomas?'

'Yes.'

'He says you're fired.'

I was silent.

'Hell's teeth, Thomas, defend yourself.'

'I warned Howard yesterday not to shoot his mouth off, but I think now that he'd already done it.'

'Two weeks ago he tried to get the moguls to fire you, if you remember. I pacified them then. But *this*!' Words failed him.

I began finally to protest. 'We're on target for time. We're within budget. The company themselves insisted on story changes. I'm making a commercial motion picture, and it isn't true that there are rows and discord, except with Howard himself.'

'What's he saying?' Nash demanded impatiently.

'I'm sacked.'

Nash snatched the phone out of my hand.

'O'Hara? This is Nash. You tell those brain-deads who are our masters that I did not say what the *Drumbeat* says I did. Your boy is doing an OK job on this movie and if you take him off it at this stage you *will* get a bummer of a film, and what's more, they can whistle for me to sign with them ever again.'

Aghast, I snatched the phone back. 'Nash, you can't do that. O'Hara, don't listen to him.'

'Put him back on the line.'

I handed the phone over, shaking my head. Nash listened to O'Hara for a while and finally said, 'You told me to trust him. I do. This movie has a good feel. Now you trust *me*, trust my nose in these matters.'

He listened a bit longer, said 'Right' and pressed the power-off button.

'O'Hara says he'll call you back in five hours when they will have talked it through in Hollywood. They're going to hold a breakfast meeting there at nine o'clock, when the big-wigs are all up. O'Hara will sit in on a conference call.'

'Thank you,' I said.

He smiled briefly. 'My reputation is at stake here, same as yours. I don't want my green light turning amber.'

'It never will.'

'Bad reviews give me indigestion.'

We walked with the patient official across the track and up to the stewards' privacy. Heads turned sharply all the way as racegoer after racegoer did a double take at the sight of Nash. We had asked for no advance

92

publicity – the parent film company was security hyper-conscious – so that only the top echelon knew whom to expect. I was glad, I found, to have an anonymous face.

They hadn't waited lunch. Even for mega-stars, racing time tables couldn't be changed. About twenty stewards and friends were at their roast beef and suitable Yorkshire pudding.

From behind the forks the welcome was as warm and impressed as the most inflated ego could desire, and Nash's ego, as I was progressively discovering, was far more normal and unassuming than seemed consistent with his eminence.

I'd been in awe of him before I'd met him. I'd metaphorically approached him on my knees, and I'd found, not the temperamental perfectionist I'd been ominously told to expect, but essentially the man I'd seen him play over and over again on the screen, a man, whatever the role or the make-up, of sane intelligence, mentally tough.

I forlornly hoped that the Doncaster stewards and their wives and other guests weren't avid readers of *Drumbeat*'s 'Hot from the Stars', and with relief I saw that the two papers most in evidence were the *Racing Gazette* and the *Daily Cable*, both of them lying open at the obituary page for Valentine.

Nash and I shook a fair number of hands and were seated in prestigious places, and while Nash asked a dumbstruck waitress for fizzy mineral water, nearly causing her to faint from her proximity to the sexiest eyes in screendom, I read both farewells to Valentine, and found they'd done the old man proud. Cremation, the *Gazette* also noted, was set for 11 a.m., Monday, and a memorial service would be arranged later. If I were truly out of work, I thought gloomily, I could go to both.

By the coffee stage, the *Drumbeat*'s pages were fluttering across the table and inevitably someone commiserated with Nash over the mess his director was making of his film. My own identity, remarked on round the table behind sheltering hands, produced universally disapproving stares.

Nash said with authority, his expert voice production easily capable of silencing other conversations, 'Never believe what you read in the papers. We're making an excellent film in Newmarket. We're being bad-mouthed by a spiteful little man. I did *not* say what I am reported to have said, and I have complete confidence in Thomas here. I shall complain to the paper and demand they print a retraction.'

'Sue them,' someone said.

'Perhaps I will.'

'And as for you, Thomas,' said one of the stewards whom I knew personally, '*you* must definitely sue.'

I said, 'I'm not sure that I can.'

'Of course you can!' He stabbed at the pages with a forefinger. 'This is defamatory in the extreme.'

I said, 'It's difficult to sue anyone for asking questions.'

'*What?*'

'Those defamations are written carefully in the form of questions. The question marks tend to take the certainty out of the slurs.'

'I don't believe it!'

A head further along the large table was gravely

nodding. 'A scurrilous suggestion, if it is expressed as a question, may or may not be considered libel. There are grey areas.'

My steward friend said blankly, 'That's not justice!'

'It's the law.'

'You knew that?' Nash said to me.

'Mm.'

'Did Howard know it?'

'Whoever wrote that piece certainly did.'

Nash said, '*Shit!*' and not a single face objected.

'What Nash really needs,' I said, 'is a reliable tip for the Lincoln.'

They laughed and with relief turned to the serious business of the day. I half-heard the knowledgeable form-talk and thought that five hours could be a long torture. Barely forty minutes of it had so far passed. My pulse still raced from anxiety. My whole professional life probably hung on whether the moguls who would be bidden to the breakfast table were putting in a good night's sleep. Saturday morning. Golf day. I would be doubly unpopular.

I went down with Nash and a couple of the stewards' other lunch guests to see the horses walking round the parade ring before the first race. Nash looked at the horses: the racecrowd progressively looked at Nash. He seemed to take the staring for granted, just as he would have done back home in Hollywood, and he signed a few autographs for wide-eyed teenagers with pleasant politeness.

'How do I put a bet on?' he asked me, signing away.

'I'll do it for you if you like. Which horse, how much?'

'Hell knows.' He raised his eyes briefly and pointed to a horse being at that point mounted by a jockey in scarlet and yellow stripes. 'That one. Twenty.'

'Will you be all right if I leave you?'

'I'm a grown boy, you know.'

Grinning, I turned away, walked to the Tote, and bet twenty pounds to win on the horse called Wasp. Nash, waiting for me to retrieve him, returned with me to the stewards' room, from where we watched Wasp finish an unobtrusive fifth.

'I owe you,' Nash said. 'Pick me one yourself for the next race.'

The races as always were being shown on closed-circuit television on sets throughout the bars and the grandstands. A set in the stewards' room was busy with a replay of the just-finished race, Wasp still finishing fifth, the jockey busy to the end.

I stared breathlessly at the screen.

'Thomas? *Thomas*,' Nash said forcefully in my ear, 'come back from wherever you've gone.'

'Television,' I said.

Nash said ironically, 'It's been around a while, you know.'

'Yes, but ...' I picked up a copy of the *Racing Gazette* that was lying on the table and turned from Valentine's obituary to the pages laying out the Doncaster programme. Television coverage of the day's sport, I saw, was, as I'd hoped, by courtesy of a commercial station that provided full day-by-day racing for grateful millions. For the big-race opening of the Flat season, they would be there in force.

'Thomas,' Nash repeated.

'Er . . .' I said, 'how badly do you want to save our film? Or, in fact . . . me?'

'Not badly enough to jump off a cliff.'

'How about an interview on TV?'

He stared.

I said, 'What if you could say on television that we're *not* making a bummer of a movie? Would you want to do it?'

'Sure,' he said easily, 'but it wouldn't reach every reader of the *Drumbeat*.'

'No. But what if O'Hara could get the interview transmitted to Hollywood? How about the moguls seeing it at breakfast? Your own face on the screen might tip things where O'Hara's assurances might not. Only . . . how do you feel about trying?'

'Hell, Thomas, get on with it.'

I went out onto the viewing balcony and pressed the buttons to get O'Hara: and let me not get his message service, I prayed.

He answered immediately himself, as if waiting for calls.

'It's Thomas,' I said.

'It's too early to hear from Hollywood.'

'No. It's something else.' I told him what I'd suggested to Nash, and he put his finger at once on the snags.

'First of all,' he said doubtfully, 'you'd have to get the TV company to interview Nash.'

'I could do that. It's getting the interview onto the screen in the Hollywood conference room that I'm not sure of. Live pictures get transmitted regularly from England to the States, but I don't know the pathways.

If we could get to an LA station we could have a tape rushed round for our moguls to play on a VCR . . .'

'Thomas, stop. I can fix the LA end. The transmission from England . . .' he paused, sucking his teeth. 'What station are we talking about?'

I told him. 'The people they'll have here are an outside broadcast unit. They'll have engineers and camera crews and a producer or two and three or four interviewers and commentators, but they won't have the authority or the equipment to transmit overseas. The OK would have to come from their headquarters, which are in London. They'll have Doncaster races on their screen there. They can transmit to anywhere. Their number will be in the phone book . . .'

'And you need me to use my clout.' He sounded resigned, seeing difficulties.

'Um,' I said, 'if you want *Unstable Times* to reach the cinema, it might be worth trying. I mean, it's your picture too, you know. Your head on the block for engaging me.'

'I see that.' He paused. 'All right, I'll start. It's a hell of a long shot.'

'They've been known to win.'

'Is Nash with you?'

'Five paces away.'

'Get him, would you?'

Nash came outside and took the phone. 'I'll do the interview. Thomas says he can fix it, no problem.' He listened. 'Yeah. Yeah. If he says he can, I guess he can. He doesn't promise what he can't deliver. O'Hara, you get off your ass and put Thomas and me into that meeting. It's damn stupid to let that son-of-a-bitch Tyler sink the ship.' He listened again, then said, 'Get it done, O'Hara. Hang the expense. I'll not be beaten by that *scribbler*.'

I listened in awe to the switched-on power of the ultimate green light and humbly thanked the fates that he saw me as an ally, not a villain.

He disconnected, handed the phone back to me and said, 'Where do we find our interviewer?'

'Follow me.' I tried to make it sound light-hearted, but I was no great actor. Nash silently came with me down to the unsaddling enclosure, from where the runners of the just-run race had already departed.

'Do you know who you are looking for?' he asked, as I turned my head one way and another. 'Can't you ask?'

'I don't need to,' I said, conscious, even if Nash ignored it, of everyone looking at *him*. 'This television company travels with a race-caller, a paddock commentator who talks about the runners for the next race, and someone who interviews the winning jockeys and trainers afterwards, and it's him I'm looking for ... and I know him.'

'That's something.'

'And there he is,' I said, spotting him. 'Coming?'

I slid then between the groups of people chatting in the railed area outside the weighing-room; slid where the groups parted like the Red Sea to clear a path for Nash. My acquaintance, the interviewer, began to say hello to me, saw who I was with and ended with his mouth open.

'Nash,' I introduced, 'this is Greg Compass: Greg ... Nash Rourke.'

Greg came to his senses like any seasoned television performer should and with genuine welcome shook the hand that had fired a hundred harmless bullets.

'He's here to see the Lincoln,' I explained. 'How about some inside information?'

'Gallico,' Greg suggested promptly. 'He's bursting out of his skin, so they say.' He looked thoughtfully at Nash and without pressing him asked, 'Do you mind if I say you're here? I expect Thomas told you I do the ghastly chat stuff for all the couch potatoes?'

'I did tell him, yes.'

'Thomas and I,' Greg explained, 'used to ride against each other, when I was a jockey and we were young.'

'You're all so tall,' Nash exclaimed.

'Jump jockeys are mostly taller. Ex-jump jockeys get to be racing commentators or journalists, things like that. Live it first. Talk about it after.' He was comically self-deprecating, though in fact he'd been a top career jockey, not an amateur like me. He was forty, slender, striking, stylish. He took a breath. 'Well . . .'

'You can certainly say I'm here,' Nash assured him.

'Great. Um . . .' He hesitated.

'Ask him,' I said, half-smiling.

Greg glanced at me and back to Nash. 'I suppose . . . I couldn't get you in front of my camera?'

Nash gave me a dry sideways look and in his best slay-them gravelly bass said that he saw no reason why not.

'I did hear you were in Newmarket, making a film,' Greg said. 'I suppose I can say so?'

'Sure. Thomas is directing it.'

'Yes. Word gets around.'

I pulled a folded *Drumbeat* page from my pocket and handed it to Greg.

'If you'll let him,' I said, 'Nash would very briefly like to contradict what's written in that "Hot from the Stars" column.'

Greg read it through quickly, his expression darkening from simple curiosity to indignation.

'Difficult to sue,' he exclaimed. 'It's all questions. Is it true?'

'It's true the film story is different from the book,' I said.

Nash assured him, 'I didn't say those things and I don't think them. The film is going well. All I'd like to say, if you'll let me, is that one shouldn't believe newspapers.'

'Thomas?' Greg raised his eyebrows at me. 'You're using me, aren't you?'

'Yes. But that column's assassinating me. If Nash can say on screen that it's not true, we can beam him to the money-men in Hollywood and hope to prevent them from taking the column seriously.'

He thought it over. He sighed. 'All right, then, but very casual, OK? I'll put you both together in shot.'

'Innocence by association,' I said gratefully.

'Always a bright boy.' He looked at his watch. 'How about after the Lincoln? An hour from now. After I've talked to the winning trainer and jockey and the owners, if they're here. We could slot it in at that point. I'll tell my producer. Thomas, you remember where the camera is? Come there after the Lincoln. And Thomas, you owe me.'

101

'Two seats for the première,' I said. 'Without you, there may not be one.'

'Four seats.'

'A whole row,' I said.

'Done.' Greg looked at Nash. 'What is this over-hyped buffoon of an ineffectual bullyboy really like as a director?'

'Worse,' Nash said.

We did the interview, Nash and I side by side. Greg introduced us to the viewers, asked if Nash had backed the winner of the Lincoln – Gallico – congratulated him and said he hoped Nash was enjoying his visit to Britain.

Nash said, 'I'm making a film here. Very enjoyable.' He nodded affably. He added a few details casually, as Greg had wanted, but left no listeners in doubt that the racing film we were making in Newmarket was going well.

'Didn't I read an uncomplimentary report . . .?' Greg prompted quizzically.

'Yes,' Nash agreed, nodding. 'Words were put into my mouth that I never said. So what else is new? Never believe newspapers.'

'You're playing a trainer, aren't you?' Greg asked the questions we had asked him to ask as if he'd just that minute thought of them. 'How's it going with the riding?'

'I can sit on a horse,' Nash smiled. 'I can't ride like Thomas.'

'Do you ride in the film?' Greg asked me helpfully.

102

'No, he doesn't,' Nash said, 'but he takes a horse out on the Heath to gallop it sometimes. Still, I can beat him at golf.'

The affection in his voice said more than a thousand words. Greg wound up the interview good-naturedly and expertly handed on the couch potatoes to the paddock commentator for profiles of the next race's runners.

'Thank you,' I said, 'very much.'

'A row of seats,' he nodded. 'Don't forget.' He paused, and added cynically, 'Do you play golf, Thomas?'

'No.'

'I can always beat him,' Nash confirmed.

'You're a double act!' Greg said.

O'Hara had watched the interview in the television company's headquarters in London, and he buzzed my telephone before I'd found a quiet spot for reaching him.

'Brilliant!' he said, almost laughing. 'Brotherly love all over the screen. Not a dry eye in the house.'

'Will it work?'

'Of course it will work.'

'Will it get to the meeting in time?'

'Cancel the anxiety, Thomas. The people here have been real helpful. Their fee would launch a Hubble telescope, but the moguls will see the show with their wheaties.'

'Thanks, O'Hara.'

'Give me Nash.'

I handed the phone over and watched Nash deliver a series of nods and yeses.

'Yes, of course he suggested my lines,' Nash said, 'and he got that pal of his to ask the right questions. How? Hell knows. The old jockey network, I guess.'

The last few races crawled by and, having thanked our hosts, we flew back to Newmarket with still no further word from O'Hara. After-breakfast time in Los Angeles. What were the moguls doing?

'Stop biting your nails,' Nash said.

His chauffeured Rolls took us back to Bedford Lodge, where Nash suggested I join him in his rooms so that we might both hear what O'Hara might report.

The film company had engaged four comfortable suites in the hotel; the best for Nash, one for Silva, one for me and one (often empty) for O'Hara or other visiting mogul. Rooms in the hotel were provided for Moncrieff and for Howard: the rest of the approximately sixty people working on the film, those in scene-setting, wardrobe, make-up, those in technical trades, those who were assistants or production staff or couriers, all those inescapably involved were staying in various other hotels, motels or private lodgings. Most of the stable lads were housed in a hostel. The horse-master/assistant trainer went home to his wife. The overall logistics of keeping everyone fed and working within union guidelines were, thankfully, not my job.

Nash's rooms looked out over pleasant gardens and provided large armchairs fit for soothing limbs made weary by hours of pretending to be someone else; or rather by hours of waiting around in order to pretend to be someone else, for five minutes or so, now and then. Moncrieff and I might work frantically non-stop. Actors stood around getting bored, waiting for us to be ready. Actors, lengthily immobile, grew tired, while Moncrieff and I did not.

Nash sank into his favourite armchair and for about the four-hundredth time looked at his watch.

Five hours had gone. Almost six. I'd spent a great deal of the time sweating.

My mobile phone buzzed. My mouth went dry. Buzz, buzz.

'Answer it!' Nash commanded crossly, seeing my reluctance.

I said, 'Hello.' More of a croak.

'Thomas?' O'Hara said. 'You're not fired.'

Silence.

'Thomas? Did you hear? Get on with the film.'

'I . . . er . . .'

'For hell's sake! Is Nash there?'

I handed the phone to the green light whose reaction to the news was a robust, 'I should damn well think so. Yes, of course he's been worried, he's only human.'

He gave me the phone back. O'Hara said, 'There are strings attached. I have to spend more time in Newmarket supervising you. One of the big boys is coming to visit, in order to be satisfied that their money is being spent reasonably. They waffled on for far too long about who they could put in to direct in your place. But in the end your television clip did the trick. Nash convinced them. They still think he can do no wrong. If Nash is happy, they'll keep you on.'

'Thanks.'

'I'm coming back to Newmarket tomorrow. It's a goddam nuisance as I was planning to fly to LA, but there it is. Like you said, it's my head on the block alongside yours. What will you be doing tomorrow morning?'

'Horses galloping on the Heath.'

'And Nash?'

'Sitting on a horse, watching. In the afternoon, we ferry the horses to Huntingdon racecourse. Monday we set up and rehearse the crowd scenes at the races. Some of the crews are moving to motels around Huntingdon, but Nash and I, and a few others, are staying in our rooms here in Newmarket.'

'How far is it?'

'Only about thirty-eight miles. Where do you want to sleep?'

'Newmarket.' No hesitation. 'Get yourself a driver, Thomas. I don't want you falling asleep at the wheel with those long hours you work.'

'I like to drive myself, and it's not very far.'

'Get a driver.'

It was an order. I said OK. I was grateful to be still employed. He said, 'See you, fellow,' and I said, 'Thanks, O'Hara,' and he left one further report: 'Howard will have his claws well clipped. Stupid son of a bitch.'

'There you go,' Nash said, smiling, when I switched the phone off. 'Drink? Eat with me, why not?'

Nash had most of his meals alone upstairs, brought by room service. Unlike most actors he had a solitary streak to which, because of his wife's absence, he had given free rein. Surprised, therefore, but pleased not to

106

be dining alone myself, I stayed for soup, lamb and claret and a step into a positive friendship that I wouldn't, a couple of weeks earlier, have thought likely.

Relaxed after the day's troubles, I decided to make a brief call on Dorothea, to see if she needed anything, before my scheduled meeting with Moncrieff to plan the morning's activities on the Heath.

I expected to find a quiet sorrowful house. Instead, when I arrived there, I found flashing lights, a police car, and an ambulance.

CHAPTER SIX

A policeman barred my attempt to walk up the concrete path.

'What happened?' I asked.

'Clear the path, please, sir.' He was young, big, businesslike, and unsympathetic with unknown members of the public. He had kept – and was keeping – a small crowd of onlookers from stepping too close to the goings-on.

I tried again. 'The people who live here are my friends.'

'Stand back, if you please, sir.' He scarcely looked at me, unintentionally impressive, a large physical barrier that I had no inclination to fight.

I retreated through the curious crowd and from behind them used my constant companion, the portable telephone, to ring Dorothea's number. After what seemed a very long time a distressed woman's voice said, 'Hello.'

'Dorothea?' I said. 'It's Thomas.'

'Oh. Oh, no, I'm Betty. Where are you, Thomas? Can you come?' I explained I was outside but obstructed and in a few seconds she was hurrying down the path to collect me. The large policeman stepped aside, shrugging, not caring one way or the other, and I hastened with Betty towards the front door.

'What's happened?' I asked her.

'Someone broke in. It's *terrible* . . . they've nearly killed Dorothea . . . how *could* they? Dr Gill has just come and the police too and there's so much blood and they're taking photographs and it's all *unbelievable . . .*'

We went into the house which looked inside as if it had been swept through by a tornado.

Valentine's bedroom by the front door had been wrecked: drawers were upturned on the floor, their contents scattered. The wardrobe stood open, empty. Pictures had been torn from the walls, their frames smashed. Mattress and pillows were ripped, guts spilling.

'It's all like this,' Betty wailed. 'Even the bathrooms and the kitchen. I must go back to Dorothea . . . I'm afraid she'll die . . .'

She left me and vanished into Dorothea's bedroom where I with hesitation followed, stepping round a wide drying sea of blood in the hall.

I needn't have felt I might be intruding: the room was full of people. Robbie Gill obstructed my view of most of Dorothea, who was lying unspeaking but in shoes and stockings on the sliced ruins of her bed. Two ambulancemen filled half the available space with a stretcher on wheels. A uniformed policewoman and a photographer were busy. Betty threaded a way into the throng, beckoning me to follow.

Robbie Gill glanced up, saw me, nodded recognition and took a pace back with the result that I saw all of

Dorothea, and became sickened and overwhelmingly angry.

She was bleeding, swollen and unconscious, with great gashes in the flesh of her cheek and forehead and a red mess where her mouth was.

'Her right arm's broken,' Robbie Gill dictated to the note-taking policewoman. 'She has internal injuries . . .' He stopped. Even for a doctor, it was too much. Dorothea's clothes were ripped open, her old breasts and stomach bare, two slashed wounds on her body bleeding copiously, one so deep that a bulge of intestines protruded through the abdomen wall, a glistening pale swelling island in a wet scarlet ocean. The smell of blood was overpowering.

Robbie Gill took sterile dressings from his bag and told everyone except the policewoman to leave. She herself looked over-pale, but stood her ground as the rest of us silently obeyed.

Betty was shaking, tears on her cheeks.

'I came over to make sure she'd given herself something to eat. She doesn't take care of herself, now Valentine's gone. I came in through the back door, into the kitchen, and it's *wrecked* . . . it's terrible . . . and I *found* her, she was bleeding on the floor in the hall, and I thought she was dead . . . so I phoned Dr Gill because his number is right beside the phone in the kitchen, and he brought the police here and the ambulancemen . . . and they carried her into the bedroom. Do you think she'll be all right?' Her anxiety shook her. 'She won't die, not like this. How *could* anyone do this?'

I had imagined and I had filmed scenes as bad or worse, but the blood we'd used had often been lipstick dissolved in oil – to give it viscosity – and intestines made of inflated sausage skin, and sweat sprayed through an atomiser onto grey-greasepainted faces.

More people came, apparently plain-clothes policemen. Betty and I retreated to Dorothea's sitting-room where, again, comprehensive chaos paralysed thought.

'How could anyone *do* this?' Betty repeated numbly. '*Why* would anyone do it?'

'Did she have anything valuable?' I asked.

'Of course she didn't. Just her little knick-knacks. Trinkets and souvenirs. They've even torn the photo of her and Bill's wedding. How *could* they?' She picked up the ruins of a photo frame, crying for her friend's pain. 'And her pretty pink vase . . . it's in splinters. She loved that vase.'

I stared at the pink pieces, and then went down on one knee and fruitlessly searched the carpet around them.

'I've put the key in the pink vase in my sitting-room.'

Dorothea's voice spoke clearly in my memory. The key of Valentine's study, in safekeeping to prevent her son Paul from taking the books.

Bitterly but silently swearing I went along the passage and pushed open the study's half-closed door. The key was in the lock. Inside, Valentine's sanctum had been ravaged like the rest of the house; everything breakable had been demolished, everything soft slashed, all his photographs destroyed.

Every book had gone.

I opened the cupboard where I knew he kept the scrapbooks containing every column he'd ever written for newspapers.

Every shelf was bare.

Betty, trembling, put her hand on my arm and said, 'Dorothea told me Valentine wanted you to have his books. Where have they gone?'

With Paul, I automatically thought. But he *couldn't* have inflicted such wounds on his mother. A pompous, bombastic man, yes; but not to this extent vicious.

I asked Betty, 'Where is Paul? Her son.'

'Oh, dear! Oh, dear! He went home yesterday. He doesn't know ... And I don't know his number ...' She swayed. 'I can't bear it.'

'Don't worry,' I said. 'Sit down. I'll find his number. I'll get you some tea. Where's your husband?'

'It's his darts night ... at the pub.'

'Which pub?'

'Oh, dear ... The Dragon.'

First things first, I thought, heading for the kitchen. Hot sweet tea prevented a lot of breakdowns from shock. No figure of authority stopped me, though the little house seemed crowded with them. I took the cup and saucer to Betty who held them clattering in both hands as she sat in Valentine's room.

In the old man's fortunately unshredded phone book I looked up The Dragon's number and spoiled Betty's husband's treble twenty by asking him to come home quickly. Then I searched around for Paul's number and ran it to earth on the notepad attached to the extension phone in the kitchen.

Paul answered, and I listened to his obnoxious voice with relief. If he were at home in Surrey he couldn't have attacked his mother a hundred miles away in Newmarket, not with her wounds so recent and bleeding. Even if she lived, she couldn't have mentally recovered from being attacked by her own son.

He sounded as appalled as he ought to be. He announced he would set off at once.

'I don't know which hospital they'll take her to,' I said.

'Is she going to die?' he interrupted.

'Like I told you, I don't know. Hold on for a bit and I'll get Dr Gill to talk to you.'

'Useless man!'

'Stay on the line,' I said. 'Wait.'

I left the kitchen, found the plain-clothes men starting to blow dust on things for fingerprints and hovered until Dorothea's door opened to let out the policewoman who was beckoning to the men to bring back the stretcher.

I said to her, 'Mrs Pannier's son is on the telephone. Please can Dr Gill talk to him?'

She looked at me vaguely and retreated into Dorothea's room with the ambulance people, but it seemed that she did pass on the message because presently Robbie Gill opened the bedroom door again and asked me if Paul were actually on the line.

'Yes,' I confirmed. 'He's waiting to talk to you.'

'Tell him I won't be long.'

I relayed the message to Paul. He was impatiently displeased. I told him to wait and left him. Angry and anxious about Dorothea, and concerned about the missing books, I found reassuring Paul impossible. I couldn't even be decently sympathetic. I was sure he wouldn't give the books back unless I took him to court, and even then I had no list of what I'd lost.

Robbie Gill accompanied Dorothea on the rolling stretcher right out to the ambulance, solicitously making sure she was gently treated. Then, looking stern, he came back into the house, strode down the hall to where I waited by the kitchen door, walked over to the central table and picked up the receiver.

'Mr Pannier?' he asked, then grimaced crossly as Paul spoke on the other end.

'Mr Pannier,' Robbie said forcefully, 'your mother has been beaten about the head. She's unconscious from those blows. Her right arm is broken. In addition, she has knife wounds to her body. I am sending her to Cambridge ...' he named the hospital ... 'where she will receive the best attention. I cannot tell you whether or not she will survive.' He listened with disgust to Paul's reply. 'No, she was not sexually assaulted. I have done everything possible. I suggest you check with the hospital later. It is now out of my hands.' He thrust the receiver back into its cradle, compressed his mouth as if physically restraining himself from swearing, and squeezed his eyes with finger and thumb.

'How is she really?' I asked.

He shrugged wearily, his expression relaxing. 'I don't know. She put up a fight, I should think. Tried to defend herself with her arm. It's odd ... it's almost as if she had *two* assailants ... one that hit her arm and her head with something hard and jagged, and one that used a knife. Or perhaps there was only one assailant, but with two weapons.'

'It's a useless question,' I said, 'but *why* attack her?'

'A dear good old lady! The world's grown vicious.

114

Old ladies get attacked. I detest that son of hers. I shouldn't say that. Pay no attention. He wanted to know if she'd been raped.'

'He's the ultimate four-letter case.'

'The police want to know why the whole house is in this state.' He waved an arm at the devastation around. 'How do I know? They weren't poor, they weren't rich. Poor old bodies. They relied on you lately, you know. They loved you, in a way. Pity *you* weren't their son.'

'Valentine was part of my childhood.'

'Yes. He told me.'

'Well . . . what happens next?'

'The police are talking about attempted murder, because of the knife wounds. But . . . I don't know . . .'

'What?' I prompted, as he hesitated.

'It may be fanciful . . . I don't know if I'll say it to the police . . . but it would have taken so little to finish her off. Just one stab in the right place.' He paused. 'You saw her, didn't you?'

'Yes, when you moved back from her bed.'

He nodded. 'I thought so. You saw those slashes. Two of them, one relatively superficial, one very deep. The first one cut her clothes open. Why wasn't there a third? You know what I think? I think it was an *aborted* murder. I think he changed his mind.'

I stared

'You can call me crazy,' he said.

'No, I think you're clever.'

'I've seen knife murders. They often look like frenzy. Dozens of stab wounds. Deranged mind at work. They can't stop. Do you see?'

115

'Yes,' I said.

'I don't know why I'm telling you. Pay no attention. With luck Dorothea will live to tell us herself.'

'How much luck does she need?'

'Frankly,' he said dispiritedly, 'quite a lot. Concussion's unpredictable. I don't think she has intra-cranial bleeding, but I can't be sure. But that abdominal wound ... it's bad ... it depends on infection ... and she's eighty next month ... but she's well in herself ... healthy for her age, I mean. I've grown fond of them both, though I used to fight with Valentine on the surface, obstinate old cuss.'

I thought Robbie Gill a good doctor, and I said so. He brushed off my words.

'Can I ask you something?' I said.

'Of course.'

'Well ... how long ago was Dorothea attacked?'

'How long ago?'

'Yes. I mean, was she attacked *before* the trashing of the house? All this damage must have taken quite a while to achieve. Or had she been out, and come back at the wrong moment? Or did someone try to beat some information out of her and go too far, and then pull the place apart looking for whatever he wanted?'

'Hey, slow down,' he protested. 'You think like a policeman.'

Like a film-maker, I thought. I said again, 'How long since she was attacked?'

He pursed his lips. 'The house was trashed first.'

We digested it in silence.

'You're sure?' I asked finally.

Gill said, 'Judging from the comparatively small

116

amount of swelling and the rate of bleeding, Dorothea hadn't been in that state very long before her friend Betty found her. I came at once when Betty phoned me. I wasn't much longer than five minutes on the way. Betty might be lucky that she didn't arrive here ten minutes sooner.' He sighed. 'It isn't our problem, I'm glad to say. We can leave it to the police.'

'Yes.'

He looked at his watch and said it had been a long day, and I agreed with that too. When he told the police he was leaving, they decided to take his fingerprints. They took mine also, and Betty's: for elimination, they said. They wrote brief statements from Betty and me, and we told them Paul's fingerprints would be everywhere, like our own.

Betty's husband came to collect her with wide consoling arms, and at length I drove back to Bedford Lodge and downed a medicinal large one with Moncrieff.

Summoned by Ed on my say-so, all available crews, technicians, wardrobe people and actors (except Nash) gathered in the stable yard at dawn on Sunday morning.

I mounted a wooden chair to address them and, in the fresh ever-moving East Anglian air, wondered how Shakespeare could have expected Henry V's words before Agincourt to be heard by any but the nearest knights, given the clinking noises of armour on horseback and the absence of microphones.

I at least had a megaphone, equipment perhaps overfamiliar to my audience.

117

'I expect,' I said loudly, when movement in the company had diminished to restless impatience, 'that most of you have by now read yesterday's "Hot from the Stars" column in the *Daily Drumbeat*.'

I reaped stares, nods, and a good many sardonic smiles. No overt sneers. Something, at least.

'As you can guess,' I went on, 'the column badly disturbed our parent company in Hollywood. Fortunately our producer assured them that you are all doing a very good job here. Some of you may like it, some may not, but Hollywood has confirmed that I continue to direct. Nash Rourke has told them he is in favour of this. In consequence, nothing has changed. Whether or not you agree with the *Drumbeat*'s assessment of my character, if you want to continue to be employed on this enterprise, you will please make a private commitment to give this film your best shot. For all our sakes, the creation of a well-made, visually exciting commercial motion picture should take priority over any personal feelings. I want you to be able in the future to say with *satisfaction* that you worked on this film. So it's back to business as usual, which means will the lads now saddle the horses and everyone else continue with the schedule that Ed has distributed. OK? Good.'

I lowered the megaphone, stepped off the chair and turned my back to the company to join Moncrieff, who had been standing behind me in support.

'Socked it to them,' he approved with irony. 'We could make a film of making this film.'

'Or a book,' I said.

Our female star, Silva Shawn, loped across the stable

118

yard to join us. As usual, when not dressed in character, she wore flapping dark voluminous layers of clothes reaching to her ankles, with black Doc Marten boots below and a charcoal hat above, a hat that looked like a soft collapsed topper sitting on her eyebrows. She walked with long strides and arrived at most meetings with her shapely chin thrust forward in the body language of belittle-me-if-you-dare.

O'Hara had strongly warned me not to pay her any compliment she could possibly construe as sexual harassment, which I found difficult to comply with, as the adjectives which sprang first and naturally to my mind, apart from delicious, were divine, bewitching and ultra-desirable: but 'Never call her darling,' O'Hara had instructed.

'Why did you pick her if she's so touchy?' I'd asked him, and he had said succinctly, 'She can act.'

To date, her acting in the film had chiefly consisted of the notably explicit bedroom scenes with Nash (punctuated by No, no, no, moans from Howard) that we had captured the previous week. We had in fact faithfully adhered to Howard's script in the matter of words: what infuriated him was that I had ignored his intention to have Nash and Silva deliver their lines fully clothed. He had set their restrained show of affection in the drawing-room. I had transferred it to the bedroom, letting the verbal restraint remain, but contrasting it with growing physical desire. Silva, without self-consciousness ('bodies are natural'), had allowed delicately lit shots of her nudity in the bathroom. The rushes had quickened many pulses, including my own.

119

Whether she chose to admit it or not, there was a sensual quality in Silva's acting diametrically opposite to her chosen off-screen stance.

She had been away from Newmarket for the past week fulfilling an unbreakable commitment somewhere else, but was due to ride a horse on the Heath that morning, making use of an equestrian skill she was proud of. As happened in almost all films, we were not shooting the scenes chronologically: the coming encounter between the trainer and Cibber's wife was their first, their meeting, all innocence at the start but with, in no time, a promise developing in their eyes.

Silva said disapprovingly, 'I hope you got me a good horse.'

'He's fast,' I said, nodding.

'And good looking?'

'Of course.'

'And well trained?'

'I've been riding him myself.'

Without comment she transferred her near-universal disapproval to Moncrieff, whom she considered a male chauvinist despite his spectacular ability to make even ugly women look beautiful on screen.

After so many years spent studying female curves one might have expected Moncrieff to have grown an impervious skin, but every time we'd worked together he had fallen in love with the leading lady, and Silva looked like being no exception.

'Platonic,' I'd advised him. 'Strictly hands off. OK?'

'She needs me,' he'd pleaded.

'Light her and leave her.'

120

'Such cheekbones!'

Silva had fortunately so far given him the reverse of encouragement. I'd noticed from the first day I met her that she looked with more favour on men with suits, ties, short haircuts and clean-shaven faces, an inclination that should ensure the comparative invisibility of straggle-bearded, shambling, sloppily-dressed Moncrieff.

'I think,' I said to Silva politely, 'they're expecting you in make-up.'

She demanded, 'Are you telling me I'm late?'

I shook my head. 'The meeting has set everyone back. But I hope to finish the Heath scenes by lunchtime.'

She loped off, skirts flapping, making her own sort of statement.

'Gorgeous,' Moncrieff breathed.

'Dangerous,' I said.

Nash arrived, yawning, in his Rolls, and went into the house to the wardrobe and make-up departments. He was followed into the stable yard almost immediately by a man of very similar build, riding a bicycle which braked hard with a spraying of gravel beside Moncrieff and me.

'Morning,' the newcomer said briefly, dismounting. No deference in sight.

'Good morning, Ivan,' I answered.

'Are we still in business?'

'You're late,' I said.

He rightly took the comment as disapproval and wordlessly retreated, with his bicycle, into the house.

121

'I don't like him,' Moncrieff said. 'Saucy bugger.'

'Never mind. Make him look like St George, a shining champion.'

Nash himself had great presence just sitting on a horse but any speed faster than a walk revealed deficiencies, so for distance shots of him trotting or cantering we were using a stuntman, Ivan, instead. Ivan made a living riding in front of cameras and had picked up a truculent manner that would prevent his ever getting further in his profession. He had a habit, I'd been told, of holding forth in pubs about how *close* he was to Nash Rourke, for whom he had doubled on an earlier picture. Nash this, Nash that, Nash and I . . . In actual fact, they met seldom and conversed less. Ivan had mushroomed a relationship from a few short businesslike exchanges.

Trainers in many other racing centres drove out in Land-Rovers to watch their strings work, but on Newmarket's mainly roadless Heath it was still the norm to oversee everything from horseback and there was no doubt Nash looked more imposing in the saddle than operating a four-wheel drive. The mega-star's sex appeal brought in the pennies. My job was to make it powerful while looking natural, which in Nash's case wasn't hard.

Moncrieff was driven off up one of the few roads in a camera truck, with a second crew following, to positions we'd agreed the previous evening. The string of horses would canter up a hill, be followed broadside by one camera and head-on by a second as they came over the brow into the low-in-the-sky sunlight; rather, I hoped, like an orchestral flourish of brass after

122

a muted but lyrical introduction. I often heard sound-tracks in my head long before any composer approached them.

Ed, knowing to the minute when to start the action, remained down by the stable. Though I could easily have driven, I chose to ride up onto the Heath to join Moncrieff; and I rode the horse we'd allotted to Silva, to get its back down: that is to say, to warm him up so that he would go sweetly with her and not buck. Silva might be proud of her riding, but O'Hara wouldn't thank me for getting her dumped on her exquisite backside.

The terrible Ivan was to canter alone to the brow of the hill, riding Nash's usual mount. He was to stop there, turn his horse, and stand silhouetted against the brightening sky. I'd asked him particularly not to waste the precious light-slot by getting it wrong.

He'd been insulted that I should expect him to get it wrong.

'Don't then,' I said.

I joined Moncrieff by the truck positioned halfway up the hill, and breathed sighs of relief when Ivan obliged us with a beautifully ridden canter up the hill, stopping and turning at the right place, horse and rider stark and splendidly black against a halo of gold.

'Holy Moses,' Moncrieff said, intently looking through the lens. 'It's a beaut.' He ran a long fifteen seconds' worth before cutting.

'Again?' I suggested.

Moncrieff checked that the film had run properly through the camera gate and shook his head. 'It was about perfect.'

'Great. Print. Let's reload fresh stock for the next long shot of the rest of the horses.'

I called down to Ed on our walkie-talkie system, told him to stick to schedule, had the shot numbered as always by the clapper board operator and watched while the string was filmed streaming uphill at a fast canter. I called up the out-of-sight camera over the brow of the hill to start rolling, but perfection was an elusive quality and it was only after I'd ridden over the hill myself to organise things from up there, only after some huffing and puffing and two retakes, that I got my flourish of trumpets.

With the crowd shots at last in the can, everyone on horseback milled around waiting for clearance and instructions. Ivan was still importantly riding Nash's horse, but a little apart, and I myself was now down on foot conferring with Moncrieff, eyes concentrating on his records of exposed footage.

I didn't see what happened. I heard an indignant shout from Ivan and a clamour from other voices. I sensed and felt a lot of startled movement among the riders, but at first I assumed it to be the sort of everyday commotion when one in a company of horses lets fly with his heels at another.

Ivan, swearing, was picking himself up off the ground. One horse with its rider detached itself from the group and raced off over the hill in the direction of Newmarket town. I thought with irritation that I'd need to rap a knuckle or two and grudged the waste of time.

Ivan came storming up to me with his complaint.

'That *madman*,' he said furiously, 'came at me with a knife!'

'He can't have done.'

'Look, then.' He raised his left arm so that I could see his jacket, the tweed coat identical to that usually worn in the training scenes by Nash. At about waist level the cloth was cut open for seven or eight inches from front to back.

'I'm telling you!' Ivan was rigid with fear on top of indignation. 'He had a *knife*.'

Convinced and enormously alarmed, I glanced instinctively to find the horse I'd been riding, but he was being led around a good way off. Nearest in the matter of transport stood one of the camera trucks, though pointing in the wrong direction. I scrambled behind its steering wheel, made a stunt-worthy three-point turn and raced across the turf in the direction of Newmarket, coming into view of the fleeing horseman in the distance as soon as I was over the hilltop.

He was too far ahead for me to have a realistic chance of catching up with him. Over grass, a horse was as fast as the truck; and he had only to reach the town and to slow to a walk to become instantly invisible, as Newmarket was threaded through and through with special paths known as horse-walks which had been purpose-laid to allow strings of horses to transfer to the gallops on the Heath from their stables in the town without having to disrupt traffic on the roads. Any rider moving slowly on a horse-walk became an unremarkable part of the general scenery, even on a Sunday morning.

It crossed my mind that I should perhaps try to catch him on film, but the camera on the truck was bolted to face backwards, as normally it was driven along in front

125

of its subject, filming advancing cars, people or horses. If I stopped to turn the truck and change places to operate the camera my quarry would be too far off even for blow-ups, if not entirely out of sight.

I was just about to give up when the distant horse was suddenly and violently reined to a halt, the rider reversing his direction and starting back towards me. The truck's engine raced. His head came up. He seemed to see me speeding down the hill towards him. He whirled his horse round again and galloped towards Newmarket at an even faster pace than before.

Even though the distance between us had closed, he'd travelled too far towards safety. It was already hard to distinguish his outline against the buildings ahead. I had to admit to myself that I wasn't going to catch him, and if so I would settle for second best and try to discover what had made him stop and reverse.

I braked the truck to a standstill as near as I could judge to the place where he'd turned, then jumped out onto the grass, trying to see what he might have seen, that could have been important enough to interrupt his flight.

He'd been facing the town. I looked that way and could see nothing to alarm him. There seemed no reason for him to have doubled back, but no one escaping at that pace would have stopped unless he had to.

If I were filming it . . . why might he stop?

Because he'd *dropped* something.

The uphill stretch of well-grassed exercise ground was as wide as an airport runway and almost as long. I couldn't be sure I was in the right place. If the rider had dropped something small I could search all day. If he had dropped something insignificant I wouldn't see any importance in anything I might come across. Yet he had *stopped*.

I took a few irresolute strides. There was simply too much space. Grass all round; miles of it. I looked up the hill, to the brow, and saw all the film horses and riders standing there, like Indians appearing on the skyline in an old pioneer movie. The sun was rising behind them.

I'd dropped my walkie-talkie up there in my hurry. I decided to drive the truck back up the hill, having left a mark where I was currently standing, and get all the lads to walk down in that strung-out sideways fashion, to see if they could find anything odd on the ground.

I marked the spot by taking off my light blue sweater and dropping it in a heap: anything smaller couldn't be seen. I walked back to climb into the truck.

The sun rose brilliantly over the hill, and in the grass twenty paces ahead of me, something *glinted*.

I went on foot to see what it was, as nothing should glint where racehorses worked; and I stood transfixed and breathless.

The escaping rider had dropped his *knife*.

No wonder he'd tried to retrieve it. I stared down at the thing which lay on the turf in front of my toes, and felt both awed and repelled. It was no ordinary knife. It had a wide double-edged blade about eight inches long, joined to a handle consisting of a bar with four finger holes like substantial rings attached to one side of it. The blade was steel and the grip yellowish, like dulled brass. Overall the knife, about a foot long, was thick, strong, frightening and infinitely deadly.

I looked up the hill. The lads still stood there, awaiting instructions.

One behaves as one is, I suppose. I returned to the truck, climbed into it and drove it round until it stood over the knife, so that no one could pick up that weapon or dislodge it; so that no horse could step on it and get cut.

Then I hopped into the back of the truck, set the camera rolling, and filmed the line of horsemen standing black against the risen sun.

Even though I was again staring unemployment in its implacable face, it seemed a shame to waste such a shot.

CHAPTER SEVEN

I rearranged the day.

Everyone returned to the stable yard except Moncrieff, whom I left stationed behind the steering wheel of the camera truck with strict instructions not to move the wheels even if it were demanded of him by irate men whose job it was to keep vehicles off the Heath. I had transgressed appallingly, I told him, by driving on the hallowed gallops. He was not to budge the truck an inch.

'Why not?'

I explained why not.

'Knife?' he said disbelievingly.

'Someone really did mean harm to Nash.'

'Impossible!' Moncrieff exclaimed, though more in protest than disbelief.

'Tennis players, skaters, John Lennon,' I said. 'Who's safe?'

'Shit.'

Without choice, though reluctantly, I phoned the police, headlines bannering themselves in my head – 'Jinx strikes Newmarket film again'. *Shit*, indeed. I met them in the stable yard where all the lads were waiting in groups and Ivan had come to grandiose terms with his possible nearness to injury.

The policemen who presently arrived were different from those who had come to attend Dorothea. I wondered how odd it would strike the force eventually to have been called to two knife incidents within twenty-four hours, however unconnected the events might appear. I wondered if they would realise I'd been on the scene of both.

Nash, beseeched by Ed, came out of the house in costume and make-up and stood side by side with Ivan. The policemen looked from one to the other and came, as we all had, to the only possible conclusion. In carefully matched riding breeches, tweed jacket and large buckled crash helmet, they looked from ten paces identical. Only the slash along the side of Ivan's jacket distinguished them easily.

I said to Nash, '*This* may put paid to the film.'

'No one is hurt.'

'Someone was out to get you.'

'They didn't manage it,' he said.

'You're pretty calm.'

'Thomas, I've lived through years of danger of this sort. We all do. The world's full of crazy fanatics. If you let it worry you, you'd never go out.' He looked across to where the police were writing down what the lads were telling them. 'Are we going on with today's work?'

I hesitated. 'How will Silva react?'

'Tough.'

I smothered a smile. 'Do you want to come out on the Heath and see what someone intended to stick into

you? And do you realise that from now on you have to
have a bodyguard?'

'No. I never have a bodyguard.'

'No bodyguard, no film. Very likely, no film anyway,
once Hollywood gets to hear of this.'

He looked at his watch. 'It's the middle of the night
over there.'

'You'll go on, then?'

'Yes, I will.'

'In that case, as soon as we can,' I said gratefully.

Ed came across and said the police wanted to speak
to the person really in charge. I went over: they were
both older than I and seemed to be looking around for
a father figure to relate to. I was not, it appeared, their
idea of authority. O'Hara would have fitted their bill.

The lads had told them that an extra horseman had
joined their group while they were haphazardly circling
after their third canter over the hill. They'd thought
nothing much of it, as with film-making the normal
routine of training-stable life was not adhered to. The
newcomer, dressed in jeans, anorak and crash helmet,
had blended in with themselves. It was only when Ivan's
horse had reared away, and Ivan himself had shouted
and fallen off, that they'd thought anything was wrong.
No one seemed to have seen the slash of the blade.

They couldn't do much towards describing the extra
man. Crash helmets with heavy chin straps effectively
hid half the face. The newcomer also, they remembered,
had been wearing jockey's goggles, as many of them
frequently did themselves to shield their eyes from dust
and kicked-up debris. They thought he might have been
wearing gloves: nothing unusual in that, either.

Had I anything to add, the police wanted to know.

'He could ride well,' I said.

They seemed to find that unimportant, being used to the many skills of Newmarket, though I thought it significant.

'He wasn't a jockey,' I said. 'He was too heavy. Too thickset.'

Description of features? I shook my head. I hadn't seen his face, only his back view galloping away.

I waited until they had let the lads and the camera crew disperse out of earshot before I told them about the knife.

We drove up the road to get as near as possible to the camera truck which still stuck out like an illegal sore thumb. Thanks only to its being Sunday, I guessed, no groundsmen were hopping up and down in rage. Leading the police vehicle, I took Nash with me in my car, breaking all the film company's rigid insurance instructions. What with one thing and another, who cared?

Moncrieff backed the camera truck ten feet. The police peered in silence at the revealed peril. Moncrieff looked shocked. Nash grew still.

'He dropped it,' I explained. 'He turned to come back for it. Then he saw me chasing him and decided on flight.'

Nash said, 'He lunged at Ivan with *that*?'

I nodded. 'You'll have a bodyguard from now on.'

He looked at me and made no further protest. One of the policemen produced a large paper bag and with care not to smudge possible fingerprints lifted the knife from the grass.

'There weren't any touts,' I remarked.

'What?' asked Nash.

'Every day except Sunday there are watchers down there on the edge of the town, with binoculars.' I pointed. 'Information is their trade. They know every horse on the Heath. They pass tit-bits of training progress to newspapermen and to bookmakers. If they'd only been here today, our knifeman wouldn't have been able to vanish so easily.'

One of the policemen nodded. 'So who knew, sir, that Mr Rourke would be out here this Sunday morning?'

'About sixty people,' I said. 'Everyone working on the film knows the shooting schedule a couple of days in advance.' I paused. 'There *were* a few people out watching, as there always are with film-making, but we have staff moving them away as far as possible if we don't want them in shot. Then, too, we started work today before sunrise.' I looked round the Heath. Despite our activity, few people were about. Cars went past us on the road without slowing. The Heath looked wide and peaceful, the last place for death.

As Nash had pointed out, no one had been hurt. The police took their notes, the knife and their possible theories back into Newmarket and, with a feeling of imminent doom sitting like vultures on our shoulders, I summoned the camera crews back to work and made the magical initial meeting of Nash and Silva come to life.

It was nearly three in the afternoon by the time we'd finished on the Heath. Just as I returned to the stables four large motor horseboxes arrived to transport to

Huntingdon racecourse all the horses, their saddles, bridles, rugs and other gear and their feed and bedding, besides the lads and their own travel bags. Our horse-master seemed to be managing fine. Despite the early morning upset everyone involved seemed to hum in a holiday mood.

O'Hara banished the temporary euphoria, arriving in the yard by car and scrambling out angrily to demand of me loudly, 'What in hell's teeth's going on?'

'Going to Huntingdon,' I said.

'*Thomas*. I'm not talking about goddam Huntingdon. It's on the car radio that some maniac attacked Nash with a knife. What in buggery happened?'

I tried to tell him but he was too agitated to listen.

'Where's Nash?' he demanded.

'In the house getting his make-up off.'

He strode impatiently away and through the house's rear door, leaving me to re-start the transportation and set the wagon-train rolling, even though the pioneers no longer sang.

Moncrieff was supposed to be having a rare after-noon off. I told him he deserved it and to scarper, which he rapidly did, hoping O'Hara wouldn't reappear too soon.

Alone for a change, I leaned against the bottom half of a stable door, listening to the unaccustomed silence and thinking of knives. Valentine's old voice murmured in my head . . . 'I left the knife with Derry . . .'

The world was full of knives.

Who was Derry?

O'Hara and Nash came out of the house together looking more cheerful than I'd feared.

'I spent half the night talking to Hollywood,' O'Hara announced. 'I reminded them that yanking the director in mid-film almost inevitably led to critical disaster, as reviewers always latch onto that fact firstly and spend most of their column speculating on how much better it would have been to have left things alone.'

'However untrue,' Nash commented dryly.

'In this case,' O'Hara told him firmly, 'you said, if I remember, that if they sacked Thomas they sacked you too.'

'Yeah. Crazy.'

O'Hara nodded. 'Anyway, I'll be plugging the line that the attack on the stuntman is *positive* publicity, not bad. By the time this movie gets to distribution, the public will be fired up to see it.'

He sounded, I thought, as though he had had to convince himself first, but I was certainly not going to argue.

I asked instead, 'Do you need me around, then, for the next several hours?'

'I guess not.' He sounded doubtful, stifling curiosity.

'Late Sunday afternoon,' I explained, 'is a fairly mellow time for surprise calls on farmers.'

O'Hara worked it out. 'Jackson Wells!'

'Right.' I turned to Nash. 'Do you want to meet the man you're playing?'

'No, I do *not*,' he said positively. 'I do *not* want to pick up the crusty mannerisms of some bitter old grouch.'

As I didn't want him to, either, I felt relieved rather than regretful. I said, 'I'll be back by ten this evening. I've a meeting scheduled then with Moncrieff and Ziggy Keene.'

135

'Ziggy who?' Nash asked.

'Stuntman,' I said. 'No one better on a horse.'

'Better than Ivan?'

I smiled. 'He costs ten times as much and he's worth twenty.'

'This beach business?' O'Hara asked.

I nodded.

'What beach business?' Nash wanted to know.

'Don't ask,' O'Hara told him humorously. 'Our boy has visions. Sometimes they work.'

'What vision?' Nash asked me,

'He can't tell you,' O'Hara answered for me. 'But when he sees it, so will we.'

Nash sighed. O'Hara went on, 'Talking of seeing, when will today's dailies be ready?'

'Tomorrow morning, as usual,' I assured him. 'When the van comes back.'

'Good.'

We were sending our exposed film to London every day by courier, to have it processed there overnight in a laboratory specialising in Technicolor. The film travelled each way in a London-based van, with the driver and an accompanying guard spending their nights in London and their days in Newmarket: and so far the arrangement had thankfully proved hitchless.

Each day, after seeing the previous day's rushes, I entered on a complicated chart the scenes and takes that I thought we should use on screen, roughly editing the film as I went along. It both clarified my own mind and saved a great deal of time in the overall editing period later on. Some directors liked to work with the film's appointed editor always at hand making decisions throughout on the dailies, but I preferred to do it myself, even if sometimes it took half the night, as it gave me more control over the eventual product. The rough cut, the bones and shape of the finished film, would be in that way my own work.

Stand or fall, my own work. Life on the leaning tower.

I set off westwards from Newmarket with only a vague idea of where I was headed and an even vaguer idea of what I would say when I got there.

Perhaps postponing the moment, but anyway because the city lay on my route, I drove first into Cambridge and stopped at the hospital housing Dorothea. Enquiries on the telephone had produced merely 'She's comfortable' reports, which could mean anything from near death to doped to the eyeballs and, predictably, my arrival at the nurses' desk gained me no access to their patient.

'Sorry, no visitors.'

Nothing would budge them. Positively no visitors, except for her son. I could probably speak to *him*, if I liked.

'Is he here?' I asked, wondering why I should be surprised. Nothing, after all, would unstick Paul from a full-blown crisis.

One of the nurses obligingly went to tell him of my presence, coming back with him in tow.

'Mother is not well enough to see you,' he announced proprietorially. 'Also, she is sleeping.'

We eyed each other in mutual dislike.

'How is she?' I asked. 'What do the doctors say?'

'She is in intensive care.' His bulletin voice sounded over-pompous, even for him.

I waited. In the end he amplified, 'Unless there are complications, she will recover.'

Great, I thought. 'Has she said who attacked her?'

'She is not yet lucid.'

I waited again, but this time without results. After he began to show signs of simply walking off to end the exchange, I said, 'Have you seen the state of her house?'

He answered with a frown, 'I went there this morning. The police took my fingerprints!' He sounded outraged.

'They took mine also,' I said mildly. 'Please return my books.'

'Do *what*?'

'Return Valentine's books and papers.'

He stared with a mixture of indignation and hatred. 'I didn't take Valentine's books. *You* did.'

'I did *not*.'

He glared righteously. 'Mother locked the door and refused – *refused* – to give me the key. Her own son!'

'The key was in the open door last night,' I said. 'And the books had gone.'

'Because *you* had taken them. I certainly did *not*.'

I began to believe his protestations of innocence, unlikely as they were.

But if he hadn't taken the things, who on earth had? The damage inside the house and the attack on Dorothea spoke of violence and speed. Moving a wall of books and cupboardfuls of papers out of the house spoke of thoroughness and time. And Robbie Gill had been sure the rampage had happened before the attack on Dorothea.

None of it made any sense.

'Why,' I asked, 'were you so extremely anxious to get your hands on those books?'

Somewhere in his brain warning bells sounded. I'd directed too many actors not to recognise the twitch of eye muscles that I'd so often prompted. Paul, I thought, had a motive beyond greed, but apart from seeing that it existed, I was not going to get any further.

'It's best to keep family possessions in the family,' he pontificated, and fired a final shot before stalking off. 'In view of my mother's condition, the cremation planned for tomorrow morning has been indefinitely postponed. And do not plague her or me by coming here again. She is old and frail and *I* will look after her.'

I watched his large back-view bustle away, self-importance in every stride, the fronts of his suit jacket swinging out sideways in the motion.

I called loudly after him, 'Paul!'

He stopped reluctantly and turned, standing four-square in the hospital passage and not returning. 'What is it now?'

A forty-two-inch waist at least, I thought. A heavy leather belt held up his dark grey trousers. Cream shirt, diagonally striped tie. The podgy chin tilted upwards aggressively.

'What do you want?'

'Nothing,' I said. 'Never mind.'

He shrugged heavily with exasperation, and I went

thoughtfully out to my car with my mind on telephones. I wore my mobile clipped to my belt, ready at all times. Paul, I'd noticed, carried a similar mobile, similarly clipped to his heavy belt.

Yesterday evening, I remembered, I'd been glad for Dorothea's sake that Paul had answered from his Surrey home when I'd told him of the attack on his mother. Surrey was rock-solid alibi land.

If I'd liked or even trusted Paul it wouldn't have occurred to me to check. As it was, I strove to remember the number I'd called, but could get no further than the first four digits and the last two, which wasn't going to connect me anywhere.

I rang the operator and asked if the four first numbers were a regional exchange in Surrey.

'No, sir,' a crisp female voice said. 'Those numbers are used for mobile telephones.'

Frozen, I asked if she could find me Paul Pannier's mobile number: he lived near Godalming; the last two digits were seven seven. Obligingly, after a short pause for searching, she told me the numbers I'd forgotten, and I wrote them down and made my call.

Paul answered curtly, 'Yes?'

I said nothing.

Paul said, 'Who are you? What do you want?'

I didn't speak.

'I can't hear you,' he said crossly, and switched off his instrument.

So much for Surrey, I thought grimly. But even Paul – *even Paul* – couldn't have slashed open his mother.

Sons had been known to murder their mothers . . .

But not fat forty-five-year-old men with inflated self-esteem.

Disturbed, I drove westwards to Oxfordshire and set about looking for Jackson Wells.

With help again from directory enquiries I discovered his general location and, by asking at garages and from people out walking dogs, I arrived in the end at Batwillow Farm, south of Abingdon, south of Oxford, sleepy and peaceful in the late Sunday afternoon.

I bumped slowly down a rutted unmade lane which ended in an untidy space outside a creeper-grown house. Weeds flourished. A set of old tyres leaned against a rotting wooden shed. An unsteady-looking stack of fencing timber seemed to be weathering into disintegration. A crusty old grouch of a man leaned on a farm gate and stared at me with disfavour.

Climbing out of the car and feeling depressed already, I asked, 'Mr Wells?'

'Eh?'

He was deaf.

'Mr Wells,' I shouted.

'Aye.'

'Can I talk to you?' I shouted

Hopeless, I thought.

The old man hadn't heard. I tried again. He merely stared at me impassively, and then pointed at the house.

Unsure of what he intended, I nevertheless walked across to the obvious point of access and pressed a conspicuous doorbell.

There was no gentle ding-dong as with Dorothea:

141

the clamour of the bell inside Batwillow Farm set one's teeth rattling. The door was soon opened by a fair young blonde girl with pony-tailed hair and to-die-for skin.

I said, 'I'd like to talk to Mr Jackson Wells.'

'OK,' she nodded. 'Hang on.' She retreated into a hallway and turned left out of my sight, prompting the appearance presently of a lean loose-limbed blond man looking less than fifty.

'You wanted me?' he enquired.

I looked back to where the old deaf grump still leaned on the gate.

'My father,' the blond man said, following my gaze.

'Mr Jackson Wells?'

'That's me,' he said.

'Oh!'

He grinned at my relief with an easy-going light-heartedness a hundred miles from my expectations. He waited, untroubled, for me to introduce myself, and then said slowly, 'Have I seen you somewhere before?'

'I don't think so.'

'On the television,' he said doubtfully.

'Oh. Well – were you watching the Lincoln at Doncaster yesterday?'

'Yes, I was, but . . .' He wrinkled his forehead, not clearly remembering.

'My name,' I said, 'is Thomas Lyon, and I was a friend of Valentine Clark.'

A cloud crossed Jackson Wells's sunny landscape.

'Poor old bugger died this week,' he said. My name finally registered. 'Thomas Lyon. Not him that's making the film?'

142

'Him,' I agreed.

'I did see you on the telly yesterday, then, with Nash Rourke.'

He summed me up in a short silence, and rubbed the top of his nose indecisively on the back of his hand.

I said, 'I don't want to do you any harm in the making of this film. I came to ask you if there is anything you particularly don't want said. Because sometimes,' I explained, 'one can invent things – or think one invents them – that turn out to be damagingly true.'

He thought it over and finally said, 'You'd better come in, I reckon.'

'Thank you.'

He led me into a small room near the door; a room unlived in and furnished only with an upright piano, a piano stool, a hard wooden chair and a closed cupboard. He himself sat on the piano stool and waved me to the chair.

'Do you play?' I asked civilly, indicating the piano.

'My daughter does. Lucy, you met her.'

'Mm,' I nodded. I took a breath; said, 'Actually, I came to ask you about Yvonne.'

'Who?'

'Yvonne. Your wife.'

'Sonia,' he said heavily. 'Her name was Sonia.'

'It was Yvonne in Howard Tyler's book.'

'Aye,' he agreed. 'Yvonne. I read it. The book.'

He seemed to feel no anger or grief, so I asked, 'What did you think of it?'

Unexpectedly, he laughed. 'Load of rubbish. Dream

lovers! And that upper-class wimp in the book, that was supposed to be me! Cobblers.'

'You're going to be far from a wimp in the film.'

'Is it true, then? Nash Rourke is *me*?'

'He's the man whose wife is found hanged, yes.'

'You know what?' The sunniness shone in his manner and the smile in his eyes surely couldn't be faked. 'It's all so bloody long ago. I don't give a piss what you say in the film. I can hardly remember Sonia, and that's a fact. It was a different life. I left it behind. Did a bunk, if you like. I got fed up with the whole bloody shooting match. See, I was twenty-two when I married Sonia and not yet twenty-five when she died, and I was only a kid really. A kid playing at being a big Newmarket racehorse trainer. After that business, people started taking their horses away, so I packed it in and came here instead, and this life's OK, mate, no regrets.'

As he seemed to discuss it quite easily I asked, 'Why ... er ... why did your wife die?'

'Call her Sonia. I don't think of her as my wife. My wife's here in this house. Lucy's mother. We've been wed twenty-three years now and we'll stay that way.'

There was an obvious self-contentment in his whole personality. He had the weathered complexion and thread-veined cheeks of an outdoors man, his eyebrows dramatically blond against the tanned skin. Blue eyes held no guile. His teeth looked naturally good, even and white. No tension showed in his long limbs or sturdy neck. I thought him no great brain, but one of nature's lucky accidents, a person who could be happy with little.

144

'Do you mind me asking about her?' I said.

'Sonia? Not really. I can't tell you why she died, though, because I don't know.'

That was, I thought, the first lie he'd told me.

'The police had me in,' he smiled. 'Helping with their enquiries, they told the press. So of course everyone thought I'd done it. Questions! Days of them. I just said I didn't know why she died. I said it over and over. They did go on a bit. They thought they'd get me to confess, see?' He laughed. 'Seems they do sometimes get fools to confess to things they haven't done. I can't see how that happens, can you? If you haven't done something, you just keep on saying it. In England, leastwise. No actual thumbscrews, see? They ban actual thumbscrews here, see?' He laughed again at his joke. 'I told them to piss off and find out who really killed her, but they never managed *that*. They couldn't see farther than getting me to confess. I mean, it was daft. Would *you* confess to murdering someone if you hadn't?'

'I don't think so.'

''Course you wouldn't. Hour after hour of it! I stopped listening. I wouldn't let them work me up into a state. I just sat there like a lump and told them to piss off at regular intervals.'

'They must have loved it,' I said dryly.

'You're taking the mickey!'

'Indeed, I'm not,' I assured him. 'I think you were great.'

'I was young,' he said cheerfully. 'They kept waking me up in the night. Silly sods didn't realise I was often up half the night with sick horses. Colic. Stuff like that.

I just nodded off when they frothed on about Sonia. It narked them no end.'

'Mm,' I agreed, and asked tentatively, 'Did you *see* . . . Sonia . . . I mean . . . er . . .'

'Did I see her hanging? No, I didn't. I saw her in the morgue, hours after they took her down. They'd made her look peaceful by then.'

'So it wasn't you who found her?'

'No. Reckon I was lucky, there. One of my stable lads found her while I was driving north to York races. The police drove me back and they'd already decided I'd killed her. She'd been in a box we weren't using at that point. The lad that found her brought his food up for a week after, poor sod.'

'Did you think she'd hanged herself?'

'It wasn't like her.' He showed a very long-lived old doubt. 'There was a stack of hay bales there she could have jumped off of.' He shook his head. 'No one ever did know the truth of it and, tell you no lie, it's better that way. I read in that *Drumbeat* rag that you're trying to find out. Well, I'd just as soon you didn't, to be honest. I don't want my wife and Lucy stirred up. Not fair to them, it isn't. You just get on and make up what story you like for your film. As long as you don't make out I killed her, it'll be all right with me.'

'In the film you do *not* kill her,' I said.

'That's fine, then.'

'But I have to say why she died.'

He said without heat, 'I told you, I don't know why she died.'

'Yes, I know you did, but you must have *thought* about it.'

146

He gave me an unadulteratedly carefree smile and no information, and I had a clear picture of what the interrogating police had faced all those years ago: a happy unbroachable brick wall.

'In Howard Tyler's book,' I said, 'Yvonne daydreams about jockey lovers. Where ... I mean ... have you any idea where he got that idea?'

Internally this time, Jackson Wells laughed. 'Howard Tyler didn't ask me about that.'

'No,' I agreed. 'He told me he hadn't tried to see you at all.'

'No, he didn't. First I knew of it, people were saying that that book, *Unstable Times*, was about me and Sonia.'

'And did she ... well ... daydream?'

Again the secret, intense amusement. 'I don't know,' he said. 'She might have done. That whole marriage, it was a sort of make-believe. We were kids playing at grown-ups. That writer, he got us dead wrong. I'm not complaining, mind.'

'But the dream lovers are so striking,' I persisted. 'Where did he get the idea?'

Jackson Wells thought it over without any apparent anxiety.

'I reckon,' he told me at length, 'you should ask that stuck-up sister of hers.'

'Sister ... do you mean Rupert Visborough's widow?'

He nodded. 'Audrey. Sonia's sister. Audrey was married to a member of the Jockey Club and never let me forget it. Audrey told Sonia not to waste herself on me. I wasn't good enough for her, see?' He grinned, not

147

caring. 'When I read that book I heard Audrey's prissy voice all through it.'

Stunned by the simple depth of that perception I sat in silence wondering what to ask him next; wondering whether I should or could ask why the hanging death of an obscure young sister-in-law had so thoroughly and permanently blighted Rupert Visborough's chances of political life.

How unacceptable in Westminster, in fact, were mysteriously dead relations? Disreputable family misfortunes might prove an embarrassment, but if the sins of sons and daughters could be forgiven, surely the more distant unsolved death should have been but a hiccup.

Before I'd found the words, the door opened to reveal Lucy, sunny like her father.

'Mum wants to know if you want anything, like for instance drinks.'

I took it as the dismissal Mum had intended, and stood up.

Jackson Wells introduced me to his daughter with 'Lucy, this is Thomas Lyon, the personification-of-evil film-maker, according to yesterday's *Drumbeat*.'

Her eyes widened and, with her father's quiet mischief, she said, 'I saw you on the telly with no horns or tails in sight! How cool to be making a film with Nash Rourke.'

I said, 'Do you want to be in it?'

'What do you mean?'

I explained that we were recruiting the local inhabitants of Huntingdon to be 'crowd' at our version of a race meeting held on the course.

'We need people to ooh and aah . . .'

'And scream "shift your arse"?' she grinned.

'Exactly.'

'Dad?'

Her father's instinct was to say no. As he shook his head I said, 'No one needs to know who you are. Give your name as Batwillow . . . and, incidentally, what is a batwillow?'

'A tree you make cricket bats from,' Lucy said, as if my question revealed my stupidity.

'You're kidding me?'

'Certainly not,' her father said. 'Where do you think cricket bats come from? They grow on trees.'

They watched my face. 'We grow the willows in wetlands near the brook,' he said. 'This farm has grown batwillows for generations.'

Growing cricket bats, it seemed to me, entirely fitted his nature: wide shoulders hitting carefree sixes over the boundary with fast balls solidly blocked to prevent the breaking of the wicket.

Lucy's mother appeared with curiosity in the doorway, a friendly woman in fawn trousers and an enormous brown sweater over a cream polo-neck. Unconscious style, I thought, just like her daughter.

Jackson Wells explained my presence. His wife enjoyed the tale.

'Of course, we'll all come,' she said decisively, 'if you promise we'll see Nash Rourke!'

'How corny can you get?' Lucy demanded of her.

I said, 'Tomorrow at two o'clock we hold crowd rehearsals. Nash might be there, can't promise. On Tuesday and Wednesday we shoot the crowd scenes.

We offer breakfast, lunch and expenses to everyone who turns up, and Nash Rourke will definitely be there.'

'It's near a two-hour drive from here to Huntingdon racecourse,' Jackson Wells protested.

'You're outvoted, Dad,' Lucy told him. 'What time Tuesday? Would it be OK if we miss tomorrow's rehearsal?'

I gave them one of my cards, writing on the back 'Priority entry. Batwillow family.' 'Nine in the morning, on Tuesday,' I said. 'Follow the crowd, who'll know what to do. When we break for lunch, use this card, and find me.'

'Wow,' Lucy said.

She had freckles on her nose. Quizzical blue eyes. I wondered how mature she was on the piano.

I said to her father, 'Do you know why anyone would do violence to get this film abandoned?'

He answered blandly, 'Like I heard on the radio? Someone tried to take a knife to your star? Total madman. To my knowledge, no one's afraid of your film.'

I thought that that was probably the second lie he'd told me, or at least the second I'd noticed.

Lucy said, 'Can Dad's brother come as well?'

Her father made a dismissive gesture and said, 'He wouldn't want to.'

'Yes, he would.' To me she said, 'My Uncle Ridley lives in Newmarket. He goes to the cinema all the time, and he'd *rave* to be in a film with Nash Rourke.'

'Then bring him in with you,' I agreed. 'We need the largest crowd we can get.'

Her parents, I saw, didn't share her enthusiasm for her Uncle Ridley.

'Is he free,' I asked, fishing, 'to spend a day at Huntingdon on Tuesday or Wednesday?'

Lucy guilelessly answered, 'Uncle Ridley bums around, Dad says.'

Her father shook his head at her shortage of worldliness and amplified, 'My brother Ridley breaks in horses and acts as a general nagsman. He's not exactly high-powered, but he makes a living.'

I smiled, half interested. 'I'll be glad to meet him.' I paused, and returned to what more closely concerned me. 'Could you lend me a photo of ... er ... Sonia? Just so we don't make Yvonne too like her in the film.'

'Haven't got one,' Jackson Wells said promptly.

'Not even ... Excuse me,' I said to Mrs Wells apologetically, '... not even a wedding photo?'

'No,' Jackson Wells said. 'They got lost when I moved here.' His eyes were wide with innocence, and for the third time I didn't believe him.

CHAPTER EIGHT

Driving towards Newmarket and working out times, I thought I might squeeze in an empty half-hour before my ten o'clock meeting, and accordingly telephoned Dr Robbie Gill, whose number I did remember clearly from Dorothea's heavy black help-summoning handwriting.

'Do you feel,' I asked, 'like a quick jar somewhere?'

'When?'

I'd worked it out. 'I'm in my car. I'll hit Newmarket around nine-thirty. Any good? I have to be at Bedford Lodge at ten.'

'Is it important?'

'Interesting,' I said. 'About Dorothea's attacker.'

'I'll square it with my wife.' His voice smiled, as if that were no problem. 'I'll come to Bedford Lodge at nine-thirty and wait in the lounge.'

'Great.'

'I heard someone attacked Nash Rourke with a knife.'

'As good as. It was his stand-in, though. And no harm done.'

'So I gathered. Nine-thirty, then.'

He clicked off, his Scottish voice as brusque as ever: and red-headed and terrier-like, he was patiently waiting in the entrance lounge when I got back to Bedford Lodge.

'Come upstairs,' I said, shaking his hand. 'What do you drink?'

'Diet coke.'

I got room service to bring up his fizzy tipple and for myself poured cognac from a resident bottle. This film, I thought fleetingly, was driving me towards forty per cent proof.

'Well,' I said, waving him to an armchair in the neat sitting-room, 'I went to see Dorothea in Cambridge this afternoon and found my way barred by our friend Paul.'

Robbie Gill grimaced. 'She's basically my patient, and he's barring my way too, as far as possible.'

'What can I do to preserve her from being shanghaied by him as soon as she's capable of being transported by ambulance? She told him, and me, that she didn't want to move into this retirement home he's arranging for her, but he pays no attention.'

'He's a pest.'

'Can't you slap a "don't move this patient" notice on Dorothea?'

He considered it doubtfully. 'No one would move her at present. But a few days from now . . .'

'Any which way,' I said.

'How much do you care?'

'A good deal.'

'I mean . . . moneywise.'

I looked at him over my brandy glass. 'Are you saying that an application of funds might do the trick?'

He replied forthrightly, as was his Scottish nature. 'I'm saying that as her doctor I could, with her permission, shift her into a private nursing home of my choice if I could guarantee the bills would be paid.'

'Would it break me?'

He mentioned an alarming sum and waited without censure for me to find it too much.

'You have no obligation,' he remarked.

'I'm not poor, either,' I said. 'Don't tell her who's paying.'

He nodded. 'I'll say it's free on the National Health. She'll accept that.'

'Go ahead, then.'

He downed his diet coke. 'Is that the lot?'

'No,' I said. 'If I draw something for you, tell me what you think.' I took a large sheet of writing paper, laid it on the coffee table, and drew a picture of the knife I'd found on the Heath. A wickedly knobbed hand grip on eight sharp inches of steel.

He looked at the drawing in motionless silence.

'Well?' I asked.

'A knuckle-duster,' he said, 'that grew into a knife.'

'And Dorothea's injuries?' I suggested. He stared at me. I said, 'Not two assailants. Not two weapons. This one, that's both a blunt instrument *and* a blade.'

'Dear God.'

'Who would own such a thing?' I asked him. He shook his head mutely.

'Do you know anyone called Derry?'

He looked completely perplexed.

I said, 'Valentine once mentioned leaving a knife with someone called Derry.'

Robbie Gill frowned, thinking. 'I don't know any Derry.'

I sighed. Too many people knew nothing.

He said abruptly, 'How old are you?'

'Thirty. And you?'

'Thirty-six.' He smiled wryly. 'Too old to conquer the world.'

'So am I.'

'Ridiculous!'

'Steven Spielberg,' I said, 'was twenty-seven when he made *Jaws*. I'm not him. Nor Visconti, nor Fellini, nor Lucas. Just a jobbing storyteller.'

'And Alexander the Great died at thirty-three.'

'Of diet coke?' I asked.

He laughed. 'Is it true that in America, if you die of old age, it's your fault?'

I nodded gravely. 'You should have jogged more. Or not smoked, or checked your cholesterol, or abstained from the juice.'

'And then what?'

'And then you exist miserably for years with tubes.'

He laughed and rose to go. 'I'm embarrassed,' he said, 'but my wife wants Nash Rourke's autograph.'

'Done,' I promised. 'How soon can you realistically move Dorothea?'

He thought it over. 'She was attacked yesterday evening. She's been sleepy from anaesthetic all day today. It was a bad wound ... they had to remove part of the intestine before repairing the abdomen wall. If it all goes well she'll be fully awake tomorrow and briefly on her feet the day after, but I'd say it will be another week before she could travel.'

'I'd like to see her,' I said. 'The wretched Paul must sleep *sometimes*.'

'I'll fix it. Phone me tomorrow evening.'

Moncrieff, Ziggy Keene and I set off at four-thirty the next morning, heading north and east to the Norfolk coast.

Ed, instructed by O'Hara, had found me a driver, a silent young man who took my car along smoothly and followed the instructions I gave him as I map-read beside him in the front passenger seat.

Moncrieff and Ziggy slept in the back. Into the boot we'd packed the heavy camera Moncrieff could carry on his shoulders like a toy, also a cold-box full of raw film and a hot-box full of coffee and breakfast. The outside air was cold; the warm car soporific. I was glad, after a while, of the driver.

We cleared Norwich and headed across the flat lands towards the North Sea, skirting the Broads and sliding eventually through the still-sleeping village of Happisburgh and slowing down a narrow lane that ended in sand dunes.

Moncrieff and Ziggy climbed stiffly out of the car and shivered. It was still completely dark outside the range of the car's lights, and the coastal breeze was as unrelenting as ever.

'You said to bring warm clothes,' Moncrieff complained, zipping himself into a fur-lined parka. 'You said nothing about playing Inuits.' He pulled the fur-lined hood over his head and thrust his hands into Arctic-issue gauntlets.

156

Leaving the driver with his own separate breakfast in the car, the three of us walked onwards through the sand dunes towards the open shore, Moncrieff carrying the camera and the film box, I leading with the hot-box and Ziggy between us toting polystyrene rectangles for sitting insulation on cold salt-laden ground.

'How did you find this godforsaken place?' Moncrieff grumbled.

'I used to come here as a boy.'

'Suppose it had sprouted casinos?'

'I checked.'

Beyond the range of the car's lights we paused to establish night vision, then went on slowly until the sand dunes fell away, the breeze freshened, and the sound of the restless waves spoke of timeless desolation.

'OK,' I said, 'if there's any shelter, sit in it.'

Moncrieff groaned, took a pallet from Ziggy and folded himself with oaths into a shallow hollow on the sea side of the last dune. Ziggy, tougher and taciturn, found a similar place near him.

Ziggy, Ukrainian by birth, had from the nursery proved so spectacularly acrobatic on horses that he had been sent to the Moscow Circus school at the age of eight, and there, far from his rural roots, had received a first class education along with endless practice in his special skill. Every pupil in the school, boys and girls alike, received daily ballet lessons to teach graceful movement in the circus ring. Ziggy could in consequence have joined any ballet company anywhere, but nothing interested him except horses.

Ziggy at twenty-two had left the circus behind:

circuses everywhere had left town. Never political, though a favoured son, he had somehow travelled with his trade to America, and it was there that I'd seen him first, turning somersaults on a cantering horse one afternoon in an ill-attended practice for the Ringling Brothers in Madison Square Garden.

I'd offered him a job in my rodeo film and, despite union protests, I'd secured him. I'd shortened his unpronounceable surname to Keene, and he'd quickly earned such a brilliant reputation in the horse stunt business that nowadays I had to beg him for his time.

Slender, light and wiry, he took the Norfolk chill in his stride. Child's play, I supposed, after the Russian steppes. Alternately morose and laughing, he was intensely Ukrainian in temperament, and often told me he would return soon to his roots, a threat receding as years passed. His roots, as perhaps he acknowledged, were no longer there.

At a fairly brief meeting the evening before, I'd outlined what we were looking for.

'Film the sunrise!' Moncrieff exclaimed lugubriously, 'We don't have to drive seventy miles for that! What's wrong with the Heath outside the door?'

'You'll see.'

'And the weather forecast?'

'Cold, windy and clear.'

His objections, I knew, were not from the heart. Every lighting cameraman knew that directors could be both unreasonable and unmovable when it came to specific locations. If I'd demanded the slopes of K2, he would have sworn and strapped on his crampons.

I said, 'As it's the time of the vernal equinox, the sun

will rise due east. And that' – I consulted the small compass I'd brought – 'is straight over there.' I pointed. 'At the moment, looking directly out to sea, we are facing a bit further north. The coast runs from north-west to south-east, so when the sun rises, horses galloping along the sand from our left will be back-lit, but will also have the sun very slightly in their faces.'

Moncrieff nodded.

'Can you catch gleams of sun in their eyes?'

'Close?'

'Heads, necks and manes in shot.'

'Thomas,' Ziggy said, the bass notes in his voice always a surprise from the slightness of his body, 'you ask for wild horses.'

I'd asked him the previous evening to picture them and to suggest where we might find some. The trouble with sudden visions was that I'd had no idea of the scene while we were at the pre-production stage, and so had not arranged a wild herd in advance. Wild horses didn't grow on batwillows.

Circus horses, Ziggy had said. Too fat and sleek, I'd objected. Moorland ponies no good, he'd said: too slow and stupid. Think, I'd urged him. Tell me in the morning.

'Thomas,' Ziggy said, as always emphasising the second syllable of my name, 'I think it must be *Viking* horses, from Norway.'

I gazed at him. 'Did you know that Viking ships once regularly raided this coast?'

'Yes, Thomas.'

Viking horses. Perfect. Where on earth could I get any? From Norway, of course. So easy.

I asked him, 'Have you ever worked with Norwegian horses?'

'No, Thomas. But I think they are not true wild. They are not ridden, but they are, I think, handled.'

'Could you ride one without a saddle?'

'Of course.' There wasn't a horse alive, his expression said, that wouldn't do what he asked.

'You could ride one in a nightgown and a long blonde wig?'

'Of course.'

'Bare feet?'

He nodded.

'The woman is *dreaming* she is riding the wild horse. It must be romantic, not real.'

'Thomas, she will *float* on the horse.'

I believed him. He was simply the best. Even Moncrieff stopped grumbling about our mission.

We ate our hot vacuum-packed bacon breakfast rolls and drank steaming coffee while the black sky slowly greyed and lightened and grew softly crimson far out at sea.

With adjusted eyes we watched the world take shape. Around us and at our backs the irregularly heaped sand dunes were revealed as being patches of scrubby marram grass, fringes of long dried stalks leaning in the wind. Slightly below us the sand remained powdery, unwashed by the tide, but blowing back to add to the dunes; and below that, hard-packed sand stretched away to distant white-fringed waves.

The tide, I reckoned, was as low as it ever went. Too low, really, for the best dramatic effect. One week ahead, the tide at dawn would be high, covering the sand. We needed, I thought, to arrange to film the horses on a mid-tide day: better, I supposed, during an ebb tide, as a flooding tide could race over these flat sands and maroon the cameras. Say ten days to the next mid-tide ebb at dawn. Too soon. Add two weeks to the next opportunity; twenty-four days. Perhaps.

I told Ziggy the time frame. 'We need the horses here on the beach twenty-four days from now. Or else fourteen days later; thirty-eight days. OK?'

'I understand,' he agreed.

'I'll send an agent to Norway to arrange the horses and the transport. Will you go with him, to make sure we get the sort of horses we need?'

He nodded. 'Best to have ten,' he said. 'Or twelve.'

'See what you can find.'

Moncrieff stirred, abandoning breakfast in favour of art. Faint horizontal threads of clouds were growing a fiercer red against the still grey sky, and as he busied himself with camera speed and focus, the streaks intensified to scarlet and to orange and to gold, until the whole sky was a breath-gripping symphony of sizzling colour, the prelude to the earth's daily spin towards the empowerment of life.

I had always loved sunrise: was always renewed in spirit. For all my life I'd felt cheated if I'd slept through dawn The primaeval winter solstice on bitter Salisbury Plain had raised my childhood's goose pimples long before I understood why; and it had ever seemed to me that dawn-worship was the most logical of primitive beliefs.

The glittering ball rimmed over the horizon and hurt one's eyes. The brilliant streaks of cloud flattened to grey. The whole sun, somehow losing its magic, nevertheless lit a shimmering pathway across the ruffled surface of the sea, and Moncrieff went on filming, breathing deeply with satisfaction. Slowly on the wind, he and I became aware of a deep rhythmic humming that grew into a melody seeming age-old and sad: and as if of one mind we understood and laughed.

Ziggy was *singing*.

This was a dangerous coast as, flat as it looked, a few miles out to sea unrelenting sandbars paralleled the shore; underwater invisible hazards, shipwrecking the unwary. Graveyards in the coastal villages were heaped with memorials to sailors drowned before accurate depth charts were invented.

Too much background music, I decided, would ruin the atmospheric quality of this historic shore. All we would need would be the wind, the waves, the clip of the horses' hooves, and perhaps Ziggy's own distant song, or maybe a haunting plaintive chant from Norway. This was to be a dream: did one ever hear whole orchestras in dreams?

Fulfilled in all sorts of ways, the three of us were driven back to Newmarket where everyday reality returned to the hotel lobby in the unwelcome shape of our author, Howard Tyler.

Howard was not repentant but incensed. The round glasses flashed as if with their own anger. The prissy little mouth puckered with injured feelings of injustice. Howard the great writer could produce temper tantrums like a toddler.

Moncrieff, at the sight of him, evaporated into the woodwork. Ziggy, communing only with himself, loped off on foot towards the Heath and horses. Howard stood in my path, flushed with grievance.

'O'Hara says the company will sue me for breach of contract!' he complained. 'It's not *fair*.'

I said reasonably, 'But you *did* breach your contract.'

'No, I didn't!'

'Where did the *Drumbeat* get its opinions from?'

Howard opened his baby lips and closed them again.

'Your contract,' I reminded him, 'forbids you to talk about the film to outsiders. I did warn you.'

'But O'Hara can't sue me!'

I sighed. 'You signed with a major business corporation, not personally with O'Hara. The corporation has lawyers with flints for souls whose job it is to recover for the company any money they can squeeze from the most minor breaches of contract. They are not kind compassionate fellows who will pat you forgivingly on the back. They can imagine damages you never thought of. You opened your undisciplined mouth to some avidly listening ear, and whether you've done any real box-office damage or not, they're going to act as if you've cost the company millions, and they'll try to recover every penny they are contracted to pay you, and if you're really unlucky, more.'

It seemed finally to get through to him that his gripe would prove expensive.

'Then *do* something,' he insisted. 'Tell them no harm was done.'

'You as near as dammit cost me not just this job but any work in the future.'

163

'All I said was . . .' his voice died.

'All you said was that I was a tyrannical buffoon wasting the film company's money.'

'Well . . . I didn't mean it.'

'That's almost worse.'

'Yes . . . but . . . you've *mangled* my book. And as an author I have *moral* rights.' The air of triumph accompanying these last words made my next statement sound perhaps more brutal than I would have let it if he'd shown the slightest regret.

With vanishing patience I said, 'Moral rights give an author the right to object to derogatory alterations being made to his work. Moral rights can be waived, and invariably this waiver is included in agreements between screenplay writers and film production companies. Often the screenplay writer is given the right to remove his name from the credits if he hates the film enough, but in your case, Howard, it's your name they're specifically paying for, and you waived that right also.'

Stunned, he asked, 'How do you know?'

'I was given a sight of your contract. I had to know where we each stood.'

'*When?*' he demanded. 'When did you see it?'

'Before I signed a contract myself.'

'You mean . . . *weeks* ago?'

'Three months or more.'

He began to look bewildered. 'Then . . . what can I do?'

'Pray,' I said dryly. 'But for a start, you can say who you talked to. You can say how you got in touch with the writer of "Hot from the Stars". Who did you reach?'

164

'But I . . .' He seemed not far from tears. 'I *didn't*. I mean, I didn't tell the *Drumbeat*. I didn't.'

'Who, then?'

'Well, just a friend.'

'A *friend*? And the friend told the *Drumbeat*?'

He said miserably, 'I suppose so.'

We had been standing all this time in the lobby with Monday morning coming and going around us. I waved him now towards the lounge area and found a pair of convenient armchairs.

'I want some coffee,' he said, looking round for a waiter.

'Have some later, I haven't got time. Who did you talk to?'

'I don't think I should say.'

I felt like shaking him. 'Howard, I'll throw you to the corporation wolves. And besides that, I'll sue you personally for defamation.'

'She said questions weren't libellous.'

'She, whoever she is, got it at least half wrong. I don't want to waste time and energy suing you, Howard, but if you don't cough up some answers pronto you'll get a writ in tomorrow's mail.' I took a breath. 'So, who is *she*?'

After a long pause in which I hoped he faced a few realities, he said, 'Alison Visborough.'

'Who?'

'Alison Vis – '

'Yes, yes,' I interrupted. 'I thought her name was Audrey.'

'That's her mother.'

I shook my head to clear it, feeling I'd left my senses back on Happisburgh beach.

165

'Let's get this straight,' I said. 'You poured out your grudges to Alison Visborough, whose mother is Audrey Visborough, who is the widow of the deceased Rupert Visborough, known in your book as Cibber. Right so far?'

He nodded unhappily.

'And,' I said, 'when you read Rupert Visborough's obituary, and got the idea for your book, you did *not* go to see Jackson Wells, whose wife hanged, but you *did* go to see the dead woman's sister, Audrey Visborough.'

'Well . . . I suppose so.'

'Yes or no?'

'Yes.'

'And it was she who told you about her sister having dream lovers?'

'Er . . .'

'*Howard!*'

'Look,' he said, with a recurrence of petulance, 'I don't have to answer all these questions.'

'Why ever not?'

'They wouldn't like it.'

'Audrey and Alison wouldn't, do you mean?'

He nodded. 'And Roddy.'

'Who's Roddy?'

'Alison's brother.'

Give me strength, I thought. I said, 'Is this right? Rupert Visborough married Audrey; they had a daughter Alison and a son Roddy?'

'I don't see why you make it sound so difficult.'

'But you didn't put the children in your book.'

'They're not *children*,' Howard objected. 'They're as old as I am.'

166

Howard was forty-five.

'When you bitched to Alison,' I asked, 'why did she get your complaints printed in the *Drumbeat*? And how?'

He stood up abruptly. 'I didn't know she was going to do it. I didn't ask her to. If you want to know, I was shocked when I read the paper. I didn't mean what I said to her to be published like that.'

'Have you talked to her since?'

He said defensively, 'She thought she was helping me.'

'Shit,' I said.

He took offence and stalked off, heading for the way out to the world.

With a feeling of medium irritation I went upstairs and found my message light flashing. O'Hara, it seemed, would be pleased by my appearance in his suite.

I walked the carpeted passages. 'Did you know,' he asked, opening his door to my knock, 'that Howard is back?'

We discussed Howard. O'Hara's use of words was profligate.

'Howard told me,' I said, only half successfully damming O'Hara's flow, 'that he poured out his woes to a lady friend who promptly relayed them to the *Drumbeat* but without his knowledge.'

'What?'

I told O'Hara about the Visboroughs.

He repeated in disbelief, '*Audrey, Alison and Roddy?*'

'And God knows who else.'

'Howard,' he pronounced heavily, 'is off his trolley.'

'He's naive. Doesn't make him a bad writer.'

O'Hara agreed gloomily. 'Dream lovers are naive.' He thought things over. 'I'll have to discuss his breach of contract again with the moguls. I suppose you've never met this disastrous Alison?'

I shook my head.

'Someone will have to switch on her lights.'

'Mm,' I paused. 'You?'

O'Hara ducked it. 'What time do you have, yourself?'

'Oh, no,' I protested. 'We know her opinion of *me*.'

'All the same,' O'Hara smiled, 'if you want to, you can charm the birds off the trees.'

'I don't know where she lives.'

'I'll find out,' he promised, 'and you can do the damage control.'

He seemed all of a sudden happier. Suing Howard would have dragged on and on and could well have alienated the very lending-library customers his name was supposed to attract into the cinema. Never attack anyone, old Valentine had once written, unless you've counted the cost of winning.

O'Hara asked if I'd found Jackson Wells, but seemed disappointed in the sweetness and light of his household.

'Do you think he murdered his wife?' he asked curiously.

'No one could ever prove it.'

'But do *you* think he did?'

I paused. 'I don't know.'

O'Hara shrugged the thought away and, as he wanted to see the previous day's rushes, we drove along to the stable yard. There, in the vast house, one small room had been rigged for projection, with a screen and six chairs but no luxury. The windows were blacked out to foil peepers, and the reels of previously printed film were secured in racks in there by every fancy lock and fireproofing invented. The moguls had in this case spent lavishly: no one could afford to start shooting all over again.

That morning I worked the projector myself. O'Hara sat impassively while the horses galloped up the training hill and breasted it into sunlight. I'd been right, I saw, about the third attempt, and my flourish of trumpets looked great. Moncrieff had stopped the cameras after that. The only shot left on the reel was the one I'd made myself; the line of horses on the skyline, black against sunshine. The worst of luck, I thought, that with all that raw film in our possession, we had no footage at all that included the rider whose frightful knife had slashed at Ivan.

O'Hara cursed over it, but hindsight, as always, was an unfruitful regret.

I left that reel for the regular projectionist to rewind, and set going the stuff we'd done later, the 'first meeting' of Nash and Silva.

As always with dailies, the sound quality was imperfect; marrying the eventual soundtrack to the pictures came later, in the post-production stage. Dailies, in any case, with two or three or more takes printed of a single scene, could only be judged by experts, rather like wine buyers discerning an eventual vintage in the harsh juice straight from fermentation. O'Hara even made appropriate sucking noises with his teeth as he watched Silva

169

joltingly rein-in her horse, nearly knocking down Nash as he, the trainer, stood near his own horses; watched her dismount, jerk off her helmet and speak her lines with the character's initial aggravation awakening to quick sexual interest; watched the smile curve the blissful mouth in a way that would quadruple her sticker price next time out.

'Good girl,' O'Hara murmured, pleased.

Nash, bareheaded in riding clothes, did his own lines in platinum, close to priceless.

Howard, goaded into writing this scene, which had of course not appeared in the book, had nevertheless written exchanges of a quality entirely to justify his high placing in the film's credits. Moncrieff had lit the faces with creative skill and had, as agreed, shot the horses slightly out of focus to give sharp prominence to each human figure in close-up. Somehow the uncaring, oblivious nature of the horses lent contrast and comment to the vivid emotion developing near them. A brief, fleeting impression, but an addition to the mood. Not bad, overall.

The reel ended, I switched the projector off and the regular lights on and waited for O'Hara's verdict.

'Tell you something,' he said casually, 'if you're not careful we'll have a success on our hands.'

'A bit early to say.' I was pleased, all the same, at his compliment.

'How do you get on personally with Silva?' O'Hara asked, standing and stretching, preparing to leave.

'She does ride very well,' I said. 'I told her that I thought so.'

'And you did not, I hope, tell her she rides as well as any man.'

I laughed. 'I'm not suicidal.'

'She looks good on screen.'

I nodded. 'You were right, she can act. She knows where the camera is. She's professional, she listens to me, she did the nude scene on the closed set last week with cool naturalness, she's ambitious in a sensible way and I can tiptoe round the feminism.'

'And do you like her?'

'It's not necessary.'

'No, but do you?'

I smiled. 'If I told her I liked her she'd smack my face.'

'That's no answer.'

'Then yes, I do like her. Actually, very much. But she doesn't want to be liked. She wants to be thought a good actress. Which she is. A merry-go-round, don't you think?'

'She's sleeping with me,' O'Hara said.

I looked, in a moment of stillness, at the craggy strength of his face and physique, understood the magnetic sexual quality of power, and said without resentment, 'Are you telling me, hands off?'

He calmly nodded. 'Hands off.'

'OK.'

He made no more of it. It altered little. We went upstairs to see how far the art director and his department had gone with dismantling the Jockey Club enquiry-room set, ready to construct an approximation of the Athenaeum dining-room in the space.

Several of the upstairs walls had earlier been removed, with steel joists now holding up the roof. Many of the ceilings also had been cut out to allow for overhead lights and cameras. The house's owner was warming himself with his nicely stuffed bank account while trusting his beams and plaster would reassert themselves later.

The Athenaeum dining-room remained embryonic but would be ready with tables, waiters and roast beef on our return from Huntingdon.

O'Hara said, 'I met Moncrieff in the passage at the hotel this morning after you returned from the ocean. Incredibly, he was *humming*. He said he'd seen a revelation and that you were sending Ziggy to import a herd of wild horses from Norway. Say it's not true.'

I laughed. 'It's true. Viking horses. If we have ten or twelve, we can make them look like fifty. I'll send Ziggy with an agent to find some. They'll come over in horseboxes on the ferry from Bergen.'

'But,' O'Hara asked reasonably, 'wouldn't it be cheaper to use *local* wild horses?'

'First of all,' I said, 'there aren't any. Second, genuine Viking horses will be worth their weight in publicity.'

O'Hara picked his way across wobbling scraps of scenery and stood looking out of a high window at the grey-green expanse of the Heath. He turned eventually: I couldn't see his expression against the light.

'I'll arrange it,' he said. 'I'll send Ziggy. You just get on with the movie.'

I said with satisfaction, 'Right,' and we made our way as colleagues down to the stable yard, signing out as usual with the guard on the outer door and crossing to the car.

'Did you know,' I said conversationally, 'that they used to hang witches?'

O'Hara stopped in mid-stride and after a pause said, 'Howard didn't suggest such a thing in the book, did he?'

'No. I'm surprised, really, that he didn't. It would have gelled with the dream lovers, don't you think?'

O'Hara blinked.

'The last witch was hanged in Merrie England in 1685,' I said. 'By then they had strung up over a thousand people accused of witchcraft, mostly women. I looked it up. Witchcraft itself went on for a long time after that. Goya was painting witches flying, around the year eighteen hundred. People still follow the old practices to this day. I'd think it improbable that a witch-hanging took place in Newmarket only twenty-six years ago, but there's no harm in Howard inserting a scene or two to sow doubt.'

CHAPTER NINE

Unexpectedly glad after all to have a driver, I travelled to Huntingdon making notes for the rehearsals ahead and thinking over my second conversation with Howard. He had been in his room when I returned with O'Hara and had agreed to come along to my sitting-room, but with bad grace.

'Howard,' I pointed out, 'your name is immovable on this film. You can write brilliantly. Whether or not you disapprove of its plot, the *words* in this film are mostly yours, and you'll be judged by them.'

'Some are *yours*,' he objected.

'I prefer yours. I only write what you won't.'

He could glare, but not dispute it.

'So,' I said without fuss, 'please will you write a scene suggesting that the dead wife was hanged for being a witch.'

He was outraged. 'But she *wasn't* a witch.'

'How do you know?'

'She was Audrey Visborough's sister!' His tone said that that settled matters beyond doubt.

'Think it over, Howard. Put the thought into some-

174

one's mouth. Into someone's head. Just a shot of a magazine article might do the trick. Headline – "Is witchcraft dead?" Something like that. But don't place your scene in the Jockey Club enquiry room, they've already struck that set.'

Howard looked as if he might comply: he even looked interested.

'Her real name was Sonia,' I said.

'Yes, I know.'

'Did the Visboroughs tell you?'

'Why shouldn't they?' His prickles rose protectively. 'They were all very helpful.'

I forbore to say that the *Drumbeat* was as unhelpful as one could get, and went on my way.

My assistant director, Ed, who normally had one assistant of his own, now had, as usual for crowd scenes, several extra deputised helpers. The townspeople of Huntingdon, having streamed to the racecourse in highly satisfactory numbers, were being divided, positioned and generally jollied along by Ed who had been given, and had passed on, my emphatic instruction that the people who had come should be *happy*, and should want to return the next day, and the next. Lollipops were to be dangled. Fun was to be had. Nash – ah, Nash *himself* – would sign autographs now and then.

The people in charge of Huntingdon racecourse had been welcoming and obliging. Contracts, payment, insurance, safety precautions, police: all had been arranged. Provided we finished and vacated the place by Friday, they would give us, if they could, everything we asked for. Repairs, if any were needed, could then be done before they opened the gates to bona fide racing the following Monday.

Our horses, our jockeys, our crowds, our drama, had realistically to play their parts by Thursday evening. Tight, but possible.

I prayed for it not to rain.

Ed chose people to stand in the parade ring in groups, looking like owners and trainers. Others were directed to crowd round and stare. Genuine professional steeplechase jockeys appeared in the parade ring in racing colours and scattered to each group. They weren't the absolute top jockeys, but tough, reliably expert and being well paid. Our lads led round the horses, saddled, rugged and carrying number cloths. It all began to look like a race meeting.

The real thing, of course, would be filmed separately on the following Monday, with Ed in charge of wide, establishing shots of full stands, large crowd movement and bookmakers shouting the odds. Cut in with our own scenes, the joins of real to acted would be invisible – given no rain.

Cibber stood in the parade ring with his wife (Silva), and I positioned Nash's stand-in within easy scowling distance. Moncrieff rolled his camera around on a dolly to get interesting architectural background. It all, as ever, took time, but as soon as possible I sent the townspeople home. Boredom was my enemy; bore them, and they wouldn't return. Every child received a helium balloon on leaving (UNSTABLE TIMES in blue on silver), given with jokes and thanks.

The jockeys had been asked to stay in the parade

ring for a briefing. I found them standing stiffly in a group there, their attitude distrustful and surly.

Not understanding this, I began, 'Just pretend it's a normal race tomorrow. Do everything you normally do on the way down to the start.'

One of them almost belligerently interrupted, 'Is it true you raced once as an amateur?'

'Well, yes, for three seasons.'

'Why did you stop?'

I frowned. It wasn't their business to ask such questions, and certainly not like an inquisition, but I needed their cooperation, so I said mildly, 'I went to Hollywood to make films of horses instead.'

Silence.

'What's the matter?' I asked.

After a long pause, one of them told me, 'It says about you in the *Drumbeat* . . .'

'Ah.' Light arrived. I looked at the cool faces, all highly cynical. I needed these jockeys to ride their hearts out the next day; and I could see with absolute clarity that they weren't going to.

How odd, I thought, that I'd feared losing my authority over the film crews, but in fact had had little difficulty in re-establishing it, only to find now that I'd lost it among men I thought I understood. I asked if they'd watched the Lincoln and seen me talking to Greg Compass. None had. They'd been too busy working, they said. They'd been riding in races.

I said, 'If any of you has doubts about doing a good job for me tomorrow, I'll race him here and now.'

I didn't know I was going to say it until I did. Once said, there was no going back.

They stared.

I said, 'I'm not incompetent or a buffoon or a tyrant. Newspapers tell lies. Surely you know?'

They loosened up a little and a few began staring at their boots instead of my face, but one of them slowly and silently unbuttoned his shiny green and white striped shirt. He took it off and held it out. Underneath he wore the usual thin blue sweater, with a white stock round his neck.

I unclipped the walkie-talkie from my belt and whistled up Ed.

'Where are you?' I asked.

'In the stables.'

'Good. Send three of the horses back, will you, with racing saddles and bridles, each led by a lad.'

'Sure. Which three?'

'The three fastest,' I said. 'And find the doctor we brought with us. Ask him to come to the parade ring.'

'You don't have to be an effing hero,' one of the jockeys said. 'We get your point.'

The one who'd removed his colours, however, still held them out as a challenge.

I unzipped my navy windproof jacket, took it off, and dropped it on the grass. I pulled off my sweater, ditto, and unbuttoned my shirt, which followed. I wore no jersey underneath, but I didn't feel my bare skin chill in the wind: too much else to think about. I put on the offered green and white stripes and pointed to the stock. Silently, it was handed over, and I tied it neatly, thanking my stars that I remembered how.

As it had been only a rehearsal that afternoon, and

all on foot, no one carried a whip and none of the
jockeys was wearing the normal shock-absorbing body
protector that shielded fallen riders from horses'
hooves. No one mentioned this absence. I buttoned the
shirt and pushed the tails down inside my trousers; and
I was passed a crash helmet with a scarlet cap.

Ed, in the distance, was walking back with three
horses.

Moncrieff suddenly arrived at my elbow and
demanded, 'What in hell are you doing?'

'Going for a ride.' I put on the helmet and left the
strap hanging.

'You can't!'

'Be a pal and don't film it in case I fall off.'

Moncrieff threw his arms out and appealed to the
jockeys. 'You can't let him. Tell him to stop.'

'They've read the *Drumbeat*,' I said succinctly, 'and
do we want one hell of a race tomorrow, or do we not?'

Moncrieff understood all right, but made ineffectual
noises about insurance, and moguls, and O'Hara, and
what would happen to the movie if I broke my neck.

'Do shut up,' I said.

'Thomas!'

I grinned at him. I said to the jockeys, 'Two of you
might care to race with me. Sorry I can't take you all
on, but we have to race the whole string tomorrow and
they'll need to be fresh. So just two. Whoever you like.
We'll go one circuit over the fences, not the hurdles,
just as long as there's no one roaming about on the
course where they shouldn't be.'

Silence.

Privately amused, I waited until Ed had drawn near with the horses and had got over his shock at my explicit clothes.

'Ed, get a car out onto that road beside the far rails,' I showed him where, 'and drive round behind us. Take our doctor with you in case one of us falls.' I pointed. 'There he is. He's coming now.'

Ed looked stricken. I unclipped both the walkie-talkie and my mobile phone from my belt, and gave them to him to look after.

'I don't believe this,' Moncrieff said.

A jockey said, 'We could lose our licences, racing you.'

'No, you can't,' I contradicted. 'You're employed by the film company, and you're out here for a rehearsal. We have permission from everyone for you to jump round the course. You're just doing it a day earlier than planned. There's a doctor in attendance, as we promised in your agreements. Who'll come with me?'

They had lost the worst of their antagonism but I'd thrown the challenge back in their faces, and they weren't having *that*. Two of them started for the horses and left me the third.

'O'Hara will *kill* you,' Moncrieff told me.

It so happened that they'd left me the horse that Silva had ridden the previous morning: the undisputed fastest of our bunch. I'd ridden him often at a canter and, according to his history, he was supposed to know how to jump.

'You haven't any breeches or boots,' Ed said, looking with bewilderment at my ordinary trousers and brown shoes.

'The horse won't mind,' I said. A little light-headedness, I thought, wasn't a bad idea in the circumstances.

The horse's lad gave me a leg up, as he'd done many times. I tightened the girth and lengthened the stirrup leathers, and buckled the strap of my helmet.

The two jockeys holding me to my word were mounted and ready. I laughed down at the ring of other faces that had suddenly reverted to a better humour.

'You're a right lot of bastards,' I said, and I got several grins back.

As none of the gates was locked we walked the horses without hindrance out to the track. The one-and-a-half-mile circuit ran right-handed, with nine assorted jumps on the way. I hadn't raced for eleven years. I was crazy. It felt great.

Nasty long words like irresponsibility swam like worms into the saner regions of my mind. I did carry this multi-million motion picture on my shoulders. I did know, arrogance aside, that the soufflé I was building would collapse if the cooker were switched off.

All the same, it seemed to me somehow that I'd grown old a long time ago after too brief a youth. For perhaps three minutes I would go back to my teens.

Ed, car and doctor followed us onto the course.

One of my opponents asked me, 'How much do you weigh?'

'Enough to give me an excuse for losing.'

'Bugger that,' he said, and pointed his horse towards the task and dug him in the flanks with his heels.

I followed him immediately. I'd have no second chance, and I felt the old controlled recklessness swamp through brain and body as if I'd never been away.

181

I thought of the man in front as Blue, because of his colours, and the one behind me as Red. We'd had all the shiny shirts especially made for the film for eye-appeal and distinguishability, and the wardrobe people had given us the goods.

Both Blue and Red were younger than I and had not yet started their careers by the time I'd left. They were intent, I saw at once, on making no allowances, and indeed, if they had done so, the whole enterprise would have been without purpose. I simply dredged my memory for a skill that had once come naturally, and judged my horse's stride before the first of the fences with an easy practice I'd thought long forgotten.

There was speed and there was silence. No banter, no swearing from the others. Only the thud of hooves and the brush through the dark birch of the fences. Only the gritting determination and the old exaltation.

My God, I thought in mid-air, why ever did I give this up? But I knew the answer. At nineteen I'd been too tall and growing too heavy, and starving down to a professional riding weight had made me feel ill.

Half a mile and two jumps later I felt the first quiver of unfitness in my muscles and remembered that both Blue and Red had been at racing peak for several months. The speed they took in their stride used all my strength. We'd rounded the bottom turn and had straightened three abreast into the long far side before I seriously considered that I'd been a fool – or at least definitely foolhardy – to set off on this roller-coaster, and I jumped the next four close-together fences concentrating mainly on desperately keeping my weight as far forward as possible.

Riding with one's centre of gravity over the horse's shoulder was best for speed aerodynamically, but placed the jockey in a prime position for being catapulted off forwards if his mount hit a fence. The alternative was to slow the pace before jumping, sit back, let the reins slide long through one's fingers, and maybe raise an arm up and back to maintain balance before landing. An habitually raised arm, termed 'calling a cab', was the trade-mark of amateurism. To do it once couldn't be helped, but five or six raised arms would bring me pity, not in the least what I was out there trying to earn. I was going to go over Huntingdon's jumps with my weight forward if it killed me.

Which of course it might.

With this last mordant thought, and with straining muscles and labouring lungs, I reached the long last bend towards home: two more fences to jump, and the run-in and winning post after.

Experienced jockeys that they were, Blue and Red had waited for that last bend before piling on the ultimate pressure. I quickened with them, determined only not to be ignominiously tailed-off, and my mount responded, as most thoroughbreds do, with an inbred compulsion to put his head in front.

I don't know about the others, but I rode over the last two fences as if it mattered like the Grand National; but even so, it wasn't enough. We finished in order, Red, Green, Blue, flat out past the winning post, with half a length and half a length between first and second and second and third.

We pulled up and trotted back to the gate. I felt weak enough for falling off. I breathed deeply through

183

my nose, having told many actors in my time that the most reliable evidence of exhaustion was to gasp with the mouth open.

With Blue and Red leading the way, we rejoined the other jockeys. No one said much. We dismounted and gave the reins to the lads. I could feel my fingers trembling as I unbuckled the helmet and hoped the jockeys couldn't see. I took off the helmet, returning it to the man who'd lent it, and brushed sweat off my forehead with my thumb. Still no sound above half-heard murmurs. I unbuttoned the striped colours, forcing my hands to the task, and fumbled too much over untying the stock. Still with breaths heaving in my belly, I handed shirt and stock back, and took my own clothes from someone who'd lifted them from the grass. I hadn't the strength to put them on, but simply held them over my arm.

It struck me that what everyone was feeling, including myself, was chiefly embarrassment, so I made my best stab at lightness.

'OK!' I said. 'Tomorrow, then? You'll race?'

Blue said, 'Yes', and the others nodded.

'Fine. See you.'

I raised a smile that was genuine, even if only half wattage, and turned away to walk over to where Moncrieff, curse him, was trying to pretend he hadn't had a video camera on his shoulder the whole time.

A voice behind me called, 'Mr Lyon.'

I paused and turned. Mr Lyon, indeed! A surprise.

The one with the green and white stripes said, 'You did make your point.'

I managed a better smile and a flap of a hand and plodded across the grass to Moncrieff.

'Shit,' he said.

'Anything but. We might now get a brilliant race tomorrow. They're not going to let themselves do worse than a panting amateur.'

'Put your shirt on, you'll die of cold.'

But not of a broken neck, I thought, and felt warm and spent and thunderously happy.

Ed gave me back the mobile phone saying that O'Hara had called while he, Ed, was driving round the course, and had wanted to know where I was.

'What did you tell him?' I asked.

'I said you were riding. He wants you to call him back.'

'Right.'

I set off towards my car and its driver and called O'Hara as I went. He had spent time with Howard, it seemed, who was now enthusiastic over the witchcraft angle and wanted it emphasised. Scenes were positively dripping off his pen.

'Yeah,' I said, 'but restrain him. Witches do not hang *themselves*, and we still need our designated murderer.'

'You have,' O'Hara said dryly, 'a habit of putting your finger on the button.' He paused briefly. 'Howard told me where Alison Visborough lives.'

'Did you bargain with him? A deal?'

'It's possible,' O'Hara said stiffly, 'that we may not wring the last cent out of him.'

I smiled.

'Anyhow, go see her, will you? Some place in Leicestershire.'

'When? We're shooting all day tomorrow.'

'Uh, now. Howard phoned her. She's expecting you.'

'*Now?* Can't someone else do it?'

I'd been up since four that morning and it was by now five-forty in the afternoon and I needed a shower and I felt knackered, to put it politely. Leicestershire began a lot of miles in the wrong direction.

O'Hara said, 'I thought you'd be interested to meet her, and she has her mother living with her.'

'The Audrey?'

O'Hara confirmed it. 'Silva's character in the movie.'

'Well . . . yes, I'm interested. OK, I'll go. What's the address?'

He told it to me in detail, phone number included. 'Howard's busting a gut trying to be helpful.'

'I'll bet.'

O'Hara said, changing the subject, 'Ed said you were riding?'

Amused by his oblique question, I answered, 'I rode round the course with a couple of the jockeys for them to see what we'll be needing tomorrow.'

'You take care.'

'Sure,' I said. 'Always.'

We said goodbye and I walked onwards to the car, making another phone call, this time to Robbie Gill.

'Thomas Lyon,' I said, when I reached him. 'How's my girl?'

'Still in intensive care. I've liaised with her surgeon. He's slapped a "Do not move" notice on her, which should hold while she needs drip feeds. Two or three days, anyway. I can't stand that son of hers. What a bully!'

'What's he been doing?'

'The nurses threaten a mutiny. He's so bloody *lordly*.'

'Is Dorothea awake yet?'

'Yes, she's talked briefly to the police. Apparently the last thing she remembers is setting off to walk home from supper with a widowed friend who lives only a quarter of a mile away. They watch TV together sometimes and she felt like company with Valentine gone. Lucky she wasn't at home earlier.'

'I guess so. Perhaps.'

'Perhaps,' he agreed.

'Anything else?' I asked.

'Nothing. I asked the police. They gave me the sort of guff which means they haven't a clue.'

'I'd like to see her.'

'I told her that you'd been asking. She was obviously pleased. Perhaps tomorrow evening, or the next day.'

'I'll phone you,' I said.

I reached the car, delivered the change of plans to the driver and consulted the road map. A matter of turn right onto the A14, go north-west, skirt Kettering, press onwards. Forty miles perhaps to Market Harborough. Wake me when we reach that point, I said, and went to sleep on the back seat.

Alison Visborough's hideaway proclaimed her personality from the gateposts onwards. A crumbling tarmac drive led to an old two-storey house, brick-built, poss-

187

ibly eighteenth century, but without distinction. Fields near the house were divided into many paddocks, all fenced with weathered wooden rails, some occupied by well-muscled but plain horses. A larger paddock to one side held a variety of flakily-painted gates, poles and fake walls, the paraphernalia of show jumping. At the far end, a man in a tweed jacket and high-domed black riding hat cantered a horse slowly round in a circle, looking down and concentrating on the leading foreleg, practising dressage. A child, watching him, held a workaday pony by the reins. Lesson, it appeared, being given and received.

Everything about the place looked tidy and efficient and spoke of a possible shortage of funds.

My driver drew up outside the undemonstrative front door. He had said he would check that we had arrived at the right place, but he had no need to. The door opened before he could reach it, to reveal a full-bosomed middle-aged woman dressed in jodhpurs, shirt and dull green sweater, accompanied by two half-grown Labrador dogs.

'Mr Lyon?' Her voice reached me, loud, imperious, displeased.

My driver gestured to the car, out of which I unenthusiastically climbed.

'I'm Thomas Lyon,' I said, approaching her.

She shook my hand as an unwelcome social obligation and similarly invited me into her house, leaving my driver to look after himself.

'I am Alison Visborough. Howard warned me to expect you,' she announced, leading me into a cold tidy room furnished with hard-stuffed, blue-green armchairs and sofas which looked inviting but repelled boarders, so to speak. I perched on the inhospitable edge of one of them, and she on another. The dogs had been unceremoniously left in the hall.

'You are younger than I expected,' she pronounced, her vowels unselfconsciously plummy. 'Are you sure you are who you say?'

'Quite often.'

She stared.

I said, 'I'm not the ogre you described to the *Drumbeat*.'

'You were driving Howard to despair,' she said crisply. 'Something had to be done. I did not expect all this fuss. Still less did I intend to bring trouble to Howard. He has explained that your wretched film company are angry with me, but when I perceive an injustice, I must speak out.'

'Always?' I asked with interest.

'Of course.'

'And does it often get you into trouble?'

'I am not to be deterred by opposition.'

'For Howard's sake,' I said, 'could you write a short apology to the film company?'

She shook her head indignantly, then thought it over, and finally looked indecisive, an unusual state for her, I guessed.

She had short dark hair with grey advancing, also unafraid brown eyes, weathered skin, no lipstick and ringless work-roughened hands. A woman hard on herself and on everyone else, but admired by Howard.

I asked, 'Who did you talk to, who works for the *Drumbeat*?'

She hesitated again and looked not over-pleased. 'I didn't say,' she grudgingly answered, 'exactly what she wrote in the paper.'

'She?'

'She's an old acquaintance. We went to the same school. She works on the "Hot from the Stars" team, and I thought it would *help* Howard in his fight against you. *She* didn't write what was printed. She just passed on the information to one of the columnists, as she always does. She gathers the material, you see, and then it gets *sensationalised*, she explained to me, by someone whose job it is to do that.'

Sensationalised. What a process! Yet without it, I supposed, Howard's gripe wouldn't have been worth the space.

'How long,' I enquired, 'have you known Howard?'

'Why do you want to know?'

'I only wondered about the length of your commitment to him.'

With a touch of the belligerence I was coming to expect, she said, 'I can be committed to a good cause within five minutes.'

'I'm sure.'

'Actually, we've known Howard since he came to visit us after Daddy died.'

The word Daddy came naturally: it was only I who found it odd and incongruous in someone of her age.

'He came to see your mother?'

'Principally, I suppose so.'

'Because of the obituary?'

She nodded. 'Howard found it interesting.'

'Mm.' I paused. 'Have you any idea who wrote that obituary?'

'Why do you want to know?'

I shrugged. 'Interest. It seemed to me it was written from personal feelings.'

'I see.' She let seconds pass, then said, 'I wrote that myself. It was edited by the paper, but the gist of it was mine.'

'Was it?' I was non-committal. 'You wrote about your father's potential career being blighted by Sonia's death?'

'Yes, I did.'

'You wrote as if you cared.'

'Of *course* I cared,' she said vehemently. 'Daddy would never discuss it with me, but I knew he was bitter.'

'Uh,' I said, 'but why did Sonia's death make him give up politics?'

Impatiently, as if it were self-evident, she said, 'Scandal, of course. But he would never talk about it. He would never have let this film be made. Rodbury and I were also against it, but we were powerless. The book was Howard's, not ours. Our name, Daddy's name, doesn't appear in it. Howard says you *forced* him to make the ridiculously untrue changes to his work, so of course I felt someone had to stop you. For Howard's sake and, yes, for Daddy's memory, I had to do it.'

And nearly succeeded, I thought.

I said, without trying to defend either myself or film company policy, 'Excuse me, but who is Rodbury?'

'My brother, Roddy.'

191

Roddy, of course.

'Could I possibly,' I asked, 'meet your mother?'

'What for?'

'To pay my respects.'

It hung in the balance, but it wasn't left to her to decide. The half-closed door was pushed open by a walking stick in the hands of a thin seventyish lady with a limp. She advanced slowly and forbiddingly and, while I rose to my feet, informed me that I was a monster.

'You are the person, aren't you,' she accused with tight lips, 'who says I was unfaithful to my husband with Jackson Wells? *Jackson Wells!*' There was a world of outraged class-distinction in her thin voice. 'Dreadful man! I *warned* my sister not to marry him, but she was headstrong and wouldn't listen. He wasn't good enough for her. And as for you thinking that I ... I ...' Words almost failed her. 'I could hardly even be *civil* to the man – and he was almost twenty years *younger* than I.'

She shook with vibrant disapproval. Her daughter rose, took her mother's arm and helped her towards one of the chairs whose overstuffed firmness suddenly made sense.

She had short white curling hair and high cheek-bones, and must once have been pretty, but either pain or a general disapproval of life had given her mouth a pinched bad-tempered downturn. I thought of Silva and her glowing beauty, and reckoned the two women would probably not want to meet.

I said without emphasis, 'The film company discussed with Howard Tyler the changes they wished made to certain elements of the published book. I did not myself arrange them. I was engaged after the main changes had been agreed. Still, I think they were necessary and that they'll make a strong and entertaining motion picture, even though I understand your reservations.'

'*Reservations!*'

'Disapproval, then. But as your own name is nowhere used, and as the film is fiction, not many will connect you to it.'

'Don't be ridiculous. We are the laughing stock of Newmarket.'

'I don't think so,' I said. 'It was all so long ago. But I would like to ask you a question, and I do hope you will help with the answer, as it might soften for you your understandable outrage. Did your sister Sonia lead the strong fantasy life that Howard gave her in the book? Was she a dreamy young woman in real life?'

While the older woman hesitated, Alison said, 'I've never met her husband and I don't remember her much at all. I was only fourteen.'

'Sixteen,' her mother corrected sharply.

Alison darted a barb of irritation at her mother, who looked faintly complacent. An uneasy mother–daughter friction existed, I saw, that was only half-stifled by good manners. Alison, odd though it seemed for one of her disposition, was woman enough to want me to believe her younger.

'Dreams?' I prompted.

'My sister,' Audrey Visborough pronounced repressively, 'tended to fall for any man in breeches. She would drool over men she could never have. Very silly. I daresay I mentioned it to Howard when he first came here. Jackson Wells looked good in breeches and of course he was flattered when Sonia made eyes at him. It was no basis for a marriage.'

I said, 'Er . . .' without opinion.

'I at least prevented my daughter from making the same mistake.'

Alison, the unmarried daughter, flashed her a glance full of old and bitter resentment.

I cleared my throat diplomatically and asked, 'Do you by any chance have a photograph of your sister?'

'I don't think so.'

'Not even from when you were both young?'

Audrey said severely, 'Sonia was a late and unexpected child, born when I was already grown. She was pleasant enough to begin with, I suppose. I didn't see much of her. Then I married Rupert, and really . . . ! Sonia's behaviour became *insupportable*. She wouldn't *listen* to me.'

'But . . . when she died in that way . . .?' I left the question open, ready for any response.

Audrey shuddered a little. 'Horrible,' she said, but the word and the shudder were automatic, the emotion dead from age.

'Do you have any idea why she died?' I asked.

'We have said over and over again that we do not.'

'And,' Alison added in the same manner, 'it is disgraceful that you and your film should be intruding on our lives.'

Audrey nodded vigorously: mother and daughter were agreed on that, at least.

I asked Alison, 'For Howard's sake, then, will you

194

write the short note of explanation to the film company?'

With asperity she countered, 'You don't care about Howard. You just care about yourself.'

With patience I spoke the truth. 'Howard writes a good screenplay. His name is on the film. If he is worried about being sued by the film company he will not do himself justice in scenes which still need expanding. He admires you, Miss Visborough. Give him a chance to do his best work.'

She blinked, rose to her sturdy feet, and left the room, closing the door behind her.

Her mother gave a cough of implacable distrust and said, 'May I ask why you want a photograph of my sister?'

'It would help because then I could be sure the actress who plays her in the film will not look like her. If your sister had red hair, for instance, we could get the actress a black wig.'

Every response seemed to be squeezed out of her against her will. She said, however, 'My sister had naturally mousey-brown hair. She disliked it and dyed it any colour she could think of. My husband had a fierce disagreement with her once when she came here with a green crewcut.'

I managed not to smile. 'Upsetting,' I said.

'I do not care what you say about Sonia,' she went on, 'but I mind very much that you are denigrating my husband's achievements. Ga-ga! He was *never* ga-ga. He was a man of sense and wisdom, with a spotless reputation.'

195

And I had no need to wonder what he'd looked like, as there were photographs of Rupert Visborough at various ages in silver frames on almost every surface in the room. He'd been handsome, upright and humourless: no twinkle in any of the eyes. I thought with a small twinge of guilt that I was going to make of Cibber something Visborough had never been; a charging bull travelling out of control to self-destruction.

The sitting-room door opened to reveal, not Alison returning, but an unprepossessing man in hacking jacket and jodhpurs who entered as if thoroughly at home, crossing to a tray holding glasses and a single bottle of whisky. He poured from bottle to glass and took a swig before looking me over and waiting for an introduction.

'Roddy,' Audrey Visborough said from conditioned social reflex, 'this man is Thomas Lyon, who is making that wretched film.'

Roddy Visborough had his glass to his face so that I couldn't see his expression, but his body stiffened in annoyance. He was, I thought, the dressage rider from the show-jumping paddock: a man of medium height, neither fat nor thin, uncharismatic, with scanty grey-brown hair, going bald.

He lowered the glass to chest level and offensively said, 'Bugger off.' He said it phonetically, as bugger *orf*.

Audrey Visborough made not the slightest protest. She remarked, merely, 'Mr Lyon is leaving shortly.'

Her son sank the rest of his undiluted drink and poured a second. 'What are you doing here?' he said. 'You're upsetting my mother.'

I answered, 'I came to help straighten things out for Howard Tyler.'

196

'Oh, him.' Roddy Visborough smiled superciliously. 'Seems keen on Alison. I can't think what he sees in her.'

His mother made no comment.

I thought that what Howard saw in Alison was a staunch woman who took a realistic but none too happy view of the world. There had been unlikelier alliances.

Alison herself returned with a white envelope which she held out for me to take. I thanked her: she nodded unenthusiastically and turned to her brother, asking, 'How did the lesson go?'

'The child's stupid.'

'We need her custom.'

'I do not need your criticism.'

Alison looked as if this level of brotherly love was customary. To me, rather to my surprise, she explained, 'We prepare horses and riders for eventing and show jumping. We keep horses and ponies here at livery.'

'I see.'

'*I* don't live here,' Roddy said with a sort of throttled grudge. 'I have a cottage down the road. I only work here.'

'He's the show jumper,' Alison said, as if I should have heard of him. 'I employ him to teach.'

'Ah,' I said vaguely.

'This house is mine,' Alison said. 'Daddy left our family home to me in his will. Mummy, of course, is now my guest.'

I looked carefully at Alison's face. Under the no-nonsense exterior she let me see a buried but definite glimmer of mischief, of extreme satisfaction, of perhaps the sweetest revenge for a lifetime of snubs.

CHAPTER TEN

Next morning I awoke with a groan, every muscle stiffly lecturing me on the folly of proving points. I winced down towards my car but was stopped in the lobby by Nash, O'Hara and Moncrieff, who seemed to have been holding a conference.

O'Hara didn't say good morning, he said, 'You're goddam crazy, you know that.'

I turned disillusioned eyes on Moncrieff, who said, 'Yeah, well, nothing's off the record, you're always saying so yourself.'

Nash said, 'Midnight last night, when you'd gone to bed, Moncrieff played us the video.'

I pinched sleepy eyes between finger and thumb and asked O'Hara if he'd faxed Alison's letter to Hollywood, as he'd intended.

He nodded. 'If Howard stays in line, he's off the hook.'

'Good.' I paused. 'OK. Today, then. It's not raining. We can shoot the race as planned. We can only do it once, so anyone loading fogged film or getting his f-stops wrong will be blindfolded for the firing squad. Moncrieff, I'll sincerely kill you if your crews bugger it up.'

O'Hara said, 'Did you phone that TV guy, Greg Compass, yesterday?'

I thought back and nodded. 'From Huntingdon. I couldn't reach him.'

'He sent a message. The reception desk says you didn't call down for it.'

He handed me a piece of paper on which a phone number was written, and a time, 9 a.m.

By nine o'clock, each of us travelling in his own car with driver, we had long reached Huntingdon racecourse. Greg, as good as his message, answered immediately I phoned.

I said, 'I wanted to thank you for Saturday.'

'No sweat. I gather you're still running things.'

'Sort of.' I explained about the Huntingdon scenes and invited him to come and drape his familiar figure in shot, if he cared to.

'When?'

'Today, tomorrow or Thursday. Any or all.'

'Too busy,' he said.

'Never mind, then.'

'Fee?'

'Of course.'

'I'll be with you tomorrow.' He laughed and clicked off, and I wondered if it would cost me another row of seats.

I drove round the track with Moncrieff to check the positions of the cameras and, in places, lights. Apart from our own two usual crews, we had rented three more cameras on dollies and planted two others, unmanned, in the fences for close action. Moncrieff himself would be on the camera truck, driving round ahead of the horses, filming them from head on. The last of the rented equipment was high on the stands from where it would follow the action from start to winning post. As always with scenes that could only be shot once, there would be glitches, but enough, I fervently hoped, would be usable.

Ed having briefed the jockeys to wait for me, I found them gathered in the jockeys' changing room, kitted as for an ordinary race. Fourteen of them. Every single one.

'Morning,' I said, matter of factly.

'Morning.'

No one referred to the day before. I said, 'I know Ed's given you the gen but we'll just go over it once more. From your point of view, it will be a race like most others. Two miles over fences. You'll circle around at the starting gate, and the starter will call you into line. The starter is an actor. He's been well rehearsed, but if he makes a balls of it, don't stop and go back. Just keep on racing.' I paused. 'Same as usual, there's a groundsman and an ambulanceman at every fence. The groundsmen and the ambulancemen are the real thing. The ambulance is real. So is the doctor. So is the vet. All the spectators out on the course and at the fences will be professional extras. All the crowds on the stands will be townspeople. OK so far?'

They nodded.

'Our fourteen horses are all fairly fit but, as you know, they were chosen for a safe jumping record and bought cheaply. They won't break any sound barriers, and the three of them that raced yesterday may not stay the course today. If you want to you can draw lots in a minute to see who gets which horse; one to fourteen on the number cloths.'

The faces were businesslike. They agreed to draw lots.

'This race won't work,' I said, 'unless you yourselves make it good. You want to be able to show the video of it all to your families, let alone see it in the cinema. You'll all get a CD or video tape later.'

'Who's got to win?' one of them asked.

'Didn't Ed tell you?'

They shook their heads.

'It's got to be a bona fide race. Whoever wins, those are the colours we'll put on the actor who's playing the jockey in close-up. This actor looks OK sitting on a horse and he can trot at a pinch. Sorry, but it's he who'll be led into the unsaddling enclosure in the winner's colours. But ... er ... to make up for it, the one of you who wins this race will get a percentage same as usual. When you pull up, come off the course through the usual gate. All the also-rans can unsaddle in the usual place. There'll be some extras there acting as owners and trainers. The lads will take the horses. Just behave as normal. The first four will be led off towards the winner's enclosure. Any questions?'

'What if we fall?' It was Blue who asked.

'Why did you all turn up?'

Some laughed and some swore. No tension any more.

'Have fun,' I said.

One asked, 'And where will you be?'

I said with audible regret, 'I'll be watching from the

ground.' I paused. 'If you can possibly avoid it, don't give us any flagrant grounds for an enquiry. There's no enquiry in the script. Try not to cross. OK?'

I went outdoors through the deserted weighing-room that on a real race day would have been crowded with officials and trainers, and I watched for a moment the helpful people of Huntingdon arrive in droves, all dressed in racegoing clothes and carrying, in impressive numbers, binoculars. Ed, I saw, had done a fine job.

One of the film personnel came up to me and handed me an envelope, saying it was urgent. I thanked him perfunctorily, and he'd gone before I'd opened the message.

I unfolded the inside sheet of contents, and read the words:

Stop making this film or you will die by the knife today.

Oh, delightful.

It looked like a computer printout on anonymous white office paper.

O'Hara appeared, wanting to discuss a detail or two, and asked what was the matter. 'Why are you frozen?'

I gave him the missive. 'I've had death threats before,' I pointed out.

'Those were after the movie had been distributed. But we have to take this seriously.' He flicked the page with a fingernail. 'What are we going to do about it?'

'What do you suggest?'

'If you leave the set,' O'Hara said plainly, 'the movie

202

automatically goes into recess. It would give us all time to find this bozo and slap him behind bars.'

'We can't stop the filming,' I said. 'After the *Drumbeat* article and the knife on the Heath ... one more panic and the moguls will take complete fright and yank the whole movie for ever.'

O'Hara suspected it was true, but worriedly said, 'This letter doesn't just say you'll die, it says you'll die *today*.'

'Mm.'

'Thomas, you're no good to us dead.'

'What strikes me,' I said, half-smiling at his pragmatism, 'is that whoever sent this note doesn't actually want to kill me, he wants to stop the film without being driven to drastic action. If he – or, I suppose, she – meant to stop the film by killing me, why not just do it? Why the preliminary melodrama? We'll ignore it and press on.'

'I'll at least get you a bodyguard, like Nash.'

Nash, that day, had not one but two bodyguards in attendance but, as I reminded O'Hara, both of these bodyguards were well known to us.

'If you bring in a stranger, you're risking what you're trying to avoid,' I said. 'In classic cases, it's the bodyguards themselves that kill the victim.' I tried a lie that I hoped would be true, and said, 'I don't think I'm in much danger, so just forget it.'

'Difficult.' He was mildly relieved, all the same, by my decision.

'Keep the paper,' I told him, 'and keep the envelope.' I gave it to him. 'And let's get on with the film.'

'I still don't like it.'

Nor did I, much; but delivering a death *threat* took little organisation or courage, and delivering a death by knife took both.

The knife intended for Nash had been incompetently dropped. Cling to that. Forget – for Christ's sake forget – the intestines spilling out of Dorothea.

'Who gave you the letter?' O'Hara asked.

'One of the grips. I've seen him around but I don't know his name.'

There was never time to know the names of the between sixty and a hundred people working on a film on location. I hadn't learned even the names of the horses, neither their registered names, nor the names the lads called them, nor their invented names for the film. I didn't know the jockeys' names, nor those of the bit-part actors. It was faces I remembered, horses' faces, jockeys' faces, actors' faces from way back: my memory had always been chiefly visual.

I did forget for a while about the death threat: too much else to do.

As always with scenes involving two or three hundred people, the race took forever to set up. I spent ages on the walkie-talkie checking the status of each far-flung section but, at last, towards noon, everything seemed to be ready. The lads brought the horses from the stables and the jockeys mounted their balloted numbers and cantered down to the start.

I decided to ride on the camera truck with Moncrieff, to be nearer the action: and to guard my back, I cravenly and privately acknowledged.

Ed, equipped with loudspeaker, alerted the Hunting-don multitude to put on raceday faces and cheer the finish. The commentary, we had explained, would be missing; we had to record it separately and afterwards. Nevertheless, Ed urged, cheer whoever won.

Eventually it was he who shouted, 'Action', the command reverberating through the stands, and I, with raised pulse, who found myself begging unknown deities for perfection.

There were flaws, of course. One of the rented cameras jammed, and one of the two planted in fences got kicked to oblivion by a horse, but the race started tidily, and it was joyously clear from the first that my quasi-colleagues were playing fair.

They had seen me on the truck, when it was positioned for the start, seen me sitting on the edge of the roof of the cab, to get the best of views. They'd waved, in a way, I thought, to reassure me, and I'd waved back; and they did indeed ride their hearts out all the way round.

We had the truck driven for a lot of the way so that the camera was barely six feet from the leading horses' heads, then speeded it up to give a longer view, then slowed again, varying the angles.

Two horses fell on the backstretch second time round. I looked back with anxiety, but both jockeys got to their feet, the loose horses adding the unpremeditated facets that in the end proved the contest real.

The other riders again piled on the pressure rounding the last bend, and again they rode flat out over the last two fences and stretched every sinew to win. The finish was even faster and closer than the day before, but distinguishably Blue, Green with White Stripes, and Yellow crossed the line in the first three places; and as the truck slowed I could hear the crowd shouting them home as if they'd gambled their shirts. Those jockeys had ridden with an outpouring of courage that left me dry-mouthed and breathless, grateful beyond expression, bursting with admiration.

As agreed, when they jogged the tired horses back to unsaddle, another of Moncrieff's cameras continued to film them. I couldn't walk into shot to thank them, and thanks, in any form, would have been inadequate.

'Hell's teeth,' Moncrieff exclaimed, moved by the proximity to the speed and sweating commitment. 'And they do that for a *living*?'

'Day in, day out, several times an afternoon.'

'Crazy.'

'There's nothing like it,' I said.

We changed the actor-jockey into Blue's colours and had him led into the winner's enclosure, to applause from a throng of mixed extras and townspeople. We had to do the unsaddling at that point, while the horses still steamed and sweated and stamped from the excitement of racing. We filmed Nash patting the winner's neck. We filmed the actor-jockey unbuckling the saddle while showing, to my mind, a lot too much clumsiness. We filmed the four horses being rugged and led away by the lads; and we broke for lunch.

Nash, bodyguard close, signed a host of good-natured autographs, mostly on the racecards we'd lavishly distributed.

O'Hara, again at my elbow, breathed in my ear, 'Satisfied?'

'Are you?'

'Nash and I watched the race from up in the stewards' box. Nash says those first three jockeys rode beyond the call of duty.'

'Yes, they did.'

'He says it will give fantastic bite to the victory of *his* horse over Cibber's.'

'It'll drive Cibber mad.'

'The final straw?'

'Almost. Cibber can't stand to have his best horse beaten into second place like that by the man he hates.'

'When I read the revised script, I thought Howard had overdone the hate. I couldn't see any race inducing that level of paranoia.'

'Hate can corrode the soul to disintegration.'

'Maybe. But to show that, you needed an *exceptional* race ...' His voice tailed off momentarily. '... and I guess you got it,' he finished, 'in your own way.'

I half-smiled. 'Let's find some lunch.'

'You're having it in the stewards' box with Nash and me. Do you realise I could have come up behind you just now and put a knife through your ribs? Do you realise we have roughly three hundred strangers here wandering around?'

I did realise. I went with him and lunched high up in safety.

By the time we returned to ground level and to work, one of Ed's assistants had found the grip who'd passed on the letter. Some kid had given it to him. What kid? He looked around, bewildered. Kids were all over the place. The grip had no recollection of age, sex or

207

clothes. He'd been busy with the unloading of scenery for the following day.

'Shit,' O'Hara said.

Another of the film personnel approached as if apologetically and held out a card towards me. 'Some people called Batwillow say you're expecting them.' He looked across to where the little group stood. Jackson Wells, his wife and Lucy, and a man I didn't know.

I took the card and waved them over and had time only to say to O'Hara, 'This is our hanged lady's real husband,' before shaking their hands. They had come dressed for the races and Jackson Wells himself, in tweeds and trilby, looked indefinably more a trainer than a farmer. He introduced the stranger as 'Ridley Wells, my brother.' I shook a leathery hand.

Ridley Wells was altogether less striking than Jackson, both in colouring and personality, and he was also, I thought, less intelligent. He blinked a lot. He was dressed in riding clothes as if he had come straight from his work, which Jackson described to O'Hara as 'teaching difficult horses better manners'.

Ridley nodded, and in an accent stronger than his brother's, said self-pityingly, 'I'm out in all weathers on Newmarket Heath, but it's a thankless sort of job. I can ride better than most, but no one pays me enough. How about employing me in this film?'

Jackson resignedly shook his head at Ridley's underlying chip-on-the-shoulder attitude. O'Hara said sorry, no job. Ridley looked as if he'd been badly treated; a habitual expression, I guessed. I could see why Jackson hadn't welcomed Ridley's inclusion in the day's proceedings.

Jackson still had, it seemed, the old professional trainer's eye, because after a few 'nice days' and so on, he said, 'That was some race those jocks rode. More electrifying than most of the real thing.'

'Could you see that?' O'Hara asked interestedly.

'Didn't you hear the cheering? That was no act, either. "Cheer the winner," we were told, but the cheers came easy as pie.'

'Be darned,' O'Hara said, no horseman himself. He looked at my guests thoughtfully and said impulsively to me, 'Keep the Batwillow family around you, why not?'

He meant, use them as bodyguards. He hadn't heard Jackson Wells tell me he'd have preferred not to have the film made. I felt safe, though, with his wife and daughter, so I wrapped them as a living shield around me, Mrs Wells on one arm, Lucy on the other, and walked them all off to meet Nash.

Although Nash hadn't wanted to meet the man he was playing, I introduced them straightforwardly, 'Jackson Wells – Nash Rourke,' and watched them shake hands with mutual reservations.

They were in several ways superficially alike: same build, same age bracket, same firm facial muscles. Jackson was blond where Nash was darker, and sunnily open, where Nash, from long mega-star status, had grown self protectively wary. Easier with the women, Nash autographed racecards for wife and daughter and effortlessly melted their hearts. He signed for Ridloy also, and didn't take to him.

We were due to film Nash walking up the steps to the stands to watch (supposedly) his horse run in the race. Slightly to O'Hara's dismay, he invited Mrs Wells and Lucy to stand near him, in front of the bodyguards, for the scene. Ridley, unasked, followed them up the steps, which left Jackson Wells marooned on his feet by my side, looking as if he wished he hadn't come.

'It hasn't occurred to your wife,' I said.

'What hasn't?' he said, but he knew what I meant.

'That she's standing next to you, twenty-six years ago.'

'They're the wrong age,' he said brusquely. 'We were all kids at the time. And you're right, I don't like it.'

He bore it, however, standing rigid but quiet, while Nash, taking over from his stand-in, walked up the steps and turned on exactly the right spot to bring his face into Moncrieff's careful lighting. We shot the scene three times and I marked the first and third takes to be printed: and O'Hara stood all the while at my left elbow, riding shotgun, so to speak.

I grinned at him. 'I could get me some armour,' I said.

'It's no laughing matter.'

'No.'

One can't somehow believe in one's own imminent death. I hadn't stopped the film and I went on shooting bits of it all afternoon; and for ages at a time, like ten minutes, I stopped thinking about steel.

At one point, waiting as ever for lights and camera to be ready, I found myself a little apart from the centre of activity, standing beside Lucy, gazing into her amazing blue eyes and wondering how old she was.

She said suddenly, 'You asked Dad for a photo of Sonia so that you didn't copy her exactly in the film.'

'That's right. He hadn't kept any.'

'No,' she agreed. 'But ... well ... I've got one. I found it one day jammed at the back of a drawer. I meant to give it to Dad, but he won't talk about Sonia. He won't let us mention her, ever. So I just kept it.' She opened the small handbag swinging from her shoulder and handed me a creased but clearly distinguishable snapshot of a pretty girl and a good-looking young man, not Jackson. 'You won't make Yvonne look like her, will you?'

Shaking my head, I turned the photo over and read the pencilled information on the back, 'Sonia and Pig.'

'Who is Pig?' I asked.

'No idea,' Lucy said. 'I've never heard Dad mention him. But that's Dad's handwriting, so he must have known him, long ago.'

'Long ago before you were born.'

'I'm eighteen,' she said.

I felt old. I said, 'Could I borrow the photo for a while?'

She looked doubtful. 'I don't want to lose it.'

'Until tomorrow?' I suggested. 'If you came here again tomorrow ...'

'I don't think there's a chance. Dad didn't really want to come at all. He only gave in to Mum so that she could meet Nash Rourke.'

'Could you and your mother come tomorrow?'

'She won't do anything if Dad doesn't like it.'

'And you?'

'I don't have a car of my own.'

'Lend me the photo for an hour, then.'

She brightened and agreed, and I gave the photo to

Moncrieff with an on-my-knees expression, begging him to do me a clear negative from which we could get a positive print. It would take the usual day for travelling to London to the laboratory for development, but with reasonable luck I'd have it back in the morning.

In the morning. Die today. Shut up, I thought.

'Do you,' I asked Lucy later, 'have a computer and a printer at home?'

'Of course we do,' she answered, puzzled. 'No one can farm without one, nowadays. The paperwork drives Dad *loco*. Why do you ask?'

'Just wondered. We use one here all the time.' I enlarged on it, defusing my enquiry. 'Every inch of film, every lens used, every focal stop . . . we have a script supervisor entering the lot. We can lay our hands on any frame of film that way, and also make sure we have continuity if we shoot the next scene days later.'

She nodded in partial understanding and said, 'And who are all those odd people you see on the credits? Grips, gaffers . . . who are they?'

'Grips move scenery. The gaffer is in charge of the lighting equipment. The most important chap at the moment is the production manager. He's the person who arranges for vehicles and scenery and props and all sorts of things to be in the right place when we need them.'

'And you,' she said with unflattering doubt, 'are in overall charge of the whole thing?'

'I and the producer.' I pointed to O'Hara. 'No us, no film.'

She said baldly, 'Dad said so, but Mum thought you were too young.'

'Are you always so frank?'

'Sixteen was hell,' she said. 'Tongue-tied. Not long ago I broke out of the egg.'

'Congratulations.'

'Dad says I talk nonsense.'

'No better time for it. Stay and have dinner. I'll take you home later.'

'Sorry.' The response was automatic, the blue eyes full of the warnings she'd been given about date-rape and such. 'Not on our own.'

I smiled wryly. I'd thought only of not being knifed, not of bed. I'm losing it, I thought, wanting my life saved by an eighteen-year-old still half in the cradle. I fetched her snap from Moncrieff – thumbs up, he said – and returned it to her.

'I didn't mean,' she said awkwardly, sixteen surfacing again after all. 'I mean, I don't want to offend you . . .'

'But no casting couches. It's all right.'

She blushed and retreated, sane and confused, to her parents, and I thought bed wouldn't have been such a bad idea after all.

The trouble with making films, I acknowledged, was the way the occupation gobbled time. For the three months of any pre-production, I worked flat out to put the film together, choosing locations, getting the feel – the vision – in place, altering the screenplay, living with the characters. During production, like now, I worked seven days a week with little sleep. Post-production – the recording of music and sound effects, the cutting together of scenes and parts of scenes to make an impact and tell a story, the debates and the meetings and the previews – all of those often had to be scrambled into just a further three months. And with one film done, another crowded on my heels. I'd made three films lately in under two years. This new one had by far the biggest budget. I loved the work, I was lucky to be wanted, I felt no flicker of regret: I just didn't seem to have time to look for a wife.

One day, I guessed, it might happen like a thunderbolt. The skies, however, had to date vouchsafed only scattered showers, and Lucy looked like a continuing drought.

Someone unexpectedly knocked my elbow. I whirled round with surging heartbeat and found myself face to face with Moncrieff.

'Jumpy!' he said, watching me reach for composure. 'What were you expecting? A tiger?'

'With claws,' I agreed. I got things under control and we discussed the next scene.

'Are you all right?' Moncrieff asked, puzzled. 'Not ill?'

Not ill, I thought, but plain scared. I said, 'Everything's fine. But ... er ... some nutter wants to get the film stopped, and if you see anyone in my area raising a blunt instrument, give me a holler.'

His eyebrows rose. 'Is that why O'Hara has been standing behind you whenever he can?'

'I guess so.'

He thought it over. 'Nasty knife, that, on the gallops.' A pause. 'It got effing close to Ivan.'

'Do me a favour and don't remind me.'

'Just keep my eyes open?'

'Got it.'

We lit and shot some non-speaking takes of Nash's emotions during the race. The block of crowd behind

214

him, mostly bona fide extras but some townspeople, also Mrs Wells, Lucy, Ridley and Nash's bodyguards, responded faithfully to Ed's exhortations, looking for each shot to where he pointed, oohing and aahing, showing anxiety, showing excitement and finally cheering wildly as they watched in memory the horses racing to the finish.

All of the faces except Nash's would be very slightly out of focus, thanks to Moncrieff's wizardry with lenses. One of his favourite lenses had to be focused principally on the light in the actor's eyes. Everything else on the actor's head would be a tiny shade fuzzy, his neck, hair, the lot.

'The daylight's going,' Moncrieff told me eventually, though to any eye but his the change was too slight to notice. 'We should wrap for today.'

Ed through his megaphone thanked the citizens of Huntingdon for their work and invited them back for the morrow. They clapped. Happy faces all round. Nash signed autographs with the bodyguards at his shoulders.

Lucy, glowing with the day's pleasures, walked to where I was checking through the following day's schedule with O'Hara, and handed me a flat white box about a foot long by three inches wide, fastened shut with a rubber band.

'What is it?' I asked.

'I don't know,' she said. 'A boy asked me to give it to you.'

'What boy?'

'Just a boy. A present, he said. Aren't you going to open it?'

O'Hara took it out of my hands, stripped off the

rubber band and cautiously opened the box himself. Inside, on a bed of crunched-up white office paper, lay a knife.

I swallowed. The knife had a handle of dark polished wood, ridged round and round to give a good grip. There was a businesslike black hilt and a narrow black blade nearly six inches long: all in all, good looking and efficient.

'Wow,' Lucy said. 'It's beautiful.'

O'Hara closed the box without touching the knife and, restoring the rubber band, stuck it in his outside jacket pocket. I thought it was better to get a knife in a box than in the body.

'We should stop all boys from leaving,' O'Hara said, but he could see, as I could, that it was already too late. Half of the crowd had already walked homewards through the gates.

'Is something the matter?' Lucy asked, frowning, sensing our alarm.

'No,' I smiled at the blue eyes. 'I hope you've had a good day.'

'Spectacular!'

I kissed her cheek. In public, she allowed it. She said, 'I'd better go, Dad's waiting,' and made a carefree departure, waving.

O'Hara took the white box from his pocket and carefully opened it again, picking out of the raised lid a folded strip of the same white paper. He handed it to me and I looked at its message.

Again a computer print out, it said, 'Tomorrow'.

*

216

O'Hara and I walked out together towards the cars and I told him about Dorothea and her injuries. I described again for him, as I had two days earlier, the knife that had been dropped on the Heath.

He stopped dead in mid-stride. 'Are you saying,' he demanded, 'that your friend was attacked with *that* knife? The one on the Heath?'

'I don't know.'

'But,' he protested, bemused, 'what possible connection could there be between her and our film?'

'I don't know.'

'It can't have been the same knife.' He walked on, troubled but certain.

'The only connection,' I said, going with him, 'is the fact that long ago Dorothea's brother Valentine put shoes on Jackson Wells's racehorses.'

'Much too distant to have any significance.'

'And Valentine said he once gave a knife to someone called Derry.'

'Hell's teeth, Thomas, you're rambling.'

'Yes. Valentine was at the time.'

'Valentine was what?'

'Rambling,' I said. 'Delirious.'

I killed the Cornish boy . . .

Too many knives.

'You are *not*,' O'Hara said strongly, 'going to get knifed tomorrow.'

'Good.'

He laughed. 'You're a jackass, Thomas.'

He wanted me to travel in his car, but I called Robbie Gill's mobile and found I could briefly see Dorothea, if I arrived by seven.

At the hospital the egregious Paul had positioned himself in a chair outside the single room into which Dorothea had been moved. He rose heavily to his feet at the sight of me, but to my surprise made none of the objections I was expecting.

'My mother wants to see you,' he said disapprovingly. 'I've told her I don't want you here, but all she does is cry.'

There had been, I thought, a subtle change in Paul. His pompous inner certainty seemed to have rocked: the external bombast sounded much the same, but half its fire had gone.

'You're not to tire her,' he lectured. 'Five minutes, that's all.'

Paul himself opened Dorothea's door, and came in with me purposefully.

Dorothea lay on a high bed, her head supported by a bank of pillows, her old face almost as colourless as the cotton except for dark disturbing bruises and threadlike minutely stitched cuts. There were tubes, a bag delivering drops of blood, another bag of clear liquid, and a system that allowed her to run painkillers into her veins when she needed it. Her hold on life looked negligible. Her eyes were closed and her white body was motionless, even the slow rise and fall of her chest seeming too slight to register on the covering sheet.

'Dorothea,' I said quietly. 'It's Thomas. I've come.'

Very faintly, she smiled.

Paul's loud voice broke her peace. 'I've told him, Mother, that he has five minutes. And, of course, I will remain here at hand.'

218

Dorothea, murmuring, said she wanted to talk to me alone.

'Don't be silly, Mother.'

Two tears appeared below her eyelids and trembled in the lashes.

'Oh, for heaven's sake,' Paul said brusquely. 'She does that all the time.' He turned on his heel and gave her her wish, seeming hurt at her rejection. 'Five minutes,' he threatened as a parting shot.

'Paul's gone,' I said, as the door closed behind him. 'How are you feeling?'

'So tired, dear.' Her voice, though still a murmur, was perfectly clear. 'I don't remember how I got here.'

'No, I've been told. Robbie Gill told me.'

'Robbie Gill is very kind.'

'Yes.'

'Hold my hand, dear.'

I pulled the visitor's chair to her side and did as she asked, vividly remembering Valentine's grasp of my wrist, exactly a week ago. Dorothea, however, had no sins to confess.

'Paul told me,' she said, 'that someone tore my house apart, looking for something.'

'I'm afraid so. Yes, I saw it.'

'What were they looking for?'

'Don't you know?'

'No, dear. The police asked me. It must have been something Valentine had. Sometimes I think I know. Sometimes I think I hear him shouting at me, to tell him. Then it all goes away again.'

'Who was shouting?'

She said doubtfully, 'Paul was shouting.'

'Oh, no.'

'He does shout, you know. He means well. He's my son, my sweet baby.' Tears of weakness and regret ran down her cheeks. 'Why do precious little babies grow ...?' Her question ended in a quiet sob, unanswerable. 'He wants to look after me.'

I said, 'Did Robbie Gill talk to you about a nursing home?'

'So kind. I'd like to go there. But Paul says ...' She stopped, fluttering a white hand exhaustedly. 'I haven't the strength to argue.'

'Let Robbie Gill move you,' I urged. 'In a day or two, when you're stronger.'

'Paul says ...' She stopped, the effort of opposing him too much.

'Just rest,' I said. 'Don't worry. Just lie and drift and get stronger.'

'So kind, dear.' She lay quiet for a long minute, then said, 'I'm sure I know what he was looking for, but I can't remember it.'

'What Paul was looking for?'

'No, dear. Not Paul.' She frowned. 'It's all jumbled up.' After another pause she said, 'How many knives did I have?'

'How many ...?'

'The police asked me. How many knives in the kitchen. I can't remember.'

'No one knows how many knives they have in the kitchen.'

'No. They said there weren't any knives in the house with blood on them.'

'Yes, I see.'

220

'Perhaps when I go home I'll see which knife is missing.'

'Yes, perhaps. Would you like me to tidy your house up a bit?'

'I can't ask you.'

'I'd like to do it.'

'Paul wants to. He keeps asking. He gets so angry with me, but I don't know who has the key. So silly, isn't it? I can't go home because I haven't got the key.'

'I'll find the key,' I said. 'Is there anything you want from there?'

'No, dear. I just want to be at home with Valentine.' The slow tears came. 'Valentine's dead.'

I stroked her soft hand.

'It was a photo album,' she said suddenly, opening her eyes.

'What was?'

'What they were looking for.' She looked at me worriedly, pale blue shadows round her eyes.

'What photo album?'

'I don't know. I haven't got one, just some old snaps I keep in a box. Some pictures of Paul when he was little. I never had a camera, but friends gave me snaps . . .'

'Where's the box?'

'In my bedroom. But it's not an *album* . . . I didn't think of it before. Everything's so confusing.'

'Mm. Don't let it worry you. And Robbie Gill will be cross if I tire you, let alone Paul.'

A smile shone briefly in the old eyes. 'I might as well be tired. I've nothing else to do.'

I laughed. 'It's just a shame,' I said, 'that Paul took

Valentine's books after all. He swears he didn't, but he must have done because they aren't in the house.'

Dorothea frowned. 'No, dear, Paul didn't take them.'

'Didn't he?' I was sceptical. 'Did he send someone else?'

'No, dear.' Her forehead wrinkled further. 'Valentine wanted you to have his books and I know he would have been furious if Paul had taken them because he wasn't very fond of Paul, only put up with him for my sake, such a pity.'

'So . . . who took them?'

'Bill.'

'Who?'

'Bill Robinson, dear. He has them safe.'

'But Dorothea, who is Bill Robinson, and where and why does he have the books?'

She smiled guiltily. 'I was afraid, you see, dear, that Paul would come back and persuade me to let him take them. He tires me out sometimes until I do what he wants, but he's my son, dear, after all . . . So I asked Bill Robinson to come and pick them all up and put them in his garage, and he's a chum of mine, dear, so he came and took them, and they'll be quite safe, dear, he's a nice young man, he mends motorbikes.'

CHAPTER ELEVEN

I went to bed after midnight, thinking that although I had not died today, it was now already tomorrow.

Nash and I had eaten dinner together in harmony over his scenes-to-come in the parade ring, where his jockey would be wearing blue, while Cibber's would be in the green and white stripes.

After the evening preparation for the Jockey Club enquiry scene, Nash had, without baldly saying so, let me realise that he much preferred to rehearse everything with me in private, so that on set little needed to be asked or answered, his performances being already clear in his mind. I didn't know if he worked in this way with every director, but between the two of us it was notably fruitful in regard to his readiness for every shot. That we were saving time and running ahead of schedule was in this way chiefly his doing.

As usual I'd spent the last two hours of the evening with Moncrieff, putting together with him the plan of positions and lights for the parade-ring cameras, also for those catching the pre-race routines of horses being saddled and led from the saddling boxes, being led round the parade ring, being de-rugged and mounted.

Multiple cameras, though not cheap in themselves, also saved time: I would later cut together, from several lengthy shots, the snippets and pieces that in shorthand would give an overall impression of the whole pre-race tension. The slap of leather straps into buckles, the brushing of oil to gloss the hoof, the close shots of muscle moving below shining coat. It needed only two seconds of graphic visual image to flash an impression of urgency and intent, but it took maybe ten long minutes of filming to capture each.

Pace had a lot to do with good film-making. There would be no flash-flash-flash over the dream/fantasy sequences, only a slowly developing realisation of their significances.

Well . . . so I hoped.

While my silent young driver took me towards Huntingdon in the morning I thought of Dorothea's preservation of Valentine's books, and of the new uncertainty beneath Paul's bluster. He hadn't tried to cut short my visit to the patient: the five allowed minutes had stretched to ten, until I myself thought that she'd talked enough.

Paul had walked with me from her room to the hospital exit, his breath agitated and deep as if he wanted to say something but couldn't bring himself entirely to the point. I gave him time and opportunity, but he was not, as his uncle had been, desperate enough for confession.

Paul was shouting, Dorothea had said. For her sake, I hoped to God she'd got things mixed up.

At Huntingdon racecourse, before eight o'clock, the gates were already wide open to admit the local inhabitants. Breakfast, provided free for all-comers via the film's caterers, ran to endless hot dogs out of a raised-sided van. The weather, though cold, still smiled. Cheerful faces abounded. I needn't have worried that the townspeople would be too bored to return: word of mouth had acted positively and we ended with an even larger crowd than on the day before.

The publicity department of the film company had provided five hundred T-shirts, one to be given that day to thank every local helper on departure – (much to my amusement the front of each T-shirt carried the slogan, UNSTABLE TIMES in large letters, but if one looked closely at some extra tiny letters it read UNSTABLE AT ALL TIMES) – and I began to think they hadn't ordered enough.

The Huntingdon racecourse officials having been generous and helpful throughout, we had had unlimited access to everything we'd wanted. I was so keen not to abuse their welcome that I'd screwed O'Hara's arm to provide an army of scavengers to clean up all trash left by us.

'They'll have their own cleaning staff,' he'd protested. 'We're paying them, after all.'

'Goodwill is beyond price.'

He'd instructed the production manager to have the place left spotless.

The weighing-room and the jockeys' changing-rooms were already unlocked when I arrived on the course, and the wardrobe people were there too, laying out the jockeys' bright colours alongside their breeches and boots.

We had had all their gear made especially for the

film, not just the colours. Everything except the racing saddles, which had been hired, belonged to the company.

There were twenty sets across the board, as we'd allowed for tears and spares and hadn't, at time of ordering, known how many horses we would end with. In the changing-rooms I found that none of the jockeys had already arrived – they'd been called for nine o'clock – and I had no difficulty at all in scooping up what I wanted and locking myself privately into the bathroom.

I had taken with me two of the body protectors designed to save fallen jockeys from the worst effects of kicks. Stripped down to shirt and underpants, I put on the first and zipped it up the front.

In essence, the body protector was a blue cotton lightweight waistcoat padded throughout with flat polystyrene oblongs, about six inches by four, by half an inch thick. The polystyrene pieces, stitched into place, covered the trunk from the neck to below the waist, with a further extension at the back to cover the coccyx at the base of the spine. From there a soft wide belt led forward between the legs to fasten to the vest in front, a scheme which prevented the protector from being displaced. Extra pieces led like epaulettes over the shoulders and down the upper arms, to be fastened round the arm with Velcro.

Although I'd taken the largest available, the protector fitted tight and snugly. When I put the second on top, the front zip wouldn't meet to fasten across my chest; a problem I half solved by straining my trousers over both protectors and cinching my waist with my belt to hold everything together. I ended feeling like a hunch-shouldered quarterback, but with my ordinary sweater on top and my windproof blue jacket fastened over all, I didn't in the mirror look much bigger.

I had no idea how a jockey's kick protector would stand up to a knife, but psychologically an inch of polystyrene and four layers of sturdy cotton cloth was better than nothing, and I couldn't afford to spend the whole busy day worrying about something that would probably not happen.

I'd happily ridden flat out over jumps round the racecourse without a body protector, risking my neck. I would as happily have done it again. Odd how fear had different faces.

Outside, Moncrieff had already positioned his camera on its dolly for the first scene of the day, which was the exodus of the jockeys from the weighing-room on their way out to the parade ring before the race. Halfway along their path a child extra was to dash forward to offer an autograph book to the actor-jockey. Ed, directing a second camera, would film the jockey's friendly reaction in close-up, registering his face, his blue colours, and his nice-guy status, while the other jockeys went on their way through the shot behind him.

In the event we shot the sequence twice, though thanks to rehearsal it went smoothly the first time. Insurance, though, to my mind, was never wasted.

Between the two takes, I talked to the jockeys, joining them where they waited in the weighing-room. I thanked them for their brilliant race the day before and they made nothing of it, joking. All prickliness had vanished absolutely. They called me Thomas. They said several of them would be racing over the course for real at the Huntingdon meeting the following Monday, but it would be the old nitty-gritty, not the joys of make-believe land. Any time I made another racing film, they said with typically mocking humour, they would stampede in the opposite direction.

When they were recalled for the retake walk to the parade ring, I went out before them and watched from beside Moncrieff: then with the two printable shots in the can Moncrieff took the camera and crew into the parade ring itself, where the camera could swivel on a turntable to take an almost 360-degrees view of the horses being led round. I stood in the centre of the ring beside him, overseeing things.

As always it was the setting up that took the time: the positioning of extras playing the small groups of owners and trainers, the extras playing racing officials and stewards, the townspeople filling the viewing steps round the ring, the rehearsing of the jockeys so that each went to an allotted owner, the ensuring that the jockeys of the two deadly rivals would arrive in the ring together – the actor-jockey in blue, the other in green and white stripes – and part at a designated spot to join the two groups containing Nash and Cibber.

Nash's main two bodyguards, dressed as owners, carried binoculars as if they would rather have had guns. The apparently elderly lady completing that group was a twenty-eight-year-old martial arts champion with lioness instincts.

Cibber's group included Silva dressed as befitted a Jockey Club member's wife in well-cut wool coat, knee-high boots and fur hat; warm and pretty in the chill wind. Cibber's 'trainer', off-course, taught judo. O'Hara had taken these precautions. My own shadow, the one he'd insisted on, the evening before, stood beside me in the ring, looking dim. He was supposed to be a black-belt but I had more faith in polystyrene.

Later in the day we would do close-ups of Cibber's acrid fury at having to suffer Nash, his wife's lover, in unbearable proximity: close-ups of Silva looking lovingly at Nash, goading poor Cibber further; close-ups of Nash behaving with good manners, neutral towards Cibber, circumspect with Silva; short essential close shots that would take an age to light.

Meanwhile, with the horses being led round the ring and with everyone in their allotted places, we filmed the entry of the jockeys. Miraculously they all went to the right groups, touched their caps to the owners, made pretence conversations, watched the horses; behaved as jockeys do. The actor-jockey in blue joined Nash. Green and white stripes went to Cibber. No one tripped over cables, no one wandered inappropriately into shot, no one swore.

'Hallelujah,' Moncrieff breathed, sweating beside me when Ed yelled 'Cut.'

'And print,' I added. 'And do it again.'

We broke for lunch. Nash, in the centre of the parade ring, signed autographs one by one for a well-behaved but apparently endless single line of people, shepherded closely by one of Ed's assistants. O'Hara, the bodyguard and the lioness formed a human wall round the mega-star's back.

We ate again, Nash, O'Hara and I, up high in the stewards' box.

Threats to the film apart, it had been a satisfactory morning; we all knew that the scenes had gone well.

O'Hara said, 'Howard's here, did you know?'

'Howard!' Nash exclaimed with disgust.

'A very quiet Howard,' O'Hara amplified, grimly amused. 'Howard is putty in our hands.'

'I don't think his views have changed,' I said. 'He's been frightened. He'll keep his mouth shut. I'd describe it as a plug in a volcano. There's no doubt he passionately meant what he said to Alison Visborough. He stirred her up enough to relay his gripes to her friend on the *Drumbeat* and what he said to her, that's how he still feels.'

'But,' O'Hara protested, 'he wouldn't want the film actually stopped, would he?'

'His full screenplay fee became payable on the first day of principal photography – the first day of filming in Newmarket. It's normal, of course, and it's in his contract. Finished or abandoned, the film can't earn him more money, unless it makes unlikely zillions. And I think he still wants me sacked. He's still convinced I'm butchering his bestseller.'

'Which you are,' Nash smiled.

'Yes. You don't get good meat without a good butcher.'

O'Hara liked it. 'I'll tell Howard that.'

'Better not,' I said resignedly, knowing that he would.

O'Hara's mobile phone buzzed, and he answered it. 'What? What did you say? I can't hear you. Slow down.'

He listened a brief moment more and passed the instrument to me. 'It's Ziggy,' he said. 'You talk to him. He goes too fast for me.'

'Where is he?' I asked.

O'Hara shrugged. 'He went to Norway yesterday morning. I outlined what you wanted to an agent, who whisked him off at once.'

Ziggy's voice on the telephone was as staccato as automatic rifle fire, and just as fast.

'Hey,' I said after a while, 'have I got this straight? You've found ten wild Viking horses but they must come at once.'

'They cannot come at twenty-four days, or at thirty-eight days. They are not free. They are free only next week, for the right tides. They are coming on the ferry on Monday from Bergen to Immingham.'

'Newcastle,' I corrected.

'No. The Bergen ferry goes usually to Newcastle, but for horses it must be Immingham. It is better for us, they say. It is on the River Humber. They will leave Bergen on Sunday. They have a trainer and five grooms. They are all coming in big horse vans. They will bring the horses' food. They can work on Wednesday and Thursday and on Friday they must return to Immingham. It is all arranged, Thomas. Is it good?'

'Brilliant,' I said.

He laughed happily. 'Good horses. They will run wild without bridles, but they are trained. I have ridden one without a saddle, as you want. They are perfect.'

'Fantastic, Ziggy.'

'The trainer must know where we are to go from Immingham.'

231

'Er . . . are you meaning to travel with them?'

'Yes, Thomas. This week I work with the trainer. I learn his ways with the horses. They get to know me. I will practise with a blonde wig and a nightgown. It is arranged. The horses will not then panic. Is it good?'

I was practically speechless. Good hardly described it. 'You're a *genius*,' I said.

He said modestly, 'Yes, Thomas, I am.'

'I'll arrange where the horses are to go. Telephone again on Saturday.'

He said goodbye excitedly without giving me a number where I could call him back, but I supposed the agent might help in an emergency. I relayed Ziggy's news to O'Hara and Nash and said we would have to rearrange the following week's schedule, but that it shouldn't be much problem.

'We have the hanged-wife actress working next week,' O'Hara reminded me. 'We have to complete all her scenes in fourteen days.'

I would take her to the beach, I thought. I'd have the nightgown diaphanously blowing against the sunrise. I'd have her standing on the shore, and have Ziggy galloping for her on the horse. Insubstantial. Unreal. All in her mind.

Pray for a sunrise.

'Sonia,' I said.

'Yvonne,' O'Hara corrected. 'We have to call her Yvonne. That's her name in the book and in the script.'

I nodded. 'Howard wrote the usual hanging cliché of legs and shoes swaying unsupported, with onlookers displaying shock. But I've ideas for that.'

O'Hara was silent. Nash shuddered.

232

'Don't get us an NC-17 certificate,' Nash finally said. 'We'll have to cut that scene, if you do.'

'I'm to make it tastefully horrifying?'

They laughed.

'She did hang,' I said.

Downstairs again, one of the first people I saw was Lucy Wells, who was arguing with a man obstructing her way. I walked over and asked what was the matter.

'This man,' Lucy said heatedly, 'says he has instructions not to let anyone near you.'

O'Hara's order, the man explained. I reassured him about Lucy and bore her off, holding her arm.

'I thought you weren't coming today,' I said.

'Dad changed his mind. He and Mum are both here again. So is Uncle Ridley. Wild horses wouldn't keep him away, he said.'

'I'm glad to see you.'

'Sorry I was so uncouth.'

I smiled at her blue eyes. 'A wise child,' I said.

'I am *not* a child.'

'Stay beside me,' I said. 'I'll tell Moncrieff it's OK.'

'Who's Moncrieff?'

'The Director of Photography. Very important man.'

She looked at me dubiously when I introduced her to the untidy beard and the earthquake-victim clothes, but after allowing us one old-fashioned sideways look he took a fancy to her and let her get in his way without cursing.

She looked colourfully bright in a scarlet short coat over clean new blue jeans, and mentally bright with noticing eyes and a firm calm mouth. She watched the proceedings without senseless chatter.

'I told Dad about that knife,' she told me after a while.

'What did he say?'

'Funny, that's exactly what he said. He said, "What did he say?"'

'Did he?' I considered her guileless expression. 'And what did you say I said?'

Her forehead wrinkled. 'I told him the knife looked beautiful, but you hadn't said much at all. I told Dad it hadn't pleased the producer, O'Hara, and I didn't know why.'

'O'Hara doesn't like knives,' I said, dismissing it.

'Oh, I see. Dad said it might be because someone had tried to cut Nash Rourke, like he'd heard on the radio, but it was his stand-in, not Nash himself.'

'That, too,' I agreed.

'Dad said directors don't have a stand-in,' she was teasing, unaware, 'and you don't know which they are until someone points them out.'

'Or when they come to your home.'

'Goodness, yes. Did the photo of Sonia come out all right?'

'I'm sure it did, but I won't see it until I go back to Newmarket this evening.'

She said, hesitantly, 'I didn't tell Dad. He really wouldn't like it.'

'I won't mention it. The actress playing Yvonne – that's Nash's wife, in the film – starts work on set next week. I promise she won't look like the photo. She won't upset your father.'

She smiled her appreciation and thanks, exonerated

234

from her deception. I hoped no deadly harm would come to her, but in so many lives, it did.

First on the afternoon's schedule was the last of the wide crowd shots round the parade ring; the mounting of the jockeys onto their horses and their walk out towards the course. Even though the action would in the end be peripheral to the human story, we had to get the race-day sequences right to earn credibility. We positioned the owner-trainer groups again as before, each of them attended by their allotted jockey. Moncrieff checked the swivelling camera and gently moved Lucy out of shot.

Nash arrived in the ring trailing clouds of security and detoured to tell me a friend of mine was looking for me.

'Who?' I asked.

'Your TV pal from Doncaster.'

'Greg Compass?'

He nodded. 'Outside the weighing-room. He's been yacking with the jockeys. He'll meet you there, he said.'

'Great.'

We rehearsed the mounting scene twice and shot it three times from two camera angles until the horses grew restive, and then asked all the townspeople to go round to the course side of the stands, to watch the string cantering down to the start.

During the inevitable delay for camera-positioning I left Lucy with Moncrieff and walked over to the weighing-room to meet Greg, whom I found in a milk-of-human-kindness mood, dressed in an expensive grey suit and wide open to suggestions from me that he

235

might like to earn an unexpected fee by briefly taking on his usual persona and interviewing the winning trainer; in other words, Nash.

'It won't be more than a few seconds on screen,' I said. 'Just enough to establish your pretty face.'

'Don't see why not.' He was amused and civilised; friendly.

'In half an hour?'

'Done.'

'Incidentally, do you yourself remember anything about the trainer whose wife was hanged, who we're making this saga about?'

'Jackson Wells?'

'Yes. He's here, himself, today. So is his present wife. So's his daughter. And his brother.'

'Before my time, old lad.'

'Not much,' I assured him. 'You must have been about sixteen when Jackson stopped training. You rode in your first race not long after that. So, did you hear anything from the older jockeys about ... well ... anything?'

He looked at me quizzically. 'I can't say I haven't thought about this since last Saturday, because of course I have. As far as I know, the book, *Unstable Times*, is sentimental balls. The jockeys who knew the real Yvonne were not dream lovers, they were a randy lot of activists.'

I smiled.

'You knew?' he asked.

'It sort of stands to reason. But they're still going to be dream lovers in the film.' I paused. 'Do you remember any names? Do you by any chance know *who*?'

'By the time I'd dried behind the ears in the changing-room, no one was saying *anything*. All scared at being sucked into a murder. Clams weren't in it.' He paused. 'If Jackson Wells himself is truly here today, I'd like to meet him.'

'His daughter says he's here.'

I refrained from asking him why he wanted to meet Jackson Wells but he told me anyway. 'Good television. Rivet the couch potatoes. Good publicity for your film.'

'Jackson Wells isn't keen on the film.'

Greg grinned. 'All the better, old lad.'

I returned to Moncrieff with Greg in tow and promptly lost Lucy's attention to the smooth commentator's allure. Lucy promised breathlessly to take him to find her father and, when they'd gone, Moncrieff and I went back to work.

We shot the scenes of the horses walking out onto the course and cantering off to the start. One of the horses bolted. One of the saddles slipped, dumping its rider. One of the rented cameras jammed. The crowd grew restive, the jockeys lost their cool and Moncrieff cursed.

We got it done in the end.

I walked with drained energy back towards the weighing-room and found O'Hara there, talking to Howard.

Howard, to my complete astonishment, had brought with him his three friends: Mrs Audrey Visborough, her daughter Alison and her son Roddy.

O'Hara gave me a wild look and said, 'Mrs Visborough wants us to stop making the film.'

I said to Howard, 'Are you mad?' which might not

have been tactful but summed up my exasperation. I'd been afraid of a stiletto through the heart, and Howard had brought clowns.

All three of them, however, wore unremarkable race going clothes, not white cone hats, bobbles and red noses. Audrey Visborough leaned on her cane and continued with her complaint.

'Your director, Thomas Lyon,' she flicked me a venomous glance, 'has obviously no intention whatever of either returning to the facts or of stopping making this travesty of a film. I demand that you order him to cease at once.'

Howard shuffled from foot to foot and ineffectually said, 'Er . . . Audrey.'

O'Hara, restraining himself amazingly, told her that he hadn't the power to stop the film himself (which I guessed he actually had) and that she should write her objections directly to the moguls of the film company: in other words, to the top.

She announced that she would do that, and demanded names and addresses. O'Hara obligingly handed her two or three business cards with helpful and soothing advice that slid over her consciousness without sticking. Audrey Visborough felt personally and implacably insulted by the film's plot, and nothing would satisfy her short of preventing its completion.

Alison stood to one side of her, nodding. Roddy looked weakly supportive but from the glances he gave his mother I would have guessed he cared a good deal less than she did about the scurrilous suggestion that she would *ever* have contemplated going to bed with the unspeakable lower-class Jackson Wells.

I said to Howard, 'Why on *earth* did you bring them here?'

'I couldn't stop them,' he said huffily. 'And I do agree with Audrey, of course, that you have made her almost *ill* with disgust.'

'You agreed to the plot changes,' I pointed out. 'And you yourself wrote the love scenes between Nash and Silva.'

'But they were supposed to be quiet, in the drawing-room, not rutting about in bed.' His voice whined with self pity. 'I wanted to *please* the Visborough family with this film.'

With a second twinge of guilt I reflected that his troubles with Audrey Visborough hadn't yet reached a peak.

I said to her daughter, Alison, 'Would you care to watch a scene being shot?'

'Me?' She was surprised and glanced at her mother before answering. 'It won't change our minds. This film is a disgrace.'

When I moved a pace away in irritation, however, she took a pace after me.

'Where are you going?' her mother demanded sharply. 'I need you here.'

Alison gave me a dark look and said, 'I'll work on Mr Lyon.'

She walked resolutely beside me, sensible in tweed suit and flat shoes, earnestly committed to just causes.

'Daddy,' she said, 'was a *good* man.'

'I'm sure.'

'Not easy going,' she went on with approbation. 'A man of principle. Some people found him boring, I

239

know, but he was a good father to me. He believed that women are very badly treated by the English system of leaving family inheritances chiefly to sons, which is why he left his house to me.' She paused. 'Rodbury was furious. He's three years older than I am and he'd taken it for granted he would inherit everything. He had been generously treated all his life. Daddy bought all his showjumpers for him, and only insisted that Rodbury should earn his own keep by giving lessons. Perfectly reasonable, I thought, as Daddy wasn't unduly rich. He divided his money between the three of us. None of us is rich.' She paused again. 'I expect you wonder why I'm telling you this. It's because I want you to be fair to Daddy's memory.'

I couldn't be, not in the way she wanted.

I said, 'Think of this film as being about fictional people, not about your father and mother. The people in the film are not in the least like your parents. They are not *them*. They are inventions.'

'Mummy will never be persuaded.'

I took her with me into the parade ring where Moncrieff as ever was busy with lights.

'I'm going to show you two people,' I said to Alison. 'Tell me what you think.'

She looked puzzled, but her gaze followed where I pointed to a nearby couple, and she looked without emotion at Cibber, a sober fifty, and at lovely young Silva in her well-cut coat and polished narrow boots and bewitching fur hat.

'Well?' Alison demanded. 'They look nice enough. Who are they?'

'Mr and Mrs Cibber,' I said.

'*What?*' She whirled towards me, halfway to fury. Then, thinking better of a direct physical attack, turned back thoughtfully and simply stared.

'Beyond them,' I said, 'is Nash Rourke. He plays the character loosely based on Jackson Wells.'

Alison speechlessly stared at the broad-shouldered heart-throb whose benign intelligence was unmistakable from twenty feet.

'Come with me,' I said.

Dazed, she followed, and I took her to where Greg Compass and Lucy seemed finally to have found Lucy's father.

'These people,' I told Alison, 'are Greg Compass, who interviews racing people on TV.'

Alison briefly nodded in recognition.

'This family,' I said neutrally, 'are Mr and Mrs Jackson Wells and their daughter, Lucy.'

Alison's mouth opened but no words came out. Jackson Wells, good-looking and smiling, stood between his two wholesome, well-groomed women, waiting for me to complete the introduction.

'Alison Visborough,' I said.

Jackson Wells's sunny face darkened. He said, almost spitting, '*Her* daughter!'

'You see,' I said to Alison, 'Jackson Wells dislikes your mother as intensely as she dislikes *him*. No way in real life would they ever have had a love affair. The people in this film are *not them.*'

Alison remained dumb. I took her arm, wheeling her away.

'Your mother,' I said, 'is making herself ill. Persuade her to turn her back on what we are doing. Make her

241

interested in something else, and don't let her see the completed film. Believe that I mean no disrespect to her or to your father's memory. I am making a movie about fictional people. I have some sympathy with your mother's feelings, but she will not get the film abandoned.'

Alison found her voice. 'You are ruthless,' she said.

'Quite likely. However, I admire you, Miss Visborough, as Howard does. I admire your good sense and your loyalty to your father. I regret your anger but I can't remove its cause. Cibber in the film is not a nice man at all, I have to warn you. All I can say again is, don't identify him with your father.'

'Howard did!'

'Howard wrote Cibber as a good man without powerful emotions. There's no conflict or drama in that. Conflict is the essence of drama ... first lesson of film-making. Anyway, I apologise to you and your mother and brother, but until last week I hardly knew you existed.'

'Oh, Roddy!' she said without affection. 'Don't worry about *him*. He doesn't care very much. He and Daddy were pretty cold to each other. Too different, I suppose. Rodbury – and I call him by his full name because Roddy sounds like a nice little boy, but he would never let me join in his games when we were children, and other girls were so wrong when they said I was *lucky* having an older brother – ' She broke off abruptly. 'I don't know why I said that. I don't talk to people easily. Particularly not to people I disapprove of. Anyway, Rodbury wouldn't care what you said about Daddy as long as *he* didn't lose money over it.

He only pretends to Mummy that he cares, because he's always conning her into buying things for him.'

'He's not married?'

She shook her head. 'He boasts about girls. More talk than action, I sometimes think.'

I smiled at her forthright opinion and thought of her unfulfilled life: the disappointing brother, the adored but distant father, the mother who'd prevented a perhaps unsuitable match. An admirable woman overall.

'I like you, Miss Visborough,' I said.

She gave me a straight look. 'Stop the film, then.'

I thought of her feelings, and I thought of knives.

'I can't,' I said.

We completed the day's shooting schedule in time to hold the semi-planned good-public-relations final auto-graphing session outside the weighing-room. Nash, Silva and Cibber scribbled there with maximum charm.

Many Huntingdon residents were already wearing their UNSTABLE AT ALL TIMES T-shirts. Good humour abounded all around. The envisaged orderly line of autograph hunters dissolved into a friendly scrum. O'Hara signed books and racecards presented to him by people who knew a producer when they saw one, and I, too, signed my share. Howard modestly wrote in proffered copies of his book.

The happy crowd roamed around. Nash's body-guards were smiling. The lioness tried to stop him being kissed. My black-belt stood at my left hand so that I could sign with my right.

I felt a thud as if someone had cannoned into me, a

knock hard enough to send me stumbling forward onto one knee and from there overbalancing to the ground. I fell onto my right side and felt the first pain, sharp and alarming, and I understood with searing clarity that I had a knife blade in my body and that I had fallen onto its hilt, and driven it in further.

CHAPTER TWELVE

O'Hara, laughing, stretched his hand down to help me up.

I took his hand in my right, and reflexly accepted his assistance, and he saw the strong wince round my eyes and stopped laughing.

'Did you hurt yourself?'

'No.' His pull had lifted me back to my knees. I said, 'Lend me your jacket.' He wore an old flying type of jacket, army-coloured, zip fronts hanging open. 'Jacket,' I repeated.

'What?' He leaned down towards me from his craggy height.

'Lend me your jacket.' I swallowed, making myself calm. 'Lend me your jacket and get my driver to bring my car right up here to the weighing-room.'

'Thomas!' He was progressively concerned, bringing his head lower to hear me better. 'What's the matter?'

Clear-headed beyond normal, I said distinctly, 'There is a knife in my side. Drape your jacket over my right shoulder, to hide it. Don't make a fuss. Don't frighten the moguls. Not a word to the press. Don't tell the police. I am not dead, and the film will go on.'

He listened and understood but could hardly believe it. 'Where's the knife?' he asked as if bewildered. 'You look all right.'

'It's somewhere under my arm, above my elbow. Do lend me your jacket.'

'I'll get our doctor.'

'No, O'Hara. *No*. Just the jacket.'

I put, I suppose, every scrap of the authority he'd given me into the words that were half plea, half order. In any case, without further objection, he took off his windproof jacket and draped it over my shoulder, revealing the heavy-knit army-coloured sweater he wore underneath.

Other eyes looked curiously our way. I put my left hand on O'Hara's arm, as he was facing me, and managed the endless inches to my feet. I concentrated on his eyes, at the same height as my own.

'The bastard,' I said carefully with obvious anger, 'is not going to succeed.'

'Right,' O'Hara said.

I relaxed infinitesimally, but in fact bloody-mindedness was the best anaesthetic invented, and too much sympathy would defeat me quicker than any pain from invaded ribs.

O'Hara sent one of Ed's assistants to bring my car and reassuringly told a few enquirers that I'd fallen and wrenched my shoulder but that it was nothing to worry about.

I saw a jumbled panorama of familiar faces and couldn't remember any of them having been near enough for attack. But crowd movement had been non-stop. Anyone I knew in England, or anyone they had employed – and professionals were for hire and invisible everywhere – could have stood among the autograph hunters and seized the moment. I concentrated mostly on remaining upright while rather wildly wondering what vital organs lay inwards from just above one's right elbow, and realising that though my skin might feel clammy from the shock waves of an outraged organism, I was not visibly leaking blood in any large quantities.

'Your forehead's sweating,' O'Hara observed.

'Never mind.'

'Let me get the doctor.'

'You'll get Greg Compass and television coverage, if you do.'

He was silent.

'I know a different doctor,' I promised. 'Where's the car?'

Ed returned with it pretty soon, though it seemed an age to me. I asked him to thank everyone and see to general security, and said we would complete the close-ups the next day.

He nodded merely and took over, and I edged gingerly into the rear seat of the car.

O'Hara climbed in on the other side. 'You don't need to,' I said.

'Yes, I do.'

I was glad enough of his company, and I gave him a number to call on his telephone, taking the mobile from him after he'd pressed buttons.

'Robbie?' I said, grateful not to get his message service. 'Thomas Lyon. Where are you?'

'Newmarket.'

'Um ... could you come to the hotel in an hour? Fairly urgent.'

'What sort of urgent?'

'Can't say, right now.'

O'Hara looked surprised, but I nodded towards our driver, who might be economical with words, but was far from deaf.

O'Hara looked understanding, but also worried. 'One of the moguls from LA has arrived at the hotel and will be waiting for us.'

'Oh.' I hesitated, then said, 'Robbie, can you make it Dorothea's house instead? It's for a Dorothea sort of job, though not so radical.'

'You've got someone with you, listening, that you don't want to know what you're talking about? And it's a knife wound?'

'Right,' I said, grateful for his quickness.

'Who's the patient?'

'I am.'

'Dear God ... have you got a key to Dorothea's house?'

'I'm sure her friend Betty must have one. She lives nearly opposite.'

'I know her,' he said briefly. 'One hour. Dorothea's house. How bad is it?'

'I don't know the internal geography well enough, but not too bad, I don't think.'

'Abdomen?' he asked worriedly.

'No. Higher, and to one side.'

'See you,' he said. 'Don't cough.'

I gave the phone back to O'Hara, who stifled all his questions with worry and difficulty. I sat sideways, propping myself as firmly as possible against the motion of the car, but all the same it was a long thirty-eight miles that time from Huntingdon to Newmarket.

I gave the driver directions to Dorothea's house. Robbie Gill's car was there already, Robbie himself opening the front door from inside when we pulled up, and coming down the path to meet us. O'Hara arranged with the driver to return for us in half an hour while I uncurled out of the car and steadied myself unobtrusively by holding Robbie's arm.

I said, 'We're not keen for publicity over this.'

'So I gathered. I haven't told anyone.'

He watched O'Hara get out of the car and give the driver a signal to depart, and I said briefly, 'O'Hara . . . Robbie Gill,' which seemed enough for them both.

We walked up the path slowly and into the empty but still ravaged house. Dorothea, Robbie said, had told him of my offer to start tidying up. We went into the kitchen where I sat on one of the chairs.

'Did you see the knife?' Robbie asked. 'How long was the blade?'

'It's still in me.'

He looked shocked. O'Hara said, 'This is some crazy boy.'

'O'Hara's producing the film,' I said. 'He would like me stitched up and back on set tomorrow morning.'

Robbie took O'Hara's jacket off my shoulder and knelt on the floor to take a closer look at the problem.

'This is like no knife I ever saw,' he pronounced.

'Like the one on the Heath?' I asked.

'Different.'

'Pull it out,' I said. 'It hurts.'

Instead he stood up and said something to O'Hara about anaesthetics.

'For Christ's sake,' I said impatiently, 'just ... pull ... it ... out.'

Robbie said, 'Let's take an inside look at the damage, then.'

He unzipped my dark blue windcheater and cut open my sweater with Dorothea's kitchen scissors, and came to the body protectors underneath.

'What on earth – ?'

'We had death threats,' I explained, 'so I thought ...' I closed my eyes briefly and opened them again. 'I borrowed two of the jockeys' body protectors. In case of kicks.'

'*Death threats?*'

O'Hara explained, and asked me, 'What made you think of these padded jackets?'

'Fear,' I said truthfully.

They almost laughed.

'Look,' I said reasonably, 'this knife had to go through my windproof jacket, a thick sweater, two body protectors designed to minimise impact and also one shirt in order to reach my skin. It has cut into me a bit but I'm not coughing blood and I don't feel any worse than I did an hour ago, so ... Robbie ... a bit of your well-known toughness ... please ...'

'Yes, all right,' he said.

He spread open the front of the body protectors and found my white shirt wet and scarlet. He pulled the shirt apart until he could see the blade itself, and he raised his eyes to me in what could only be called horror.

'What is it?' I said.

'This blade ... it's *inches* wide. It's pinning all the layers into your side.

'Go on then,' I said. 'Get it out.'

He opened the bag he'd brought with him and picked out a pre-prepared disposable syringe which he described briefly, sticking the needle into me, as a painkiller. After that he sorted out a surgical dressing in a sterile wrapping. The same as for Dorothea, I thought. He checked his watch to give the injection time to work, then tore off the wrapping and positioned the dressing ready inside my shirt and with his left hand tugged on the protruding handle of the knife.

I didn't budge and in spite of the injection it felt terrible.

'I can't get enough leverage from this angle,' Robbie said. He looked at O'Hara. 'You're strong,' he said. 'You pull it out.'

O'Hara stared at him, and then at me.

'Think of moguls,' I said.

He smiled twistedly and said to Robbie, 'Tell me when.'

'Now,' Robbie said, and O'Hara grasped the knife's handle and pulled until the blade came free.

Robbie quickly put the dressing in place and O'Hara stood as if stunned, holding in disbelief the object that had caused me such trouble.

'Sorry,' Robbie said to me.

I shook my head, dry mouthed.

O'Hara laid the knife on the kitchen table, on the discarded wrapping from the dressing, and we all spent a fairly long silence simply looking at it.

Overall it was about eight inches long, and half of

251

that was handle. The flat blade was almost three inches wide at the handle end, tapering to a sharp point. One long side of the triangular blade was a plain sharp cutting edge: the other was wickedly serrated. At its wide end the blade extended smoothly into a handle which had a space through it big enough to accommodate a whole hand. The actual grip, with undulations for fingers to give a better purchase, was given substance by bolted-on, palm-width pieces of dark, richly-polished wood: the rest was shiny metal.

'It's heavy,' O'Hara said blankly. 'It could rip you in half.'

A stud embellishing the wider end of the blade bore the one word, 'Fury'.

I picked up the awful weapon for a closer look and found it was indeed heavy (more than half a pound, we soon found, when Robbie weighed it on Dorothea's kitchen scales) and, according to letters stamped into it, had been made of stainless steel in Japan.

'What we need,' I said, putting it down, 'is a knife expert.'

'And what you need first,' Robbie said apologetically, 'is a row of staples to stop the bleeding.'

We took off all my protective layers for him to see what he was doing and he presently told me consolingly that the point of the blade had hit one of my ribs and had slid along it, not slicing down into soft tissue and through into the lung. 'The rib has been fractured by the blow but you are right, and lucky, because this injury should heal quite quickly.'

'Cheers,' I said flippantly, relieved all the same. 'Maybe tomorrow I'll get me a bullet-proof vest.'

252

Robbie mopped a good deal of dried blood from my skin, damping one of Dorothea's tea towels for the purpose, then helped me into my one relatively unharmed garment, the windproof jacket.

'You look as good as new,' he assured me, fitting together the bottom ends of the zip and closing it upwards.

'The mogul won't notice a thing,' O'Hara agreed, nodding. 'Are you fit enough to talk to him?'

I nodded. It was necessary to talk to him. Necessary to convince him that the company's money was safe in my hands. Necessary to confound all suggestion of 'jinx'.

I said, 'We do, all the same, have to find out just who is so fanatical about stopping the film that he – or she – will murder to achieve it. It's possible, I suppose, that the knife was meant only to frighten us, like yesterday's dagger, but if I hadn't been wearing the protectors . . .'

'No protection and an inch either way,' Robbie nodded, 'and you would likely have been history.'

'So,' I said, 'if we take it that my death was in fact intended, I absolutely *must* find out who and why. Find it out among ourselves, I mean, if we're not bringing in the police. Otherwise . . .' I hesitated, then went on, '. . . if the reason for the attack on me still exists, which we have to assume is the case, they – he or she or they – may try again.'

I had the feeling that the thought had already occurred to both of them, but that to save my peace of mind they hadn't liked to say it aloud.

'No film is worth dying for,' O'Hara said.

'The film has stirred up mud that's been lying quiet for twenty-six years,' I said. 'That's what's happened. No point in regretting it. So now we have the choice of either pulling the plug on the film and retiring in disarray – and where is my future if I do that? – or . . . er . . . sifting through the mud for the facts.'

'But,' Robbie said doubtfully, 'could you really find any? I mean, when it all happened, when it was fresh, the police got nowhere.'

'The police are ordinary people,' I said. 'Not infallible supermen. If we try, and get nowhere also, then so be it.'

'But how do you start?'

'Like I said, we look for someone who knows about knives.'

It had been growing dark while we spoke. As Robbie crossed to flip the light switch, we heard the front door open and close, and footsteps coming heavily along the passage towards us.

It was Paul who appeared in the kitchen doorway: Paul annoyed, Paul suspicious, Paul's attention latching with furious astonishment onto my face. The indecisiveness of our last meeting had vanished. The bluster was back.

'And what do you think *you're* doing here?' he demanded. 'I've told you to stay away, you're not wanted.'

'I told Dorothea I would tidy up a bit.'

'I will tidy the house. I don't want you here. And as for you, Dr Gill, your services aren't needed. Clear out, all of you.'

It was O'Hara's first encounter with Paul Pannier; always a learning experience.

'And where did you get a key from?' he demanded aggrievedly. 'Or did you break in?' He looked at O'Hara directly for the first time and said, 'Who the hell are you? I want you all out of here at once.'

I said neutrally, 'It's your mother's house and I'm here with her permission.'

Paul wasn't listening. Paul's gaze had fallen on the table, and he was staring at the knife.

There was barely a smear of blood on it as it had been more or less wiped clean by its outward passage through many layers of polystyrene and cloth, so it seemed to be the knife itself, not its use, that was rendering Paul temporarily speechless.

He raised his eyes to meet my gaze, and there was no disguising his shock. His eyes looked as dark as his pudgy features were pale. His mouth had opened. He found nothing at all to say but turned on one foot and stamped away out of the kitchen down the hall and out through the front door, leaving it open behind him.

'Who was *he*?' O'Hara asked. 'And what was that all about?'

'His mother,' Robbie explained, 'was savagely cut with a knife in this house last Saturday. He may think that somehow we've found the weapon.'

'And have you?' O'Hara turned to me. 'What was it you were trying to tell me yesterday? But this isn't the knife you found on the Heath, is it?'

'No.'

He frowned. 'I don't understand any of it.'

That made two of us; but somewhere there had to be an explanation. Nothing happened without cause.

I asked Robbie Gill, who was tidying and closing his medical case, 'Do you know anyone called Bill Robinson who mends motorbikes?'

'Are you feeling all right?'

'Not a hundred per cent. Do you?'

'Bill Robinson who mends motorbikes? No.'

'You know the town. Who would know?'

'Are you serious?'

'He may have,' I explained briefly, 'what this house was torn apart for.'

'And that's all you're telling me?'

I nodded.

Robbie pulled the telephone towards him, consulted a notebook from his pocket, and pressed some numbers. He was passed on, relay by relay, to four more numbers but eventually pushed the phone away in satisfaction and told me, 'Bill Robinson works for Wrigley's garage, and lives somewhere in Exning Road. He tinkers with Harley Davidsons for a hobby.'

'Great,' I said.

'But,' O'Hara objected, 'what has any of this to do with our film?'

'Knives,' I said, 'and Valentine Clark knew Jackson Wells.'

'Good luck with the mud,' Robbie said.

The mogul proved to be a hard-nosed thin businessman in his forties with no desire even to look at the growing reels of printed film. He didn't like movies, he said. He

256

despised film actors. He thought directors should be held in financial handcuffs. Venture capital was his field, he said, with every risk underwritten. Wrong field, I thought.

He had demanded in advance to have an accounting for every cent disbursed or committed since the first day of principal photography, with the result that O'Hara's production department had spent the whole day itemising such things as food, transport, pay for stable-lads, lipsticks and light bulbs.

We sat round the dining table in O'Hara's suite, I having made a detour to my own rooms to exchange my windproof jacket for a shirt and sweater. Robbie had stuck only a light dressing over the mended damage. I still felt a shade trembly, but apparently nothing showed. I concentrated on justifying Ziggy's fare and expenses in Norway, while sipping mineral water and longing for brandy.

'Wild horses!' the mogul exclaimed in near-outrage to O'Hara. 'You surely didn't sanction bringing horses all the way from Norway! They're not in the script.'

'They're in the hanged woman's fantasy,' O'Hara explained flatly. 'Her dream life is what the company thought best about the plot, and what you expect on the screen. Viking horses hold glamour for publicity, and will earn more than they cost.'

O'Hara's clout silenced the mogul, who scowled but seemed to realise that if he antagonised his high-grade producer beyond bearing, he would lose him and scupper the whole investment. In any event, he moderated his aggressive approach and nodded through the bonus for the winning jockey with barely a grimace.

The accounts audited, he wanted to discuss Howard.

I didn't.

O'Hara didn't.

Howard proving to be usefully out of the hotel, the subject died. I excused myself on the grounds of the regular evening meeting with Moncrieff, and the mogul said in parting that he trusted we would have no further 'incidents', and announced that he would be watching the action the next morning.

'Sure,' O'Hara agreed easily, hardly blinking. 'The schedule calls for dialogue and close-ups, and several establishing shots of people walking in and out of the weighing-room at Huntingdon racecourse. No crowd scenes, though, they're in the can. No jockeys, they've finished also. The horses will be shipped back here tomorrow afternoon. Thanks to fine weather and Thomas's good management, we'll be through with the racetrack scenes a day early.'

The mogul looked as if he'd bitten a wasp. I wondered, as I left, just what would make him happy.

The Moncrieff session swelled with the arrival of both Nash and Silva, each wanting to continue with the private rehearsals. Nash had brought his script. Silva wore no lipstick and a feminist expression. I wondered what she and O'Hara were like together in bed, a speculation that didn't advance my work any, but couldn't be helped.

We went through the scenes. Moncrieff and Nash discussed lighting. Silva thrust forward her divine jaw and to her pleasure Moncrieff assessed her facial bones in terms of planes and shadows.

I drank brandy and painkillers with dedication: possibly medicinally a bad combination, but a great distancer from tribulation. When everyone left I went to bed half-sitting up, and stayed awake through a lot of o'clocks, throbbing and thinking and deciding that in the near future I would stand with my back to a wall at all times.

O'Hara woke me from a troubled sleep by phoning at seven-thirty. Late.

'How are you doing?' he asked.

'Lousy.'

'It's raining.'

'Is it?' I yawned. 'That's good.'

'Moncrieff phoned the weather people. It should be dry this afternoon. So we could watch all the Huntingdon rushes this morning, when the van comes from London.'

'Yes . . . I thought the mogul couldn't be bothered.'

'He's going to London himself. He's not keen on waiting for Huntingdon this afternoon. He told me everything seems to be going all right with the movie now, and he'll report back to that effect.'

'Jeez.'

O'Hara chuckled. 'He thought you were business-like. That's his highest word of praise. He says I can go back to LA.'

'Oh.' I was surprised by the strength of my dismay. 'And are you going?'

'It's your movie,' he said.

I said, 'Stay.'

After a pause he said, 'If I go, it shows you're totally

259

in command.' Another pause. 'Think it over. We'll decide after the dailies. See you at eleven o'clock in the screening room. Will you be fit enough?'

'Yes.'

'I sure as hell wouldn't be,' he said, and disconnected.

By nine I'd decided against the great British breakfast and had located Wrigley's garage on a town road map: by nine-fifteen my driver had found it in reality. There was a canopy over the petrol pumps: shelter from rain.

Bill Robinson had long hair, a couple of pimples, a strong East Anglian accent, a short black leather jacket covered in gold studs and a belt of heavy tools strung round his small hips. He took in the fact that I had a chauffeur and offered opportunist respect.

'Wha' can I do for yer?' he enquired, chewing gum.

I grinned. 'Mrs Dorothea Pannier thinks you're a great guy.'

'Yeah?' He moved his head in pleasure, nodding. 'Not such a bad old duck herself.'

'Did you know she's in hospital?'

His good humour vanished. 'I heard some bastard carved her up.'

'I'm Thomas Lyon,' I said. 'She gave me your name.'

'Yeah?' He was wary. 'You're not from that son of hers? Right turd, that son of hers.'

I shook my head. 'Her brother Valentine left me his books in his will. She told me she'd trusted them to you for safekeeping.'

'Don't give them to no one, that's what she said.' His manner was determined and straightforward. I judged it would be a bad mistake to offer him money, which

260

conferred on him saintly status in the modern scheme of things.

'How about,' I said, 'if we could get her on the phone?'

He could see nothing wrong in that, so I used the mobile to reach the hospital and then, with many clicks and delays, Dorothea herself.

She talked to Bill Robinson in his heavy leather gear and studs, and Bill Robinson's face shone with goodness and pleasure. Hope for the old world yet.

'She says,' he announced, giving me my phone back, 'that the sun shines out of your arse and the books are yours.'

'Great.'

'But they aren't here,' he said. 'They're in the garage at home.'

'When could I pick them up?'

'I could go home midday in my lunch hour.' He gazed briefly to one side at a gleaming monster of a motorbike, heavily wheel-chained to confound would-be thieves. 'I don't usually, but I could.'

I suggested buying an hour of his time at once from his boss and not waiting for lunch.

'Cor,' he said, awestruck; but his boss, a realist, accepted the suggestion, and the money, with alacrity, and Bill Robinson rode to his house in my car with undoubted enjoyment.

'How do you know Dorothea?' I asked on the way.

'My girlfriend lives next door to her,' he explained simply. 'We do errands sometimes for the old luv. Carry her shopping, and such. She gives us sweets like we were kids.'

261

'Er,' I said, 'how old are you, then?'

'Eighteen. What did you think of my bike?'

'I envy you.'

His smile was complacent, and none the worse for that. When we reached his home ('Ma will be out at work, the key's in this thing what looks like a stone'), he unlocked a padlock on the solid doors of a brick-built garage and revealed his true vocation, the care and construction of bikes.

'I buy wrecks and rebuild them,' he explained, as I stood inside the garage gazing at wheels, handlebars, twisted tubing, shining fragments. 'I rebuild them as good as new and then I sell them.'

'Brilliant,' I said absently. 'Do you want to be in a film?'

'Do I what?'

I explained that I was always looking for interesting backgrounds. Would he mind moving some of the parts of motorbikes out of the garage into his short driveway and getting on with some work while we filmed Nash Rourke walking down the street, thinking? 'No dialogue,' I said, 'just Nash strolling by and pausing for a second or two to watch the work in progress. The character he's playing will be walking through Newmarket, trying to make up his mind about something.' I was looking for real Newmarket backgrounds, I said.

'Nash *Rourke*! You're kidding me.'

'No. You'll meet him.'

'Mrs Pannier did say you were the one making the film they're talking about. It was in the *Drumbeat*.'

'The tyrannical bully-boy? Yes, that's me.'

He smiled broadly. 'Your books are in all those boxes.' He pointed to a large random row of cartons that announced their original contents as TV sets, electrical office equipment, microwave ovens and bread-making machines. 'A ton of paper, I shouldn't wonder. It took me the whole of Saturday morning to pack it all and shift it here, but Mrs Pannier, dear old duck, she made it worth my while.'

It was approbation rather than a hint, but I said I would do the same, particularly if he could tell me which box held what.

Not a snowball's chance, he said cheerfully. Why didn't I look?

The task was too much, both for the available time and my own depleted stamina. I said I'd wrenched my shoulder and couldn't lift the boxes, and asked him to stow as many as possible in the boot of the car. He looked resignedly at the rain but splashed backwards and forwards efficiently, joined after hesitation by my driver who buttoned his jacket closely and turned up his collar.

The car, including the front passenger seat, absorbed half of the boxes. I asked what he'd used to transport them on Saturday.

'My dad's little old pick-up,' he said. 'It needed three journeys. He takes it to work weekdays, so I can't borrow it till this evening.'

He agreed to load and deliver the rest of the boxes in the pick-up, and in cheerful spirits came along to the hotel and helped the porter there stack the cartons in the lobby.

'Do you mean it about me being in your film?' he asked on the way back to Wrigley's garage. 'And ... *when*?'

'Tomorrow, maybe,' I said. 'I'll send a message. I'll fix it with your boss, and the film company will pay you a fee for your help.'

'Cor,' he said.

Nash, Silva and Moncrieff all joined O'Hara and me to watch the Huntingdon rushes.

Even without much sound the crowd scenes looked like an everyday race meeting and the race itself was still remarkable for the Victoria Cross riding of the jockeys. The race had been filmed successfully by five cameras and semi-successfully by another. There was easily enough to cut together a contest to stir the pulses of people who'd never seen jump-racing at close quarters: even Silva gasped at one sequence, and Nash looked thoughtful. Moncrieff fussed about shadows in the wrong places, which no one else had noticed.

The close shots with dialogue showed Silva at her most enticing. I praised her interpretation, not her looks, and got a brief nod of acknowledgment. The two days' work, all in all, had been worth the effort.

After the end of the rushes the film developers had joined on the thirty seconds' worth Moncrieff had shot of Lucy's photo. Large and in sharp focus, the two faces appeared on the screen.

'Who are they?' O'Hara asked, perplexed.

'The girl on the left,' I said, 'is Yvonne. Or rather, she was Sonia Wells, the girl who hanged. The real one.'

'Christ,' O'Hara said.

'And who's the man?' Nash asked.

'His name is Pig, I think.' I explained about Lucy's photo. 'I promised her that Yvonne wouldn't look like Sonia.'

The girl on the screen had curly light-brown hair, not a green crewcut or other weirdness. We would give Yvonne a long straight blonde wig and hope for the best.

The screen ran clear. We switched on the lights, talked about what we'd seen and, as always, went back to work.

Later at Huntingdon a photographer, who'd been engaged by the company to chart progress for the publicity department, brought a set of eight- by ten-inch prints for O'Hara to see. He and I took them into the weighing-room and sat at a table there, minutely searching the snapshots with a magnifying glass.

We saw nothing of any help. There were photos of Nash signing in the end-of-the-day autograph session. A shot of Howard looking smug, inscribing his own book. Silva being film-star charming. Greg signing race-cards. A shot of O'Hara and myself standing together. The lens had been focused every time on the main subject's face: people around were present, but not warts and all.

'We need blow-ups of the crowd,' O'Hara said.

'We're not going to get nice clear views of the Fury.'

Morosely, he agreed, but ordered blow-ups anyway.

No more knives appeared, in or out of bodies. We filmed the remaining scenes and shipped out the horses. We made sure the whole place was shipshape, thanked Huntingdon racecourse management for their kindnesses, and were back in Newmarket soon after six o'clock.

The message light inexorably flashed in my sitting-room: whenever did it not?

Robbie Gill wanted me to phone him, urgently.

I got his answer service: he would be available at seven.

To fill in the time I opened the tops of a few of the cartons of Valentine's books, which now took up a good deal of the floorspace, as I'd particularly asked for them not to be put one on top of another. I'd forgotten, of course, that bending down used chest muscles also. On my knees, therefore, I began to inspect my inheritance.

There was too much of it. After the first three boxes had proved to hold part of the collection of biographies and racing histories, after I'd painstakingly taken out every volume, shaken it for insertions and replaced it, I saw the need for secretarial help; for a record keeper with a lap-top computer.

Lucy, I thought. If I had a fantasy, I would materialise her in my sitting-room, like Yvonne's dream lovers. Lucy knew how to work a computer.

Impulsively I phoned her father's house and put a proposition to his daughter.

'You told me you'd left school and are waiting to do a business course. Would you care for a two-week temporary job in Newmarket?' I explained what I needed. 'I am not trying to seduce you,' I said. 'You can bring a chaperon, you can stay anywhere you like, you can drive home every day to Oxfordshire if you prefer. I'll pay you fairly. If you don't want to do it, I'll get someone local.'

She said a shade breathlessly, 'Would I see Nash Rourke again?'

Wryly, I promised that she would. 'Every day.'

'He's . . . he's . . .'

'Yes,' I agreed, 'and he's married.'

'It's not *that*,' she said disgustedly. 'He's just . . . nice.'

'True. What about the job?'

'I could start tomorrow.'

The boxes could wait that long, I thought.

At seven I phoned Robbie Gill's number again and reached him promptly.

'Which do you want first,' he asked, 'the good news or the appalling?'

'The good. I'm tired.'

'You don't surprise me. The good news is a list of names of knife experts. Three in London, two in Glasgow, four in Sheffield and one in Cambridge.' He read them all out and took away what little breath I could manage with a broken rib.

I said weakly, 'Say that Cambridge one again.'

He repeated it distinctly. 'Professor Meredith Derry, lecturer in mediaeval history, late of Trinity College, retired.'

Derry.

Knives . . .

'Do you want the appalling?' Robbie asked.

'I suppose I have to hear it?'

'Afraid so. Paul Pannier has been murdered.'

CHAPTER THIRTEEN

'*Murdered?*'

''Fraid so.'

'Where? And . . . er . . . how?'

As if it were inevitable, the Scots voice informed me, 'He was killed in Dorothea's house . . . with a knife.'

I sighed; a groan. 'Does Dorothea know?'

'The police sent a policewoman to the hospital.'

'Poor, poor Dorothea.'

He said bluntly, 'She won't be bullied any more.'

'But she loved him,' I protested. 'She loved the baby he'd been. She loved her little son. She will be devastated.'

'Go and see her,' Robbie said. 'You seem to understand her. I never could see why she put up with him.'

She needed a hug, I thought. She needed someone to hold her while she wept. I said, 'What about Paul's wife, Janet?'

'The police have told her. She's on her way here now, I think.'

I looked at my watch. Five past seven. I was sore and hungry and had tomorrow's shots to discuss with Nash and Moncrieff. Still . . .

'Robbie,' I said, 'does Professor Derry have an address?'

'There's a phone number.' He read it out. 'What about Dorothea?'

'I'll go to see her now. I could be at the hospital in about forty minutes. Can you fix it that they'll let me see her?'

He could and would. Who had discovered Paul's murder, I asked.

'I did, damn it. At about three o'clock this afternoon I went to pick up a notebook that I left in Dorothea's kitchen last night. I called to get the key again from her friend Betty, but she said she didn't have the key any more, she'd given it to Paul this morning early. I went across to Dorothea's house and rang the bell – that ruddy quiet ding-dong – and no one came, so I went round the back and tried the kitchen door, and it was open.' He paused. 'Paul was lying in the hall on almost the exact spot where Betty found Dorothea. There wasn't any blood, though. He'd died at once and he'd been dead for hours. He was killed with what looked like one of Dorothea's big kitchen knives. It was still in him, driven deep into his chest from behind at a point not far above his right elbow . . .'

'*Robbie*,' I said, stunned.

'Yes. Almost the same place as you. The handle was sticking out. An ordinary chef's knife handle, nothing fancy. No Fury. So I phoned the police and they kept me hanging about in that house all afternoon, but I couldn't tell them why Paul had gone there. How could I know? I couldn't tell them anything except that it looked to me as if the knife had reached his heart and stopped it.'

I cleared my throat. 'You didn't tell them about . . . me?'

'No. You didn't want me to, did you?'

'I did not.'

'But things are different now,' he said dubiously.

'Not if the police find Paul's killer quickly.'

'I've got the impression that they don't know where to look. They'll be setting up an incident room, though. There will be all sorts of questions. You'd better be ready for them, because you were there in that house after Dorothea was attacked, and they have your fingerprints.'

'So they have.' I thought a bit and asked, 'Is it against the law not to report having a knife stuck into you?'

'I don't really know,' Robbie said, 'but I know it's mostly against the law to carry a knife like the Fury in a public place, which is what O'Hara did when the two of you took it away with you last night. He could be liable for a fine and six months in jail.'

'You're kidding?'

'No. There are fierce laws now about carrying offensive weapons, and you can't get anything much more offensive than a Fury.'

'Forget you ever saw it.'

'So easy.'

We had cleaned the kitchen the evening before by bundling the body protectors, my shirt, my sweater and Robbie's medical debris into a trash bag, knotting the top; and we'd taken it with us, casually adding it to the

271

heap of similar bags to one side of Bedford Lodge, from where mountains of rubbish and empty bottles were cleared daily.

Robbie in farewell said again he would tell the nurses it was OK to let me in to see Dorothea, and asked me to phone him back later.

Promising I would, I said goodbye to him and dialled the number of Professor Meredith Derry who, to my relief, could be brought to the phone and who would acquiesce to a half-hour's worth of knife-expertise, especially if I were paying a consultancy fee.

'Of course,' I said heartily. 'Double, if it can be this evening.'

'Come when you like,' the professor said, and gave me an address and directions.

Dorothea's grief was as deep and pulverising as I'd feared. The tears flowed the minute she saw me, weak endless silent tears, not howls and sobs of pain, but an intense mourning as much for times past as for present loss.

I put my arm round her for a while and then simply held her hand, and sat there in that fashion until she fumbled for a tissue lying on the bed and weakly blew her nose.

'Thomas.'

'Yes, I know. I'm so sorry.'

'He wanted what was best for me. He was a good son.'

'Yes,' I said.

'I didn't appreciate him enough . . .'

'Don't feel guilty,' I said.

'But I do. I can't help it. I should have let him take me with him as soon as Valentine died.'

'No,' I said. 'Stop it, dearest Dorothea. You are not to blame for anything. You mustn't blame yourself.'

'But *why*? Why would anyone want to kill my Paul?'

'The police will find out.'

'I can't *bear* it.' The tears came again, preventing speech.

I went out of her room to ask the nurses to give Dorothea a sedative. She had already been given one. No more without a doctor's say-so, they said.

'Then get a doctor,' I told them irritably. 'Her son's been murdered. She's feeling guilty.'

'Guilty? Why?'

It was too difficult to explain. 'She will be seriously ill by morning if you don't do something.'

I went back to Dorothea thinking I'd wasted my breath, but ten minutes later one of the nurses came in brightly and gave her an injection, which almost immediately sent her to sleep.

'That satisfy you?' the nurse asked me with a hint of sarcasm.

'Couldn't be better.'

I left the hospital and helped my driver find the way to Professor Derry. The driver was on time-and-a-half for evening work and said he was in no hurry at all to take me home.

Professor Derry's retirement was no gold-plated affair. He lived on the ground floor of a tall house divided horizontally into flats, himself occupying, it

273

transpired, a study, a bedroom, a bathroom and a screened-off kitchen alcove, all small and heavy looking in brown wood, all the fading domain of an ancient academic living frugally.

He was white haired, physically stooped and frail, but with eyes and mind in sharp array. He waved me into his study, sat me down on a wooden chair with arms and asked how he could help.

'I came for information about knives.'

'Yes, yes,' he interrupted. 'You said that on the phone.'

I looked around but could see no phone in his room. There had, however, been one – a pay phone – out in the hallway, shared with the upstairs tenants.

I said, 'If I show you a drawing of a knife, could you tell me about it?'

'I can try.'

I took the drawing of the Heath knife out of my jacket pocket and handed it to him folded. He opened it, flattened it out and laid it aside on his desk.

'I have to tell you,' he said with many small, rapid lip movements, 'that I have recently already been consulted about a knife like this.'

'You are an acknowledged expert, sir.'

'Yes.' He studied my face. 'Why do you not ask who consulted me? Have you no curiosity? I don't like students who have no curiosity.'

'I imagine it was the police.'

The old voice cackled in a wheezy sort of laugh. 'I see I have to reassess.'

'No, sir. It was I who found the knife on Newmarket Heath. The police took it into custody. I didn't know

274

they had consulted you. It was curiosity, strong and undiluted, that brought me here.'

'What did you read?'

'I never went to university.'

'Pity.'

'Thank you, sir.'

'I was going to have some coffee. Do you want some coffee?'

'Yes. Thank you, I'd like some.'

He nodded busily, pulled aside the screen, and in his kitchen alcove heated water, spooned instant powder into cups and asked about milk and sugar. I stood and helped him, the small domesticity a signal of his willingness to impart.

'I didn't care for the two young policemen who came here,' he said unexpectedly. 'They called me Granddad. Patronising.'

'Stupid of them.'

'Yes. The shell grows old, but not the inhabiting intellect. People see the shell and call me Granddad. And *Dearie*. What do you think of *Dearie*?'

'I'd kill 'em.'

'Quite right.' He cackled again. We carried the cups across to the chairs. 'The knife the police brought here,' he said, 'is a modern replica of a trench knife issued to American soldiers in France in the First World War.'

'Wow,' I said.

'Don't use that ridiculous word.'

'No, sir.'

'The policemen asked why I thought it was a replica and not the real thing. I told them to open their eyes. They didn't like it.'

'Well . . . er . . . how did you know?'

He cackled. 'It had "Made in Taiwan" stamped into the metal. Go on, say it.'

I said, 'Taiwan wasn't called Taiwan in World War One.'

'Correct. It was Formosa. And at that point in its history, it was not an industrial island.' He sat and tasted his coffee, which, like mine, was weak. 'The police wanted to know who owned the knife. How could I possibly know? I said it wasn't legal in England to carry such a knife in a public place, and I asked where they had found it.'

'What did they say?'

'They didn't. They said it didn't concern me. Granddad.'

I told him in detail how the police had acquired their trophy and he said, mocking me, 'Wow.'

I was becoming accustomed to him and to his crowded room, aware now of the walls of bookshelves, so like Valentine's, and of his cluttered old antique walnut desk, of the single brass lamp with green metal shade throwing inadequate light, of rusty-green velvet curtains hanging from great brown rings on a pole, of an incongruously modern television set beside a worn old typewriter, of dried faded hydrangeas in a cloisonné vase and a brass Roman-numeralled clock ticking away the remains of a life.

The room, neat and orderly, smelled of old books, of old leather, of old coffee, of old pipe smoke, of old man. There was no heating, despite the chilly evening. An old three-barred electric fire stood black and cold. The professor wore a sweater, a scarf, a shabby tweed jacket with elbow patches, and indoor slippers of brown checked wool. Bifocals gave him sight, and he had meticulously shaved: he might be old and short of cash, but standards had nowhere slipped.

On the desk, in a silver frame, there was an indistinct old photograph of a younger himself standing beside a woman, both of them smiling.

'My wife,' he explained, seeing where I was looking. 'She died.'

'I'm sorry.'

'It happens,' he said. 'It was long ago.'

I drank my unexciting coffee, and he delicately brought up the subject of his fee.

'I haven't forgotten,' I said, 'but there's another knife I'd like to ask you about.'

'What knife?'

'Two knives, actually.' I paused. 'One has a handle of polished striped wood that I think may be rosewood. It has a black hilt and a black double-edged blade an inch wide and almost six inches long.'

'A *black* blade?'

I confirmed it. 'It's a strong, purposeful and good-looking weapon. Would you know it from that description?'

He put his empty cup carefully on his desk and took mine also.

He said, 'The best-known black-bladed knife is the British commando knife. Useful for killing sentries on dark nights.'

I nearly said 'Wow' again, not so much at the content of what he said, but at his acceptance that the purpose of such knives was death.

'They usually come in olive-khaki webbing sheaths,' he said, 'with a slot for a belt and cords for tying the bottom of the sheath round the leg.'

'The one I saw had no sheath,' I said.

'Pity. Was it authentic, or a replica?'

'I don't know.'

'Where did you see it?'

'It was given to me, in a box. I don't know who gave it, but I know where it is. I'll look for "Made in Taiwan".'

'There were thousands made in World War Two, but they are collectors' items now. And, of course, in Britain one can no longer sell, advertise or even give such knives since the Criminal Justice Act of 1988. A collection can be confiscated. No one who owns a collection will have it on display these days.'

'Really?'

He smiled dimly at my surprise. 'Where have you been, young man?'

'I live in California.'

'Ah. That explains it. Knives of all sorts are legal in the United States. Over there, they have clubs for aficionados, and monthly magazines, and shops and shows, and also one can buy almost any knife by mail order.' He paused. 'I would guess that the trench knife the police showed me came here illegally from America.'

I waited a few seconds, thinking things over, and then said, 'I'd like to draw another knife for you, if you have a piece of paper.'

He provided a notepad and I drew the Fury, giving it its name.

Derry looked at the drawing in ominous stillness, finally saying, 'Where did you see this?'

'In England.'

'Who owns it?'

'I don't know,' I said. 'I hoped you might.'

'No, I don't. As I said, anyone who owns such a thing in Britain keeps it invisible and secret.'

I sighed. I'd hoped much from Professor Derry.

'The knife you've drawn,' he said, 'is called the Armadillo. Fury is the manufacturer's mark. It's made of stainless steel in Japan. It is expensive, heavy and infinitely sharp and dangerous.'

'Mm.'

After a silence, I said, 'Professor, what sort of person likes to own such knives, even in secret? Or, perhaps, particularly in secret?'

'Almost anyone,' he said. 'It's easy to buy this knife in the United States. There are hundreds of thousands of knife buffs in the world. People collect guns, they collect knives, they like the feeling of power . . .' His voice faded on the edge of personal revelation and he looked down at the drawing as if unwilling for me to see his eyes.

'Do you,' I asked carefully, without inflection, 'own a collection? A collection left over, perhaps, from when it was legal?'

'You can't ask that,' he said.

A silence.

'The Armadillo,' he said, 'comes in a heavy black leather protective sheath with a button closure. The sheath is intended to be worn on a belt.'

'The one I saw had no sheath.'

'It isn't safe, let alone legal, to carry it without a sheath.'

'I don't think safety was of prime importance.'

'You talk in riddles, young man.'

'So do you, Professor. The subject is one of innuendo and mistrust.'

'I don't know that you wouldn't go to the police.'

'And I,' I said, 'don't know that you wouldn't.'

Another silence.

'I'll tell you something, young man,' Derry said. 'If you are in any danger from the person who owns these knives, be very careful.' He considered his words. 'Normally knives such as these would be locked away. I find it disturbing that one was *used* on Newmarket Heath.'

'Could the police trace its owner?'

'Extremely unlikely,' he said. 'They didn't know where to begin, and I couldn't help them.'

'And the Armadillo's owner?'

He shook his head. 'Thousands will have been made. The Fury Armadillo does, I believe, have a serial number. It would identify when a particular knife was made and one might even trace it to its first owner. But from there it could be sold, stolen or given several times. I cannot envisage these knives you've seen being allowed into the light of day if they were traceable.'

Depressing, I thought.

I said, 'Professor, please show me your collection.'

'Certainly not.'

A pause.

I said, 'I'll tell you where I saw the Armadillo.'

'Go on, then.'

His old face was firm, his eyes unblinking. He promised nothing, but I needed more.

'A man I knew was murdered today,' I said. 'He was killed in a house in Newmarket with an ordinary kitchen knife. It is his mother's house. Last Saturday, in the same house, his mother was badly slashed by a knife, but no weapons were found. She lived, and she's recovering in hospital. On the Heath, as I told you, we believe the star of our picture was an intended victim. The police are investigating all three of these things.'

He stared.

I went on. 'At first sight there seems to be no connection between today's murder and the attack on the Heath. I'm not sure, but I think that there may be.'

He frowned. 'Why do you think so?'

'A feeling. Too many knives all at once. And . . . well . . . do you remember Valentine Clark? He died of cancer a week ago today.'

Derry's stare grew ever more intense. When he didn't answer I said, 'It was Valentine's sister, Dorothea Pannier, who was slashed last Saturday, in the house she shared with Valentine. The house was ransacked. Today her son Paul, Valentine's nephew, went to the house and was killed there. There is indeed someone very dangerous roaming around and if the police find him – or her – quickly . . . great.'

Unguessable thoughts occupied the professor's mind for whole long minutes. Finally he said, 'I became interested in knives when I was a boy. Someone gave me a Swiss Army knife with many blades. I treasured it.' He smiled briefly with small mouth movements. 'I was a lonely child. The knife made me feel more able to deal with the world. But there you are, that's how I think many people are drawn towards collecting, especially collecting weapons that one could use if one were ... bolder, perhaps, or criminal. They are a crutch, a secret power.'

'I see,' I said, as he paused.

'Knives fascinated me,' Derry went on. 'They were my companions. I carried them everywhere. I had them strapped to my leg, or to my arm under my sleeve. I wore them on my belt. I felt warm with them, and more confident. Of course, it was adolescence ... but as I grew older, I collected more, not less. I rationalised my feelings. I was a student, making a serious study, or so I thought. It went on for very many years, this sort of self-confidence. I became an acknowledged expert. I am, as you know, *consulted*.'

'Yes .'

'Slowly, some years ago, my need for knives vanished. You may say that at about sixty-five I finally grew up. Even so, I've kept my knowledge of knives current, because consultancy fees, though infrequent, are welcome.'

'Mm.'

'I do still own a collection, as you realise, but I seldom look at it. I have left it to a museum in my will. If those young policemen had known of its existence, they had the power to take it away.'

'I can't believe it!'

With the long-suffering smile of a tutor for a dim student, he pulled open a drawer in his desk, fumbled around a little and produced a photo-copied sheet of paper, finely printed, which he handed to me.

I read the heading. PREVENTION OF CRIME ACT 1953. OFFENSIVE WEAPONS.

'Take it and read it later,' he said. 'I give this to everyone who asks about knives. And now, young man, tell me where you saw the Armadillo.'

I paid my dues. I said, 'Someone stuck it into me. I saw it after it was pulled out.'

His mouth opened. I had really surprised him. He recovered a little and said, 'Was this a *game*?'

'I think I was supposed to die. The knife hit a rib, and here I am.'

'Great God.' He thought. 'Then the police have the Armadillo also?'

'No,' I said. 'I've good reasons for not going to the police. So I'm trusting you, Professor.'

'Tell me the reasons.'

I explained about the moguls and their horror of jinxes. I said I wanted to complete the film, which I couldn't do with police intervention.

'You are as obsessed as anybody,' Derry judged.

'Very likely.'

He wanted to know where and how I had – er, *acquired* – my first-hand knowledge of the knife in question, and I told him. I told him about the body protectors, and all about Robbie Gill's ministrations; all except the doctor's name.

When I stopped, I waited another long minute for his reaction. The old eyes watched me steadily.

He stood up. 'Come with me,' he said, and led the way through a brown door to an inner room, which proved to be his bedroom, a monastic-looking cell with a polished wood floor and a high old-fashioned iron bed with a white counterpane. There was a brown wooden wardrobe, a heavy chest of drawers and a single upright chair against plain white walls. The right ambience, I thought, for a mediaevalist.

He creaked down onto his knees by the bed as if about to say his prayers, but instead reached under the bedspread at floor level, and tugged.

A large wooden box on casters slowly rolled out, its dusty lid padlocked to the base. Roughly four feet long by three wide, it was at least a foot deep, and it looked formidably heavy.

The professor fumbled for a key ring which bore four keys only, and removed the padlock, opening the lid until it leaned back against the bed. Inside there was an expanse of green baize, and below that, when he removed it, row upon row of thin brown cardboard boxes, each bearing a neat white label with typewritten words identifying the contents. He looked them over, muttering that he hadn't inspected them for months, and picked out one of them, very much not at random.

'This,' he said, opening the narrow brown box, 'is a genuine commando knife, not a replica.'

The professor's commando knife was kept safe in bubble packing but, unwrapped, looked identical to the one sent to me as a warning, except that this one did have its sheath.

'I no longer,' he said unnecessarily, 'keep my knives on display. I packed them all away when my wife died, before I came here. She shared my interest, you see. She *grew* to be interested. I miss her.'

'I'm sure you do.'

He closed the commando knife away and opened other treasures.

'These two knives from Persia, they have a curved blade, and handles and sheaths of engraved silver with lapis lazuli inserts. These are from Japan . . . these from America, with carved bone handles in the shape of animal heads. All hand-made, of course. All magnificent specimens.'

All lethal, I thought.

'This beautiful knife is Russian, nineteenth century,' he said at one point. 'Closed, like this, it resembles, as you see, a Fabergé egg, but in fact five separate blades open from it.' He pulled out the blades until they resembled a rosette of sharp leaves spreading out from the base of the egg-shaped grip, itself enamelled in blue and banded in fine gold.

'Er . . .' I said, 'your collection must be valuable. Why don't you sell it?'

'Young man, read the paper I gave you. It can be *illegal* to sell these things. One may now only give them to museums, not even to other individuals, and then only to museums that don't make a profit from exhibiting them.'

'It's amazing!'

'It stops law-abiding people in their tracks, but criminals take no notice. The world is as mediaeval as ever. Didn't you know?'

'I suspected it.'

His laugh cackled. 'Help me lift the top tray onto the bed. I'll show you some curiosities.'

The top tray had a rope handle at each end. He

grasped one end, I the other and, at his say-so, we lifted together. The tray was heavy. Not good, from my point of view.

'What's the matter?' he demanded. 'Did that hurt you?'

'Just the Armadillo,' I apologised.

'Do you want to sit down?'

'No, I want to see your knives.'

He knelt on the floor again and opened more boxes, removing the bubble wrapping and putting each trophy into my hand for me to 'feel the balance'.

His 'curiosities' tended to be ever more fearsome. There were several knives along the lines of the American trench knife (the genuine thing, 1918) and a whole terrifying group of second cousins to the Armadillo, knives with whole-hand grips, semi-circular blades and rows of spikes, all dedicated to tearing an opponent to shreds.

As I gave each piece back to him he re-wrapped it and restored it to its box, tidying methodically as he went along.

He showed me a large crucifix fashioned in dark red cloisonné, handsome on a gold chain for use as a chest ornament, but hiding a dagger in its heart. He showed me an ordinary-looking belt that one could use to hold up one's trousers: ordinary except that the buckle, which slid easily out into my hand, proved to be the handle of a sharp triangular blade that could be pushed home to kill.

Professor Derry delivered a grave warning. 'Thomas . . .' (we had progressed from 'young man') 'Thomas, if a man – or woman – is truly obsessed with knives, you must expect that *anything* he or she carries on their person may be the sheath of a knife. One can get key rings, money clips, hair combs, all with hidden blades. Knives can be hidden even under the lapels of a coat, in special transparent sheaths designed to be stitched onto cloth. A dangerous fanatic will *feed* on this hidden power. Do you at all understand?'

'I'm beginning to.'

He nodded several times and asked if I would be able to help him replace the top tray.

'Before we do that, Professor, would you show me one more knife?'

'Well, yes, of course.' He looked vaguely at the seas of boxes. 'What sort of thing do you want?'

'Can I see the knife that Valentine Clark once gave you?'

After another of his tell-tale pauses, he said, 'I don't know what you're talking about.'

'You did know Valentine, didn't you?' I asked.

He levered himself to his feet and headed back into his study, switching off the bedroom light as he went: to save electricity, I supposed.

I followed him, and we resumed our former positions in his wooden armchairs. He asked for my connection with Valentine, and I told him about my childhood, and about Valentine recently leaving me his books. 'I read to him while he couldn't see. I was with him not long before he died.'

Reassured by my account, Derry felt able to talk. 'I knew Valentine quite well at one time. We met at one of those ridiculous fund-raising events, all for a good cause, where people stood around with tea or small glasses of bad wine, being civil and wishing they could go home. I hated those affairs. My dear wife had a soft heart and was always coaxing me to take her, and I couldn't deny her . . . So long ago. So long ago.'

I waited through his wave of regret and loneliness, unable to comfort the nostalgia.

'Thirty years ago, it must be,' he said, 'since we met Valentine. They were raising funds to stop the shipment of live horses to the Continent to be killed for meat. Valentine was one of the speakers. He and I just liked each other . . . and we came from such different backgrounds. I began reading his column in the newspapers, though I wasn't much interested in racing. But Valentine was so *wise* . . . and still an active blacksmith . . . a gust of fresh air, you see, when I was more used to the claustrophobia of university life. My dear wife liked him, and we met him and his wife several times, but it was Valentine and I who *talked*. He came from one sort of world and I from another, and it was perhaps because of that that we could discuss things with each other that we couldn't have mentioned to our colleagues.'

I asked without pressure, 'What sort of things?'

'Oh . . . medical, sometimes. Growing old. I would never have told you this once, but since I passed eighty I've lost almost all my inhibitions, I don't *care* so much about things. I told Valentine I was having impotency problems, and I was not yet sixty. Are you laughing?'

'No, sir,' I said truthfully.

'It was easy to ask Valentine for advice. One *trusted* him.'

'Yes.'

'We were the same age. I asked him if he had the

288

same problem but he told me his problem was the opposite, he was aroused by young women and had difficulty in controlling his urges.'

'*Valentine?*' I exclaimed, astonished.

'People hide things,' Derry said simply. 'My dear wife didn't really mind that I could no longer easily make love to her, but she used to joke to other people about how *sexy* I was. Such a dreadful word! She wanted people to admire me, she said.' He shook his head in love and sorrow. 'Valentine told me a doctor to go to. He himself knew of all sorts of ways to deal with impotence. He told me he'd learned a lot of them from stud farms! He said I must be more light-hearted and not think of impotence as an embarrassment or a tragedy. He told me it wasn't the end of the world.' He paused. 'Because of Valentine, I learned to be content.'

'He was great to so many people,' I said.

The professor nodded, still reminiscing. 'He told me something I've never been able to verify. He swore it was true. I've always *wondered* ... If I ask you something, Thomas, will you answer me truthfully?'

'Of course.'

'You may be too young.'

'Try me.'

'In confidence.'

'Yes.'

Nothing, I'd told Moncrieff, was ever off the record. But confessions were, surely?

The professor said, 'Valentine told me that restricting the flow of oxygen to the brain could result in an erection.'

289

He waited for my comment, which took a while to materialise. I hesitantly said, 'Er . . . I've heard of it.'

'Tell me, then.'

'I believe it's a perversion that comes under the general heading of auto-erotic mania. In this case, self-inflicted partial asphyxia.'

He said impatiently, 'Valentine told me that thirty years ago. What I'm asking you is, does it work?'

'First hand, I don't know.'

He said with a touch of bitterness, 'Because you've never needed to find out?'

'Well, not yet, no.'

'Then . . . has anyone told you?'

'Not first hand.'

He sighed. 'I could never face doing it. It's one of those things I'm never going to know.'

'There are others?'

'Don't be stupid, Thomas. I am a mediaevalist. I know the facts that were written down. I try to feel my way into that lost world. I cannot smell it, hear it, live it. I can't know its secret fears and its assumptions. I've spent a lifetime learning and teaching at second hand. If I went to sleep now and awoke in the year fourteen hundred, I wouldn't understand the language or know how to cook a meal. You've heard the old saying that if Jesus returned to do a replay of the Sermon on the Mount, no one now living would understand him, as he would be speaking ancient Hebrew with a Nazareth carpenter's accent? Well, I've wasted a lifetime on an unintelligible past.'

'No, Professor,' I protested.

'Yes,' he said resignedly. 'I don't think I any longer

care. And I no longer have anyone to talk to. I can't talk to boring social workers who think I need looking after, and who call me "dearie". But I find I'm talking to *you*, Thomas, and I'm an old fool who should know better.'

'Please go on talking,' I said. 'Go on about Valentine.'

'These last years, I haven't seen him much. His wife died. So did mine. You might think it would have drawn us together, but it didn't. I suppose it was our wives who had arranged our meetings. Valentine and I just drifted apart.'

'But,' I said, 'years ago ... he knew you were interested in knives?'

'Oh yes, of course. He was enthusiastic about my collection. He and his wife used to come over to our house and the women would chat together and I would show Valentine the knives.'

'He told me he gave you one.'

'He *told you* ...?' —

'Yes.'

The professor frowned. 'I remember him saying I wasn't ever to say who had given me that knife. He said just to keep it in case he asked for it back ... but he never asked. I haven't thought about it. I'd forgotten it.' He paused. '*Why* do you want to see it?'

'Just curiosity ... and fondness for my old friend.'

The professor thought it over, and said, 'I suppose if he told you, he wouldn't mind.'

He got to his feet and returned to the bedroom, with me on his heels. The light went on dimly; an economical bulb.

'I'm afraid,' my host said doubtfully, 'that there are three levels of knives in this chest, and we have to lift out the second tray to reach the knife you want to see. Are you able to lift it out onto the floor? It doesn't have to go up onto the bed.'

I assured him I could, and did it left-handed, a shade better. The third layer, revealed, proved not to be of brown cardboard boxes but of longer parcels, each wrapped only in bubble plastic, and labelled.

'These are mostly swords,' Derry said. 'And sword-sticks, and a couple of umbrellas with swords in the handles. They were a defence against footpads a hundred or two hundred years ago. Now, of course, they are illegal. One has nowadays to allow oneself to be mugged.' He cackled gently. 'You mustn't hurt the poor robber, you know.'

He surveyed the labels, running his fingers along the rows.

'Here we are. "Present from V.C."' He lifted out a bubble-wrapped package, snapped open a sellotaped fastening and unrolled the parcel to reveal the contents.

'There you are,' Professor Derry said, 'that's Valentine's knife.'

I looked at it. It was like no knife I'd ever seen. It was at least fifteen inches long, possibly eighteen. Its blade, double-edged and clearly sharp, took up barely a third of the overall length and was of an elongated flat oval like a spear, with a sharp spear's point. The long handle was narrow and was twisted throughout its length in a close spiral. The end of the spiral had been flattened into a circular embellishment, perforated with several holes.

'It's not a knife,' I said. 'It's a spear.'

Derry smiled. 'It's not meant for throwing.'

'What was it for?'

'I don't know. Valentine simply asked me if I'd like to put it in my collection. It's hammered steel. Unique.'

'But where would he buy such a thing?'

'Buy it?' The full cackle rang out. 'Have you forgotten Valentine's trade? He was a smith. He didn't buy it. He *made* it.'

CHAPTER FOURTEEN

Early Friday morning I worked in peace from four o'clock to six-thirty in the projection room, cutting scenes into rough order, a process that apart from anything else always told me what necessary establishing shots hadn't been provided for in the screenplay. A five-second shot here and there could replace, also, patches of dialogue that hadn't gone well. I made notes, fiddled about, hummed with contentment, clarified the vision.

By six-thirty Moncrieff was setting up the cameras in the stable yard, by seven the horses (back from Huntingdon) were out at exercise on the Heath, by seventhirty the wardrobe and make-up departments were at work in the house, and at eight-thirty O'Hara's car swept into the yard with the horn blowing.

The lads, back from the Heath to groom and feed their charges, came out of the open-doored boxes at the summons. Wardrobe and make-up appeared. The camera crews paused to listen. Actors and extras stood around.

Satisfied, O'Hara borrowed Ed's megaphone and announced that the Hollywood company was pleased with the way things were going, and that as he himself was now leaving for Los Angeles, Thomas Lyon would be in sole charge of the production.

He handed the megaphone back to Ed, waved everyone away to resume work, and gave me a challenging stare.

'Well?' he said.

'I'd rather you stayed.'

'It's your film,' he insisted. 'But you will please not go anywhere without your driver and your bodyguard.' He looked around. 'Where are they, anyway?'

'I'm safe here,' I said.

'You are not to think you're safe *anywhere*, Thomas.' He handed me a key, explaining it was his hotel key. 'Use my rooms if you need them. The two knives are in the safe in there The combination is four five, four five. Got it?'

'Yes . . . but how will I reach you?'

'Phone my secretary in LA. She'll know.'

'Don't go.'

He smiled. 'My airplane leaves at noon. See you, guy.'

He climbed into his car with finality and was driven away, and I felt like a junior general left in charge of a major battlefield, apprehensive, half confident, emotionally naked.

The schedule that morning was for some of the earliest scenes of the film, the arrival of the police to investigate the hanging. Moncrieff set about lighting the actors some in and some out of police uniform – explaining exactly where he wanted them to stop and turn towards the camera. He and they would be work-

295

ing from the plans and diagrams we'd drawn the evening before on my return from Cambridge.

Leaving Ed to supervise, I drove back to Bedford Lodge for a quiet breakfast in my rooms and found my driver and black-belt distractedly pacing the lobby and fearing the sack.

'Calm down,' I said. 'Your day starts in an hour.'

'Mr O'Hara said . . .'

'One hour,' I reiterated, and went upstairs thinking that as they hadn't saved me from the Armadillo I might do equally well on my own.

Room service brought my breakfast and a visitor, Robbie Gill.

'I should be listening to chests and prescribing cough mixture,' he said. 'My receptionist is dealing with a seething line of disgruntled patients. Take your clothes off.'

'Do what?'

'Sweater and shirt off,' he repeated. 'Undo your trousers. I've come to save your unworthy life.'

Busily he unpacked things from his case, moving my croissant and coffee aside and eating my ham with his fingers.

'Hope you're not hungry,' he said, munching.

'Starving.'

'Too bad. Get undressed.'

'Er . . . what for?'

'Number one, fresh dressing. Number two, knife-proof vest. I tried to get a proper bullet-and-knife-proof vest but neither the police nor the army would let me have one without bureaucracy, so we'll have to trust to home made.'

I took off my sweater and shirt and he removed the dressing, raising his eyebrows at the revealed scenery but appearing not displeased.

'You're healing. Is it sore?'

'The broken rib is.'

'Only to be expected,' he added, and stuck on a new dressing. 'Now,' he said, 'what do you know about Delta-cast?'

'Nothing.'

'It's used instead of the old plaster of Paris for fractured arms and legs. It's rigid. It's a polymer, actually, and porous, so you won't itch. A knife won't go through it.'

'A bullet?'

'That's another matter.'

He worked for half an hour, during which time we discussed Dorothea and Paul, and came to no useful conclusions, though I explained how, via Bill Robinson, I was now surrounded by the army of boxes containing Valentine's books.

At the end of Robbie's work I was encased from chin to waist in a hard sleeveless jacket that I could take off and put on in two halves and fasten with strips of Velcro.

When I protested at its height round my neck he said merely, 'Do you want your throat cut? Wear a polo-necked sweater. I brought you this thin white one, in case you hadn't got one.' He handed it over as if it were nothing.

'Thanks, Robbie,' I said, and he could hear I meant it.

He nodded briefly. 'I'd better get back to my mob of

coughers, or they'll lynch me.' He packed things away. 'Do you think your hanged lady was lynched?'

'No, I don't think so.'

'Did you trawl any useful mud with Professor Derry?'

'The knife that bust my rib is called an Armadillo. The one with the finger holes, from the Heath, is a replica from World War One. The police had already asked the professor about it.'

'Wow.'

'The professor's about eighty-five. He told me not to say wow.'

'He sounds a riot.'

'We got on fine, but he doesn't know who owns the Armadillo.'

'Take care,' he said, leaving. 'I'm around if you need me.'

I ate what was left of my breakfast, dressed slowly, shaved and gradually got used to living like a turtle inside a carapace.

At about the time I was ready to leave again the people at the reception desk phoned up to tell me that a young woman was asking for me. She thought I was expecting her. A Miss Lucy Wells.

'Oh, yes.' I'd temporarily forgotten her. 'Please send her up.'

Lucy had come in jeans, sweater, trainers and pony-tail, chiefly with the cool eighteen-year-old young lady in charge but with occasional tongue-tied lapses. She looked blankly at the multitude of boxes and wanted to know where to begin.

I gave her a lap-top computer, a notebook, a biro and a big black marker pen.

'Give each box a big number,' I said, writing 'I' with the marker pen on a microwave oven carton. 'Empty it out. Write a list of the contents on the pad, enter the list on the little computer and then put everything back, topping each box with the list of contents. On another page, write me a general list, saying, for example, "Box I, books, biographies of owners and trainers." OK?'

'Yes.'

'Shake out each book in case it has loose papers inside its pages, and don't throw anything away, not even pointless scraps.'

'All right.' She seemed puzzled, but I didn't amplify.

'Order lunch from room service,' I said. 'Don't leave any papers or books lying around when the waiter comes. OK?'

'Yes, but why?'

'Just do the job, Lucy. Here's the room key for here.' I gave it to her. 'If you leave this room, use the key to return. When I come back I'll bring Nash Rourke in for a drink.'

Her blue eyes widened. She wasn't a fool. She looked at the boxes and settled for the package I'd offered.

I went back to work, driver and bodyguard giving me a lot less confidence than Delta-cast. We spent all morning in the stable yard, with Nash patiently (both in and out of character) dealing with the actors playing at police.

The initial police doubts, called for in the script, took an age to get right. 'I don't want these policemen to appear *thick*,' I pleaded, but it was the actors, I concluded, who were slow. I'd had no hand in casting minor characters; the trick was to make the dumbest poodle jump through the hoops.

Moncrieff swore non-stop. Nash could turn and get the light across his forehead right every time, but Nash, I reminded my fuming director of photography, wasn't called a mega-star for nothing.

The level of muddle was not helped by the arrival of the real police asking why my fresh fingerprints were all over Dorothea's house. We could have played it for laughs, but no one was funny. I proved to have an alibi for whenever it was that Paul had died (they wouldn't or couldn't say exactly when) but the stoppage ate up my lunch hour.

Back at work we progressed at length to the first arrival (by car) of Cibber, and to his planting of suspicions against Nash in the (fictional) police mind. Cibber was a good pro, but inclined still to tell inappropriate fruity jokes and waste time. 'Sorry, sorry,' he would breezily say, fluffing his words without remorse.

I hung on grimly to forbearance and walked twice out onto the Heath breathing deeply with sore rib twinges while Moncrieff's men loaded the cameras for the eighth take of a fairly simple sequence. I phoned Wrigley's garage and asked if Bill Robinson could have the afternoon off, and I spoke to Bill himself, thanking him for the second safe delivery of the boxes and asking him to open his home garage and bring bits of motorbike out onto his drive.

'We've decided to film your stuff after dark,' I said.

'Can you spare us the evening? And will you have your big bike at home?'

Natch, fine, yes indeedy, and cor, he said.

Tired and a shade dispirited I called it a day at five-thirty in the afternoon and invited Nash to my Bedford Lodge rooms for a reviver.

'Sure,' he agreed easily, and greeted Lucy with enough warmth to tongue-tie her into knock knees.

'How did you get on?' I asked her, explaining the task briefly to Nash; and she apologised for being slow and having completed only five boxes. She had just discovered that one of the boxes held some clippings about Sonia's death. Wasn't that extraordinary? Box six, she said. She hadn't had time to go through them.

'That's fine,' I said. 'Come again tomorrow, will you? Are you going right home at nights? Or perhaps staying with your Uncle Ridley?'

She made a face. 'Not with him. Actually,' she blushed perceptibly, 'I'm staying here in this hotel. They had a room free and Dad agreed. I hope that's all right?'

'It's splendid,' I said moderately, knowing enthusiasm would frighten her. 'What about Sunday, day after tomorrow?'

'I can stay until the job's finished,' she said. 'Dad said it was better.'

'Good for Dad,' Nash smiled.

'He's awfully interested,' Lucy said, and after a pause added, 'It's really odd, Mr Rourke, imagining you as my dad.'

Nash smiled, the eyelids crinkling. Despite his preg-

301

nant wife, he didn't look at all like anyone's dad, certainly not Lucy's.

We drank briefly together and split up, Nash yawning as he went and saying the slavedriver (T. Lyon) wanted him out working again in a couple of hours. Lucy, without making an issue of it, excused herself at the same time. Staying in the hotel, she was telling me, meant no more than convenience.

When she'd gone I looked at her master list of the boxes' contents. Since they had been well jumbled up on the journeys, and since she had started methodically at one end, the six boxes she'd worked on held mixed and random contents.

Box I. Form books. Flat racing.
Box II. Biographies, trainers, owners and jockeys.
Box III. Form books. National Hunt racing.
Box IV. Weekly columns, *Racing Gazette*.
Box V. Books, annuals, racing history.

With unstoppable curiosity I knelt on the floor and opened Box III, National Hunt form books, and found that by happy chance it contained the records of two of the years when I'd been racing.

A British racing form book, built up week by week throughout the season with loose-leaf inserts tied between soft leather covers, contained details of every single race run, identifying each runner by name, trainer, jockey, weight carried, age and sex, and giving a start-to-finish commentary of performance.

There was no gainsaying the form book. If the form

books said Mr T. Lyon (the Mr denoting amateur status) had finished fifth a long way back, it was no good Mr T. Lyon in memory thinking he'd ridden a close contest to be beaten by half a length. Mr T. Lyon, I read with nostalgia, had won a three-mile steeplechase by two lengths at Newbury, the horse carrying ten stone six. The underfoot conditions that day had been classified as 'soft', and the starting price had been 100–6, Mr T. Lyon's mount having unaccountably beaten the hot favourite (weighted out of it, carrying 20 lbs more). Mr T. Lyon, I remembered, had been ecstatic. The crowd, who'd mostly lost their bets, had been unenthusiastically silent.

I smiled. Here I was, twelve years later, clad in Delta-cast and trying not to be killed: and I didn't think I'd ever been happier than on that cold long-ago afternoon.

Valentine had put a red exclamation mark against my winner, which meant that he personally had fitted the horse with shoes especially for racing, probably on the morning of the race.

Horses wore thin aluminium shoes for racing, much lighter and thinner than the steel shoes they needed in the stable and out at exercise. Farriers would routinely change the shoes before and after a race.

Owing to chance, the form books in Box III went back only as far as my seventeenth birthday. For the Mr T. Lyon debut at sixteen to turn up, I would have to wait for Lucy.

I opened Box I, Flat racing form books, and found that in this instance the books were older. These, indeed, covered the few years when Jackson Wells had been training in Newmarket: one of them covered the year of Sonia's death.

Fascinated, I looked for Valentine's red dots (runners) and red exclamation marks (winners) and found my grandfather's name as trainer all over the place. Twenty-six years ago, when I'd been four. A whole generation ago. So many of them gone. So many horses, so many races, lost and forgotten.

Jackson Wells hadn't had large numbers of runners and precious few winners, as far as I could see. Jackson Wells hadn't had a regular jockey either: only successful wealthy stables could afford to retain a top-flighter. Several of the Wells horses had been ridden by a P. Falmouth, several others by D. Carsington, neither of whom I'd heard of, which wasn't surprising.

On the day of his wife's death, Jackson Wells had set off to York races where a horse from his stable had been entered. I looked up the actual day and found his horse hadn't started and was listed as a non-runner. Trainer Wells had been on his way back to Newmarket when they'd run the race without him.

I flicked forward through the pages. Valentine's dots for Jackson Wells were scattered and diminishing in number. There was only one exclamation mark, a minor race on a minor track, ridden by the minor jockey, D. Carsington.

'A winner is a winner,' my grandfather always said. 'Never despise the lowliest.'

I put the form books back in the box, dutifully collected my guardian shadows from the lobby, and went by car to Betty's house to ask if she by any chance

304

had Dorothea's key. She shook her head. *Poor* Dorothea; that poor man, Paul.

Betty's husband wasn't grieving for Paul. If I wanted to start tidying Dorothea's house, he said, he could open her door in no time. Betty's husband was an all-round handyman. A little how's-your-father and a shove, he said, would circumvent most locks, and consequently he and I soon went from room to ravaged room righting the mess as best we could. The police, he said, had taken their photos and their fingerprints and left. The house, such as it was, and crammed with bad memories, was Dorothea's to come home to.

I spent most time in her bedroom, looking for the photographs she said she kept in a box. I couldn't find them. I told Betty's husband what I was looking for – Dorothea's only mementos of Paul when young – but neither of us succeeded.

'Poor love,' Betty's husband said. 'That son of hers was a brute, but she would never hear a strong word against him. Between you and me, he's no loss.'

'No . . . but who killed him?'

'Yeah, I see what you mean. Gives you a nasty feeling, doesn't it, some geezer running around with a knife?'

'Yes,' I said. 'It does.'

I stood in the dark street outside Bill Robinson's garage, with the black-belt at my back facing the crowd that had inevitably collected.

There were bright lights inside the garage where Bill Robinson himself stood, dressed in his accustomed black leather and studs and looking selfconscious. The monster Harley Davidson stood to one side. Pieces of a second, that Bill was rebuilding, lay in clumps on the drive. Moncrieff was busy pointing arc lamps and spots to give dramatic shadows and gleams, and Nash's stand-in walked to the designated point and looked towards the garage. Moncrieff lit his profile first, and then a three-quarter-face angle, one side bright, the other in darkness, only the liquid sheen of an eye showing.

Nash arrived, walked up beside me and watched.

'You pause,' I said. 'You're wondering how the hell you're going to get out of the fix you're in. You're psyching yourself up. OK?'

He nodded. He waved a hand towards the scene. 'It's striking,' he said, 'but why a bike?'

'It's what our movie is about.'

'How do you mean? There aren't any bikes in it, are there?'

'Fantasy,' I said. 'Our movie is about the need for fantasy.'

'The dream lovers?' he suggested doubtfully.

'Fantasy supplies what life doesn't,' I said casually. 'That boy there with his bike is eighteen, good natured, has a regular job, carries his elderly neighbour's shopping home for her, and in his fantasy life he's a hell raiser with roaring power between his legs and the gear and the studs. He's playing at what he wouldn't really like to be, but the imagining of it fills and satisfies him.'

Nash stood without moving. 'You sound as though you approve,' he said.

'Yes, I do. A good strong fantasy life, I'd guess, saves

306

countless people from boredom and depression. It gives them a feeling of being individual. They invent themselves. You know it perfectly well. You *are* a fantasy to most people.'

'What about serial killers? Aren't they fantasists?'

'There's a hell to every heaven.'

Moncrieff called, 'Ready, Thomas,' and Nash, without comment, went to the place from where he would walk into shot, and pause, and turn his head, and watch Bill Robinson live in his courage-inducing dreamland.

Ed went round explaining the necessity of silence to the neighbours. He shouted, 'Turn over.' The cameras reached speed. Ed yelled, 'Action.' Nash walked, stopped, turned his head. Perfect. Bill Robinson dropped a piece of exhaust pipe out of nervousness and said, 'Sorry.'

'Cut,' Ed said, disgusted.

'Don't say "sorry",' I told Bill Robinson, walking towards the garage to join him. 'It doesn't matter if you drop something. It doesn't matter if you swear. It's normal. Just don't say "sorry".'

He grinned. We shot the scene again and he fitted two shining pieces of metal together as if he hadn't got fifty people watching.

'Cut,' Ed yelled with approval, and the neighbours cheered. Nash shook Bill Robinson's hand and signed autographs. We sold a lot of future cinema tickets, and no one stuck a knife in my back. Not a bad evening, overall.

Returning to Bedford Lodge, Nash and I ate room-service dinner together.

'Go on,' he said, 'about the need for fantasy.'

'Oh ... I ...' I hesitated, and stopped, unwilling to sound a fool.

'Go on,' he urged. 'People say ... in fact *I* say ... that play-acting isn't a suitable occupation for a serious man. So tell me why it is.'

'You don't need me to tell you.'

'Tell me why you make fantasies, then.'

'Have some wine.'

'Don't duck the issue, dammit.'

'Well,' I said, pouring lavishly, 'I wanted to be a jockey but I grew too big. Anyway, one day I went to see a doctor about some damage I'd done to my shoulder in a racing fall, and she asked me what I wanted to do with my life. I said "be a jockey" and she lectured me crossly on wasting my time on earth frivolously. I asked her what occupation she would recommend and she sternly told me that the only profession truly helpful and worthwhile was medicine.'

'Rubbish!'

'She scorned me for wanting to be merely an entertainer.'

Nash shook his head.

'So,' I said, 'I rationalised it, I suppose. I'm still an entertainer and always will be, I guess, and I've persuaded myself that I do at least as much good as tranquillisers. Everyone can go where their mind takes them. You can live in imaginary places without feeling the real terror or the real pain. I make the images. I open the door. I can inflame ... and I can heal ... and comfort ... and get people to understand ... and, for

God's sake, don't remember a word of this. I've just made it up to entertain you.'

He drank his wine thoughtfully.

'And in this movie that we're engaged in,' I said, 'the dream lovers make the spurned wife's existence happier. They're the best way she can face her husband's affair with her own sister. They're her refuge ... and her revenge.'

He smiled twistedly. 'My character's a shit, isn't he?'

'Human,' I said.

'And are you going to sell Howard on her suicide?'

I shook my head. 'I'm sure she didn't kill herself. But don't worry, your character will avenge her death and come up smelling of roses.'

'Has Howard written those extra scenes?'

'Not yet.'

'You're a rogue, Thomas, you know that?'

We finished dinner peaceably, and together with Moncrieff mapped out the next day's scenes, which were due to take place in the Athenaeum's look-alike dining-room, happily by now built and ready.

After that meeting I un-Velcroed my restricting knife-repeller with relief and washed without soaking the dressing, and in sleeping shorts thought I'd just take a quick look at the newspaper cuttings about Sonia's death before inching into bed: and two hours later, warmed by a dressing gown, I was still sitting in an armchair alternately amused and aghast and beginning to understand why Paul had desperately wanted to take away Valentine's books and why Valentine, perhaps, hadn't wanted him to have them. In leaving them to me, a comparative stranger, the old man had thought to safeguard the knowledge contained in them, since I couldn't have understood the significance of the clippings and might simply have thrown them away, a task he should have done himself but had left too late, until his progressing illness made action impossible.

Paul had wanted Valentine's books and papers, and Paul was dead. I looked at the Delta-cast jacket standing empty and mute on a table and felt a strong urge to fasten it on again, even at two in the morning.

In describing Sonia to me, Valentine had called her a mouse, but that couldn't have been how he'd thought of her when she was alive. The folder of clippings about her held two large photographs, both the likenesses of a vividly pretty young woman with a carefree spirit and, I would have said, considerable carnal knowledge.

One of the photographs was an expert, glossy, eight by ten black and white version of the coloured photo Lucy had lent me of 'Sonia and Pig'. In Valentine's photo the young man's presence had been deleted. Sonia smiled alone.

The second photo was of Sonia in her wedding dress, again alone, and again with nothing virginal about her eyes. My mother, of all people, had once instructed me about the difference: once a woman had slept with a man, she said, the woman would develop little pouches in her lower eyelids which would show when she smiled. Sonia was smiling in both pictures, and the small pouches were there unmistakably.

Valentine had said the book made her out to be a poor little bitch and, in saying that, he'd intended to mislead. The folder held clippings about her death from a myriad of newspapers and, in the most derogatory of the various accounts, in those most overtly speculatory about Mrs Wells's fidelity to Jackson, someone – and it had to have been Valentine himself – had stricken the accounts through and through with red biro and had written No! No! as if in pain.

I took everything out of the Sonia folder and found that beside the photos and the whole sheaf of newspaper cuttings, there were two frail dried roses, a brief note about shoeing which started 'Darling Valentine', and a wisp of creamy lace-edged panties.

Valentine had confessed he'd been too easily aroused by young women, Professor Derry had said. According to Valentine's own collection of memories, one of those young women had been Sonia Wells.

Poor old sod, I thought. He had been sixty, nearly, when she died. I was young enough to have considered sixty the far side of acute sexual obsession: Valentine enlightened even from beyond the grave.

The emotional vigour of the thick Sonia file blinded me for a long while to the slim folder underneath which lay at the bottom of the box: but this folder proved, when I read the contents carefully, to be raw explosive material in search of a detonator.

In search of myself.

I slept for five hours, put on the carapace, went back to work. Saturday morning. I struck it off in my mind's

311

calendar as Day Nineteen of production, or almost a third of my time allowed.

It rained all day, which didn't matter as we were engaged indoors in the Athenaeum dining-room, shooting the scene where Cibber's suspicions of his wife's canoodling gelled into inescapable certainty. Cibber and Silva endlessly said yes please and no thank you to actor-waiters; chewed endless mouthfuls of food, and in Silva's case spitting them out immediately I said 'Cut'; drank endless sips of wine-coloured water; waved (in Cibber's case) to unidentified acquaintances across the room; conducted a conversation of concentrated spite with rigidly smiling lips and a vivid awareness of social status. Jockey Club membership, to Cibber, meant not publicly slapping your wife's face in the most conservative dining-room in London.

Howard, I thought, as I listened and watched, had surpassed himself in understanding and reproducing the constraints of class on the potentially dangerous ego of a rejected male.

Silva sneered at Cibber with her eyes, her mouth saccharine. Silva told him she couldn't bear his hands on her breasts. Cibber, destroyed within, looked around to make sure the waiters hadn't heard. Both players gave the film enormously good value for money.

Breaking for lunch, with the close-ups to do in the afternoon, I returned for a respite to Bedford Lodge and found Nash in my rooms sprawling in an armchair and having an easy time with Lucy. She, in consequence, had, as her morning's work, itemised the contents of barely one and a half cartons.

'Oh, hallo,' she greeted me from her knees, 'what would you like me to do with three boxfuls of huge old encyclopaedias?'

'How old?'

She pulled out one large volume and investigated. 'Forty years!' Her voice made forty years unimaginable. Nash reflexly winced.

'Just label them and leave them,' I said.

'Right. Oh . . . and I haven't come across any photo albums, that you wanted me to look for, but I did find a lot of snaps in an old chocolate box. What do you want me to do with those?'

'In a chocolate box . . .?'

'Well, yes. It's got flowers on the lid. Pretty old.'

'Er . . . where's the box?'

She opened a carton that had once held a fax machine, and from it produced several box files full of ancient racecards and newspaper clippings of winners that Valentine had regularly shod. 'Here's the chocolate box,' Lucy said, lifting out and handing me a faded and battered gold-coloured cardboard box with flowers like dahlias on the lid. 'I didn't make a list of the photos. Do you want me to?'

'No,' I said absently, taking off the lid and finding small ancient pictures inside, many in long-ago faded colours with curling edges. Pictures of Valentine and his wife, pictures of Dorothea and her husband, a photo or two of Meredith Derry and his wife, and several of Dorothea with her child: with her nice-looking little boy, Paul. Pictures when life was fine, before time loused it up.

'How about ordering us all some lunch?' I said.

Nash did the ordering. 'What do you want to drink, Thomas?'

'Lethe,' I said.

'Not until you've finished the movie.'

'What's Lethe?' Lucy asked.

Nash said, 'The river in the underworld that, if you drink it, makes you sleep and forget about living.'

'Oh.'

'For ever,' Nash added. 'But Thomas doesn't mean that.'

Lucy covered non-comprehension in activity with the marker pen.

At the bottom of the chocolate box, I came across a larger print, the colours still not razor sharp, but in a better state of preservation. It was of a group of young people, all looking about twenty. On the back of the photo were two simple words – 'The Gang'.

The Gang.

The Gang consisted of five young men and a girl.

I sat staring at it for long enough for the other two to notice.

'What is it?' Nash asked. 'What have you found?'

I handed the photo to Lucy, who glanced at it, did a double take and then exclaimed, 'Why, that's Dad, isn't it? How *young* he looks.' She turned the photo over. 'The Gang,' she read aloud. 'That's his handwriting, isn't it?'

'You'd know better than I would.'

'I'm sure of it.'

'Who are the people with him? Who are the Gang?' I asked.

She studied the picture. 'That's Sonia, isn't it? It must be.'

Nash took the photo out of Lucy's hand and peered at it himself, nodding. 'That's definitely your father, and the girl looks like the photo you lent us ... and that boy next to her, that's the other one in that photo ... that's surely "Pig".'

'I suppose so,' Lucy said doubtfully. 'And that one on the end, he looks like ...' She stopped, both unsure and disturbed.

'Like who?' I asked.

'He's not like that any more. He's, well ... *bloated* ... now. That's my Uncle Ridley. He looks lovely there. How *awful*, what time does to people.'

'Yes.' Nash and I said it in unison. An endless host of barely recognisable old actors and actresses lived on in Hollywood in inelastic skins, everything sagging but the memory of glamour, their youthful selves mocking them relentlessly from rented videos and movie channels.

'Who are the others?' I asked.

'I don't know them,' Lucy said, handing the photo back to me.

I said, 'They look people of your age.'

'Yes, they do.' She found it unremarkable. 'Do you want me to repack this box?'

'Yes, please. But leave out the chocolate box.'

'OK.'

Lunch came and we ate. Ziggy phoned the hotel from Norway.

'I cannot reach O'Hara's number,' he complained.

'He's gone back to LA,' I said. 'How are the horses?'

'Working well.'

'Good. The production department has found a disused stable yard for them to stay in, only ten miles from our beach.' I fished a piece of paper out of an inner pocket and spelled the address for him patiently, letter by letter. 'Phone me after you've landed at Immingham on Monday if you have any problems.'

'Yes, Thomas.'

'Well done, Ziggy.'

He laughed, pleased, and departed.

I left Nash and Lucy drinking coffee and, taking with me both 'The Gang' photo and the lower file from the previous night's reading, went along to O'Hara's suite, let myself in with his key and stowed Valentine's mementos in the safe, with the knives. All the rooms in the hotel were equipped with individual small safes, which each guest could set to open to his own choice of combination. I hardly liked to acknowledge the instinct for extra security that led me to use O'Hara's safe instead of my own, but anyway, I did it.

Still in O'Hara's rooms I looked up the number of Ridley Wells in the local phone directory, and tried it, but there was no answer.

On returning to my own rooms I found Nash, on the point of leaving, announcing that he was going to spend the afternoon watching racing on TV while betting by phone with a bookmaker I'd arranged for him.

'Is it still on, for tonight?' he asked, pausing in the doorway.

'Certainly is, if the rain stops, which it is supposed to.'

'How do you expect me to ride a horse in the goddam dark?'

'There will be moonlight. Moncrieff's arranging it.'

'What about goddam rabbit holes?'

'There aren't any on Newmarket's gallops,' I assured him.

'But what if I fall *off*?'

'We'll pick you up and put you back in the saddle.'

'I hate you sometimes, Thomas.' He grinned and went on his way. I left Lucy up to her elbows in decades of form books, collected my minders in the lobby and was bowled the short mile back to the stables.

On my way back to 'The Athenaeum' I detoured into the downstairs office, used chiefly by Ed, where we had the business paraphernalia of telephones, faxes, and large-capacity copier, and asked the young woman operating everything there to keep on trying Ridley Wells's number for me, and if he returned home and answered the summons, to put the call through to me upstairs immediately.

'But you said never to do that, in case the phone rang during a shot.'

'We can re-shoot,' I said. 'I want to catch this man. OK?'

She nodded, reassured, and I went upstairs to re-coax Cibber and Silva into their most venomous faces.

Ridley Wells answered his telephone at three-thirty, and sounded drunk.

I said, 'Do you remember you asked our producer, O'Hara, if we had any riding work for you in our film?'

'He said you hadn't.'

'Right. But now we have. Are you still interested?' I

mentioned a fee for a morning's work large enough to hook a bigger fish than Ridley, and he didn't even ask what the job entailed.

I said, 'We'll send a car for you tomorrow morning at seven. It will bring you to the stables where we're keeping our horses. You don't need to bring anything with you. We'll supply you with clothes from our wardrobe department. We'll supply the horse for you to ride. We don't want you to do anything out of the ordinary or dangerous on the horse. We're just short of a rider for a scene we're shooting tomorrow.'

'Got you,' he said grandly.

'Don't forget,' I insisted.

'Mum's the word, old boy.'

'No,' I said. 'Mum's *not* the word. If you're not sober in the morning, then no job and no fee.'

After a pause he said, 'Got you,' again, and I hoped he meant it.

When we'd finished the close-ups and the day's work was safely on its way to London for processing I ran the previous day's rushes in the screening room, happy for Bill Robinson's sake that he and his monster bike positively quivered with shining power, filling Nash's character with the determination he needed if he were to take action.

From fantasy, courage, I thought. I wanted the film to assert that old idea, but without ramming it down anyone's throat. I wanted people to see that they had always known it. To open doors. A door-opener; that was my function.

It stopped raining more or less at the time forecast – miraculous – and Moncrieff busied himself in the stable yard supervising the loading of cameras, films, lights and crews onto trucks for the 'moonlit' shots of Nash on the Heath.

Nash arrived to the minute, no surprise, and came out of the house half an hour later in riding clothes and night-time make-up, carrying his helmet and demanding a thoroughly tranquillised mount.

'If your fans could only hear you!' I remarked dryly.

'You, Thomas,' he said, smiling, 'can go try 6G in a brake turn at low level.'

I shook my head. Nash could fly fast jet aircraft – when not under a restrictive contract in mid-film – and I couldn't. Nash's pre-mega-star hair-raising CV included air force service in fighters, all part of his mystique.

'The scene comes a night or two before the motor-bikes,' I said. 'You have been accused. You are worried. OK?'

He nodded. The screenplay had included the night-on-the-horse scene from the beginning, and he was prepared.

We drove the camera truck slowly up the road by the hill, Nash in the saddle beside us (the horse in dim 'moonlight') looking worried and thoughtful. We then filmed him sitting on the ground with his back to a wind-bent tree, the horse cropping grass nearby. We'd more or less finished when the thick clouds unexpectedly parted and blew in dramatic shapes across the real full moon, and Moncrieff turned his camera heavenwards for more than sixty seconds, and beamed at me triumphantly through his straggly beard.

The long day ended. Back at Bedford Lodge I found

three more boxes itemised, plus a note from Lucy saying she hoped I didn't mind but her parents wanted her home for Sunday after all. Back Monday, she wrote.

Box VIII. Form books. Flat racing.
Box IX. Horseshoes.
Box X. Encyclopaedias, A–F.

The horseshoes were actual horseshoes, each saved in a plastic bag and labelled with the name of the horse that had worn it, complete with winning date, racecourse and event. Valentine had been a true collector, squirrelling his successes away.

I pulled out the first of the encyclopaedias without anything particular in mind and, finding a slip of paper in it acting as a bookmark, opened it there. *Autocrat*: an absolute ruler. Multiple examples followed.

I closed the book, rested my head against the back of my armchair, decided it was time to take off the Delta-cast and drifted towards sleep.

The thought that galvanised me to full wakefulness seemed to come from nowhere but was a word seen peripherally, unconsidered.

Autocrat . . .

Further down the page came *Auto-erotism*.

I picked the volume out of the box and read the long entry. I learned much more than I wanted to about various forms of masturbation, though I could find nothing of much significance. Vaguely disappointed, I started to replace the bookmarker, but glanced at it and kept it in my hand. Valentine's bookmarker bore the one word 'Paraphilia'.

I didn't know what paraphilia was, but I searched through several unopened boxes and finally found the P volume of the encyclopaedia, following where Valentine had directed.

The P volume also had a bookmark, this time in the page for *Paraphilia*.

Paraphilia, I read, consisted of many manifestations of perverted love. One of them was listed as 'erotic strangulation – the starvation of blood to the brain to stimulate sexual arousal'.

Valentine's knowledge of self-asphyxia, the process he had described to Professor Derry, had come from this book.

'In 1791 in London,' I read, 'at the time of Haydn, a well-known musician died as a result of his leaning towards paraphilia. One Friday afternoon he engaged a prostitute to tie a leash round his neck which he could then tighten to the point of his satisfaction. Unfortunately he went too far and throttled himself. The prostitute reported his death and was tried for murder, but acquitted, as the musician's perversion was well known. The judge ordered the records of the case not to be published, in the interests of decency.'

One lived and learned, I thought tolerantly, putting the encyclopaedia back in its box. Poor old Professor Derry. Just as well, perhaps, that he hadn't acted on Valentine's information.

Before throwing them both away I glanced at Valentine's second bookmark. On the strip of white paper he'd written, 'Tell Derry this' and, lower down, 'Showed this to Pig'.

I went along to O'Hara's room, retrieved the folder

and 'The Gang' photograph from the safe, and sat in his armchair looking at them and thinking long and hard.

Eventually, I slept in his bed, as it was safer.

CHAPTER FIFTEEN

The film company's car brought Ridley Wells to the stables on time and sober the next morning. We sent him into the house to the wardrobe department, and I took the opportunity to telephone Robbie Gill on my mobile.

I expected to get his message service at that early hour, but in fact he was awake and answered my summons himself.

'Still alive?' he asked chattily.

'Yes, thank you.'

'So what do you need?'

As always with Robbie, straight to the point.

'First,' I said, 'who gave you the list of knife specialists?'

'My professional colleague in the police force,' he said promptly. 'The doctor they call out locally. He's a randy joker, ex-rugger player, good for a laugh and a jar in the pub. I asked him for known knife specialists. He said the force had drawn up the list themselves recently and asked him if he could add to it. He couldn't. The people he knows who carry knives tend to be behind bars.'

'Did he attend Dorothea?'

'No, he was away. Anything else?'

'How is she?'

'Dorothea? Still sedated. Now Paul's gone, do you still want to pay for the nursing home?'

'Yes, I do, and I want to see her soon, like this afternoon.'

'No problem. Just go. She's still in a side ward because of Paul, but physically she's healing well. We could move her by Tuesday, I should think.'

'Good,' I said.

'Take care.'

I said wryly, 'I do.'

In the stable yard the lads were readying for morning exercise, saddling and bridling the horses. As it was Sunday, I told them, we would again have the Heath gallops more or less to ourselves, but we wouldn't be filming exactly the same scenes as the week before.

'You were all asked to wear what you did last Sunday,' I said. 'Did you all check with our continuity girl if you couldn't remember?'

I got nods.

'Fine. Then all of you will canter up the hill and stop where you stopped and circled last week. OK?'

More nods.

'You remember the rider who came from nowhere and made a slash at Ivan?'

They laughed. They wouldn't forget it.

'Right,' I said, 'today we don't have Ivan, but we're going to stage that attack ourselves, and put it into the film. Today it will be a fictional affair. OK? The knife used will not be a real knife but one that's been made out of wood by our production department. What I want you to do is exactly the sort of thing you were doing last Sunday – circling, talking, paying not much attention to the stranger. Right?'

They understood without trouble. Our young horse-master said, 'Who is going to stand in for Ivan?'

'I am,' I said. 'I'm not as broad-shouldered as him or as Nash, but I'll be wearing a jacket like the one Nash usually wears as the trainer. I'll be riding the horse Ivan rode. When we're ready with the cameras, the man playing the knife-attacker will mount and ride that slow old bay that finished last in our race at Huntingdon. The lad who usually rides him will be standing behind the cameras, out of shot. Any questions?'

One asked, 'Are you going to chase him down the hill on the camera truck, like last week?'

'No,' I said. 'He will gallop off down the hill. The camera will film him.'

I handed over command, so to speak, to the horse-master, who organised the mounting and departure of the string. Ed and Moncrieff were already on the Heath. I went into the wardrobe section to put on Nash's jacket and, Ridley being ready, took him with me in my car up the road to the brow of the hill. Ridley and I, out of the car, walked over to the circling horses, stopping by the camera truck.

'What we need,' I told Ridley, 'is for you to ride into the group from somewhere over there . . .' I pointed. 'Trot into the group, draw a make-believe knife from a sheath on your belt, slash at one of the group as if you intended to wound him badly, and then, in the ensuing mêlée, canter off over the brow of the hill and down the wide training ground towards the town. OK?'

Ridley stared, his eyes darkly intense.

'You will slash at *me*, OK? I'm standing in for Nash.'

Ridley said nothing.

'Of course,' I told him pleasantly, 'when this scene appears in the finished film it will not look like one smooth sequence. There will be flashes of the knife, of horses rearing, of jumbled movement and confusion. There will be a wound. There will be blood. We will fake those later.' Ed brought various props across to where I stood with Ridley, and handed them to him one by one.

'Make-believe knife in sheath on belt,' Ed said, as if reading from a list. 'Please put on the belt.'

As if mesmerised, Ridley obeyed.

'Please practise drawing the knife,' I said.

Ridley drew the knife and looked at it in horror. The production department had faithfully reproduced the American trench knife from my drawing, and although the object Ridley held was light-weight and of painted wood, from three paces it looked like a heavy knuckle-duster with a long blade attached to its index finger side.

'Fine,' I said non-committally. 'Put it back in its sheath.'

Ridley fumbled the knife back into place.

'Helmet,' Ed said, holding it out.

Ridley buckled on the helmet.

'Goggles,' Ed offered.

Ridley put them on slowly.

'Gloves.'

Ridley hesitated.

'Anything the matter?' I asked.

Ridley said 'No' hoarsely, and accepted a leg-up onto our slowest nag.

'Great,' I said, 'off you go, then. When Ed yells "Action", just trot straight towards me, draw the knife, take a slash, and canter away fast towards Newmarket. Do you want a rehearsal, or do you think you can get it right first time?'

The helmeted, be-goggled, gloved figure didn't respond.

'We'll take a bet you can get it right,' I said.

Ridley seemed incapable of action. I asked the lad whose horse he was riding to lead him over to the starting point, and then let go and clear the shot. While the lad intelligently followed the instruction, the lad on Nash's horse dismounted and gave me a leg-up. The cracked rib tugged sharply. I lengthened the stirrup leathers. Moncrieff opened his floodlights to bathe the scene and augment the daylight.

Ed yelled, 'Action.'

Ridley Wells kicked his horse into a canter, not a trot. He tugged the knife free with his right hand while holding the reins with his left. He steered his mount with his legs, expert that he was, and he aimed himself straight at me, as murderously intent as one could have hoped.

The 'knife' hit my coat and the carapace beneath and because the imitation blade had no slicing power, the impact knocked the weapon flying out of Ridley's grasp.

'I've dropped it,' he shouted, and I pointed to the brow of the hill and yelled at him, 'Never mind. Gallop.'

He galloped. He sat down low in the saddle and galloped as if it were a genuine escape.

The lads on their horses crowded to the top of the hill to watch, just as before, and this time I went after the fugitive on a horse, not in a truck.

The truck was being driven down the road, camera whirring. The sequence I finally cut together for the film showed 'Nash' closely chasing his assailant; Nash with a deep bleeding wound; Nash losing his quarry, blood dripping everywhere; Nash in pain.

'*Lovely stuff*,' O'Hara breathed when he saw it. '*God*, Thomas . . .'

On this Sunday morning, however, there was no blood. I had much the faster horse and I caught up with Ridley before he could vanish into Newmarket's streets.

He reined furiously to a halt. He tore off the gloves, the goggles and the helmet and threw them on the ground. He struggled out of the anorak we'd dressed him in and flung it away from him.

'I'll *kill* you,' he said.

I said, 'I'll send your fee.'

His bloated face wavered with irresolution as if he couldn't decide whether or not to attack me there and then, but sense or cowardice prevailed, and he dismounted in a practised slide, facing me, right foot lifting over the horse's neck. He let go of the reins. He turned his back on me and walked off unsteadily in the direction of Newmarket, as if he couldn't feel his feet on the ground.

I leaned forward, picked up the dangling reins and walked both horses back to the stables.

The lads came back from the hill chattering like starlings, wide eyed.

'That man looked just the same!' 'He was the same!' 'He looked like that man last week!' 'Didn't he look just like the same man?'

'Yes,' I said.

From the wardrobe department, where I shed Nash's coat and helmet, I paid a brief visit upstairs to where the production people were stacking the Athenaeum scenery to one side and filling the space instead with a reproduction of any horse's box in the stable yard.

As a real natural box was far too small for camera, crew, lights and technicians, let alone a couple of actors, we were fabricating our own version. It was as if a box had been divided into thirds, then spread apart, leaving a large centre area for camera manoeuvring. One third had the split door to the outer world (back projection of the stable yard), one portion contained a manger and water bucket. One, the largest, encompassed the place where a horse would normally stand.

The walls of the box were being constructed of actual white washed breeze blocks with an open ceiling of heavy rafters. Bales of hay, at present neatly stacked, would be placed on a platform on the rafters above the action. A floor of concrete sections covered with straw was being slotted into each setting. Artistic hoof marks and other signs of wear and habitation showed that this was a box often in use.

'How's it going?' I asked, looking round with approval.

'Ready in the morning,' they assured me. 'It'll be as solid as a rock, like you asked.'

'Great.'

Dorothea's cheeks were faintly pink; a great advance.

We had a few tears on my arrival, but not the racking distress of two days earlier. As her physical state had grown stronger, so had her strength of mind resurfaced. She thanked me for the flowers I'd brought her and said she was sick of a diet of tomato soup.

'They say it's good for me but I'm growing to hate it. It's true I can't eat meat and salad – have you ever endured a hospital salad? – but why not *mushroom*, or *chicken* soup? And none of it's home made, of course.'

She was longing, she said, to go to the nursing home dear Robbie Gill had suggested, and she hoped her daughter-in-law, Janet, would soon return home to Surrey.

'We don't like each other,' Dorothea confessed, sighing. 'Such a pity.'

'Mm,' I agreed. 'When you're well, will you go back to your house?'

Tears quivered in her eyes. 'Paul died there.'

Valentine also, I thought.

'Thomas ... I've been remembering things.' She sounded almost anxious. 'That night when I was attacked ...'

'Yes?' I prompted, as she stopped. 'What do you remember?'

'Paul was shouting.'

'Yes, you told me.'

'There was another man there.'

I drew the visitor's chair to beside her bed and sat peacefully holding her hand, not wanting to alarm her and smothering my own urgent thoughts.

I said gently, 'Do you remember what he looked like?'

'I didn't know him. He was there with Paul when I got home from Mona's house ... I'd been watching television with her, you see, but we didn't like the programme and I went home early ... and I went in by the kitchen door as usual and I was so surprised and, well – *pleased*, of course – to see Paul, but he was so *strange*, dear, and almost *frightened*, but he couldn't have been frightened. Why should he have been frightened?'

'Perhaps because you'd come home while he and the other man were ransacking your house.'

'Well, dear, Paul shouted ... where was Valentine's photo album, and I'm sure I said he didn't have one, he just kept a few old snaps in a chocolate box, the same as I did, but Paul wouldn't believe me, he kept going on about an album.'

'So,' I said, 'did Valentine ever have an album?'

'No, dear, I'm sure he didn't. We were never a great family for photos, not like some people who don't believe a thing's happened unless they take snaps of it. Valentine had dozens of pictures of horses, but it was horses, you see, that were his life. Always horses. He never had any children, his Cathy *couldn't*, you see. He might have been keener on photos if he'd had children.

I keep quite a lot of photos in a box in my bedroom. Photos of us all, long ago. Pictures of Paul . . .'

Tears came again, and I didn't tell her I hadn't been able to find those pathetically few mementos in her bedroom. I would give her Valentine's chocolate box instead.

'Did Paul say why he wanted the photo album?' I asked.

'I don't think so, dear. Everything was happening so fast and the other man was so *angry*, and shouting too, and Paul said to me – so *frightening*, dear, but he said, "Tell him where the album is, he's got a knife."'

I asked quietly, 'Are you sure about that?'

'I believed it was a dream.'

'And now?'

'Well, now . . . I think he must have said it. I can hear my Paul's voice . . . oh, dear . . . oh, my darling little boy.'

I hugged her while she sobbed.

'That other man *hit* me,' she said, gulping. 'Hit my head . . . and Paul was shouting, "Tell him, tell him". . . and I saw . . . he really did have a knife, that man . . . or at least he was holding something shiny, but it wasn't a real knife, he had his fingers through it . . . dirty fingernails . . . it was horrid . . . and Paul was shouting, "Stop it . . . *don't* . . ." and I woke up in the hospital and I didn't know what had happened, but last night . . . well, dear, when I was waking up this morning and thinking about Paul, well, I sort of *remembered*.'

'Yes,' I said. I paused, consolidating earlier impressions. 'Dearest Dorothea,' I said. 'I think Paul saved your life.'

'Oh! Oh!' She was still crying, but after a while it was from radiant joy, not grinding regret.

'I think,' I said, 'that Paul was so horrified by seeing you attacked with that knife, that he prevented a fatal blow. Robbie Gill thought that the attack on you looked like an *interrupted* murder. He said that people who inflicted such awful knife wounds were usually in a frenzy, and simply couldn't stop. I think Paul stopped him.'

'Oh, *Thomas*!'

'But I'm afraid,' I said regretfully, 'that it means that Paul knew the man who attacked you, and he didn't identify him to the police. In fact, Paul pretended he was in Surrey when you were attacked.'

'Oh, dear.'

'And,' I said, 'Paul tried hard to prevent you from talking to me or to Robbie, or anyone else, until he was sure you remembered nothing about the attack.'

Dorothea's joy faded somewhat but, underneath, remained.

'He changed a bit,' I said. 'I think at one point he almost told me something, but I don't know what. I do believe, though, that he was feeling remorse over what had happened to you.'

'Oh, Thomas, I do hope so.'

'I'm sure of it,' I said, more positively than I felt.

She thought things over quietly for a while and then said, 'Paul would burst out sometimes with opinions as if he couldn't hold them in any more.'

'Did he?'

'He said . . . I didn't like to tell you, Thomas, but the other day – when he was here with me – he burst out with, "*Why* did you ever have to make your film?" He was *bitter*. He said, "I would never have been attacked if you hadn't stirred everything up." Of course I asked *what* you had stirred up and he said, "It was all in the *Drumbeat*, but I was to forget what he'd said, only if anything happened to you it would be your own fault." He said . . . I'm really sorry . . . but he said he would be pleased if you were cut to ribbons like me . . . It wasn't like him, really it wasn't.'

'I did bolt him out of your house,' I reminded her. 'He didn't like me much for embarrassing him.'

'No, but . . . well, something was *worrying* him, I'm sure of it.'

I stood up and wandered over to the window, looking out aimlessly at the institutionally regular pattern of the windows in the building opposite and the scrubby patch of garden between. Two people in white coats walked slowly along a path, conversing. Extras playing doctors, I thought automatically – and realised I often saw even real life in terms of film.

I turned and asked Dorothea, 'While you've been here in the hospital, did Paul ask you about a photo album?'

'I don't think so, dear. Everything gets so muddled, though.' She paused. 'He said something about you having taken Valentine's books away, and I didn't tell him you hadn't. I didn't want to argue, you see, dear. I felt too tired.'

I told her I'd found a photo among Valentine's possessions which I had retrieved from her nice young friend, Bill Robinson – but I couldn't see that it was worth the damage to her house or to herself.

'If I show it to you,' I said, 'will you tell me who the people are?'

'Of course, dear, if I can.'

I took 'The Gang' photo out of my pocket and put it into her hand.

'I need my reading glasses,' she said, peering at it. 'That red case on the bedside table.'

I gave her her glasses and she looked without much reaction at the picture.

'Did one of those people attack you?' I asked.

'Oh no, none of those. He was much older. All these people are so young. Why!' she exclaimed, 'that's Paul! That one at the end, isn't that Paul? How young he was! So handsome, then.' She let the hand holding the photo rest on the sheet. 'I don't know any of the others. I wish Paul was here.'

Sighing, I took back the photo, replaced it in my pocket and produced the small memo pad I habitually carried.

I said, 'I don't want to upset you, but if I draw a knife will you tell me if it's the one that might have been used on you?'

'I don't want to see it.'

'Please, Dorothea.'

'Paul was killed with a knife,' she wailed, and cried for her son.

'Dearest Dorothea,' I said after a while, 'if it will help to find Paul's killer, will you look at my drawing?'

She shook her head. I put the drawing close to her hand and, after a long minute, she picked it up.

'How *horrid*,' she said, looking at it, 'I didn't see a

knife like that.' She sounded extremely relieved. 'It wasn't anything like that.'

I'd drawn for her the American trench knife from the Heath. I turned the paper over and drew the wicked Armadillo, serrated edge and all.

Dorothea looked at it, went white and didn't speak.

'I'm so sorry,' I said helplessly. 'But you didn't die. Paul loved you . . . He saved your life.'

I thought of the cataclysmic shock in Paul's face when he'd come to Dorothea's house and seen the Armadillo lying on the kitchen table. When he'd seen me sitting there, *alive*.

He'd blundered out of the house and gone away, and it was pointless now to speculate that if we'd stopped him, if we'd sat him down and made him talk, he might have lived. Paul had been near, once, to breaking open. Paul, I thought, had become a fragile danger, likely to crumble, likely to confess. Paul, overbearing, pompous, unlikeable, had lost his nerve and died of repentance.

My driver, with the black-belt beside him, aimed my car towards Oxfordshire while consulting from time to time my written directions, and I sat in the back seat looking again at 'The Gang' photo and remembering what both Dorothea and Lucy had said about it.

'They're so *young*.'

Young.

Jackson Wells, Ridley Wells, Paul Pannier, were all at least twenty-six years younger in the photo than the living men I'd met. Sonia had died twenty-six years earlier, and Sonia was alive in the picture.

Say the photo had been taken twenty-*seven* years ago – that made Jackson Wells about twenty-three, with all the others younger than that. Eighteen, nineteen, twenty: that sort of age. Sonia had died at twenty-one.

I had been four when she died and I hadn't heard of her, and I'd come back at thirty and wanted to know *why* she had died, and I had said I might try and find out, and in saying that I'd set off a chain reaction that had put Dorothea into hospital and Paul into his grave and had earned me a knife in the ribs . . . and whatever else might come.

I hadn't known there was a genie in the bottle, but genies once let out couldn't be put back.

My driver found Batwillow Farm and delivered me to Jackson Wells's door.

Lucy again answered the summons of the over-loud bell, her blue eyes widening with astonishment.

'I say,' she said, 'you didn't mind my coming home for the day, did you? You haven't come to drag me back by my ponytail?'

'No,' I smiled. 'I really wanted to talk to your father.'

'Oh, sure. Come in.'

I shook my head. 'I wonder if he would come out.'

'Oh? Well, I'll ask him.' Faintly puzzled, she disappeared into the house, to return soon with her blond, lean, farm-tanned enquiring parent looking exactly as he had looked there one week earlier.

'Come in,' he said, gesturing a welcome, happy-go-lucky.

'Come for a walk.'

He shrugged. 'If you like.' He stepped out of his

337

house and Lucy, unsure of herself, remained in the doorway.

Jackson eyed the two agile men sitting in my car and asked, 'Friends?'

'A driver and a bodyguard,' I answered. 'Film company issue.'

'Oh.'

We crossed from the house and came to rest by the five-barred gate on which deaf old Wells senior had been leaning the week before.

'Lucy's doing a good job,' I said. 'Did she tell you?'

'She likes talking to Nash Rourke.'

'They get on fine,' I agreed.

'I told her to be careful.'

I smiled. 'You've taught her well.' Too well, I thought. I said, 'Did she mention a photograph?'

He looked as if he didn't know whether to say yes or no, but in the end said, 'What photograph?'

'This one.' I brought it out of my pocket and gave it to him.

He looked at the front briefly and at the back, and met my eyes expressionlessly.

'Lucy says that's your handwriting,' I commented, taking the picture back.

'What if it is?'

'I'm not the police,' I said, 'and I haven't brought thumbscrews.'

He laughed, but the totally carefree manner of a week earlier had been undermined by wariness.

I said, 'Last week you told me no one knew why Sonia had died.'

'That's right.' The blue eyes shone, as ever, with innocence.

I shook my head. 'Everyone in that photo,' I said, 'knew why Sonia died.'

His utter stillness lasted until he'd manufactured a smile and a suitably scornful expression.

'Sonia is in that photo. What you said is codswallop.'

'Sonia knew,' I said.

'Are you saying she killed herself?' He looked almost hopeful, as well he might.

'Not really. She didn't intend to die. No one intended to kill her. She died by accident.'

'You know bloody nothing about it.'

I knew too much about it. I didn't want to do any more harm, and I didn't want to get myself killed, but Paul Pannier's death couldn't simply be ignored; and apart from considerations of justice, until his murderer had been caught I would be wearing Delta-cast.

'You all look so young in that photo,' I said. 'Golden girl, golden boys, all smiling, all with bright lives ahead. You were all kids then, like you told me. All playing at living, everything a game.' I named the light-hearted gang in the photo. 'There's you and Sonia, and your younger brother Ridley. There's Paul Pannier, your blacksmith's nephew. There's Roddy Visborough, the son of Sonia's sister, which made Sonia actually his aunt. And there's your jockey, P. Falmouth, known as Pig.' I paused. 'You were the eldest, twenty-two or twenty-three. Ridley, Paul, Roddy and Pig were all eighteen, nineteen or twenty when Sonia died, and she was only twenty-one.'

Jackson Wells said blankly, 'How do you know?'

'Newspaper reports. Doing sums. It hardly matters. What does matter is the immaturity of you all ... and the feeling some people have at that age that youth is eternal, caution is for oldies, and responsibility a dirty word. You went off to York and the others played a game ... and I think this whole gang, except you, were there when she died.'

'No,' he said sharply. 'It wasn't a gang thing. You're meaning gang rape. That didn't happen.'

'I know it didn't. The autopsy made it quite clear that there'd been no intercourse. The newspapers all pointed it out.'

'Well, then.'

I said carefully, 'I think one of those boys in some way throttled her, not meaning to do her harm, and they were all so frightened that they tried to make it look like suicide, by hanging her. And then they just – ran away.'

'No,' Jackson said numbly.

'I think,' I said, 'that to begin with you truly didn't know what had happened. When you talked to the police, when they tried to get you to confess, you could deal blithely with their questions because you knew you weren't guilty. You truly didn't know at that point whether or not she'd hanged herself, though you knew – and said – that it wasn't like her. I think that for quite a while it was a true mystery to you, but what is also evident is that you weren't psychologically pulverised by it. None of the newspaper reports – and I've now read a lot of them – not one says anything about a *distraught* young husband.'

'Well . . . I . . .'

'By then,' I suggested, 'you knew she had lovers. Not dream lovers. Real ones. The Gang. All casual. A joke. A game. I'd guess she never thought the sex act more than a passing delight, like ice cream, and there are plenty of people like that, though it's not them but the intense and the jealous that sell the tabloids. When Sonia died, your playing-at-marriage was already over. You told me so. You might have felt shock and regret at her death, but you were young and healthy and blessed with a resilient nature, and your grief was short.'

'You can't possibly know.'

'Am I right so far?'

'Well . . .'

'Tell me what happened afterwards,' I said. 'If you tell me, I promise not to put anything you say in the film. I'll keep the fictional story well away. But it would be better if I knew the truth because, like I told you before, I might reveal your innermost secrets simply by guessing. So tell me . . . and you won't find what you're afraid of on the screen.'

Jackson Wells surveyed his creeper-covered house and his untidy drive and yard, and no doubt thought of his pleasant existence with his second wife and of his pride in Lucy.

'You're right.' He sighed heavily. 'They were all there, and I didn't find out for weeks.'

I let time pass. He had taken the first great step: the rest would follow.

'Weeks afterwards, they began to unravel,' he said at length. 'They'd sworn to each other they would never

341

say a word. Never. But it got too much for them. Pig pissed off to Australia and left me with only Derek Carsington to ride my nags; not that it mattered much, the owners were leaving as if I had the pox, and then Ridley ...' He paused. 'Ridley got drunk, which wasn't a rarity even in those days, and spilled his guts from every possible orifice. Ridley *disgusts* me but Lucy still thinks he's a laugh, which won't last much longer as he'd have his hand up her skirt by now except that I've told her always to wear jeans. No fun being a girl these days, not like Sonia, she loved skirts down to her ankles and no bra most of the time and a green crewcut – and why the *hell* am I telling you this?'

I thought he might be mourning Sonia twenty-six years too late; but maybe nothing was ever too late in that way.

'She was *fun*,' he said. 'Always good for a laugh.'

'Yes.'

'Ridley told me what they'd done.' The pain of the revelation showed sharply in the sunny face. 'I as good as killed him. I thrashed him. Hit him. Beat him with a riding whip. Anything I could lay my hands on. I kicked him unconscious.'

'That was grief,' I said.

'Anger.'

'Same thing.'

Jackson stared unseeingly at time past.

'I went to see Valentine to ask him what to do,' he said. 'Valentine was like a father to all of us. A better father than any of us had. Valentine loved Sonia like a daughter.'

342

I said nothing. The way Valentine had loved Sonia had had nothing to do with fatherhood.

'What did Valentine say?' I asked.

'He already knew! He said Paul had told him. Paul was in pieces, like Ridley. Paul had told his uncle everything. Valentine said they could all either live with what they'd done or go to the police . . . and he wouldn't choose for them.'

'Did Valentine know that Roddy Visborough had been there?'

'I told him,' Jackson said frankly. 'Sonia was Roddy's *aunt*. And whatever sort of sex orgy they'd all been planning – I mean, of course, it was nothing like that, forget I said it – Roddy couldn't be dragged in, they said it was impossible. She was his aunt!'

'You all knew Valentine well,' I said.

'Yes, of course. His old smithy was only just down the road from my yard. He was always in and out with the horses and we'd drop in there at his house, all of us. Like I said, he was a sort of father. Better than a father. But everything broke up. Training died on me, and Paul left Newmarket and moved away with his mother and father, and Roddy went off to go on the show jumping circuit . . . he'd been wanting to be an assistant race-horse trainer only he hadn't yet got a job, and Pig, like I said, he'd already gone off. And then Valentine was moving too. The old smithy needed impossible roof repairs, so he had it torn down and sold the land for building. I was there one day when he was watching the builders throw the junk of a lifetime down to fill up an old well that he had in the back there, that was a danger

343

to children, and I said things were never going to be the same again. And of course they weren't.'

'But they turned out all right for you.'

'Well, yes, they did.' He couldn't repress his grin for long. 'And Valentine became the Grand Old Man of racing, and Roddy Visborough's won enough silver cups for an avalanche. Ridley's still bumming about and I help him out from time to time, and Paul got married . . .' He stopped uncertainly.

'And Paul got killed,' I said baldly.

He was silent.

'Do you know who killed him?' I asked.

'No.' He stared. 'Do you?'

I didn't answer directly. I said, 'Did any of them tell Valentine – or you – which of the four of them throttled Sonia?'

'It was an accident.'

'Whose accident?'

'She was going to let them put their hands round her neck. She was laughing, they all agreed about that. They were sort of high, but not on drugs.'

'On excitement,' I said.

His blue eyes widened. 'They were all going to . . . that's what broke them up . . . they were all going to have a turn with her, and she wanted it . . . she bet they couldn't all manage it, not like that when the lads had all ridden out for second morning exercise, not before they came back again in an hour, and not with all of the gang watching and cheering each other on, and not in a box on hay as a bed . . . and they were all crazy, and so was she . . . and Pig put his hands round her neck and kissed her . . . and squeezed . . . and she choked . . . he

344

went on too long ... and she went dark ... her skin went dark, and by the time they realised ... they couldn't bring her back ...' His voice died, and after a while he said, 'You're not surprised, are you?'

'I won't put it in the film.'

'I was so angry,' he said. 'How *could* they? How could she let them? It wasn't drugs ...'

'Do you realise,' I asked, 'that it's almost always men who die in that sort of asphyxia?'

'Oh, God ... They wanted to see if it worked the same for women.'

The total foolishness of it blankly silenced us both.

I took a breath. I said, 'The *Drumbeat* said I couldn't solve Sonia's death, and I have. So now I'll find out who killed Paul Pannier.'

He pushed himself away from the gate explosively, shouting back at me, '*How?* Leave it alone. Leave all of us alone. Don't make this pissing film.'

His raised voice brought my judo keeper out of the car like an uncoiling eel. Jackson looked both surprised and alarmed, even as I made soothing hand gestures to calm my minder's reflexes.

I said to Jackson, 'My bodyguard's like a growling dog. Pay no attention. The film company insists on him because others beside you want this movie stopped.'

'That bitch Audrey, Sonia's sneering sister, I bet *she* does, for one.'

'She above all,' I agreed.

Lucy reappeared at the front door and called to her father, 'Dad, Uncle Ridley's on the phone.'

'Tell him I'll come in a minute.'

345

I said, as she dematerialised, 'Your brother rode on the Heath this morning, for the film. He won't be pleased with me.'

'Why not?'

'He'll tell you.'

'I wish you'd never come,' he said bitterly, and strode off towards his house, his safe haven, his two normal nice women.

I spent the journey back to Newmarket knowing I'd been rash, but not really regretting it. I might think I knew who'd killed Paul, but proving it was different. The police would have to prove it, but I could at least direct their gaze.

I thought of one particular newspaper clipping that I'd found in the file now resting in O'Hara's safe.

Valentine had written it for his occasional gossip column. The paper was dated six weeks after Sonia's death, and didn't mention her.

It said:

Newmarket sources tell me that the jockey P.G. Falmouth (19), familiarly known as 'Pig', has gone to Australia, and is seeking a work-permit to ride there, hoping to settle. Born and raised near the town of his name in Cornwall, Pig Falmouth moved to Newmarket two years ago, where his attractive personality and dedication to winning soon earned him many friends. Undoubtedly he would have prospered in England as his experience increased, but we wish him great success in his new venture overseas.

This item was accompanied by a smiling picture of a fresh-faced, good-looking young man in jockey's helmet and colours; but it was the headline of the section that had been for me the drench of ice-cold understanding.

'Exit,' it said, 'of the Cornish boy.'

CHAPTER SIXTEEN

We filmed the hanging scene the following morning, Monday, in the cut-and-separated loose box upstairs in the house.

Moncrieff flung a rope over the rafters and swung on it himself to test the set's robustness, but owing to the solid breeze blocks and huge metal angle-iron braces anchoring the new walls to the old floor, there wasn't the slightest quiver in the scenery, to the audible relief of the production department. The straw-covered concrete in the set sections deadened all hollow give-away underfoot echoing noises, those reality-destroying clatterings across the floors of many a supposedly well-built Hollywood 'mansion'.

'Where did you get to after our very brief meeting last night?' Moncrieff enquired. 'Howard was looking all over the hotel for you.'

'Was he?'

'Your car brought you back, you ate a room-service sandwich while we discussed today's work, and then you vanished.'

'Did I? Well, I'm here now.'

'I told Howard you would be sure to be here this morning.'

'Thanks so much.'

Moncrieff grinned. 'Howard was *anxious*.'

'Mm. Did the Yvonne girl get here?'

'Down in make-up,' Moncrieff nodded lasciviously. 'And is she a dish.'

'Long blonde hair?'

He nodded. 'The wig you ordered. Where did you get to, in fact?'

'Around,' I said vaguely. I'd slipped my minder and walked a roundabout way, via the Heath, to the stables, booking in with the guard on the house door and telling him I wanted to work undisturbed and, if anyone asked, to say I wasn't there.

'Sure thing, Mr Lyon,' he promised, used to my vagaries, so I'd gone privately into the downstairs office and phoned Robbie Gill.

'Sorry to bother you on Sunday evening,' I apologised.

'I was only watching the telly. How can I help?'

I said, 'Is Dorothea well enough to be moved tomorrow instead of Tuesday?'

'Did you see her today? What did you think?'

'She's longing to go to the nursing home, she said, and a lot of her toughness of spirit is back. But medically . . . could she go?'

'Hm . . .'

'She's remembered a good deal more about being stabbed,' I said. 'She saw the attacker's face, but she doesn't know him. She also saw the knife that cut her.'

'*God*,' Robbie exclaimed, 'that knuckle-duster thing?'

'No. It was the one that ended in me.'

'*Christ*.'

'So, move her tomorrow if you can. Give her a false name in the nursing home. She's at risk.'

'Bloody hell.'

'She remembers that Paul interrupted the attack on her and effectively saved her life. It's comforting her. She's amazing. She's had three terrible things happen, but she'll be all right, I think.'

'Spunky old woman. Don't worry, I'll shift her.'

'Great.' I paused. 'You remember the police took our fingerprints to match them with the prints in Dorothea's house?'

'Of course I do. They took Dorothea's and her friend Betty's and her husband's and worked out Valentine's from his razor.'

'And,' I said, 'there were others they couldn't match.'

'Sure. Several, I believe. I asked my police friend how their enquiries were progressing. Dead stop, I would guess.'

'Mm,' I said. 'Some of the prints they couldn't match would have been O'Hara's, and some would have been Bill Robinson's.' I explained Bill Robinson. 'And there has to be another – Dorothea's attacker didn't wear gloves.'

Robbie said breathlessly, 'Are you sure?'

'Yes. She said she saw his hand through the knife and he had dirty fingernails.'

'*Jeeze*.'

'When he went to her house he didn't expect her to be there. He didn't plan in advance to attack her. He went to search with Paul for something Valentine might

350

have had and I guess they ripped the place to bits from fury and frustration that they couldn't find anything. Anyway, his prints must be all over the place.'

Robbie, perplexed, asked, 'Whose?'

'I'll tell you when I'm sure.'

'Don't get yourself killed.'

'Of course not,' I said.

Yvonne came upstairs at the required time, and proved to be the regulation issue semi-anorexic Californian waif beloved of moguls, a culture concept a cosmos away from the real laughing reckless Sonia.

Sonia, at her death, had worn, according to the more conservative newspapers, 'a rose-red satin slip', and, according to the titillators, in blackest type, 'A shiny scarlet mini with shoe-string shoulder straps, and black finely-strapped sandals with high rhinestone heels.'

No wonder, I'd thought, that suicide had been in doubt.

Yvonne of the dream lovers was wearing a loose white day-dress described in American fashion circles as a 'float': that is to say, it softly outlined only what it touched. She also wore, at my request, chandelier pearl and gold earrings and a long pearl necklace nearly to her waist.

She looked beautifully ethereal and spoke like Texas.

'This morning,' I said, 'we're shooting the scenes in the right sequence. That's to say, first you enter through that split door.' I pointed. 'There will be back-lighting. When Moncrieff is ready, I'd like you to stand in the doorway and turn your head slowly until we say stop, then if you'll remember that position and stop your head right there for the take, we will get a dramatic effect. You will be entering but looking back. OK? I expect you know your lines.'

She gave me a limpid unintelligent wide-eyed look: great for the film, not so good for technical speed while we made it.

'They say,' she said, 'you get mad if you have to shoot a scene more than three times. That so?'

'Absolutely so.'

'Guess I'd better concentrate then.'

'Honey child,' I said in her accent, 'you do just that and I'll earn you talk-show spots.'

'The Today Show?'

'Nothing's impossible.'

Calculation clouded the peerless violet eyes and she went quietly off to one side and studied her script.

Battle lines drawn, we proceeded. When Moncrieff was satisfied with his light placement we stood Yvonne in the doorway and moved her inch by inch until the light outside the door shone through her flimsy float to reveal her body to the camera inside: too flat-chested for my interest, but of the dreamy otherworld unreality I'd hoped for.

'Jeeze,' Moncrieff murmured, looking through his lens.

I said, 'Can you put a glint on those earrings?'

'You don't ask much!'

He positioned an inkie – an inkie-dinkie, meaning a very small spotlight – to give a glitter below her ears.

'Great,' I said. 'Everyone ready? We'll do a rehearsal. Yvonne, don't forget you're being followed by an earthy man who is parsecs away from a dream lover. You are already laughing at him in your mind, though not openly, as he has power to make Nash's life – that's to say, your film husband's life – very difficult. Just imagine you're being followed by a man you sexually despise but can't be rude to . . .'

Yvonne giggled. 'Who needs to act? I meet them every day.'

'I'll bet you do,' Moncrieff said under his breath.

'Right then,' I said, trying not to laugh, 'we'll do a walk-through. Ready? And . . .' a pause, 'go.'

Yvonne got it dead right at the second rehearsal and then we shot the scene for real twice, both times fit to print.

'You're a doll,' I told her. She liked it, where Silva might have said 'sexism' or 'harassment'. I liked women, all sorts; I'd simply discovered, as I had with male actors, that it saved time to accept, not fight, their views of themselves in the world.

In the scene Yvonne, talking to a man out of shot, had been saying she'd promised to prepare the loose box for a soon-to-arrive horse, a job she'd forgotten earlier but was now doing before joining her husband at a drinks party, to be held somewhere on his way home from the races.

So silly about her white sandals, she said, on the rough flooring. Would he please help her move the stack of hay bales, since – eyelashes fluttering – he was so much *bigger* and *stronger* than little Yvonne?

'I'd lie down and die for her,' Moncrieff observed.

'He more or less did.'

'Such a cynic,' Moncrieff told me, moving lights to a point high among the rafters.

I rehearsed Yvonne through the scene where she

353

realised the man meant business against her wishes. We trekked through surprise, discomfort, revulsion and, dangerously, mockery. I made sure she understood – and could personally relate to – every step.

'Most directors just yell at me,' she said at one point, when she'd fluffed her lines in rehearsal for the fifth or sixth time.

'You look stunning,' I said. 'All you need to do is *act stunned*. Then *laugh* at him. Some men can't bear women laughing at them. He's full of lust for you, and you think he's *funny*. What you're doing is mocking him to madness. He's going to kill you.'

Total comprehension lit her sweet features. 'Get out the strait-jacket,' she said.

'Yvonne, I love you.'

We took a long series of shots of her face, one emotion at a time, and many of negative messages of body language and of the growth of fright, of panic, of desperate disbelief: enough to cut together the ultimate terror of approaching unexpected death.

We gave Yvonne a rest for lunch, while Moncrieff and I filmed the crews slapping heavy ropes sharply over the rafters, and tying frightful knots, to show the violence, the speed, the lack of mercy that I wanted. Naturally each segment took many minutes to stage and get right, but later, in cinemas, with every successful impression strung together – slap, slap, slap – the horror of the hanging would strike the popcorn crunchers silent.

I sat beside Yvonne on a hay bale. I said, 'This afternoon we are going to tie your wrists together with that thick rope now hanging free from that rafter.'

She took it easily.

'The man has by now frightened you so much that you are almost relieved that it is your wrists he has tied.'

She nodded.

'But suddenly he pulls some slack into the rope leading from the rafter, and he loops the slack round your neck, and does it a second time, and pulls the rope tight until your pearls break and slide down inside your dress, and he leans all his weight on the free end of rope swinging from the rafter, and . . . er . . . he lifts you off your feet . . . and hangs you.'

Big-eyed, she said, 'What do I say? Do I beg? It doesn't say this.'

'You don't say anything,' I said. 'You scream.'

'*Scream?*'

'Yes. Can you?'

She opened her mouth and screamed up a hair-raising scale, alarming everyone on set and bringing them galloping to her rescue.

She giggled.

'No one rescued Yvonne,' I said regretfully, 'but no one will forget that scream.'

We filmed a brutal hanging, but short of the dreaded 'NC-17' or '18' certificates. We showed no black asphyxiated face, no terrible bloating. I got Yvonne to wriggle frantically while we suspended her from the wrists, but I filmed her only from the roped neck to her feet that frantically stretched down to the out-of-reach floor. We arranged for one of her white shoes to fall off. We turned the camera onto the shoe while the shadow of her last paroxysms fell across the whitewashed walls, and we filmed her broken pearls and one twisted earring in the straw with her bare jerking toes just above.

That done, I let her down and hugged her gratefully; and told her she was marvellous, ravishing, brilliant, moving, could play Ophelia in her sleep and would *undoubtedly* appear on the Today Show (which fortunately, later, she did).

I'd planned from the beginning to shoot the hanging separate from the murderer just in case we needed to make a radical plot re-think at a later stage. By filming murder and murderer apart, one could slot in anyone's face behind the rope. That afternoon, however, I'd invited Cibber to learn the murderer's few lines, and he arrived on set with them only vaguely in his mind, while he expansively smoked a large cigar and exercised his fruity larynx on inappropriate jokes.

He patted Yvonne's bottom. Silly old buffoon, I thought, and set about turning him into a lecherous bull.

I positioned him in the manger section, and gave him an ashtray to prevent his setting fire to the straw. We placed Yvonne so that her white dress, on the edge of the frame and out of focus from being too near the camera, nonetheless established her presence.

Moncrieff, concentrating on the lighting, added a sheet of blue gelatine across one of the spots. He looked through the lens and smiled, and I looked also, and there it was, the actor blinking, bored, waiting for us while we fiddled, but with the probability of his guilt revealed by a trick of light.

Cibber, as first written by Howard, had been a pillar

of the Jockey Club, an upright, unfortunate victim of events. Reluctantly Howard, bowing to the film company, had agreed to write a (mild!) liaison between Cibber's wife (Silva) and Nash Rourke. Equally reluctantly he had agreed that Cibber should persecute Nash for supposedly having hanged his (Nash's) wife Yvonne. Howard still didn't know that it would be Cibber himself that did the hanging. I would have trouble with Howard. Nothing new.

To me, the character of Cibber lay at the centre of the film's dynamic. The Cibber I saw was a man constrained by his position in society; a man forced by upbringing, by wealth, by the expectations of his peers to mould himself into a righteous puritan, difficult to love, incapable of loving. Cibber couldn't in consequence stand ridicule; couldn't bear to know his wife had rejected him for a lover, couldn't have waiters hearing his wife mock him. Cibber expected people to do his bidding. He was, above all, accustomed to deference.

Yet Cibber, underneath, was a raw and passionate man. Cibber hanged Yvonne in a burst of uncontrollable rage when she laughed at his attempt at rape. Appalled, unable to face his own guilt, Cibber persecuted Nash to the point of paranoia and beyond. Cibber, eventually, would be totally destroyed and mentally wrecked when Nash, after many tries, found that the one way to defeat his persecutor was to trap him into earning pitying sneers. Cibber would, at the end, disintegrate into catatonic schizophrenia.

I looked at Cibber the actor and wondered how I could ever dig out of him Cibber the man.

I started that afternoon by blowing away his complacency and telling him he didn't understand lust.

He was indignant. 'Of course I do.'

'The lust I want is uncontrollable. It's out of control, frenetic, frantic, raging, berserk. It's *murderous*.'

'And you expect *me* to show all that?'

'No, I don't. I don't think you can. I don't think you have the technique. I don't think you're a good enough actor.'

Cibber froze. He stubbed out the cigar: and he produced for the camera that day a conception of lust that made one understand and pity his ungovernable compulsion even while he killed for having it mocked.

He would never be a grandee type-cast actor again.

'I hate you,' he said.

Lucy was busy with the boxes when, on returning to the hotel, I opened the door of my sitting-room and went in, leaving it ajar.

She was on her knees among the boxes and looked up as if guiltily, faintly blushing.

'Sorry for the mess,' she said, flustered. 'I didn't think you'd be back before six o'clock, as usual. I'll just tidy this lot away. And shall I close the door?'

'No, leave it open.'

Books and papers were scattered over much of the floor, and many of them, I was interested to see, had come out of boxes she had already investigated and itemised. The folder of clippings about Sonia's death

358

lay open on the table: the harmless clippings only, as Valentine's totally revealing souvenirs were out of sight in O'Hara's safe.

'You had some messages,' Lucy said jerkily, picking up and reading from a notebook. 'Howard Tyler wants to see you. Someone called Ziggy – I think – wanted you to know the horses had come without trouble through Immingham and had reached their stable. Does that sound right? Robbie – he wouldn't give any other name – said to tell you the move had been accomplished. And the film crew you sent to Huntingdon races got some good crowd and bookmaker shots, they said.'

'Thanks.'

I viewed the general clutter on the floor and mildly asked, 'What are you looking for?'

'Oh.' The blush deepened. 'Dad said . . . I mean, I hope you won't mind, but my Uncle Ridley came in to see me.'

'In here?'

'Yes. I didn't know he was coming. He just knocked on the door and walked straight in when I opened it. I said you might not be pleased, and he said he didn't care a f—. I mean, he didn't care what you thought.'

'Did your father send him?'

'I don't know if he *sent* him. He told him where I was and what I was doing.'

I hid from her my inner satisfaction. I had rather hoped to stir Ridley to action; hoped Jackson would perform the service.

'What did Ridley want?' I asked.

'He said I wasn't to tell you.' She stood up, her blue eyes troubled. 'I don't like it . . . and I don't know what I should do.'

'Perch on something and relax.' I lowered myself stiffly into an armchair and eased my constricted neck. 'Bad back,' I said, explaining it away. 'Nothing to fuss over. What did Ridley want?'

She sat doubtfully sideways on the edge of the table, swinging a free leg. The ubiquitous jeans were accompanied that day by a big blue sweater across which white lambs gambolled: nothing could possibly have been less threatening.

She made up her mind. 'He wanted that photo of the Gang that you showed Dad yesterday. And he wanted anything Valentine had written about Sonia. He emptied out all this stuff. And,' her forehead wrinkled, 'he wanted the *knives*.'

'What knives?'

'He wouldn't tell me. I asked him if he wanted that one a boy asked me to give you at Huntingdon, and he said that one and others.'

'What did you say?'

'I said I hadn't seen any others and anyhow, if you had anything like that you would keep it locked away safely . . . and . . . well . . . he told me to wheedle out of you the combination you're using for the safe here. He tried to open it, you see . . .' She stopped miserably. 'I *know* I should never have let him in. What is it all *about*?'

'Cheer up,' I said, 'while I think.'

'Shall I tidy the boxes?'

'Yes, do.'

First catch your sprat . . .

'Lucy,' I said, 'why did you tell me what Ridley wanted?'

She looked uncomfortable. 'Do you mean, why am I not loyal to my uncle?'

'Yes, I do mean that.'

'I didn't like him saying *wheedle*. And . . . well . . . he's not as nice as he used to be.'

I smiled. 'Good. Well, if I tell you the combination number, will you please tell Ridley? And also tell him how clever you were, the way you wheedled it out of me! And tell him you do think I have knives in the safe.'

She hesitated.

I said, 'Give your allegiance one way or the other, but stick to one.'

She said solemnly, 'I give it to you.'

'Then the combination is seven three five two.'

'Now?' she asked, stretching towards the telephone.

'Now.'

She spoke to her uncle. She blushed deeply while she lied, but she would have convinced me, let alone Ridley.

When she put down the telephone I said, 'When I've finished all the work on this film, which will be in another four and a half months, I should think, would you like to spend a holiday in California? Not,' I went on hastily, 'with any conditions or expectations attached. Just a holiday. You could bring your mother, if you like. I thought you might find it interesting, that's all.'

Her uncertainty over this suggestion was endearing.

I was everything she'd been taught to fear, a young healthy male in a position of power, out for any conquest he could make.

'I won't try to seduce you,' I promised lightly. But I might end by marrying her, I thought unexpectedly, when she was older. I'd been forever bombarded by actresses. An Oxfordshire farmer's freckled-nosed blue-eyed daughter who played the piano and lapsed occasionally into sixteen-year-old awkwardness seemed in contrast an unrealistic and unlikely future.

There was no thunderbolt: just an insidious hungry delight that never went away.

Her first response was abrupt and typical. 'I can't afford it.'

'Never mind, then.'

'But . . . er . . . yes.'

'Lucy!'

The blush persisted. 'You'll turn out to be a frog.'

'Kermit's not bad,' I said, assessingly.

She giggled. 'What do you want me to do with the boxes?'

Her work on the boxes had been originally my pathway to her father. I might not need her to work on them any longer, but I'd grown to like finding her here in my rooms.

'I hope you'll go on with the cataloguing tomorrow,' I said.

'All right.'

'But this evening I have to work on the film . . . er, alone.'

She seemed slightly disappointed but mostly relieved. A daring step forward . . . half a cautious step back. But we would get there one day, I thought, and was content and even reassured by the wait.

We left through the still slightly open doorway and I walked down the passage a little way before waving her down the stairs; and, returning, I stopped to talk to my bodyguard whom O'Hara, for the company, had by now installed in the room opposite my own.

My bodyguard, half Asian, had straight black hair, black shiny eyes and no visible feelings. He might be young, agile, well-trained and fast on his feet, but he was also unimaginative and hadn't saved me from the Armadillo.

When I pushed open his unlocked door to reveal him sitting wide awake in an upright chair facing me, he said at once, 'Your door has all the time been open, Mr Lyon.'

I nodded. I'd arranged with him that if he saw my door closed he was to use my key and enter my rooms immediately. I couldn't think of a clearer or more simple demand for help.

'Have you eaten?' I asked.

'Yes, Mr Lyon.'

I tried a smile. No response.

'Don't go to sleep,' I said tamely.

'No, Mr Lyon.'

O'Hara must have dug him up from central casting, I thought. Bad choice.

I retreated into my sitting-room, left the door six inches open, drank a small amount of brandy and answered a telephone call from Howard.

He was predictably raging.

'Cibber told me you've made him the murderer! It's

impossible! You can't do it. I won't allow it! What will the Visboroughs say?'

I pointed out that we could slot in a different murderer, if we wanted to.

'Cibber says you tore him to *shreds*.'

'Cibber gave the performance of his life,' I contradicted: and indeed, of the film's eventual four Oscar nominations, Cibber won the award for Best Supporting Actor – graciously forgiving me about a year later.

I promised Howard, 'We'll hold a full script conference tomorrow morning. You, me, Nash and Moncrieff.'

'I want you to stop the film!'

'I don't have that authority.'

'What if you're *dead*?' he demanded.

I said after a moment, 'The company will finish the movie with another director. Killing me, believe me, Howard, would give this film massive publicity, but it would not stop it.'

'It's not *fair*,' he said, as if he'd learned nothing, and I said, 'See you in the morning,' and disconnected in despair.

The safe in my sitting-room, as in O'Hara's, was out of casual sight in a fitment that housed a large TV set above and a mini-bar as well as the safe below. The mini-bar held small quantities of drinks for needy travellers, spirits, wine, champagne and beer, also chocolate and nuts. The safe – my safe – held nothing. I programmed it to open at seven three five two, entrusted 'The Gang' photo into its safekeeping, and closed its door.

I sat then in the armchair in my bedroom and waited for a long time, and thought about the obligations of the confessional, and about how totally, or how little, I myself was bound by Valentine's dying and frantic admissions.

I felt the weight of the obligation of priesthood that so many priests themselves took lightly, knowing that their role absolved them from any dire responsibility, even while they dispensed regular indulgences. I had had no right to hear Valentine's confession nor to pardon his sins, and I had done both. I'd absolved him. *'In nomine Patris . . . ego te absolvo.'*

I could not evade feeling an absolute obligation to the spirit of those words. I should not – and could not – save myself with the knowledge he'd entrusted to me as a priest when he was dying. On the other hand, I could in good conscience use what he'd left me in his will.

I hadn't come across, in his books and papers, any one single revelation that could have been found by ransacking his house. The pieces had been there, but obscured and devious. I'd sorted those out a good deal by luck. I wished there were a more conclusive artifact than 'The Gang' photo with which to bait the safe, but I'd come to the conclusion that there wasn't one. Valentine hadn't written down his ultimate sin; he'd confessed it in his last lucid breaths but he had never meant it to live after him. He hadn't left any exact concrete record of his twenty-six-year-old secret.

Two and a half hours after I'd talked to Howard, my visitor arrived. He came to my sitting-room door calling my name, and when I didn't at first reply he walked in boldly and closed the door behind him. I heard it latch. I heard him open the fitment and press the buttons to open the safe.

I ambled to my bedroom door and greeted him.

'Hello, Roddy.'

He was dressed in blazer, shirt and tie. He looked a pillar of show-jumping rectitude; and he held 'The Gang' photo.

'Looking for something?' I asked.

'Er . . .' Roddy Visborough said civilly, 'yes, actually. Bit of an imposition, I'm afraid, but one of the children I teach has begged me to get Nash Rourke's autograph. Howard swears you'll ask him for it.'

He laid the photo on the table and came towards me holding out an autograph album and a pen.

It was so very unexpected that I forgot Professor Derry's warning – *anything* he possesses may hide a knife – and I let him get too close.

He dropped the autograph book at my feet, and when I automatically looked down at it, he pulled his gold-coloured pen apart with a movement too fast for me to follow, and lunged at me with it.

The revealed stiletto point went straight through my jersey and shirt and hit solid polymer over my heart.

Himself flummoxed, disbelieving, Roddy dropped the pen and reached for his tie, and with a tug produced from under it a much larger knife, fearsomely lethal, which I later saw to be a triangular blade like a flat trowel fixed to a bar which led between his fingers to a grip within his hand.

At the time I saw only the triangular blade that seemed to grow like an integral part of his fist, the wide

366

end across his knuckles, the point protruding five or more inches ahead.

He slashed at my throat instantly and found Robbie's handiwork foiling him there also, and with one quick movement flicked the blade higher so that it cut my chin and ran sharply up across my cheek to above my ear.

I hadn't meant to have to fight him. I wasn't good at it. And how could anyone fight an opponent so appallingly armed, when one had no defence except fists?

He meant to kill me. I saw it in his face. He was going to get blood on his elegant clothes. One thinks such stupid *non sequiturs* at moments of maximum peril. He worked out that I wore a body protector from neck to waist and aimed at more vulnerable areas and punched his awful triangular blade into my left arm several times as I tried to shield my eyes from damage while unsuccessfully trying to get behind him to put my right arm round his throat.

I tried to evade him. We circled the bedroom. He sought to keep himself between me and the door while he killed me.

There were scarlet splatters all over the place; a scarlet river down my left hand. I yelled with what breath I could muster for my damned bodyguard to come to my rescue and nothing happened except that I began to believe that whatever happened to Roddy afterwards I wouldn't be there to care.

I tugged the bedspread off the bed and threw it at him, and by good fortune it landed over his right hand. I sprang at him. I rolled against him, wrapping his right arm closely. I overbalanced him: I put one leg behind his and levered him backwards off his feet, and scrambled with him on the floor, enveloping him ever more deeply in the bedspread until he was cocooned in it, until I lay over him bleeding while he tried to heave me off.

I don't know what would eventually have happened, but at that moment my bodyguard finally showed up.

He arrived in the bedroom doorway, saying enquiringly, 'Mr Lyon?'

I was past answering him sensibly. I said, 'Fetch someone.' Hardly a Nash Rourke-hero sort of speech.

He took me literally, anyway. I vaguely heard him talking on the sitting-room telephone and soon my rooms seemed full of people. Moncrieff, Nash himself, large men from the Bedford Lodge kitchen staff who sat on the wriggling bedspread, and eventually people saying they were policemen and paramedics and so on.

I apologised to the hotel manager for the blood. Oh, well.

'Where the hell were you?' I asked my bodyguard. 'Didn't you see that my door was shut?'

'Yes, Mr Lyon.'

'Well then?'

'But, Mr Lyon,' he said in righteous self-justification, 'sometimes I have to go to the bathroom.'

CHAPTER SEVENTEEN

Early on Thursday morning I sat on a windy sand dune waiting for the sun to rise over Happisburgh beach.

O'Hara, back in a panic from LA, sat shivering beside me. About forty people, the various location crews, came and went from the vehicles parked close behind the dunes, and out on the wet expanse of firm sand left clean and unmarked by the ebbing tide, Moncrieff worked the cameras, lights and gantry that had been taken out there bolted onto a caterpillar-tracked orange beach-cleaning monster that could bull-doze wrecks if need be.

Far off to the left, Ziggy waited with the Viking horses. Between him and us, Ed commanded a second camera crew, one that would give us side-on shots.

We had held a rehearsal on the ebb tide the evening before and knew from the churned-up state of the sand afterwards that we needed to get the first shoot right. Ziggy was confident, Moncrieff was confident, O'Hara was confident: I fidgeted.

We needed a decent sunrise. We could fudge together an impression by using the blazing shots of the sky from the previous week; we could shine lights to get gleams in the horses' eyes, but we needed luck and the real thing to get the effect I truly wanted.

I thought over the events of the past few days. There had been a micro-surgeon in the Cambridge hospital who'd sewn up my face with a hundred tiny black stitches that at present looked as if a millipede was climbing from my chin to my hairline, but which he swore would leave hardly a scar. The gouges in my left arm had given him and me more trouble, but at least they were out of sight. He expected everything to be healed in a week.

Robbie Gill visited the hospital briefly early on Tuesday morning, taking away with him the Delta-cast jacket that had puzzled the night-nursing staff the evening before. He didn't explain why I'd been wearing it beyond. 'An experiment in porosity – interesting.' He also told me he'd mentioned to his police colleague that Dorothea could now identify her attacker, and that as two knife nuts suddenly active in Newmarket were unlikely, why didn't they try her with a photo?

I'd spent Tuesday afternoon talking to policemen, and by then (during Monday night) I'd decided what to say and what not.

I heard later that they had already searched Roddy Visborough's cottage in Leicestershire and had found it packed with hidden unusual knives. They asked why I thought Roddy had attacked me.

'He wanted the film stopped. He believes it harms his family's reputation.'

They thought it not a good enough reason for attempted murder and, sighing at the vagaries of the world, I agreed with them. Did I know of any other reason? Sorry, no.

Roddy Visborough, I was certain, would give them no other reason. Roddy Visborough would not say, 'I was afraid Thomas Lyon would find out that I connived at a fake hanging of my aunt to cover up a sex orgy.'

Roddy, 'the' show jumper, had had too much to lose. Roddy, Paul and Ridley must all have been aghast when their buried crime started coming back to haunt them. They'd tried to frighten me off first with threats, and when those hadn't worked, with terminal action.

With knives.

The police asked if I knew that Mr Visborough's fingerprints had been found all over Mrs Pannier's house, along with my own? How *extraordinary*! I said; I'd never seen Mr Visborough in her house.

They said that, acting on information, they had that morning interviewed Mrs Pannier who had identified a police photograph of Mr Visborough as being the man who had attacked her.

'*Amazing*,' I said.

They asked if I knew why Mrs Pannier had been attacked by Mr Visborough. No, I didn't.

What connection was there between her and me?

'I used to read to her blind brother,' I said. 'He died of cancer . . .'

They knew.

They wondered if the knife I'd found on the Heath, that was now in their possession, had anything to do with what had happened to me.

'We all believed it was an attempt to get the film abandoned,' I said. 'That's all.'

I believed also, though I didn't say so, that it was Roddy who had given Ridley the trench knife and told him to frighten off Nash and, through him, the film.

I believed Roddy had coerced Paul to ransack Dorothea's house with him, both of them looking for any giveaway account Valentine might have left of Sonia's death.

Roddy had been the strongest of the three of them, and the most afraid.

Prompted by Lucy, Ridley had obligingly passed on to Roddy the combination of my safe, and had told him that I knew far too much.

Roddy, as I'd hoped, had revealed himself and his involvement, the mackerel coming to the sprat. I had lured him to come, had hoped he might bring with him another esoteric knife: I hadn't meant to get myself so cut.

The police went away as if dissatisfied, but they were sure at the very least of two convictions for grievous bodily harm, and if, with all the modern available detection techniques, they couldn't prove Roddy Visborough had killed Paul Pannier, too bad. As for motive, they might conclude Paul had threatened in remorse to give Roddy away to the police for attacking Dorothea: near enough for belief. Near enough, anyway, for Dorothea to believe it, and be comforted.

On Wednesday morning I discharged myself from the hospital and returned to Newmarket to be confronted by a furious Howard and an extremely upset Alison Visborough.

'I *told* you you shouldn't have made changes to my book,' Howard raged. 'Now see what you've done! Roddy is going to *prison*.'

Alison looked in disbelief at the long millipede track up my face. 'Rodbury wouldn't have done that!'

'Rodbury did,' I said dryly. 'Did he always have knives?'

She hesitated. She was fair minded under the outrage. 'I suppose . . . perhaps . . . he was secretive . . .'

'And he wouldn't let you join in his games.'

She said 'Oh,' blankly, and began re-evaluating her brother's psyche.

Sitting on the Norfolk dunes I thought of her father, Rupert, and of his aborted political career. I thought it almost certain that the scandal that had caused his retreat was not that his sister-in-law had been mysteriously hanged, but that he'd learned – perhaps from Valentine or even from Jackson Wells – that his own son had been present at the mid-morning cover-up hanging, having intended to have sexual relations with his aunt. Rupert, upright man, had given his son show jumpers with which to redeem himself, but had stopped short of loving forgiveness and had left his own house to his daughter. Poor Rupert Visborough . . . he hadn't deserved to become Cibber, but at least he would never know.

O'Hara, huddling into his padded ex-army jacket, said that while I'd been out on the beach rehearsing the previous evening, he'd got the projectionist to show him the rushes of the hanging.

'What sort of certificate did we earn?' I asked. 'PG-13? That's what we ideally want.'

'Depends on the cutting. What gave you that view of her death?'

'Howard holds forth on the catharsis of the primal scream.'

'Shit, Thomas. That death wasn't any sort of therapy. That hanging had gut-churning vigour.'

'Good.'

O'Hara blew on his fingers. 'I hope these damn horses are worth this frigging cold.'

The eastern sky turned from black to grey. I picked up the walkie-talkie and spoke again to Ed and also to Ziggy. Everything was ready. I wasn't to worry. All would be well.

I thought of Valentine's powerful muscles, years ago.

I had kept faith with his confession. No one through me would ever learn his truth.

I left the knife with Derry....

Valentine's strength had fashioned for his great friend Professor Derry a unique knife to add to his collection: a steel knife with a spear head and a candy-twisted handle, unlike any ordinary weapon.

I killed the Cornish boy....

One of the Gang, perhaps even Pig Falmouth himself, had told Valentine how Sonia had died, and in an overwhelming, towering tidal wave of anger and grief and guilt he had snatched up the spear and plunged it deep into the jockey's body.

It had to have happened in some way like that. Valentine had loved Sonia in secret. He'd learned about paraphilia to solve Derry's impotence problem, and he'd shown the encyclopaedia article to Pig, no doubt light-heartedly – 'I say, Pig, just look at this!' – and Pig had told his friends.

I destroyed all their lives ... I guessed he might have meant he ruined their lives by giving them the idea of

374

their fatal game. They had destroyed their own lives, but guilt could lack logic.

Valentine had killed Pig Falmouth in the wild, uncontainable sort of anger and grief that had caused Jackson Wells to beat his brother Ridley near to death: and Valentine himself had then written the gossip column that reported Pig's departure to work in Australia, that everyone had believed.

Pig Falmouth, I guessed, had lain for twenty-six years at the bottom of the well that Valentine had had a firm of builders fill in to make it safe for children. Valentine had stood with Jackson Wells and watched them throw the junk of years down the hole to obliterate the carefree boy who had kissed and killed his golden girl.

Valentine had at the end unloaded his soul's burden of murder.

I laid them both to rest.

The sky's amorphous grey was slowly suffused with a dull soft crimson in the east.

Moncrieff was holding a light meter to measure the changing intensity in minutes with the dedication that won him *Unstable Times*' second Oscar, for Cinematography. Howard, nominated for Best Adapted Screenplay, lost the award by inches, as did our fourth nominee, the Art Director. O'Hara and the moguls were happy, however, and I got allotted a big-budget epic with mega-star Nash.

Over Happisburgh beach the crimson in the sky blossomed to scarlet and coloured the waves pink.

There were fewer cloud streaks than the week before, fewer brilliant gold halos against the vermilion. We would merge the two sunrises, I thought.

Away to our right, far behind Moncrieff and his cameras, the trainer of the Viking horses had spread out on the sands great bowls of horse-nuts: the wild horses would race, on our signal, to reach their breakfast, as they had been trained.

Moncrieff, raising meters high, greeted the dawn like an ancient prophet. When he lowered his arms, I was to cue the action.

The blinding sun swam upwards. Moncrieff's arms swept down.

I said, 'Action, Ed,' and 'Now, Ziggy,' into my walkie-talkie, and away down the beach the horses began their run.

We had dressed Ziggy in an all-over body suit of grey Lycra, to which, ballet trained, he'd adapted instantly. Over the body suit he wore a floating shapeless gown of translucent white silk voile, and on his head the light blonde wig. His own dark features had been transformed to blondeness by the make-up department, and he was riding, as he'd promised, without shoes, saddle or reins.

The horses accelerated, bursting into the wide silence of the deserted seascape with the thud and suction of their galloping hooves.

Ziggy knelt on his horse's withers, his head forward above the horse's straining neck. Gown and hair streamed out, gathering to themselves all the light, the grey-clad man inside seeming almost invisible, a misty shadow.

376

Moncrieff ran two head-on cameras, one set for a speed of thirty-six frames, a second, slow motion.

The rising sun shone in the horses' eyes. Light gleamed on the flying manes. The heads of the wild herd plunged forward in the urgency of racing, in the untamed compulsion to be *first*, to lead the pack. The herd parted and swept round Moncrieff, the plunging bodies close, the Viking heads wild and free.

Ziggy rode between Moncrieff and the maximum brilliance of light. On the finished film it looked as if the flying figure had evaporated there, had been absorbed and assimilated in luminescence; had become a part of the sun.

'Jesus *Christ*,' O'Hara said, when he saw it.

I cut some of the shots of the hanging scene into the wild horse sequences for the ending of the film.

Yvonne's scream dissolved into the high thin forlorn cry of a wheeling seagull.

The young woman of the fantasy lovers dreamed she was riding the wild horses as she swung to her death.